SIXTEEN TONS

A Novel

For Gerald,
Thank you for all
you've done in your own
important life
Best Wishes,
Kevi Cooly

THE REVIEWERS PRAISE *SIXTEEN TONS*

"Kevin's words bring to life the dreams and aspirations of the men, women and children who lived our labor history, a history which has been pretty well pushed aside and papered over in America... This is a part of American history that needs to be remembered." **Richard L. Trumka, President, AFL-CIO**

"Sixteen Tons is at its best when describing work, culture, leisure, and everyday life in close-knit Illinois mining communities...Strong women characters also add to the book, as does Corley's handling of immigration and race...His writing is fresh and engaging as the saga unfolds. Sixteen Tons is an entertaining way to learn a lot about this chapter in history."
Labor Notes

"Corley describes the efforts by union organizers across America in a battle for human dignity... a compelling historical novel [that] allows readers to better understand the historical context of the ongoing struggle for workers' rights in America. For those who maintain that unions have become too powerful, Corley's novel serves as a reminder that unions remain a crucial bulwark against the oppression of countless American workers. " **Illinois Times**

"...As a teacher, Corley soaked up stories of the Illinois coal fields, translating them into a readable novel of a recent past that should not be forgotten." **Grand Prairie Union News**

"Squeezed into crevices, pounding support timbers before they could even start to extract coal, and in constant peril of restless earth, runaway coal cars and "black damp" (a deadly mixture of carbon dioxide and nitrogen), the miners who powered our great country finally emerge from behind the seams."
Class Action

Published by Hard Ball Press, March, 2014.
Information available at: www.hardballpress.com
ISBN: 978-0-9911639-9-1

Cover design by Tim Sheard, Kevin Corley and D. Bass
Interior book design by D. Bass.

Dedication
For Erin, Tyson, Richelle and Krissie
Dedicated to Carl Oblinger and Cullom Davis for helping
people to understand the significance of their lives and that
history is not just about kings, queens and Presidents.
And for Kirk, Janice, Kate, Ben, Megan and Will Kettelkamp
for showing us the true meaning of courage.

SIXTEEN TONS

A Novel

Kevin Corley

HARDBALL PRESS

1

By his tenth hour in the boxcar, the senses of William Jefferson Hemings had progressed beyond the smell of cow dung and body odor. Throughout the day a little autumn light had peeked through the cracks in the boxcar walls, but now the sun was setting, casting an amber glow over the black skin of the men crowded in the windowless car. The train moved faster now that it had hit the open plain of the Illinois prairie. Despite the heat of the crowded room, the rhythmic grinding and clanking of the wheels against the railroad tracks lulled many of the weary travelers into a much-needed sleep.

William, however, had endured the clammy skin pressed against him long enough. He jerked his shoulder from beneath the sweating head of the old man next to him, grabbed a torn, gray carpetbag and stood awkwardly on stiff legs. Then, ignoring the grumbling protests of the half-naked men, he stumbled over and around them to an empty area on the far side of the boxcar.

"What the..."

"Damn, nigger!"

He ripped off his shirt and tucked it into the bag. His torso and arms bulged with muscles gained from a lifetime of physical labor.

As the train lurched, William landed hard, ripping the skin on the top of his shoulder.

A heavy boy opened his eyes and, using a huge butt, pushed the man next to him, giving William room to sit.

"They says the car next to us is empty 'cept for a few goats," the boy said. "Coulda let a few of us ride with the goats. Woulda been better than mashin' us all up in this stuffy ol' boxcar."

William shrugged.

"Name's Calvin." The boy glanced down at his bare feet.

"William." William nodded.

"Ain't got no family," Calvin said. "Just wanna make a decent livin'. Maybe meet a nice gal. Settle down. Don't even have to be pretty. Long as she's a God-fearin' woman."

William nodded slowly.

"You sure is a handsome fella with that Abe Lincoln beard," Calvin said. "Got a gal?"

William shook his head. "Just my mama and six brothers and four sisters back in Birmingham. I'm the oldest except for Rochester, and he ain't right."

Calvin nodded he understood. "Why you figure them white folk don't wanna work these here mines?"

William said, "I've gotta send money to Mama 'til Horace gets old enough to work. Then Mama says he'll take care of the family till the next one gets a job and right on down the line. Mama says I can start my own family then, but I s'pect I'll still send her a dollar now and then. Least 'til I git four or five young 'uns of my own."

Calvin lowered his eye to a small opening between two boards. "Lord, that's a purty hill up yonder. Looks like a tombstone with a picture on it."

When he moved his head, William took a turn looking through the opening. A greenish-blue mist surrounded the big hill before him. Trees with different shades of red, gold and green filled the autumn horizon. It did remind him of a cemetery, but in a happy, peaceful way. He breathed in the beauty of that moment, filling his lungs with a sense of hope he'd not felt in a long time.

The train whistle shrieked, then the brakes squealed. It was time.

<><><><><><>

Joe Harrison lay on the ground, his ear firmly pressed against the cold iron of the railroad track, his hand gripping his rifle. Of the dozens of mine workers gathered on Old Man Staple's farm, he'd been chosen to be the lookout—the one to warn when the train approached. The sprawl of the boy's long legs seemed positioned to add drama to an already dramatic situation. His tanned, handsome face had a clean innocence that reflected his eighteen years on earth. A shock of dark red hair stuck out like rooster feathers beneath a small, gray cap.

Old Herman Staples kicked one of his pigs so hard the thud caused Joe to inadvertently slide the barrel of his rifle along the track.

Without moving his body from its honored position as lookout, the young man watched the shoat grunting its way back to an almost completely dried up mud puddle that lay beneath a collapsing tin shed.

Staples showed no interest in the animal and instead continued to give the spread-eagled boy a hard stare.

"I think I hear something," Joe said without raising his head. He hoped the news would break the man's intense gaze.

The skin on Staples' face was as dark and wrinkled as a dried up hunk of beef jerky. His bluish-gray eyes showed an empty cruelty the likes of which the boy had never before seen.

"Yep, it's a comin'!" Joe shouted. He jumped up and ran to hide with the others behind an oak. Williamsburg Hill was filled with large trees, creating the ideal spot for mushroom hunting in the spring and, on this autumn day, for ambushing nigger trains.

The face next to him didn't change a wrinkle. A shiver ran through Joe's body. Had it not been for the dizziness he felt from the excitement, he would've sped back to the village of Tower Hill, and then straight on a few more miles to his home in Pana. There had been no peace in his community since the coal mine opened. When men were not being crushed to death underground by falling rock, they were killing each other

3

above ground. His own father had died in the mine when a roof collapsed. Joe had consoled himself by going to bed and pulling the covers over his head. He continued that habit every time things got rough in his community. During a strike in '96, he had slept for three days straight without even so much as a drink of water. Now that he had a job picking rock in the mine, the comfort of his bed was no alternative. He was expected to stand beside his fellow mine workers.

The sound of the train echoed across the Illinois prairie even before it came into view. Staples had said it would stop with the third boxcar just in front of the trees. No one had reason to doubt the man's accuracy. Word around the mine was that after driving mule-pulled coal cars most of his life, he had a penchant for precision.

Joe ran his hand along the barrel of the rifle. He had been given the weapon that morning and had never had an opportunity to fire it. In fact, truth be known, he had never shot any gun. He understood the basics of cocking and firing, but if everything went as planned, he was certain he would have no need to use the rifle, except maybe as a club.

When his deputies had passed out the Winchesters, Sheriff Crowley made it clear there was to be no shooting. They were only to scare the strikebreakers so they'd go back to where they came from. If miners across the coalfields of Illinois could prevent this strike from being broken, the fledgling United Mine Workers of America would develop into a worker's union with national power.

Only the week before, a twenty-minute shootout with a trainload of colored strikebreakers at Virden, Illinois, had left eight striking miners killed and over thirty wounded. Many of the scabs on the train were also wounded, but only four of the security guards had died. When the shooting got too extreme, the panicking engineer moved the train on to Springfield, but the damage was done.

There was also rumor about a second incident that had

occurred even before the Virden Massacre and just a few miles from where they now were. The mine company had brought strikebreakers in from Birmingham by way of Indiana, and even allowed the coloreds to ride in a special railroad coach.

Sheriff Crowley had referred to that incident that morning to rally the striking miners.

"You boys sent those sixty scabs scampering home a few weeks ago right from this same area." Crowley told the men as they loaded and checked their Winchesters. "I see no reason it shouldn't work this time. According to my sources, today's batch are hiding in the train's third boxcar. Well, I've done what I can to make this a peaceful situation and now I wash my hands clean of this entire affair." With those words the Sheriff had mounted his horse and reined it back toward town, his deputies following in a wagon.

Now Joe's eyes were growing wide as he watched the anticipated third boxcar of the train creep closer. A steam whistle blew two long blasts. Despite the sheriff's insistence on no violence, dozens of weapons from behind the nearby trees cocked, the sound bouncing between the trees.

A few moments later, the engine passed, spewing steam and again blasting the whistle. The conductor looked in the direction of the trees, raised his gray cap above his head and waved it towards the men in hiding.

Joe looked at old man Staples. White spittle oozed from one corner of his mouth. The wrinkled man counted the boxcars aloud as they slowly passed the tree where he was hiding.

"One."

"Two."

With the third boxcar came one last squeal of brakes as the train rolled to a complete stop. Quiet. Stillness. Even the pig that Staples had kicked lay like a statue in the security of its muddy bed. Far up on the hill, a chicken hawk hovered, almost motionless in the air as if it were also watching the train, waiting.

The long, quiet seconds passed. Finally the door to the boxcar slowly slid open. Joe thought his ears must have stopped working, because even the movement of the big door made absolutely no sound. First one black-skinned man, then another and then another appeared, sitting or squatting inside the boxcar. Many more stood behind the ones in front, all peering cautiously, the whites of their eyes wide with anticipation. Most were shirtless. The rest were stripped down to undershirts. Sweat glistened on their black skin. Joe had never in his life seen a colored person, and he was struck by how . . . how *human* they looked.

He waited for the warning gunshot from Staples. He even thought of covering one ear, but at that moment, movement did not seem justifiable.

Then, one of the shirtless black men squatting near the front rose slowly. A big, toothy, white smile broke across his face. He was a splendid specimen of manhood. He might have been a statue of Hercules with his dark beard and glistening muscles. The man's face appeared kind. Friendly.

A gunshot exploded, deafening Joe's left ear.

That single moment would be ingrained in Joe Harrison's memory for the rest of his life. His mind's eye would forever see the piece of metal traveling like an arrow rather than a bullet from the barrel of old Herman Staples' gun to the jaw of that magnificent, black man. The man's head snapped sideways, followed by his entire body as blood spewed across the face and bodies of his companions.

The next sound was like a single cannon shot as more than two-dozen gunshots tore through the strikebreakers and the boxcar. A heavy cloud of white gun smoke filled the air. Like an angry, slow-moving storm, it rolled toward the train. A moment of silence followed, but was quickly replaced by screams of those who had survived the first wave of bullets.

"Finish 'em boys!" Staples shouted as he cocked and fired and then cocked and fired over and over again while walking slowly toward the defenseless men in the boxcar. A dozen men followed him, whooping like confederate soldiers as they fired and advanced, fired and advanced. As they got closer, some of the men seemed to tire from holding their rifles at their shoulders and began to cock and fire from the hip.

Joe watched as the bodies of the black men jerked in every direction from the barrage of bullets and from the spasms of death convulsions. Only when the guns and shouting stopped did Joe realize that he had not moved an inch since the massacre began. *We were only supposed to scare the scabs.*

"You men there." Staples pointed. "Drag the niggers over to the road and load 'em on the hay wagon. You other men separate this boxcar from the others. Then turn it over and burn it."

The area was instantly a blur of movement. Men, suddenly quiet, went about their tasks as if they were setting up for a circus. Talk was minimal, and for the most part, in low voices. In a daze, Joe walked about the scene. At times he heard men chuckle but also occasionally caught the sound of a sob. A few men disappeared into the woods for a while, followed by the sound of vomiting.

"Don't forget these scabs were trying to take your jobs," Staples said to the men as they returned from the woods. "They were going to take food out of your children's mouths. They were evil and received the punishment God wanted them to have. Their souls are burning in hell at this very moment."

Joe never touched a body; never raised a finger to help. No one asked him to. He just stood and watched. When the bodies were loaded on the hay wagon and covered with a tarp, the men poured kerosene on the boxcar and someone set it on fire. Half a dozen men stood with shovels ready to scatter and bury the ashes when the fire died out. The train engine backed into the remaining boxcars and was quickly coupled. As it pulled down the tracks, the men gathered up their belongings and returned to the horses or buggies they'd arrived in. Staples walked over to Joe, firmly took his arm, and led him to a one-horse carriage waiting on the road. Joe immediately curled up on his side in the backseat, his knees against his chest.

It was a strange sight, that caravan traveling slowly up Williamsburg Hill; men on horseback rode in front of the heavily loaded hay wagon pulled by six strong horses and followed by several buggies, then by men walking. Whenever they came to a farmhouse the men on horseback rode ahead and insisted the occupants stay inside until they passed.

Up the hill they went; then down a long, grassy path that was barely wide enough for the hay wagon, and on to a pair of gravel pits that Joe recognized as being owned by one of the ambushers. Years before, he had searched for Indian arrowheads and beads in those rock gardens with his friends. There was a grassy area between the two pits that formed a nice hill for picnicking, and that was where they took those colored men. How many slain men were there? Joe didn't even know. He didn't want to know. He walked to the top of the pile of dirt and looked down at a big hole in the ground. The grave had water at the bottom from the big storm several days before. When was this hole dug? Had this all been planned?

Joe felt betrayed. Mr. Staples had been his father's friend, as had most of the men who were now unloading bodies and pitching them like bales of hay into the open pit. If his father were alive, would he have been one of those callously piling corpses into the grave?

As the last of the bodies somersaulted atop the others, a faint groan carried on the wind. Joe looked into the pit. One of the men moved.

"He . . ." Joe pointed. "That one's . . ."

Herman Staples appeared next to him and forced a shotgun into his hands. "Finish him."

Joe looked at Staples. Though he had seen that face hundreds of times over the years, he didn't recognize it. The edges of the man's mouth seemed to extend all the way to his ears, and the corner of his eyes drooped low on his face.

"You're in this, too," Staples hissed in his ear, "and by God, if you don't finish that black bastard, I'll see you buried right next to him."

Joe looked at the shotgun in his hands and almost threw it on the ground. The reason he had never before fired a gun was because he hated them. Even before this day he had seen them used by hunters and saw the devastation they created. He knew what this shotgun would do to the man lying in the pit. Despite the blood that covered the man's face, Joe recognized him as the handsome Hercules who had taken that first bullet from Staples' gun. Though his bearded jaw was half gone, the man had a look of kindness on his face. The dying man's eyes were open and he stared directly at Joe. At least half a dozen bloody holes showed on his magnificent, bare chest and stomach. He'd die soon without any help. Still, to pull the trigger and be the one to end his life . . . .

A large green grasshopper jumped onto the man's face just over his left eye. The colored man didn't even try to blink it away. He seemed to look right through the insect and into Joe's soul.

"Just shoot the grasshopper, son." one of the miners said as he threw a shovel full of dirt onto the black men.

Joe slowly raised the gun to his shoulder and cocked one of the barrels.

"Both barrels, boy," Staples said.

Joe cocked the second barrel and took aim at the grasshopper. He tried to see only the little bug, but he couldn't avoid the man's eyes.

When he pulled the triggers, the gun bucked so hard he was sure his shoulder was broken. He dropped the weapon, but still he watched the devastation he had inflicted. The grasshopper was gone—as was the entire top of the man's head.

One miner walked up to the grave, snorted mucus up his throat, hawked it into a ball inside his mouth and spit expertly into one of the dead men's faces. Another miner approached and added his own snort, hawk and spit. More men filed past the bodies even as others shoveled dirt into the faces of the dead. Snort, hawk and spit.

When it came Joe's turn, he found his mouth completely dry. He tried to move his tongue but sensed in horror that it was getting thicker and curling on its own accord toward the back of his throat. He feared he was about to swallow his tongue. He began gagging. The bitter taste of bile rose from his stomach. When he leaned forward and placed his hands on his knees, vomit spewed from his mouth in a long wave of ugly, gray chunks, some of which stuck in his throat and made him emit a second, even longer, eruption.

"Atta boy, Joe," he heard someone behind him say. "Give 'em their last meal."

With his head between his legs, Joe heard the last few men issue their own nauseating epithet over the strikebreakers' grave.

Snort, hawk, spit.

Snort, hawk, spit.

2

Antonio was the last chance to keep the Vacca name alive. As he stood at the Taylorville, Illinois, train station sporting his brown sack suit and the slouch hat he'd worn during the recent Cuba campaign, he felt optimistic that a son would soon be in the making; perhaps even in the next few hours.

Several other coal miners stood nearby also waiting for the train carrying loved ones. Most of them held bouquets. He cursed himself for not thinking to bring flowers. He proudly possessed the curly brown hair, Romanesque nose and short stature of his Italian heritage, but he regretted not inheriting the romantic nature that was common among the Latin. Love ethic did not come as easily to him as work ethic. As he walked back and forth along the wooden railway platform he was thankful that his wife, Angeline, was not a woman to require such frivolities, though he had to admit she did seem pleased when romance came without prompting.

He nodded and smiled at a few of those miners he had worked with during the past year. Like Antonio, many of them had left the West Virginia mines and come west to enjoy the benefits gained by the United Mine Workers in Illinois. Most of them were first generation immigrants from countries all across Europe. While they understood one another well enough when they talked mining, they were less accomplished when it came to casual conversation.

Joe Harrison, his work partner in the mine, had told him that language barrier wasn't always a bad thing. "Being able to claim you don't understand is mighty useful for keeping secrets," Joe had said matter-of-factly one day as they timbered a weak ceiling in the mine. Joe never told him what secrets he was talking about, but Antonio suspected it had something to do with the battles that had taken place against company scabs a year and a half ago. There seemed to be as many tall tales about murders and hidden gravesites as there were mine chambers beneath the ground in Christian County, and Joe had seen some bad things during his first two years in the mines.

Thankfully, those bloody successes had created not only somewhat better working conditions, but also higher wages in the Illinois mines. In just over a year, he had saved enough money to send for his young bride.

The train whistle shrilled through the air. A moment later, the locomotive slowly ambled its way between the trees to the east. Antonio forgot about coal mining and concentrated on the plan he had laid out for the next twenty-four hours. Antonio Vacca was a methodical planner both above and below ground. He hated wasted motion and was famous among miners for performing complicated tasks with his right hand even as his left hand did something completely different.

When the train finally chugged and squealed to a steamy stop, he watched impatiently as women and children filed down the train steps and into the arms of waiting miners.

Angeline finally appeared on the landing. She was a short, stocky girl barely out of her teens. Antonio smiled at the sight of her wearing a thick, black overcoat that was too heavy for such a mild, spring day, yet too big to fit in the carpetbags she carried.

After several long and passionate kisses, he took the bags from her and proudly set off on the half-mile walk to the land he had bought for their new home.

"Hewittville is the perfect place for us to live," he told his young bride as they followed a dirt road near the railroad tracks. "It's only a fifteen-minute walk from our house to the center of Taylorville, the county seat."

A few minutes later the young couple stood on the threshold

of a long, barren piece of land between the railroad tracks and the road. Dozens of carefully planted and well-placed trees, each about five feet high, dotted the finely plowed field.

"Let me getta this straight." Angeline Vacca put her hands on her ample hips and spoke in an Italian accent as thick as mozzarella. "You bought five acres of land, stripped it of every living thing, plowed it under, and then planted the slowest growing trees you could find?"

"Yes, I surely did." Antonio hadn't seen his wife in seven months and was too busy admiring her chubby, bare forearms to recognize her sarcasm.

"But oak trees, Antonio!" The little woman waved furiously at her round face with a funeral home fan. "We will be dead by the time they are fully grown."

"Do we do everything for ourselves, Angeline?" He emphasized every word with a hand gesture. "What about our sons? Did your father, God rest his soul, come to America to give himself a better life? No, I tell you! He was an old man when he came. He brought you and your brother Vincent to America to give you the opportunities that godless priest in Italia denied him."

"Antonio!" Angeline gasped and crossed herself. "Not in front of God!"

"It is true, and you know it!" Antonio shouted. "The priest was shady. He was not a man of God."

"He *was* of God," Angeline insisted. "We must respect his position even if we do not respect the man."

"Aah!" Antonio shook his head and pointed to a large stack of lumber across the road. "Tomorrow I build you a house. We will have to sleep on the floor, but, by golly, tomorrow night you shall have a house. Tonight we stay at the inn."

"And how will you build a house in one day, my husband?"

"You will see," Antonio said with a smile that showed off his fine white teeth. "You will see."

Sixteen Tons

<><><><><><>

At sunrise the next morning, Antonio began dragging the lumber across the road to his building site. Angeline tried to help but was immediately chastised.

"Go away!" her husband said, waving his hand with finality. "Go into town and introduce yourself to the women. When you come back this evening, we will sleep in our new home."

Angeline wanted to tell her husband how crazy he was, but she had been taught by her mother to choose her battles wisely. Besides, she was anxious to find the church. She wanted to light a candle for her safe journey from West Virginia.

Taylorville was a thriving town of five thousand souls with plenty of churches, flourmills, carriage and wagon shops, and two banks for those with money. Angeline would only need a church. The first Roman Catholic Church she stopped at had an Irish priest named Father Flannigan. The short, elderly man was friendly enough, but she wanted to be with an Italian priest even if it meant walking a little further each Sunday.

She finally found a church on the west end of town. The priest, Father Marco, wasted no time in establishing what her husband's income was. Once they had the tithes figured, Angeline handed over the nickel she had planned to use for a ham bone, said her confessions, lit a candle, and with rosary in hand, said the Our Father and ten Hail Marys the priest had ordained as penance for her sins.

Later, walking down the shady streets toward the town square, she felt saddened to think of what Antonio would think about Father Marco. In her brief conversation with the priest, she sensed the same malevolence that her husband had despised in the clerics back in Bologna. It was true that her own father had barely escaped Italy with his family when the priest, who was a capo crimini, ordered he be killed simply because he refused to pay protection money.

When Father Marco had asked her what parish she attended

14

in Bologna, she cited the name of a priest from a church in a country village, who she knew was not a consigliere of the don who had ordered her father's death sentence. Her only concern now was that someone who emigrated to Taylorville from the Bologna area might catch her in the exaggeration. She didn't think it was a real lie because she had attended the church a time or two while visiting her cousin.

In the Taylorville town square, a street vendor stood precariously on a rain barrel, telling anyone who would listen of the benefits of buying Hood's Sarsaparilla. "As a constitutional remedy, this little bottle is guaranteed to radically cure catarrh," the man said. "Yes sir, acting primarily on the blood, Hood's Sarsaparilla eradicates scrofula, salt rheum, or eczema. How about you, pretty lady? Ever had trouble with eruptions, pimples, boils, blood poisoning or just that tired feeling? This is a true nerve tonic. By purifying the blood, it feeds the nerves upon strength-giving food."

Angeline felt her cheeks burning. She believed that only her Antonio had the right to call her pretty, especially in a public place. Though she was by nature heavy, she had inherited her mother's smooth, dark complexion and long lashes that draped sparkling brown eyes. When the salesman pointed at her, she put her head down and hurried along the wooden sidewalk away from him. She felt the eyes of several onlookers burning into her back. Hopefully, if she met any of these people later, they would not remember this embarrassment.

Before she could get away, she was slowed by a woman's voice. "That's the wife of one of them dago strikebreakers that tried to take my husband's job during the last strike."

A tall, obese man stepped in front of Angeline. "That true, wop? You and your old man scabs?"

Angeline tried to step around the man, but her short legs were no match for the man's long ones, and he again quickly blocked her path. A dozen pedestrians stopped to stare at her.

"Step aside, mister," another voice broke in.

A gentle hand touched Angeline's arm. She turned to see that the second male voice had come from an extremely well dressed young man who stood in front of the most beautiful and equally well-dressed woman she had ever seen. He was thin with a gentle, white smile. The lady on his arm looked like a china doll with hazel eyes and brown hair tied back in a bun beneath a stylishly feathered cap.

"What's it to you, Eng?" the first man asked. "You never lost a job. Or have you ever even had one?"

"Well, as a matter of fact," Eng said, "the answer is no on both counts. Unless you consider the months I spent with Colonel Roosevelt in Cuba."

"I don't." The tall man growled. "Inherited money makes a man weak."

"Lucky for your children, then," Eng said and stepped toward the man.

"I just came in on the train last night," Angeline said quickly. She didn't want the gallant Mr. Eng to have to fight for her. "My husband worked the old mine for a year and just bought some land south of town. He recently got a job with the new mine and hasn't even started yet."

The obese bully never took his eyes off Eng but seemed to stand a little easier. "Then I'm only half wrong. You're still a wop, ain't ya?"

Laughing over his shoulder, the man walked away.

"Thank you, sir," Angeline said. She glanced shyly at the man and his lovely companion. "My husband would thank you too. He was also with the Rough Riders in Cuba."

"My name is Harley Eng, and this lovely lady is my wife, Lena. Like you, she is from Italy, so I'm sure you two will have a lot to discuss."

Harley tilted his slouch hat. Angeline noticed it was exactly like the one her husband wore.

"I'm Angeline Vacca."

"Ah, Antonio's wife?" Harley said. "I've already had the

pleasure of his acquaintance."

Lena touched Angeline's arm. "*Piacere di fare la vostra conoscenza,*" she said. "*Vuoi unirti a noi per un bicchiere di limonata?*"

"*Si, mi piacerebbe,*" Angeline answered with a smile.

"What are you two talking about?" Harley asked.

"You just offered to buy us both a big glass of lemonade." Lena took her new friend's hand and led her into the general store.

Angeline would never have believed that the squeaking of the door could be louder than the voices of the dozen or so people sitting at the checkered tables. By the time the screen door swung closed with a double bang, every head in the business had turned toward them and every eye seemed to be upon her. She stood for a moment, watching the men and women, thinking they would return to their conversations in a moment. They did not. Instead, they continued the awkward stare as she sat down at a table with the Engs.

Harley Eng broke the silence. "Quite the typical small-town reaction to a new face. Pay them no mind."

After what seemed several minutes to Angeline, a few of the patrons resumed talking in low voices, though she occasionally caught some of them glancing in her direction. She had no intention of ordering anything, but she kept her eyes on the one-page menu found between the salt and pepper shakers. She was so intent on the menu, she started when she noticed an elderly waitress with white hair and a crooked nose standing beside her. The woman's skin was as pale as death and she displayed absolutely no expression on her face. Angeline forced a nervous smile.

"Three lemonades, please," Harley said with his dashing smile. His face was narrow and his jaw-line squarely chiseled. Blue eyes smiled at the waitress in a happy, friendly way. Despite his carefree demeanor, the old woman turned, walked slowly toward the kitchen and whispered the order to a man in a greasy apron.

"My dear, I'm afraid my husband is not the most popular man in this town," Lena told Angeline quietly. "You see, his father once owned the old mine. When he sold it, he didn't realize the new owner would replace the older workers with cheaper labor."

"It would seem," Harley continued, "no matter how much we give back to the community, they feel we have profited from their suffering."

"You are the one who gave my husband the loan for the property," Angeline said quietly.

"And I would thank you for not sharing that around town," Harley said. "Actually, money was donated by a number of supporters of our regiment to help veterans after the war. While I do lend financial support to this cause, my primary role in your husband's loan was to give him a letter of reference."

"Were you in Cuba with my Antonio?"

"I was in H Troop and remained in Tampa during the conflict," Harley said, his face turning red. "I saw no action."

"From what my husband told me," Angeline said as the drinks arrived, "most of the action took place in the latrines."

"Yes, more men did run off that way than away from combat." Harley laughed and then caught himself. "But I really shouldn't laugh about it. More men died from diseases than from bullets in that peculiar little war."

"So," Lena said, changing the subject, "have you a home yet? You said you just got here yesterday."

"Well, yes and no." Angeline smiled. She liked the young bride instantly. "My Antonio claims he will have a house built for me by the time I get home this evening. But when I left this morning, it was little more than a pile of lumber."

"If I know your husband and the men in your community," Harley said, "you will sleep this night beneath your own roof.

<><><><><><>

That evening when Angeline came across the railroad tracks into Hewittville she was shocked to see that both Antonio and Harley Eng knew exactly what they were talking about. A dozen men were working in, on top of, and around the cutest framed house she had ever seen.

Antonio ran up and hugged her.

"How did you get so much help?" she asked. "You didn't ask them. I know you better than that."

"No," Antonio said, "I didn't ask. When they heard me hammering, they just came."

"He didn't need to ask," said one of the men passing by with a toolbox in hand. "Yer old man helped me last month when my chicken coop blew down." The man pointed with his saw at three men working on the roof. "Antonio helped shovel out the Jones' boys last January when the big blizzard hit. In fact, every man here owed your husband one thing or another."

She looked at her man in amazement. "How did you ever find time?"

Antonio laughed and waved his hands. "I don't have time. At least not time to stand here gabbing with you, my wife. Now go help those women set up dinner for our friends. We will wash up and be along shortly."

Angeline watched him hand-measure and then scratch on a two by four with a rusty nail. As he began sawing, she shook her head and hurried away to introduce herself to the women.

3

The next morning, Antonio began work at the new mine in Hewittville. Joe Harrison partnered with him as he had at the old mine. Sixteen men rode the cage to the bottom. When Antonio lit his carbide lamp and placed it on his canvass cap, he realized he'd been above ground for so long his eyes took several moments to adjust to the hazy lighting. As always, along with the cool, damp air, came coughing, especially from men who had spent much of their lives breathing the black dust.

In the entry room before him were stacks of picks, shovels, and breast augers, along with drills and bits. Since the mine was new, he didn't figure on needing to go very deep into the mine, so he didn't take a lazy man's load as several of the other men did. He and Joe had been working on a plan for days. He chose to take just the essentials this trip and come back to the entrance as he needed equipment.

Following the men through the room neck, he and Joe watched miners disappear two and three at a time into seven-foot high compartments as each team sought out the territory they would work. All of the compartments were about thirty feet by twenty feet in size, and the coal was what the miners called "on the solid." Antonio and Joe were among the last to choose their work area. They estimated they were at least a quarter-mile into the first seam.

The morning half of their day was spent timbering the compartments in their territory and laying track to the areas they would load. It was hard, laborious work, but essential to not only their safety but also to their ability to get the coal loaded in cars and pulled by mules to cages where they would be raised to the surface.

"The top seems pretty solid," Antonio told Joe after the hard morning's work. The two sat on the gravely bottom enjoying a hasty lunch followed by a leisurely cigarette. Being their first day, both men were anxious to get back to work but not so much that they were willing to forgo a smoke.

Joe agreed with Antonio. They had spent more time than normal sounding the top by pounding the flat of their picks against the ceiling and listening for the ringing that meant the top was safe. When they heard a hollow sound like a drum they would place another prop.

"Don't get careless," Joe said as he stuffed a big slice of ham in his mouth with a blackened hand. "Surest way to get kilt is to forget to sound a top."

"You ever seen a man killed?" Antonio asked.

Joe didn't answer. He rubbed his eyes with the back of his hand. Antonio was used to his partner blinking a lot with eyes that were always red and tired-looking.

"I forgot your papa died in the mine," Antonio said. "God rest his soul."

"Yes, he died in the mine, but I never seen him till they had cleaned him up and put him in his Sunday clothes." Joe looked down at his dinner bucket. "I saw death another time, though, and I don't particularly care to ever see it again."

Antonio recognized his partner's reluctance to talk so he didn't pursue the subject. Besides, negative talk never brought good luck. The miners knew they were responsible for their own safety. The mine company would do little to help them in that regard. That was why he and Joe had agreed they would not try to bring any coal up that first day. Their plan was to shoot as many compartments as they could before they left that night, let the dust settle, and then spend the next few days loading.

"We'll be eatin' a lot less dust if we shoot before we go home each night," Joe said when the two were making their plans for the new mine. The partners did become a little nervous, though, when they heard other miners shooting their territories and begin loading cars.

After lunch they went separately to different compartments and began undercutting the coal at the face. When they blasted that evening, the coal would fall in chunks that could be easily loaded. If they did their shots at the right angle, and were lucky, the coal would also be free of excessive sulfur and rock.

Antonio was more skilled at undercutting the coal than Joe. Expertly using his pick, he was able to make the horizontal slit a few inches above the floor and deep into the seam. In just over four hours, he was done with his compartments and went to help Joe finish his.

The next steps were critical and where Joe's innate skills lay. He harnessed the breast auger around his chest, and using a bit that was almost six feet long, hand-drilled into the face with a U-crank. They then poured black powder into the hole through a needle in the drill bit.

"How much powder do you think I oughta put in this shot, Antonio?"

"Oh, I'd say 'bout a cartridge and a half, maybe."

"Oh, no, that's too much."

Joe then prepared a squib by rolling a thin piece of waxed paper that was carefully mixed with just the right amount of black powder. He had been lucky enough to have the benefit of experienced miners helping him to perfect this technique. Antonio was envious of the relationship that his partner had with many of the miners in the area. They seemed to have a fraternal bond much like the one he had formed with his Rough Rider regiment in Cuba. It was as if Joe's miner friends from Pana had done battle with him.

Throughout the late afternoon, they repeated the drilling and shot preparation in various locations in their compartments. Each time, Joe would ask Antonio how much powder he thought he should use for the shots. Often as not, he would use a little more or less than his partner prescribed. Antonio never argued. He had learned to trust Joe's judgment on the matter.

After ten hours at the bottom they were finally ready to shoot their compartments and head to the surface. They shot them one at a time and made sure they were as far from each blast as possible. They also sounded the top again before entering each new compartment. Antonio had worked with a man once who thought him overly cautious.

"What are you doing?" the man scolded him when he saw him sounding the roof. "Some of that is ready to fall. If you touch it, it *will* fall."

Antonio was happy when he met Joe, a man with a similar love for living and propensity for caution.

When they were finally finished, the little Italian went to gather the picks and drill bits while Joe went to light the last shot. Under the terms of the last labor negotiations, miners were to take the tools back to the cage room with them, and the company had men who would sharpen them and have them ready the next day. To the anger of most of the workers, the company was compensated for this service by taking twenty-five cents a day from the miner's wages. The union re-negotiated this matter at every opportunity.

Joe was gone longer than Antonio knew he should be. After several minutes, he began to worry.

"Joe!" he shouted, his call echoing through the chambers.

He thought he heard a reply, but sounds bounced around so much he wasn't certain from which direction the voice had come. He moved down the room neck toward the cage, passing one compartment after another. At each entry, he shouted Joe's name and stopped a moment to listen. After doing this four times, he heard a rhythmic clanking of metal on metal. As he moved quickly forward it became louder.

"Joe!" Antonio shouted again.

"I'm here!" Joe's voice came from a nearby compartment. "My light blew out and this shots going to blow any second."

Antonio knew that if Joe's light was out, he would be in absolute darkness. "I'm coming!" he yelled.

"No, get out now!" Joe shouted back. "It's gonna blow, I tell you!"

Antonio rushed into the compartment and saw Joe frantically feeling his way along the face with his hands. When Joe saw the carbide light on the Italian's head he moved toward it, then stumbled and fell hard.

Antonio lifted his partner to his feet with one hand. "Grab the back of my shirt!" he shouted.

The two men had barely cleared the entry when the blast knocked them off their feet and flung them headfirst into the opposite wall of rock.

<><><><><><>

The first thing Antonio saw when he regained consciousness were the big, round eyes of a mule looking down at him. Someone was speaking, but it sounded distantly hollow and in words he couldn't understand. He lay there for several minutes while someone washed his face and neck with a warm, wet cloth. His forehead was wrapped in a bandage of some sort and his chest hurt so much he could barely take a shallow breath.

After several more minutes, he was finally able to understand some of the words from the man kneeling next to him. "Antonio, can you hear me? You'll be okay. Do you understand me?"

Antonio turned his head and saw that the man speaking was a fellow miner named Wittka. The man had been speaking German to his partner. That was a relief to Antonio, who had been afraid they didn't speak English or Italian in heaven.

"Joe?" Antonio whispered weakly.

"Joe's okay. He took most of the blast to his back and never went unconscious. He says you make a pretty good pillow for a scrawny dago."

It was only when Antonio saw Bill Hagley, the mine boss, storm angrily through the door that he realized they were in the mine office next to the cage.

"Are the mules hurt?" Hagley yelled at the first man he saw.

"Why, I guess the mules are fine," said Wittka's partner, a perplexed look on his face, "and I guess the men are too, if you'd like to know."

Hagley studied Antonio as if he were a big catfish a fisherman had just thrown up on shore. "Mules cost money, by God, but I can always hire another man."

Hagley left the room without another word. Antonio never saw the man again. Within six months, the mine boss was dead. Some said his wife left him for another man and old Bill Hagley killed himself by jumping off the roof of his three-story house. Others would say that he fell off the roof while peeping into the window of the house next to him where the pretty widow Stephens lived. Being an Italian who loved romance, Antonio hoped the first story was the correct one.

<><><><><><>

Angeline was half asleep when Antonio lay down on the floor beside her after his first day in the Hewittville mine. She had spent the day planting as much of the nearly five-acre garden as she could. Every muscle and every bone in her body ached. She was afraid he was going to want to take her again as he had twice the night before. He was apparently tired, though, and within seconds was snoring in her ear.

That night she dreamed that her husband built her a little booth on the corner and she sold their garden produce to miners as they walked to and from work. Angeline's mother had taught her how to cook. She would also sell tasty meals to miners, which they would put in their buckets and take down into the mine to eat. Many of them were bachelors, and many others had wives who could not cook as well as a plump, Italian woman. It was a pleasant dream.

When she awoke the next morning, Antonio had already left for the mine. She found blood on the blanket beside her shoulder and even more on a towel beside the wash basin. She didn't find out anything about the coal mine accident until she saw Bill Hagley watching her from across the road as she was bending over to plant some tomatoes.

"Did your husband go back to work today?" Hagley asked her, a cigar clenched between his teeth.

"Yes, why wouldn't he?" she asked.

"He was beat up pretty good yesterday when I saw him. He'd better be more careful. I'd hate to see a pretty little thing like you become a widow."

"He must be all right," Angeline said, hoping to coax more information out of the man. "He went to work early this morning."

"That's good." Hagley took a few steps her way. "If you ever get hard up for money and want your husband to get a little overtime, you just come by my office and ask. You don't even need to hurt his pride by telling him you talked to me. You just come see ol' Bill and I'll take care of you. You understand what I'm saying?"

When she didn't answer, Bill Hagley dropped his cigar butt on the ground and continued on down the street.

A year later, Angeline heard that after old Bill Hagley died, three coal miners quit getting overtime. Their wives had to get jobs at the new glove factory on East Main Street.

4

Eleven years after the 1898 murders of the scabs, the terrible events of Williamsburg Hill still haunted Joe Harrison's dreams.

"You sleep with your eyes open."

"What?" Joe asked. He was used to his wife making a comment followed immediately by a question. Myrna was buxom and beautiful with blond hair that fell to her waist when she let it down at night.

"Why do you sleep on your back with your eyes wide open? It kinda scares me."

Joe shut his eyes.

"I know you're not asleep 'cause your mouth's shut."

Joe opened his mouth.

"You always sleep with your mouth open like you just saw something that scared you." Myrna sat up. "What are you scared of?"

"Grasshoppers."

"I don't like Angeline," Myrna said. "Why is she always so happy? She's been pregnant ever since I've known her, and those boys of hers, my goodness."

"They do have spunk." Joe smiled as he thought of the four Vacca boys following their plump little mother through her big vegetable garden.

"I hate little boys. Would you have rather had a son than a daughter?"

Joe decided that sleeping late on his one day off in two weeks was out of the question. He rolled out of bed and threw his clothes on.

"I hate Sundays," Myrna said. "Why do people want to sit in

church on their only day off?"

<><><><><><><>

Joe stopped outside Barney's General Store. Antonio would be inside having coffee while Angeline and the boys attended Mass. Joe filled his lungs with one last drag on a cigarette, flicked it into the street and then strode through the door.

"Any news about the Cherry mine?" Joe asked as he took a chair next to his partner. Barney's had tables and chairs on one end, store goods on the other and a big, pot bellied stove in the middle. A half dozen men sat at tables talking quietly while smoking and sipping from coffee mugs.

"I heard they pulled twenty-one men out today." Antonio leaned over the coffee he held with both hands.

"Dead?"

"No, but almost."

"One of 'em died as they was bringing him up, so he don't count," Barney said as he placed a coffee and glass of water in front of Joe, and then took himself a seat in the chair next to Antonio. The storekeeper had a wall phone and an uncle who ran a store in Cherry, Illinois. They had talked twice a day since the coal mine disaster that started in the early afternoon of November 13. So far, they knew that over two hundred men had been killed and others were still trapped underground.

"I can't get Angeline to shut up about the disaster," Antonio said. "She wants me to quit mining and open a store in Hewittville. Since I built her that booth on the corner, she's been selling most everything her garden produces. Is Myrna worried about you going down in the mine again?"

Joe couldn't remember the last time he had seen Antonio talking without waving his hands. He stared at his friend who was still looking down at his tightly clutched cup. "Myrna is more worried that I sleep with my eyes open."

"You do sleep with your eyes open," Antonio said, smiling.

"I've seen it when you take a nap in the mine."

"Is that why your eyes are always red?" Barney asked.

"Do they still think the fire started in a boxcar full of hay?" Joe looked at Barney. Even though he already knew the answer, he wanted to change the subject and he knew the talkative store keep would oblige.

"They took a load of hay down to the second vein for the mules and were pushing it in a coal car," Barney said. "A spark from an oil torch on the wall must have got in the hay 'cause when they looked later, it was blazing. They didn't think nothin' of it and just pushed the car down the escarpment to the third vein. I guess they figured it would just burn out, but it didn't. I heard that someone thought he could blow the smoke out of the mine so he reversed the fan. And that was what pulled the flames up the escape shaft and set the wooden staircase on fire."

"How could anyone do such a thing?" Joe poured water in the palm of his hand and rinsed his eyes.

"I imagine they were panicked and not thinking clear," Antonio said. "Why didn't they get the men out right then?"

"By then it was spread to the timbers," Barney said. "The fire started at about one o'clock, and some of the miner's didn't even know about it until they started walking back to the cage about three o'clock. By then they were trapped."

"How do you suppose those twenty-one survived for eight days?" Antonio asked. He realized that knowing all the details might save his life one day.

"I s'pect they built a wall between them and the fire," Barney said.

Since the store keep had never been in a mine, someone must have told him about that survival technique.

"The fire would've gone out when they sealed the mine from the top," Antonio said, thinking aloud. "They probably were more concerned about the black damp."

"What's the black damp?" Barney asked.

"A mixture of carbon dioxide and nitrogen," Joe said. "Makes a deadly gas."

Barney pulled a washrag out of his dirty white apron and blew his nose, then rose and returned to the counter to wait on a customer.

"Some of those men went back down in the cage seven times to bring injured men up," Antonio told Joe. "The seventh time they raised the cage, the rescuers were all burnt to a crisp."

<><><><><><>

Harley Eng didn't have a job, but he was very busy. He had been at a stockbrokers' meeting in Peru, Illinois, when he heard about the Cherry mine disaster. Without hesitation, he rented a fast horse at a stable and rode the eight miles to the scene.

There were over a thousand people gathered around the mine yard when he arrived. Miners who were well enough to be moved were being rushed away to the closest buildings to be treated. Glassy-eyed women stood with scarves over their mouths, their children at their side, most of them crying while they looked at the dirty and often badly burnt miners being brought out. Most of the men down there had been working in teams of two—often alongside a father, son, brother or other relative. Any woman who lost one man would very likely have lost at least one other.

It was dark by the time Harley was able to get close to the cage that was sending rescuers down and then pulling them back up with a few survivors at a time. He arrived just as they were getting ready to send the elevator down for the seventh time.

"We need one more man strong enough to carry at least his own weight!" A miner on the cage shouted. The man looked exhausted but had an incredible air of authority and leadership.

"I'll go!" Harley said, raising his hand. His shout was drowned out by dozens of others, so Harley stepped forward as if he had been summoned. "My name's Eng, and I can carry three men if need be."

The leader's face was so blackened from the coal and smoke his features were barely visible. "I'm the mine boss, John Bundy, and while I'm pleased to meet you, I'm afraid you're not dirty enough for this job." He pointed at a stout young man who had donned a miner's cap. "You, Lewis, let's go."

Harley was nudged out of the cage and the designated man proudly replaced him. The cage began its descent with the twelve rescuers. The last thing he saw was the determined face of John Bundy. For the next twenty minutes, Harley helped carry injured men by way of blankets that were used as litters. After he had made his second trip from the mine yard to local houses and back, angry voices sounded around him.

"Bring 'em up!" People were shouting to the engineer in charge of the lift. "They want you to bring 'em up! The rope's shakin'!"

"That ain't the signal!" the engineer shouted back. His face looked confused and frightened. "They's supposed to ring the bell at least three times."

"Maybe it's the only signal they got!" one miner shouted. "The rope wouldn't be shakin' like that unless they wanted up. You got to bring 'em up now!"

"No!" another man shouted. "If you bring it up too soon you'll leave others behind!"

No one seemed to know what to do. Several long minutes passed with more shouting and screaming before the cage was finally started on its rapid ascent. Then there was silence except for the sound of sobs and crying children.

An angry burst of smoke and then flames spewed from the top of the cage. Four of the twelve rescuers had tried to climb out of the mine on the cables. They were lying on top of the elevator, their bodies afire. One of the bodies convulsed with violent spasms. Eight more men lay in the cage, also on fire.

Suddenly men were rushing into and onto the cage with wet

blankets to smother the flames that had completely consumed every one of the heroic men.

That was the seventh and last cage. None of the men on it were alive or recognizable. It was learned later that the body of John Bundy was among them, as was the man who took Harley's place. He was thirty-three-year-old Isaac Lewis, a liveryman, and he had left behind a wife and three young children.

<><><><><><>

Harley stayed at the scene for three days, helping where he could. He slept in the mine yard at night and ate the food the miner's wives brought the workers. They had sealed the mine immediately after the seventh cage in hopes of smothering the fire. It wasn't until the following Monday that the mine was unsealed and inspectors and rescuers wearing breathing helmets and carrying air tanks on their backs were allowed entry.

"It was supposed to be the safest mine in the world," an old woman said as she brought the men cold chunks of meat and biscuits. "It was one of the young boys who pushed the car full of hay under a torch on the wall. He was just a child and didn't know no better. There had been fires in the mine before and some of the men walked right past it like it weren't nothing. They coulda put it out, but they figured they were leavin' and they wanted to get home so let the next guy do it. They had to make those torches so they could see to work, 'cause the electric lighting had failed, don't ya see. They shoulda just come on home and worked another day, but they were used to carbide lights, so they didn't think nothing of it. They shouldn't let inexperienced young boys work down there. They shoulda just come on home and worked another day."

Harley tried to go down in the mine with the search and recovery parties.

"Thank you just the same, sir," one miner said to him as he

flicked a cigarette butt to the ground and stomped it. "We'd like to take care of our own, if you don't mind, sir."

The final death toll was two hundred and fifty-nine men and boys. Another twelve rescuers on the seventh cage trip also died. Harley Eng would forever be haunted by the thought that had it not been for his clean clothes and a man named John Bundy, he would have been among those twelve.

Most of the workers in the disaster died from the black damp, while others were consumed by fire. In one compartment they found a father and son lying on the bottom together, hugging one another in death.

5

When Harley left Cherry, he made a quick detour to Joliet, then went straight to the state capital in Springfield.

When Harley walked into his state senator's office, Winston Talbot stood and moved to the front of his desk to greet him. Talbot's head tilted back and his shoulders remained rigid. As he walked, the patriarch of the wealthiest family in downstate Illinois displayed an obvious, haughty arrogance. His stomach paunched noticeably over the top of his pants, but rather than take away from the awesomeness of the man's power, it only tended to remind people of his affluence.

"Harley," he said. "So good to see you again. To what do I owe this honor?"

"I just got back from the Cherry mine."

"Oh, yes, I heard that company had a little problem last week."

"Over two hundred miners, their wives and children had the problem." Harley tried to control himself. He forced his voice to remain calm. "The company will probably go bankrupt, but at least they are still alive."

"Yes, of course." Talbot moved back behind his desk and took a long puff on a half smoked cigar. "We will have to do a fundraiser for the families, and I would like to be the first to give. How does fifty dollars sound? That should get the ball rolling."

"Thank you, Winston. That is very generous." Harley took a seat in the leather chair and took a deep breath. "But I was thinking about something more permanent that would help miners all across the state, maybe even the country."

"Fine idea, my boy." Talbot sounded supportive, but looked less than enthusiastic. "Why don't you put some ideas in writing and leave them with my secretary?" He rose again and started back around the desk.

"I don't think so, Winston." This was the moment of truth. Harley didn't budge from his chair.

"What do you mean?"

"I mean that I'm not leaving here until you hear me out. Just consider this a stockholders meeting."

Talbot hesitated. "Did you go to the meeting last week?"

"Yes, I did, and I was sorry to see you were absent." Harley's heart was beating fast and he struggled to control his voice. "After the Cherry mine disaster, I stopped by Joliet and visited Dean Rothrock."

Talbot sat back down.

"Since I now own controlling interest in the company that you started," Harley said, becoming increasingly confident due to the startled look on the senator's face, "I thought we might have a nice, long chat about things like compensation for injured or killed workers and their families, minimum age requirements for workers, and maybe even think of a way to establish stronger safety regulations in the mines."

Winston Talbot winced. In his head he quickly began calculating figures from his investment in the company against dollars he could make through his position in the government. By the time Harley was done talking, Talbot was a new man.

<><><><><><>

The month after the Cherry mine disaster saw a long and unusually warm Indian summer. The week before Christmas, Joe spent a quiet Sunday afternoon sitting on the porch at Antonio's little house, watching Angeline gather and burn leaves in her garden. The four Vacca boys, ranging in age from two to eight, dug in a sandbox nearby. Joe was envious of his friend. He knew his own daughter, Felina, would be tearing up her toys while her mother lounged on the bed complaining about her sinuses or her back pains or one of the other popular maladies she had read about somewhere. While Myrna was infinitely more attractive than Angeline, she lacked her spunk and motherly nature.

"How do you like being pit committeeman?" Antonio asked. He took a sip of wine from his glass followed by a deep drag on a cigarette and sighed.

"It's all right, I guess," Joe said, watching his friend's reaction carefully. He had recognized over the years that when Antonio's hands stopped moving, he was about to make an adamant point.

"Does Ware take the miner's concerns seriously when you talk to him?" Antonio said, his hands still dormant.

"I suppose so." Joe sensed what was coming. His new job involved communicating concerns of the miners to Augustus Ware, the mine boss. "I don't get many grievances, though."

Antonio's hands seemed to explode, knocking over his glass of wine and dropping his cigarette. "That's because instead of going down in the mine where the workers can talk to you privately, you stand in front of the mine office as the men are leaving for the day." He emphasized each word with a chastising hand gesture. "Men are tired after work and just want to get home. You know that." He paused and met Joe's eyes. "And do you think anyone is going to talk to you when they know Ware is watching through the window of the mine office?"

"You talk like the company is against the men!" All Joe wanted was peace. Peace from his wife and now from his friend.

"You can hire another man, but, by God, mules cost money," Antonio growled. "Remember that?"

"Bill Hagley's been dead for years!" Joe filled his lungs with air to calm his words. "The company has come a long way since then, and quit waving your hands at me. I'm not the mine boss."

Antonio put his hands under his lap. "I haven't told Angeline yet." He began slowly, causing Joe to listen more closely than when the Italian waved his hands. "An agent from the company store came to me yesterday. He says Angeline can't sell her produce next summer. I guess it cuts into their profit from scrip."

Joe stared at his friend. He could understand why miners had to use the company store to buy things like black powder. Though it was marked up three times higher than they would pay somewhere else, using good powder was a matter of safety. But why would they complain about a miner's wife supplementing her family income?

In his heart, Joe knew the answer. Angeline had been telling people she wanted to start a grocery store and restaurant in Hewittville. If she did, the company would lose. Angeline's tortellinis were the best anywhere east or west of Italy.

"Tell her to quit selling," Joe said firmly.

"*What?*" Antonio took his hands out from under his lap and raveled off a stream of Italian words, many of which Joe recognized from unhappy moments down in the mine.

Joe got up, walked to the end of the porch and picked up an old coal bucket. He handed it to his friend. "Miners know how to fill a bucket. Tell Angeline to plant her garden, but tear down that booth."

That next summer, for the first time in many years, when miners walked past the Vacca house they did not see the plump Italian woman selling produce. In fact, she wasn't even outside working her garden as they walked to work in the morning or home at night. Her garden though, was rich with vegetables and more attractive than ever.

Joe Harrison knew that you couldn't put good food in front of a hungry man and expect him to ignore it. It became a custom for miners to pick what they wanted from the garden and place money in the black bucket on the porch. Joe had been right. Coal miners knew how to fill a coal bucket. Angeline made more money than she had when she worked her booth.

Kevin Corley

To show her appreciation, she began leaving a big cauldron of tortellinis on the porch.

The coal bucket filled even faster.

6

Filberto Vacca's favorite game was kick-the-can. He couldn't understand why most of the other boys would rather hit a baseball. Unfortunately, that meant he had to play it mostly with girls, although his little brother, Libero, also liked the game—but he was only four and only allowed to start school because he was smart and looked older than he was.

Filberto was glad to be six years old. He didn't think he wanted to get any older. The teacher, Mrs. Foster, was always yelling at his brother Bullo, who was ten. His other brother, Vinnie, was only eight but got paddled almost every day. In fact, Vinnie had already that morning had to wear the dunce cap and sit in the corner because he showed Missy Weir the dead frog he kept in his pocket. Missy was a year older than Filberto. He knew that, had she not screamed when she saw the frog, she would not have received a hard punch on the shoulder from Vinnie when they got outside for morning recess.

Filberto had never been paddled by the teacher and he hated dead animals. He didn't think that Missy should have screamed though, and her purple bruise did seem to even the score with Vinnie. Filberto didn't expect his brother to cause the little girl any further problems. Missy was not a very pretty girl, and he felt sorry for the way her front teeth came down over her bottom lip. But then, he himself was called Snoz because his nose was crooked from the two breaks he had sustained while playing with his brothers. Other than the nose, like his brothers, he had the curly brown hair and straight white teeth of their father.

Filberto recognized he was more sensitive about a lot of

things than the other boys. He liked school and was already in the third grade reader with Vinnie. He also liked to help his mother in the garden, especially the strawberry patch when the berries were ripe.

Libero was his best friend, just as Bullo and Vinnie were best friends. He let his little brother follow him around during recess, and today, playing kick-the-can, he showed him where to hide. Leaving Libero underneath the crawl space of the school, he snuck around through the woods trying to out-maneuver Felina Harrison, who was "it" and in charge of guarding the old soup can. Cutting through a bush to avoid some poison ivy, Filberto saw Missy with her back to a tree rubbing the shoulder that Vinnie had punched.

"Don't worry about Vinnie," Filberto whispered as he looked around for Felina. "He won't cause you anymore trouble. I'd s'pect he'll get in a fight before recess is over anyhow."

"I'm not worried about that stupid, old boy." Missy said, tears in her big, blue eyes. "I can't read. Mama said if I don't learn to read, they'll hold me back in second grade."

"Oh, getting held back don't mean nothin'," Filberto said. "Chip Howsham's been held back three times. Besides, we're all in the same classroom anyhow."

"I just don't understand letters," Missy said. "They just don't make any sense."

"I see Filberto behind that tree," Felina Harrison suddenly shouted as she ran as fast as she could toward the soup can.

Filberto was quickly on her tail and the race was on. Though the "it" girl was two years older, the little Italian had years of practice running from his brothers. Racing past Felina just before she reached the can, he kicked it a good twenty feet. Before the "it" girl could retrieve the can and return it to its original spot, Filberto and one of the three "prisoners" in jail had disappeared into the brush.

When recess was over, the teacher took Vinnie and Chip Howsham outside to the woodpile to be paddled for fighting.

They had argued over whether or not Vinnie was safe or out at second base. While she was gone, the children talked and scurried about the classroom, although they were supposed to be working on their reading.

Filberto took the opportunity to help Missy with her first grade reader.

"Filby has a girlfriend, Filby has a girlfriend," Felina Harrison sang.

The other kids in the room looked at the accused to see how they would react. Filberto glanced at Missy and saw her face turn red as a radish. He sensed that she was more than just embarrassed. A girl who had teeth like Missy probably felt that no one would ever want her. His instinct was to shout the standard line—"I wouldn't have a girlfriend that ugly!"—but Filberto Vacca's mother had always told him to think about a person's feelings before acting.

"So what if she's my girlfriend?" Filberto heard himself saying.

"Ahhgg!" Bernard Phelps shouted. "A bucktooth and a snozzola. Please don't get married and have children. Ahhgg!"

Libero jumped on Bernard's back and was still hanging on with his short arms when Bullo smacked the fifth grader in the mouth.

<><><><><><>

That evening, the four Vacca boys leaned over the woodpile, their rear ends bared.

"Mama, I wasn't even in the classroom when they got in the fight!" Vinnie protested.

"You should have been." Angeline smacked her number-two son so hard with the hickory switch her feet came off the ground along with his.

When their father came home at five o'clock, all four boys were asleep on their empty stomachs with their sore butts sticking up. As part of the punishment, their mother had made a particularly good smelling dinner.

"What did the boys do this time?" he asked his wife as she slapped a fork full of pasta onto his plate. "Even our Filberto?" he added before she could speak.

"Especially our Filberto," she said. Sauce splashed onto his shirt as the helping of meatballs bounced onto his plate from her serving spoon.

Antonio listened as his angry wife related the incident in rapid-fire Italian. She only finished as he was sopping up the last bite of sauce with a piece of garlic bread.

"Could I ask why Filberto is in trouble if all he did was help a girl with her homework?"

"Because, my husband." Angeline said. "He wanted to be beaten."

"He said he wanted to be beaten?"

"You do not know your sons, Antonio. If I had not beaten Filberto, his brothers would have resented him. Not only did he not join the fight, but he allowed his little brother to fight his battle for him."

"Are you saying he should have used violence, Angeline? Are not you the one who takes your sons to Mass every week?"

"Yes, it is the mother's job to teach her children about God." Angeline handed her husband a pair of old, heavily worn boxing gloves. "It is the father's job to teach his sons to defend themselves."

<>< ><>< ><>< >

The next Monday morning Filberto went to school with a very black eye, which he was immensely proud of. He had enjoyed the one-on-one time learning the art of fisticuffs from his father. As he and his brothers neared the corner a block from the school, he saw that Chip Howsham and Bernard Phelps were watching them and timing it so they could intersect.

"Look at the curly-headed spaghetti-snappers," Chip said with a smirk. "Is this a niggerpatch?"

"What's a niggerpatch?" Filberto asked.

"Niggerpatch," Chip repeated. "You know, where wops live."

"You must be a drugstore cowboy." Vinnie said.

"What?" Chip said, looking confused.

"One of those Johnny Bulls from England who thinks he was in America before the Indians," Vinnie said with a laugh.

"If you didn't have your brothers with you," Chip said, holding up a fist, "I'd let you have it."

Filberto touched Vinnie's arm before he could step toward the boy. "Let me handle this one," Filberto said.

Vinnie smiled and took Bernard firmly by the arm. "Let's go," he said.

When Filberto walked into the classroom ten minutes later, he was smiling ear to ear with a second black eye. Chip Howsham didn't come to school at all that day.

<><><><><><>

Although her three story, six-bedroom home was considered a mansion in Taylorville, Lena Eng loved going to the little Vacca house. She and Harley didn't fit in with the wealthy, and it seemed that most of the working class shunned them. Angeline, though, treated her as an equal and even made her help around the house or garden each time she came over.

Lena also enjoyed playing baseball or kick-the-can with the boys while the little mother kneaded and rolled dough for her pasta. It seemed that Angeline always had as much flour on her short, chubby arms as she did the blue apron that she put on immediately when entering her house and took off when leaving.

Aunt Lena, as the Vacca boys called her, longed for children. Since Harley didn't really have a job, they had plenty of time for trying. In eleven years of marriage, it just never happened. The subject came up one afternoon as Lena, Angeline and Myrna lounged on the Vacca porch.

"I'd thank my lucky stars that you don't have children if I were you," Myrna Harrison said. "Having just one girl gives me such a headache."

"I'd still like to have one," Lena said with her head down.

"Quit trying." Angeline shook her head. "Love is to be enjoyed. Bambinos will come when and if the good Lord chooses. In the meantime, take enjoyment from your man's body."

"Enjoyment?" Myrna scoffed. "I'd rather have the run off."

Angeline snuck a mischievous glance at Lena. "Let's see, diarrhea or my man's pleasure? I'll have to think about that one?"

"But, what if we never have children?" Lena asked Angeline, ignoring Myrna's comment. "I'm almost thirty years old."

"Then you will make one another happy in other ways." Angeline smiled more wickedly than Lena had ever seen. Suddenly the boys ran across the porch, whooping like Indians. "And when you get tired of that," the mother said as she grabbed a broom and smacked her slowest on the behind, "you will borrow these little rascals and my husband will give me happiness."

That next summer, Lena Eng had a little bambina to play with. She named her Angie.

7

"We don't know how to do nothin' 'cept mine for coal," the old man nicknamed Ear told Harley Eng. "This Cherry mine's done for. I lost my son and grandson down there and my wife died of a broken heart that Christmas Eve. I knew half the men who perished in that hellhole. Most of them were from the old country. Seventy-three of the men killed were Italian. Did you know that?"

"Then come to Christian County with me," Harley said. "They're opening a new mine in Jeiseyville." He turned to the twenty other men and women who sat in the pews of their church. The church had seen a resurgence of faith among the people of Cherry, Illinois. At least a half-dozen people knelt in the pews, rosaries in hand, at any given hour.

"Where will we live? I don't know anyone there," said a widow whose two sons were now old enough to work.

Harley hesitated. Here was the flaw. He had spent much of his fortune helping the surviving families, but there was a limit on how much more he could do. "There are lots of Italians living in Christian County," he said. "And there are company houses in several of the communities."

"*Company houses?*" another miner shouted. He had a violent coughing fit before continuing. "And company scrip, I suppose? Are we supposed to give away all the income that we sweat and die for so the company can get richer?"

"We got no choice," said old Ear. "I must support my son's wife until she takes a new husband. I will go."

As new mines opened up in Christian County over the next few years, much of the population of Cherry, Illinois, moved to the growing communities of Tovey, Langley, Jeiseyville and Kincaid.

Antonio Vacca told Harley Eng that the good thing about it was that these workers took mine safety as seriously as he did. Many of the older miners and the mine managers laughed at the amount of time these men spent sounding roofs and repairing props.

"Why these folks ain't miners," sneered the critics, "they're just a bunch of sounders, that's what they are."

<><><><><><>

"I was one of the women who sang my way out of jail," Mrs. Borgononi told Angeline, Lena and Myrna. The wrinkled little lady guessed her own age at somewhere around eighty, though Lena thought she looked closer to ninety.

"You must be a pretty bad singer," Myrna said. She sat at the kitchen table of the Vacca home with Mrs. Borgononi, who was holding little Angie Eng, while Lena helped Angeline prepare food.

"She's talking about the Slovak strike in Pennsylvania last year," Lena said. She liked Mrs. Borgononi and wasn't about to let Myrna's attitude prevail. "Sixteen people, mostly miners and their families, were murdered because they wanted to join the United Mine Workers."

"Well," Myrna's nose wrinkled. "I don't know what all the fuss is. You'd think those miners would just be glad to have jobs."

"My son-in-law was one of the miners," Mrs. Borgononi went on as if unaware that anyone else had been speaking. "He was paid by the ton of coal that he loaded but not the time he spent laying track, shoring up tunnels, pumping out water or even for any of the slack."

"What is slack?" Myrna asked.

"It's real small or fine coal," Angeline said, pushing her

wooden rolling pin back and forth over floury bread dough. "They only paid the miners for the larger chunks, even though the company made money on the slack."

"My Johnny spent a lot of time removing clay and slate from the coal, too," Mrs. Borgononi added. Somehow her mouth was the only part of her body that seemed to have kept its mobility in her old age. "Didn't get paid for doing that neither. Then they had those coal cars all different sizes. My goodness, I don't know how he ever made any money."

"How much did they get paid?" Lena asked loudly so the older lady could hear.

"That's what finally made the miners mad enough to try and unionize," Mrs. Borgononi said. "They lowered the wages sixteen percent to fifty-eight cents per ton-and-a-half."

"Well, what's wrong with that?" Myrna said.

"If a miner had a good day and brought out sixteen tons, that would be less than six dollars a day," Lena said. "Myrna, do you think you could have afforded that new dress you're wearing if your husband brought home six dollars a day?"

"Well," Myrna said, "I don't think it's very ladylike to talk about money, but that sounds like a lot to me."

"The mines don't work year round, do they, Myrna?" Lena said as patiently as she could. "Miners must save part of their wages for down time during the summer months."

"Besides the pay cut, our boys also had to buy the new safety lights and explosives from the company store." Mrs. Borgononi said. She shook her head sadly. "The company store—"

"Tell us about how you sang your way out of jail," Angeline prompted.

"Oh, that was Mary Jones' idea," the old woman said with a smile.

"You mean Mother Jones was there?" Angeline asked.

"Who's Mother Jones?" Lena asked. She sensed power and righteousness in the woman's very name.

"She's a famous union activist," Angeline told her. "She

travels the country helping workers who are being mistreated. But isn't she very old, Mrs. Borgononi? I can't believe she's still active."

"Oh yes, dear," Mrs. Borgononi said. "I should imagine she's a little younger than me, but she's as feisty as ever. She told our boys to go home and rest and let the women do the picketing for a while. Why, we women were harder on the strikebreakers than our men were. We knew how those scabs were taking the bread out of our children's mouths, so we really let 'em have it, I tell you.

"Well, that sheriff didn't like us out there at all, 'cause we were really mouthy, ya see, so he arrested us all for disturbing the peace. Ha! Can you imagine that? Mother Jones told us to take our babies and tiny children with us when we went to court, and you should have heard the hullabaloo. Why, those crying kids were so loud, you couldn't even hear that judge speak. He shouted, 'Thirty dollars or thirty days!'

"Why, none of us had thirty dollars, so we said we'd go to jail. That judge scowled at us and told us to get someone to watch our children, but Mother Jones told us to tell him there weren't no one to watch 'em, so I myself shouted to the judge, 'miner wives don't keep no nurse girls! God gave these children to their mothers and He held them responsible for their care.'

"By golly, he sent us to the jail in Greensburg, children and all. Boy, was that a mistake! They put us in what they called interurban cars to take us to the jail. Along the way they picked up two scabs that were walking along the road and let 'em ride in back with us. That was another mistake! As soon as that car got going, I yelled, 'Get 'em girls!' We really worked those two over! They were screaming to the motorman to stop and let 'em out, but the motorman said it was against the law for him to stop until he got to the station. That gave the women a little more time to trim the fellas, ya see. When they got to the station, those scabs looked as if they had been sleeping in the tiger cage at the zoo.

"Why, we was so happy, we was singing at the top of our lungs. A crowd of town's folk followed as they unloaded us and they joined us in singin'. I heard the sheriff of that county tell Mother Jones, 'Mother, I would rather you brought me a hundred men than those women. Women are fierce!'"

"And Mother Jones says to him, 'I didn't bring them to you, sheriff. T'was the mining company's judge sent them to you for a present.'"

"Mother Jones liked our singing so much she said, 'You sing the whole night long. You can spell one another if you get tired and hoarse. Sleep all day and sing all night and don't stop for anyone. Say you're singing to the babies. I will bring the little ones milk and fruit. Just you all sing and sing.'"

"Well, that sheriff's wife didn't like our singin' one bit. Neither did the folks in the hotels and the nearby houses. They complained to the sheriff and the sheriff complained to the judge. Finally, after five nights of non-stop singin', the judge ordered our release."

"Well," Myrna said, clearly happy the woman was done talking, "why didn't you stay in Pennsylvania if you women won?"

"Oh, we didn't win, dear." Mrs. Borgononi said. "We got out of jail, but we lost the strike this last July. The company stopped the union from coming in and fired hundreds of the strikers. My Johnny was one of them. That's why we came here, so he could work in your mine. You've got the United Mine Workers to help you."

Lena had been so moved by the story she sat in a chair at the table and watched the old woman intently. "I should like to meet this Mother Jones," she said.

"Oh, she's a character, that one is," Mrs. Borgononi said. "I told her that she needed to help women get the right to vote, and she said, 'You don't need a vote to raise hell. All you need are convictions and a voice.'"

Sixteen Tons

<><><><><><>

The next day the Vacca family got what Angeline considered their first taste of financial success.

"Why did you put the machine so high on the wall?" Angeline asked.

The telephone man looked at the five-foot tall lady and then at the rectangular, wooden box that hung vertically just above her head. It had taken him ten minutes to find the studs in the living room wall so he could secure the heavy machine.

"You need it high enough so you can stand up straight when you talk," he told her with a condescending air of authority. "It helps the person at the other end hear you."

"Oh, all right." Angeline said, nervously rubbing her chin.

"Now your ring is two longs and a short," the telephone man said. "There are a dozen other people on your line so don't pick up the ear piece unless it rings two longs and a short."

Without another word, the man packed his workbox and walked out the front door. Angeline stood looking up expectantly at the strange box hanging on the wall.

"Call someone, Mama," Bullo said. He loved machines and couldn't wait to find out how it worked. Vinnie and Libero were playing outside, while Filberto stood in the doorway eating a stalk of celery and watching silently.

"Oh my goodness, no," Angeline said. "Who would I call?"

"Well, call Aunt Lena," Filberto suggested. "She has a telephone."

Angeline's hands shook as she took the earpiece off the hook and held it firmly against her ear. When she didn't hear anyone else on the line she spun the ring handle once.

"Central? Central?" She stood on her toes and shouted into the telephone mouthpiece that arched down toward her mouth. "Yes, central, this is Angeline Vacca. Oh, Thelma? I didn't know you were Central. How are you, Thelma? Yes, well, soak it in salt water, dear. Now, I want to ring Lena Eng,

54

Thelma. Yes, yes, I'll wait."

Angeline looked at Bullo. "We have to wait until someone on Lena's party line hangs up," she told him. Several minutes went by.

"Mama," Filberto finally said quietly. "I don't think you need to keep your mouth by the mouthpiece until the person says something."

Angeline came down off her toes and leaned against the wall, but she kept the receiver pressed hard against her ear.

"*Lena?*" Angeline suddenly shouted and then realized she was away from the mouthpiece. She went back up on her toes. "Lena? Is that you, Lena Eng? This is Angeline Vacca talking." She giggled. "Yes, Angeline."

"Can you hear her, Mama?" Bullo whispered and then fell backwards when his mother gave him a hard push with the back of her hand.

"Do you want me to talk louder, Lena?" Angeline shouted. She grimaced and spoke in a quieter voice. "Oh, okay. What do you want to talk about?"

Bullo pulled up a chair, stood on it and put his head close to his mother's. She again pushed him away from the phone and he stumbled off the chair.

"I can't think of anything either!" Angeline shouted. "If you think of something you can ring me back. Oh, okay. Are you ready to stop talking? Okay, I'm going to put the listening piece down now." She stood frozen in place. A few seconds later, she shouted, *"Are you still there, Lena?* Okay, let's both hang up our pieces at the same time. I'll count to three, then we'll both hang it on the little hook. Are you ready? One, two, three..."

Angeline remained standing on her tiptoes listening in the earpiece. "Are you still there?" she finally said and then giggled. "So am I."

"Mama, just say goodbye." Bullo said.

"Oh, no, Bullo," Angeline said and pushed him away from her for a third time. "Goodbye sounds like you'll never see each other again. No, Lena, I was talking to Bullo. Listen, Lena, let's just say *ciao* when we want to quit talking. Okay? Yes, *ciao. Ciao*, dear, *ciao*."

Angeline quickly put the earpiece on its hook and stepped back. She rubbed her hands together and continued to look at the wooden box. Finally, she turned to Bullo. "Do you think she'll ring me back?"

8

One lazy Sunday afternoon following Mass and a large meal of fried chicken, mashed potatoes, corn and apple pie, the entire Vacca family sat on their porch. The boys had insisted their mother learn to cook the meal that all their friends claimed was their favorite.

"It makes us real Americans, Mama," Bullo told her the day he and his brothers got up the courage to confront their formidable little mother.

"All right," Angeline said, "I'll make it. But don't ever forget that you will still always have Italiano in your blood."

After the big dinner, the boys seemed satisfied enough to tolerate their parents' company while they digested. One lay on each of the four steps of the porch in the order of their birth, with Bullo at the top. Their parents enjoyed the slow movement of the porch swing. Antonio read the newspaper and puffed on a cigarette while Angeline darned a sock.

"Papa," Filberto said, finally breaking the silence, "do you think Henry Ford is as smart as Thomas Edison?"

Antonio lowered his newspaper and looked at his boys. He saw that Vinnie was twirling a finger around his own ear and then pointing it at Filberto. When his father gave him a stern look, Vinnie stopped immediately and turned away.

"Well, son," Antonio said, "I guess they're both smart in different ways. I think Edison's most purely an inventor, while Ford's smart at making money with his locomotives."

"I think I'd like to be like Edison," Filberto said. "But I'd want to make money so I can buy you and Mama an automobile."

"Oh, gracious sakes, Filberto." Angeline laughed. "You're

not going to make me ride in one of those infernal machines, are you?"

"Listen!" Bullo interrupted the conversation and stood up on his step. "Hear that music?"

A moment later they were all standing.

"Why, it's a marching band!" Antonio said as uniformed men walked past them down the street toward the park. Behind the band came a long crowd of people walking or with horse and buggy. An occasional flivver filled the street with smoke and loud engine noise. At the end of the procession another small band was playing while sitting on a hay wagon pulled by a half dozen horses.

"Hey, you Vaccas!" a man who worked in the mine yelled. "Everybody's going to the Chautauqua in the park. Come on, jump on the bandwagon!"

The boys looked at their mother, who looked at her husband. When he nodded, the four boys raced to the bandwagon and jumped on.

"Well," Antonio said and flipped his cigarette into a coal bucket, "so much for a relaxing Sunday. I guess we'd better get our church clothes back on and join the celebration."

<><><><><><>

Thousands of people dressed in their Sunday best had come out for the grand opening of the new Chautauqua building. The municipal band was playing on the stage while several hundred men and women sitting in rickety chairs furiously waved homemade fans to keep themselves cool.

"Sure would hold a lot of coal!" Antonio said to Angeline an hour later as they gazed at the enormous, round building in the middle of the crowded park.

"Why would they put coal in a place like that?" Myrna asked.

Joe shook his head and took his wife's arm. He gently led

her alongside Harley and Lena as the three couples walked toward the baseball field. Bullo and Vinnie were playing in a pick-up game with several other boys and young men. Nearby, Filberto had organized a game of kick-the-can and was busy hiding Libero in a bushy area near one of the pavilions.

Several large tents were set up throughout the park. Dozens of couples strolled among them, stopping occasionally to read posters that described the grand entertainment inside. One tent had a lecturer talking about a trip he'd taken to Africa. Another had dancers from Scotland. Two others had evangelists preaching, and one had a group of four men playing lively music on a guitar, a banjo, a fiddle and a bass.

"I want the boys to hear that man talk about Africa," Angeline said.

"These Chautauquas are a good way to educate people," Lena said. "I wish they had them in the town where I grew up."

Suddenly Joe spotted his daughter. At only nine years old, Felina Harrison stood out from all the children in the park. Her blond hair and clear, beautiful skin made even adult men look her way until they recognized her age. Joe didn't like that his daughter was already using her attractiveness to get the things she wanted. As the couples walked, he saw her talking to a young trumpet player near the bandwagon. The boy looked about fifteen. It didn't surprise Joe when the youth reached in his pocket, pulled out a coin and handed it to Felina. He watched his daughter grab it out of the boy's hand, and without so much as a thank you she skipped merrily away toward the taffy pull. Joe could tell that Myrna saw it too, because she quickly pointed to something in the opposite direction.

Joe had never told anyone, even his best friend Antonio, but he often had doubts that Felina was even his child. She had blond hair and a facial structure that resembled neither himself nor her mother. Hard as he had tried he found he had very little in common with Felina. Even Myrna seemed perplexed by her daughter's behavior, and though she loved the girl dearly, she clearly preferred to do so from a distance. She seemed to have fewer headaches the further she stayed from the wild and headstrong child.

<><><><><><>

Later that morning, the Vacca brothers had a nice visit as they competed in the park fishing tournament. Since Libero had broken his cane pole by using it to sword fight, he spent the time trying to make a frog jump into a Mason jar that was half full of water. Filberto had again brought up the subject of inventions and, as usual, Vinnie was in the mood to irritate his younger brother.

"I heard that everything that can be invented has been invented," Vinnie told Bullo and Filberto as they waited to get a nibble.

"Huh-uh!" Filberto said. "What about talking picture shows?"

"There'll never be picture shows that talk." Vinnie laughed.

"Sure will," Filberto said. "I'm going to invent a talking picture show." He had been obsessed with picture shows since he saw one in the spring about a boy and a girl alone on an island. His mother told him it was based on a book she'd read called *The Blue Lagoon*. The best part was when the girl threw herself in a volcano.

"How are you going to make people in a picture show talk?" Vinnie asked.

"I'm going to play one of those Gramophones with people speaking while the films running." Filberto said.

Vinnie was going to tell his brother he was stupid, but Bullo touched his arm.

"You know," Bullo whispered thoughtfully, "I think that just might work."

Libero's frog suddenly jumped and plopped like a rock into the Mason jar.

<><><><><><>

Later that afternoon, over a thousand men and their wives gathered around the new Chautauqua building to hear the guest speaker, John L. Lewis. Lewis was a fellow coal miner from Panama, Illinois, just south of Taylorville. He had been elected president of his United Mine Workers local in 1909. Samuel Gompers of the American Federation of Labor hired Lewis as a full-time union organizer in 1911. Antonio and Harley were very interested in hearing what he had to say.

"Why do you want to hear that socialist garbage?" Joe asked his friends as the three couples made their way to chairs in the big building. As the room filled, the familiar cough of coal miners echoed through billowing cigarette smoke and off the arched ceiling.

"I want to hear what he has to say about the West Virginia strike," Antonio said. "Angeline's brother, Vincent mines there. The union is strong here in Illinois, we got the best mining wages in the country, but West Virginia isn't so lucky."

Joe sat down and crossed his arms. Myrna sat beside him but started waving her butterfly fan so fast Antonio could tell she was about to get one of her headaches.

"My goodness," Myrna said when Lewis stood and walked to the podium. "Look at the size of that man's *head*. Why doesn't he trim those eyebrows?"

Antonio took a deep breath. Joe and Myrna would not hear much of John L. Lewis's speech.

With a scowl on his face and his jaw firmly set, Lewis's voice thundered through the auditorium. "Before I talk about anything else, I want to make an important announcement. The miner's angel, Mother Jones, has been released from jail."

The roar of approval made Myrna fall out of her seat onto the graveled floor. Everyone was suddenly standing and shouting, laughing, crying, hugging or slapping backs. While he embraced Angeline, Antonio saw Joe help his wife to her feet. The couple immediately began squeezing their way out of the open-air building. It took several more moments of celebration before the speaker could continue.

"Maybe some of you miners have been underground so long you haven't heard that Mary Jones and dozens of other labor leaders in West Virginia have been illegally held on trumped-up charges since early February. During that time a senator denounced her on the floor of our United States Congress saying she was the grandmother of all agitators. Well, I have news for that Senator. Mother Jones says she hopes to live long enough to be the *great-grandmother* of all agitators."

The crowd gave another rousing applause.

"I want to tell you about some threats that have been made at Mother Jones these past few weeks and how she handled them. When told they would keep her in jail for the rest of her life, our Mother Jones said, 'I can raise just as much hell in jail as anywhere.'

"When threatened with the firing squad, Mother Jones said, 'I am eighty years old and haven't long to live anyhow. Since I have to die, I would rather die for the cause to which I have given so much of my life.'

"When told she would be released if she would leave West Virginia, Mother Jones said, 'You bring your guns and put me up against that tree outside this Bastille and riddle me with bullets, but I will never surrender my rights to remain in this state as long as it suits my business to do so.'"

When another round of cheering finally subsided, Lewis continued. "Now let me tell you that I started work in an Iowa mine when I was seventeen years old, and more recently at a mine just a few miles from here. I come from the same background as many of you, so I understand what it means to be a coal miner.

"So do the miners of West Virginia. They have been fighting for the right to unionize for the last fourteen months. The

Baldwin-Felts Detective Agency has killed over fifty innocent men, women and children during that time. I want you to remember the names of Thomas, Albert and Lee Felts. They have hired over three hundred professional assassins to protect the coal company and their scabs. They have an armored car that they call the Bull Moose Special that has a mounted machine gun they use to fire into the tents of the strikers at night while they are sleeping."

A roar of condemnation arose from the crowd.

"The Governor of West Virginia has suppressed every right that is guaranteed in the First Amendment to the United States Constitution. He even suppressed all newspapers that said anything in favor of the United Mine Workers.

"Ladies and gentlemen, I hope you will join me in doing everything we can to ensure that every worker in America has the right to join a labor union. That no man will ever again be denied the freedoms of speech, press or assembly.

"Let the workers organize! Let the toilers assemble! Let their crystallized voice proclaim their injustices and demand their privileges! Let all thoughtful citizens sustain them, for the future of labor is the future of America!"

Antonio stood and cheered louder and longer than anyone in the room. Immediately after the speech, he decided to talk to his UMW representative as soon as possible about volunteering as a union organizer.

<><><><><><>

"Is it a boy kitty or a girl kitty?" Felina asked.

"I don't know," Libero said, holding the kitten to his cheek. Two other kittens with fluffy long tails purred softly as they rubbed their scent into his trousers.

"Well, take a look, silly," Felina said. She and Libero had found a good spot to hide from the kick-the-can "it" beneath a clothesline draped with sweet smelling sheets.

"Look at what?" Libero held the fuzzy animal at a distance and looked at it.

"Say, I have an idea," Felina said. "I'll show you mine if you show me yours."

"My what?" Libero asked.

"Your wee-wee, stupid," Felina said. "What else would you have that I'd want to see?"

"Why would you want to see that?" Libero asked. "Look at your own."

"I don't have one, you idiot."

"Why?" Libero said, looking horrified. "Did you break yours off?"

Felina picked up two kittens.

"Close your eyes, Libero," Felina said, a brow rising. "I have a surprise for you."

Libero closed his eyes. He had seen earlier that Felina had some licorice. When he opened his eyes a moment later, Libero let out the wildest screech of his young life. The two little kittens were hanging by their knotted tails on the clothesline above him. The animals were in a blurred battle of slashing claws and fierce bites to not only their sibling but to their own bodies. Blood squirted from their wounds onto the little boy and on the freshly laundered sheets around him. Libero continued to scream even as he reached out with both hands to try and help the poor babies. Arms suddenly grabbed around Libero's waist and pulled him away from the bloody catfight.

"Libero, quit screaming," Filberto said to his brother as the two kittens suddenly ceased to move and hung like wet socks from the clothesline.

Shaking, Libero buried his blood splattered face in his brother's shoulder and cried. He felt Filberto stroking his head. After a few minutes he looked up to see if anyone had been near enough to hear his screams.

"Everyone's running to the other end of the park 'cause someone's got an elephant," Filberto told him. "No one saw you cry."

"You won't tell Bullo or Vinnie, will you?" Libero pleaded.

"Of course not." Filberto helped his brother up. "Did Felina do that?"

Libero nodded. "I thought she was going to give me a piece of licorice."

"Felina Harrison would never give anyone anything except trouble," Filberto said as they walked toward Hewittville, "Let's get home and clean you up. No one needs to know anything about this."

"Filby," Libero asked when they reached the railroad tracks. "Felina said she doesn't have a wee-wee. How does she go pee?"

"I don't know," Filberto said and smiled, "but I'll bet if we put a garter snake in her lunch bucket, we'll find out."

9

On New Year's morning, Antonio told his wife, "They've asked me to go to Kentucky."

"Well," his wife said, staring at her blue apron, "I suppose this time you might make it past Ohio."

On his first union organizing mission to West Virginia in November, a dozen Baldwin-Felts detectives had removed him and another UMW agent named Bert Samson from the train at Cincinnati. Samson was a mild-mannered little man with thick glasses, which the detectives immediately smashed to pieces. To make matters worse, Samson began shaking and whimpering. He looked so pathetic that even one of the Baldwin-Felt thugs offered the diminutive man a handkerchief. Antonio tried to regain a degree of respect for the United Mine Workers by pulling his arm free from one of the thugs. He was rewarded with a hard kick to the stomach that knocked the wind out of him. By the time he recovered, he and the still-whimpering Samson were on a westbound train for Indianapolis. Much to the chagrin of Antonio, neither he nor Samson had any visible injuries when they reported to the UMW headquarters. He felt embarrassed to have been turned back without sporting at least a bruise or scar.

Still, the West Virginia experience left Angeline less apprehensive of his new job. She decided that union organizing was safer than working below ground.

"Maybe you'll have time to stop by Matawan and see my brother Vincent and his family," Angeline said as she threw a big slice of ham into the skillet.

"Well, I'm not going on a vacation, you know," Antonio said

a little more sharply than he intended. He coughed hard into his shirtsleeve.

"Of course not, mio caro." Angeline turned and kissed his bruised ego. "But still, the fresh mountain air might be good for your lungs."

<><><><><><>

"Well, Joe, the UMW has asked me to go to Kentucky and help organize the miners." Antonio was taking a lunch and smoke break with his partner down in the mine a few days later. "They figure I'd be recognized if I went back to West Virginia. I'm just glad they're giving me another chance."

"Why don't you tell me what happened in West Virginia?" Joe asked, as he had nearly every day for weeks.

Antonio shook his head. "Nothing good."

"They should ask *me* to go these places. I'm the pit committeeman!" Joe threw a rock against the face of the coal.

Antonio didn't answer. Both men knew that Joe hadn't been asked *because* he was the pit committeeman. Workers understood that anyone who held that position was in the pocket of the company, as were the weight-check men who decided how much pay workers received for the coal cars they sent to the surface. It was no coincidence that he and Joe had not received a single dock for having too much rock in their coal since his partner became pit committeeman.

"I will be leaving on the train next Monday," Antonio told him.

"Do you want Myrna to help watch the boys?" Joe offered, though he already knew the answer to that question, too.

"Lena said she'd help. You know how dago women stick together."

Joe's hurt was obvious, even through his blackened face. Myrna would never have agreed to help with the four rowdy boys.

"I'd appreciate it, though, if you'd take the boys hunting sometime," Antonio said. Then he remembered that Joe hated guns. He grinned. "Or maybe fishing."

<><><><><><>

The East Kentucky Coal Company mined low vein coal with seams less than two feet thick. The ceilings were so low, even in the haulageways, an average sized man could not stand upright.

When Antonio signed the big logbook he wrote his name, date of birth and ethnic group. He noted that about a third of the miners simply made an X for their name, and that the mine boss wrote "NIGGER" by the names of many of them for their ethnic group.

"I hire mostly you Italians 'cause ya'll shorter," Bruiser Carver, the mine boss, told Antonio as he turned the logbook back toward him on the big oak table of the mine office. "Had a skinny German once who was about six-three and he got stuck in a turn. We had to cut his left leg off at the knee just to get him out." The mine boss assigned Antonio a number and handed him a metal pit tag.

"What happened to him after that?" Antonio wanted to collect as many examples of company abuse as possible.

"Oh, we tied a wood crutch to his thigh and he's mining with a little fella who lost his right leg. Between the two of 'em, there ain't a vein turn small enough that one of 'em can't squeeze through." Carver studied the log for a moment. "I'm afraid I can't start you for a day or two 'cause I don't have any white men you can partner with. Unless you think you could tolerate working with a nigger."

"I sure was hoping to get started today." Antonio kicked at the shale that dotted the dark red clay. He had no quarrel with those with dark skin, but he was south of the Mason-Dixon—and he had to behave accordingly. "Guess I could tolerate one for a day or two."

"Hattie Turnipseed, get on in here!" Carver yelled to someone sitting on a wooden bench outside the mine office. The stocky man who hurried into the office was all of five feet tall and so black he wore the coal dust like a second skin. "This here's Antonio Vacca from up north. He'll be givin' you orders today. Take Mister Vacca down to level three and start in where you and Smitty worked before he got hurt this mornin'."

They left the building with dinner buckets in hand and headed toward the sloped entrance to the mine. "Ya wants me to tote yer pick and shovel down for ya, Mister Vacca?"

"I can manage," Antonio said. "And you don't need to call me 'mister.' Just 'Antonio' will be fine."

"Oh, that wouldn't do at all." Hattie handed Antonio a short handled pick and shovel from a pile of mining equipment. "I'll just call you Mister Antonio. That way we'll both be satisfied, uh-huh."

Within a short time, Antonio was convinced he'd gone beyond the call of duty by taking a job in the three-foot mines. He had hoped it would be a way to safely approach the workers with the idea of joining the union. Ducking his head, he followed the little black man along the tracks into the sloped mine. They walked steadily downward for thirty minutes and seemed to have to stoop lower at each level.

When Hattie told him to crawl on his hands and knees into a three-foot high chamber, Antonio shined the light from the lamp on his head into the tunnel and couldn't even see the back wall.

"You don't mean it," Antonio said. "There's coal in there?"

"Yes, sir, Mister Antonio, uh-huh. There be a fine face just 'bout twenty feet yonder. We blasted it last night and sounded the top this mornin'. That's how my pard got hurt. A rock fall broke his hand."

Antonio put his pick and shovel in front of him and started crawling through the narrow opening. Once in the chamber he could see that except for the low ceiling, the room was only a little smaller than he was used to back in Illinois. Hattie followed him in and immediately started hand tossing blasted chunks of coal toward the entrance. Antonio did the same. When they had a decent accumulation, Hattie backed out and started loading them in the coal car.

After half a day lying on his side on jagged rocks, Antonio's skin was scratched or torn from his neck to his ankles. The short-handled pick and shovel felt like children's tools in his hands and made undercutting the coal a slow, tedious task. Each time he and Hattie got a coal car loaded, they placed their identification number on the front of it. A Negro boy who was no more than twelve years old would hitch up a set of goats and pull the heavy boxcar through the narrow tunnels to the larger entryway. From there small ponies took the cars to the surface to be checked and weighed.

"We have an electric locomotive on the east side of the mine," Hattie told him, "but in these here low mines nothing can beat a team of goats or dogs. The joke is that if we ever get stuck down here, we'll at least have some fresh meat."

Antonio doubted that he loaded ten tons that day. When he walked up the slope that afternoon and turned in his pit tag, he learned they had been docked an entire car load for having too much slack mixed in with the coal. He'd had enough experience to know they'd been cheated.

"Don't expect to get paid too soon, neither," Hattie said as they walked toward the cleanup areas. "I didn't never get my check 'til like two months, uh-huh."

"How did you survive for two months without pay?" Antonio had learned from their talk during breaks that Hattie had a wife and four children to support.

The little man pulled a few coins out of his pocket and showed them to Antonio. The coins appeared to be aluminum and said East Kentucky Coal Company on them.

"They made me use this here scrip at the company store,"

Hattie said in a quiet voice. "By the time I finally got paid and paid them back for the scrip, then for the rent for the company house, then for the company for them sharpening my tools, I found out I had to pay ten dollars for the company doctor which we hadn't never used. I done got less than four dollars left for seven weeks of work!"

"How can you get by?" Antonio asked.

Hattie lowered his head and whispered. "We coloreds done learnt to sell our scrip to a fella who gives us fifty cents on the dollar. Then we buy from the other colored folk that farms in the area."

Hattie put a hand in front of Antonio and pointed. "Ya'll white folk clean up over yonder." The little man walked off toward a building with a sign that read "COLORED ONLY."

10

Antonio worked with Hattie for three days. During that time he learned that while the Negroes in the community were unhappy with their work conditions, they had learned to survive by helping one another. Still, at the end of the first week, Hattie made it clear as they were leaving the mine that if enough of the other workers banded together he thought most of the colored would join in.

"A lot of our older folk remember bein' slaves," Hattie said before turning to walk to his company home in the negro section of town. "Some of 'em say they was treated better as slaves than this here mine company treats us now, uh-huh."

They had taken off work early after blasting a few compartments so Antonio had the bigger part of the day ahead of him. Half a dozen white children in dirty clothes and without shoes played on the mine tipple as Antonio climbed the steep hill away from the mine yard. His own boys liked to go barefoot in the summer, but this was January—and though it was unseasonably warm, it was still a fairly cool day. The children's hair was long and uncombed. Angeline would have gone into a scissor fit had any of her sons gone out in public with hair so wild.

The town of Fancher was made up of several patch communities built between two hills. The company houses— shacks at best—were hastily built with wood from a nearby mine community that had become a ghost town when its coal vein went bad. Most of them stood precariously at odd angles along the hill. The miners had lined the inside walls with newspapers to keep out the draft blowing in from between the boards.

For the first week, Antonio allowed himself the luxury of a room in a boarding house on the edge of what was known as Frenchtown—although most of the residents were actually from Belgium. The mines and the railroad attracted a wider variety of people than he'd ever seen. Besides the usual Italians, Irish, French, Slovacs, and Germans, there were Negros as well as mountain folk—the latter of which professed no national origin other than that they were from "over yonder hill thar."

His intuition told him that getting workers from so many different experiences together into one labor union would be tricky at best. Though they communicated well enough underground, the various cultures seemed to go their separate ways once clear of the mine tipple. At least one other union organizer had blended into the community, but for security reasons neither had been given the other's name. That way if one was discovered he could not give away his comrade.

After cleaning up in a porcelain washbasin in his room and putting on clean clothes, he joined the other three tenants at the kitchen table. None of the men were miners. They looked at him as if he still had coal dust all over him.

Antonio looked down and noticed his fingernails were indeed dirty, so he tried to keep them under the table as much as possible.

None of them offered a greeting, so he dove silently into a meal of beef stew and homemade sweetbread.

Halfway through his meal, a boy of about six darted into the dining room from the parlor, followed quickly by his rotund mother, who seemed prepared to brain her son with a big bar of lye soap. She grabbed the little one by his long, unruly hair before he could open the outside door for his escape, then shoved two fingers of her other hand deep into the boy's nostrils. When he opened his mouth to scream she quickly crammed a corner of the soap so far down his throat that one of the men watching from the table began to gag on his food and quickly left the room.

The mother shouted, "This'll teach you to use that kind of language in my house, you little hoodlum!" When she ripped the soap out as forcefully as she had inserted it, one of the boy's eyeteeth popped out with it. Frothing from the corners of his mouth, the boy ran screaming and spitting from the kitchen.

Antonio hid a smile from the mother as she used the teeth-marked lye soap to vigorously wash her hands in the kitchen wash pan. The scene reminded him of home and his beloved Angeline's tussles with their own four boys. For a moment, he questioned his decision to pursue unionization in the God-forsaken hills of Kentucky. He longed to snuggle in bed beneath several layers of quilts next to his plump little wife. It was becoming more apparent than ever to him that Angeline was where he got his strength. He camouflaged a sob of sadness by coughing into the white napkin provided with the meal.

As he returned the cloth to his lap, he saw a smear of his black spit-up on it. The coal dust reminded him that his own son's lungs would most likely one day be as dark as a face in the mine. If things didn't change, they would be struggling against the same age-old company abuses as their father. If he could just help the United Mine Workers make the work environment safer, maybe it would save the life of one or more of his boys.

After his meal, Antonio went outside and sat on the top step of the high porch to smoke and to watch the sun ease itself below the trees and behind the mountain. The song of the evening birds brought more thoughts of home, but he also heard the unusual. The shrill scream of a panther echoed through the hollow, and the wind whistled as it funneled between the big boulders on the hills. When the night air became damp and turned colder, he retrieved a heavier coat from his room and headed down the hill to find a tavern where miners would be airing their complaints about the mine company. He'd had little time during the workweek to explore the town, but the weekend would bring plenty of opportunities to get to know the community.

The town boiled with activity. Dozens of children scampered about chasing dogs, cats, chickens and one another. Wagons slopped through muddy roads. Occasionally a flivver would honk, and with loud backfires, pass a startled mule, which would then have to be whipped to move again. Most people's yards had at least a few foraging chickens, and many had goats, cows or pigs, some of which were fenced or tied, but often as not were simply allowed to roam.

"Pardon." Antonio nodded toward an old gentleman leaning against a fence post whittling a stick with a pocketknife. "Can you tell me where a fella might share a drink with his fellow miners?"

"Oh, it's conversation you'd be wantin'?" the Irishman said with a singsong lilt. "Then Burton's Pub is where you'll be going. Beware, though, some o' the lads are given to drinkin' and fightin', TALKIN' tends to bore the good fellows."

Antonio entered the smoke filled pub. Inside, five tables were each occupied by four or more men each holding a tin cup in one hand and a cigarette in the other. He joined a rough group of three standing at the bar. They appeared to be hill folk who had stopped for a brew after work before walking to their homes over the ridge. The bartender drew a beer into a cup and set it on the bar before Antonio placed an order.

"Beer's all we got 'til tomorrow afternoon," the bartender said as he took the two bits Antonio had placed on the counter. "Sean O'Malley's the name."

"Antonio Vacca," Antonio said and took a long draw on the mug.

"There's four spaghetti snappers at the last table if you're lookin' for home talk," O'Malley said with a friendly grin. "The rest of the tables are filled with fine Irish gents and a few Scots."

"Or ya'll can tip a farewell jug with us if you're so inclined," a man with a well-worn hat interjected. His partners tilted their heads and stared at Antonio in a way similar to a basset hound he had once owned. "Name's Jedediah Scoggins from over yonder hill."

"You boys quitting the mine?" Antonio asked.

"Shoulda never started." Scoggins took a long chug on his tin. He wiped the foam off his upper lip with a dirty sleeve. "Company's got this one locked up. Ain't no future for an honest man."

"Any talk about doing anything about it?" Antonio said in a voice so low the three mountain men leaned forward to hear.

"Hell, half the men here don't even speak English," Scoggins said, shaking his head slowly.

Antonio waited until the bartender took a round of drinks to one of the tables, then whispered. "If there was a way to make things better, would you be willing to stick around?" He knew he was taking a risk, but there was something about these mountain men that he liked.

Scoggins leaned closer and spoke out of the corner of his tobacco filled mouth. "A Scoggins is always ready for a fight, especially if it's against those good-for-nothin' company goons. Reckon we oughta to do some conversin' on the subject. Ya had vittles yet?"

Chugging his beer in one gulp, Scoggins bid his pards goodbye and nodded for Antonio to follow. Once outside, they walked along the muddy road in silence for several minutes. Antonio became a little nervous. The UMW organizers had warned him there were often company snitches who would report a worker if he spoke out against the company. Although Scoggins didn't look like a person who would associate himself with such deceit, Antonio was a little green when it came to recognizing a man's character.

A blue heron soared overhead. The acrid smell of burning coal from the smoke stacks of the company houses filled the air. As Antonio and Scoggins approached the dilapidated building the mountain man called home, a black snake longer than a full-grown man slithered under the porch.

"Ol' Blackie scares off the copperheads." Scoggins used a finger to remove a brown chaw of tobacco and fling it on the ground. "Ain't chawin', are ya? The old lady hates tobaccy stains in the domain."

When they entered, a woman of solid proportions was scrubbing a pair of trousers on a sloping washboard inside a large tub. Her bare forearms bulged with muscles that would be envied by many miners. When she saw her husband, she immediately wrung out the britches, set the tub on the floor by the pot-bellied stove, and silently began making trips outside to fetch well water. After she had carried three buckets inside, Scoggins stripped off every stitch of his clothes, put his feet in the washtub and squatted down until his bare bottom rested on the rim. A young daughter entered from a side room with a bar of soap that was twice the size of her hand and began scrubbing furiously at the black dust on her father's back.

"What's fer supper, Ma?" the man-of-the-house moaned as he took a second bar of soap and began scrubbing his arms and shoulders.

"Beans, cornbread and fried tatters," she said, then suddenly threw a wet cloth that struck the face of a young boy Antonio had not seen sitting on the edge of an extremely large bed. "Take them shoes off, young'un. You know not to wear 'em in good weather. You think yer pa can afford fer ya to have two pairs each year? Now, give me back that warsh rag."

"Pa, I found a rattleback in the creek today." The boy hurried toward his father, holding out a small sack.

"He found a rattlesnake?" Antonio asked, pulling back a step.

"Oh, no," Scoggins said. He stood with water dripping from his body back into the tub as his wife began drying his backside with the towel she had been using on the dishes. "Show him, son."

The boy took out a small, smooth stone shaped like an airplane propeller and placed it on a flat section of the old wooden dinner table. He gave the stone a hard clockwise spin and stood back. Everyone in the room was still for a moment and watched as the stone finally slowed to a stop, began to shake a little and then made a slow, counterclockwise spin for almost three full turns.

"Why, that rattled itself backwards like a compass needle," Antonio remarked in amazement.

"Hill folk used to pay a goodly amount for one of these back in the olden days," the boy said. "They thought these stones were bewitched, but I think the rushing water from the creek wears one side down a little more than the other." He proudly held the rock up so Antonio could see both sides at once.

"Why, sure enough, you're right," Antonio said. He was amazed more by the boy's intelligent way of conversing than by the stone itself. He thought about Filberto's curiosity in science and knew his third son would have loved having someone his own age who was so smart to talk to.

"Wish the boy was old enough to figure out this workers' mess," Scoggins said as he donned a pair of overalls only slightly cleaner than the ones he had mined in all day. "Union ain't never gonna take hold in these hills. Not as long as dagos and niggers can't even work together to shore up a roof."

"You men folk oughta look in one of them word books so you'll know what union means," Ma Scoggins said without looking away from the food she placed on the table. "It don't matter to the company the color of your skin or what country you're from. You're less important to 'em than even the cheapest piece of mining equipment."

"I reckon the boy got his smarts from his Ma," Scoggins said, lighting up a corncob pipe. "So how you figure gettin' folks together on this union notion?"

"We need a spokesman for each group," Antonio said. "I worked with a colored who I think would speak for his people, me for the Italians, and you for the mountain folk."

"I'd s'pect Sean O'Malley's the one for the Irish."

"The bartender?" Antonio asked.

"His pa and a brother died in the mine," Scoggins said. He took his seat at the head of the table and motioned for Antonio to take the chair to his left. "He's made no secret of his views on the company."

"Well, that'll be a good start." Antonio sat down, and so as to avoid insulting his host, ate his second meal of the evening. "I'd hate to think the only way we'll get support is for folks to be killed in the mine first."

<><><><><><>

The following Monday morning, two Lithuanians and four boxcar-pulling dogs died in a mine cave-in. Most of the mine continued working despite the accident, and many, like Antonio, only learned about the deaths when their day's work was done. He wondered if he was the only one who found it strange that the disaster siren hadn't even sounded.

After cleaning up, he was walking up the hill when a gunshot exploded from a nearby house. As a crowd formed in front of the rickety old shack, a woman wearing black mourning clothes stepped through the doorway, blood dripping between her fingers onto the porch. She screamed a flood of words in Lithuanian, then fainted into the arms of one of the men.

"What did she say?" several people asked.

A Lithuanian miner stepped up on a porch step and faced the crowd. "The widow of one of the men who died in the mine today shot herself in the head with her husband's shotgun. Now won't you listen to me? How many of our people have to die before we do something about this injustice?"

Lowering their heads, most of the miners in the crowd slowly walked away, dinner buckets in hand. Antonio made eye contact with the dark-skinned man standing on the porch. The man's angry face glistened with tears.

A hard nudge slammed into Antonio's back.

"Move on, fella," a voice behind him said.

Antonio turned to see a well-dressed company detective holding a rifle. He looked back at the Lithuanian on the porch. The miner nodded, then turned quickly and went inside the house.

Antonio followed the others along the muddy, uphill road. He didn't stop at his boarding house but continued on to Scoggin's home. He found the mountain man sitting on a porch step smoking his corncob pipe.

"We got our Lithuanian," Antonio said.

Scoggin's blew a long cloud of smoke through his nose and mouth. "Reckon it's time for a meetin'," he said. "But first we need to pay a visit to a German fella named Rolfe Hiler."

11

A short, heavy set woman admitted Antonio and Scoggins into Hiler's home that evening. "My husband will be with you shortly," she said, pointing to a round table piled high with books and surrounded by four chairs.

"Italiano?" Antonio asked as he and the mountain man sat. He was taken aback by how much the little woman resembled Angeline. They could have been sisters.

"Yes. My name is Carmela," she told him. "I am from the Po River Valley."

The door to another room opened and a bearded man only a little taller than the woman walked in. He was balding and wore reading glasses low on his nose. Antonio stood to shake Hiler's hand, but Scoggins, who hadn't even removed his hat, remained sitting. Hiler pulled one of the chairs out and faced his two guests. Recognizing an uncomfortable moment of silence, Antonio looked at the books stacked up on the table.

"Medical books?" He asked with a smile he hoped would ease the tension.

When her husband failed to respond, Carmela said, "My husband was nearly through medical school when—"

"You men are rushing into this thing half-cocked!" Hiler said. He rubbed his beard and nose roughly with his hand. "Those Lithuanians getting killed today have the entire community ready to explode. The Baldwin thugs are chomping at the bits waiting for someone like you fellows to do something stupid. They'll be watching and ready to make an example out of some poor bastard." He stopped talking for a moment when his wife put a hand on his shoulder, then continued in a calmer voice. "Let things die down a few weeks. In the meantime, organize the different ethnic groups and help them establish leaderships. Then, when the time's right and the company is least expecting it, remind the workers of what happened today and get them fired up again."

"Hell, half the men here'll be gone by then and a whole new crew'll move in." Scoggins spat a chaw into a coffee cup on the table, causing Hiler's wife to cringe. "The time's now. If you ain't got the guts for a fight, stay home with your woman, but stay the hell out of our way!" With a look of disgust he rose from his chair, walked across the room and slammed the door as he left.

Antonio looked at the bearded man and his wife. Both were staring blankly at the books. He tried to weigh Hiler's advice against what Scoggins had said. After a long moment of silence he stood and followed the mountain man out of the house.

<><><><><><>

The turnout for the first organizational meeting took place the next night in a little clearing south of the town. It was a disappointment. Antonio had only managed to get four of his Italian countrymen to come to the conference. Scoggins brought three of the sullen-faced hill folk, and Sean O'Malley escorted two drunken Irishmen and a bottle of whiskey. Hattie Turnipseed came alone. The Lithuanian never showed.

"There's thirteen of us here," one of the mountain men said in a shaky voice. "That's bad luck, Virgil."

"You never could count good, Homer." The one named Virgil said. "There's twelve. You can't really count the nigger."

Antonio started to argue that colored folks counted just the same as the others, but he realized that then the count really would be thirteen. While he could tolerate the unlucky number, he knew the superstitious mountain men would not. It seemed strange that the success of the first union meeting might depend on a debate about the Fifteenth Amendment and the Negro's right to vote. He looked at Hattie, and with his eyes implored him to understand his silence.

"Well," Hattie said after a long moment, "the Lord Jesus started with twelve disciples so I reckon that's a good thing."

Everyone stood in silence. "I thought there were forty disciples." Virgil said finally.

"Now that's where you're wrong, Virg," Scoggins said. "There were forty knights of the round table."

The others seemed to take Scoggins' word as definitive. That settled, Antonio was just about to suggest they all introduce themselves.

A loud rustling from the woods sounded all around them. A second later they found themselves surrounded by two dozen men wearing sheets over their heads and aiming rifles at them.

Antonio felt a hard blow that knocked the wind from his lungs. He fell head first onto the ground.

"You other men, git goin!'" A scruffy voice shouted. "And spread the word that there'll be no union talk in these here hills."

The sound of men running through the snow was followed by several gunshots. Antonio rolled quickly onto his back to see if anyone was being shot, but saw the masked men were firing into the air. He was lying next to Scoggins, who was bleeding profusely from the forehead. A few yards away, Sean O'Malley and Hattie Turnipseed sat next to each other, their eyes glassy and distant.

"You okay?" Antonio asked Scoggins. He pulled a handkerchief from his coat and handed it to his friend.

"Well, well, well, what do we have here?" a man in a high, white hat said. "A wop talkin' to a hillbilly and oh, lookie, lookie. Look at the little paddy sittin' next to a smoked Irishman. You'd think they was cousins or something, wouldn't ya, Jessie?"

"Better let that one go, boss," the one called Jesse said. "Those hill folk don't take kindly to outsiders killin' their kin.

They'll come out of them hills like fleas off a wet hound dog."

"Throw him in the back of the wagon and dump him outside of town!" High Hat shouted.

A man standing behind Scoggins slammed him in the head with his rifle butt. Two other men grabbed the unconscious man by the legs and dragged him roughly through the snow and out of the glade.

"Now which of you two white boys want to die with the nigger?" High Hat said.

"Why don't we just hang 'em both?" Jesse asked.

"No, we want word to spread to the UMW what we do to union organizers." High Hat pointed his rifle between Antonio's eyes. "Maybe we should let the bartender go and kill the dago. It's never easy to find a good barkeep."

"That bartender thinks the sun comes up just to hear him crow!" Jesse shouted. "I know for a fact that he's been talking up union nonsense for months now. Hell, he waters down his whiskey anyhow, don't ya, barkeep?"

The explosion in his head prevented Antonio from hearing if O'Malley answered. When he awoke, he found himself lying on his right side. He opened his eyes to see the sun just beginning to peek between two distant hills. Feeling something rubbing the side of his head, he struggled to overcome a feeling of nausea and slowly rolled onto his back. It took him a moment to realize that the gentle caress had come from a pair of work boots that dangled just above his forehead. Horrified, he rolled out from under the big, oak tree that held the strange fruit of Sean O'Malley and Hattie Turnipseed. Their broken necks each shared one end of the same hanging rope that had been wrapped several times around a stout tree limb. As a final embarrassment, their murderers had tied their arms and legs together in a lover's embrace.

Three times Antonio tried to rise to his feet so that he could lower the two men to the ground. Even in his confused state of mind, he knew that he didn't want their bodies to be discovered in such a humiliating position. With each attempt, dizziness and nausea forced him back onto his back. On his final try, he lost consciousness completely.

<><><><><><>

"Angeline," Antonio said when he awoke and saw a pretty round face smiling down at him.

"No, Mr. Vacca, it's Carmela Hiler," the woman said. "You are in my home. My husband has been caring for you for two days."

Realizing his head was pounding with pain, Antonio brought a hand up and felt a bandage wrapped around the top of his head.

Mrs. Hiler grabbed his hand and gently returned it to his side. She took a small glass from a table next to the bed and held his head up so he could swallow its contents.

"This will help with the pain," she said.

"What happened to me?"

"My husband saved your life," she said and pulled the blanket up to his neck. "You almost died."

"My wife exaggerates," Rolfe Hiler's voice said from the doorway.

Antonio watched as the blurred image of the bearded man moved toward him and looked down at him. He felt sleepy.

"I don't think anything could have hurt that thick dago skull of yours," Hiler said.

"Who are you?" Antonio had to have some answers. "You aren't a coal miner."

"I was sent here by the United Mine Workers," Hiler said. "Now go back to sleep. We have much to discuss when you are able."

Antonio thought he saw a whirlpool of colors spinning across the ceiling. Then he went back to sleep for another two days.

Sixteen Tons

<><><><><><>

A week later, Rolfe and Carmela Hiler saw Antonio off at the train station.

"Thank you again for saving my life," Antonio said as they stood on the train platform. "You might consider being a doctor instead of a union organizer."

"That's what I've been telling him." Carmela gave Antonio a final farewell hug.

"My father died in the mines," Hiler said. "I'll not rest until I make a difference."

"I know how you feel," Antonio said as he shook the man's hand. "I guess the UMW won't be asking me for help anymore."

"Don't look back," Hiler said. "You can make a difference by inspiring the miners in your local. The UMW in Illinois is leading the way in wages and work conditions. Keep up the fight and you'll be helping us all."

"What will you do now?" Antonio asked as he picked up his grip.

"The UMW is sending me to Colorado," Hiler said as the train began to slowly move and Antonio stepped up on the platform. "Hopefully it will be a piece of cake after Kentucky."

"*Where in Colorado?*" Antonio shouted as the train began to move faster. "I'd like to write."

"A little town!" Hiler shouted, *"called Ludlow!"*

12

The first thing Rolfe Hiler saw when he and Carmela got off the train in Ludlow, Colorado, was a steel-covered car with a machine-gun mounted on it.

"They call it the Death Special," a man in a Colorado National Guard uniform told the Hilers. He had a sturdy build and a round face. "I'm Lieutenant Linderfelt, and I'm here to keep the peace. Now why don't you folks get the hell back on that damned train and keep moving?"

The couple had been warned the company intimidation would be intense. Carrying their carpetbags, they quietly walked away from the grinning, uniformed man.

When the strike started in September, the company immediately evicted the miners from the company houses. The United Mine Workers wasted no time leasing a tract of land near the mine entrance, where they set up a tent city for the strikers.

Rolfe studied the layout as they walked toward the hundreds of tents stretching in neat rows across the barren valley before them. In the distance, the Black Hills rolled off toward the mountains and the horizon beyond. The UMW had chosen an area at the mouth of the canyon where scabs would have to pass the tents to get to work each day. There had already been several deaths and injuries as a result of confrontations between the strikers and the scabs.

The tent city held twelve hundred colliers, as the miners in Colorado were called. Hundreds of campfires dotted the community, with women leaning over them to make the afternoon meal. Others scrubbed their clothes against washboards while merrily singing union songs. As he and Carmela walked past tents, he heard smatterings of several languages and smelled a variety of ethnic foods cooking. A large group of men, a few with rifles at their sides, sat on the side of a hill listening to a man speak. More children than Rolfe could count played various games, including baseball and football.

"You'd be the Hilers, I assume," a man's voice behind them said. "Sorry I couldn't meet you at the train. Our Lieutenant Linderfelt wouldn't let me through. I'm Louis Tikas."

"Pleased to meet you." Rolfe shook his hand. "We already met the Lieutenant. Not a pleasant man. This is my wife, Carmela."

"I admire a woman who would come to this God-forsaken place," Tikas said as he tipped his hat. "In fact, you're the first woman to get off that train since Mother Jones came in January. Of course, the militia tried to send her back. They even jailed her for a time."

"Mother Jones is here?" Carmela asked.

"Well, she's in hiding right now." Tikas laughed as he took Carmela's carpetbag. "She stopped by here long enough to make sure I wasn't corrupted by wine or women."

A handsome young man came up and took Rolfe's bag. "Mother Jones ran Lorena Paige right out of camp for chasin' after Mister Tikas," said the young man. "She don't like distractions during a strike. I'm Charlie Costa."

"These tents don't look too safe," Rolfe commented as he shook Costa's hand.

"No, they're not," Costa said. "In fact, several people were killed or wounded before we started digging pits inside the tents for protection at night. I dug mine about seven-foot deep for my wife, Fedelina, and our two children. They're only six and four, but having young ones around hasn't stopped the Baldwin-Felts' agents. They still enjoy firing random shots or shining bright lights at us when we're trying to sleep."

"This'll be your quarters," Tikas said. He held open a flap

to one of the smaller tents. There was a wooden platform for a floor except for a narrow hole and a small cast-iron stove.

"We had to put you next to the single women," Costa said with a little grin. "I hope that won't bother you, ma'am."

"My man is well behaved," Carmela said. Taking her bag from Costa, she began unloading a few essentials.

Rolfe turned red in the face. Costa and Tikas were short, good-looking and about thirty-years old. They both seemed of strong character and to possess robust personalities.

"What about meals?" Carmela asked. "I spotted beans in some of the pots."

"Beans are for the lucky," Costa said. "The union gives each striker four dollars a week. The food wagons come in and distribute as evenly as they can, but you can plan on losing some weight if you're here long enough."

Rolfe was thankful his wife had anticipated this and loaded their bags with dried food. After seeing the hungry look on the faces of the children, though, he didn't expect to see much of it in their own cooking pot.

That evening Rolfe went to a meeting and Carmela made her first friend. Mary Thomas was a beautiful twenty-seven year old woman with flaming red hair and two little girls. She had come to America from Wales for no more reason than to find her husband and tell him she was quitting him.

"He abandoned me with three children and one on the way," Mary told Carmela. "My fourth baby died at birth and I left my son in Wales with his father's family. They are wealthy and can give him more than I can. I will send for him when I get the money."

"Did you find your husband?" Carmela asked as she fed the girls some mashed corn and bacon.

"Yes," Mary said. "He was here in Ludlow and I told him, 'you son of a bitch, you didn't quit me, I'm quitting you!' And that killed him! He hates it that the men here chase after me, even though I'm not interested in taking another man, I like it

91

that he's jealous."

Carmela liked Mary's grit. "You sure you don't have some Italian in you?" she asked.

"Anyway, I stayed on here 'cause the strike started," Mary said. "My family were all colliers in Wales, and when I saw what these boys were up against, I decided to help all I could."

"What do you do?" Carmela asked, wondering if she also could help.

"Why, I sing for 'em!" Mary said.

The camp was growing silent as the last rays of sunlight sank behind the mountain. As women began herding their children into their tents for the night, Mary Thomas began to sing in a powerful, clear voice as beautiful as Carmela had ever heard:

> We'll win the fight today, boys,
> We'll win the fight today,
> Shouting the battle cry of union;
> We'll rally from the coal mines,
> We'll battle to the end,
> Shouting the battle cry of union.

From the hundreds of tents, women and children sang the chorus. Even the Guardsmen on the far side of the railroad tracks stood and listened as Mary Thomas' voice again rang out, while men scurried down the hill from their meeting to join in, and the whole camp united in song.

By the time the last words of the song were finished, every woman and child had disappeared into their tents.

"You'd best be tucking tight against your man in your foxhole, my dear," Mary said as she herded her two girls toward her own tent. "I doubt we'll be blessed with a quiet sleep this evening."

Carmela leaned over and kissed Rolfe hard on the mouth. "When this is over," she said softly, "will you promise to finish your medical degree?"

Rolfe smiled, took her left hand in his and kissed both their wedding rings at the same time. Carmela sighed, but she understood his answer. Rolfe Hiler was a man who finished what he started. He would get things done in his own time. For a long time she had been sensing that she needed to help guide her husband back to his medical studies. She had prayed often that God would provide her with that opportunity.

The two went into their dark shelter and felt their way along the ground to the protective hole. It was barely large enough for the small mattress, and Carmela had to lay on her side with her back to her husband. He put his arm and leg around her and pulled the blanket over them. Five minutes later the first shots rang out along with thud sounds as the bullets struck tents. The occasional blasts lasted until dawn.

<><><><><><>

By their third week, Rolfe and Carmela had grown accustomed to the gunshots at night and were able to sleep somewhat comfortably in their little burrow. Each morning Carmela checked their tent for bullet holes. In the event she found any, she quickly sewed them up. When scabs went to work in the morning and home at night, Rolfe stood on the picket line with hundreds of other men and shouted insults at them.

Meanwhile, Carmela got in the habit of helping Charlie Costa's wife Fedelina with her two children as the Greek wife washed, cooked and sewed for her husband and the other men. Fedelina was a short, rather plain-looking woman with a penchant toward caution. She was quiet and totally the opposite of her friend Mary Thomas, the darling of the tent colony. Even the women adored Mary, despite the fact so many men lusted for her.

"I've had my fill of men," Mary would tell the other women.

"Don't need any of 'em."

Mary was also the hardest worker and best organizer in the camp. When the colliers got depressed, she would lift them up with one of her songs. She was often seen exploring beyond the canyon with her two girls. She told Carmela she had made friends with an elderly couple who owned a ranch a few miles away.

"Don't be wandering too far from camp, ladies," the cautious Fedelina warned Mary and Carmela one day as they cooked over an open fire. "Did you hear about poor, old Andy Colner? He was going to the post office and was arrested by Lieutenant Linderfelt and his thugs. They gave him a pick and shovel to carry and marched him out into a canyon. The poor, old fella fell down several times and they kicked him and made him keep walking. Finally they made him dig his own grave. He begged to be allowed to go home so he could kiss his wife and children goodbye."

Fedelina leaned closer to them. "'Linderfelt said he would do all the kissing and laughed. Old Andy dug while the soldiers stood around laughing and cursing and playing craps for his tin watch. Then the old fella fainted right there in the hole he had dug. The soldiers threw some dirt on 'im and left 'im. Andy woke up later and crawled out from under that grave. There he was alone and cold. He staggered back to camp but he ain't been quite right in the head since."

Though Carmela lived in the married section of the camp, she also spent a lot of time helping the single women. She was amazed by how strong those widow's ties had become after their husbands died in the mines. They had become like an extended family working together for survival and to raise their children. None of them took offense when anyone in the community disciplined their children and always supported the discipline with a paddling of their own.

<><><><><><>

Colorado had more mine deaths in the coalmines each year than any other state. The lack of enforced safety measures was one of the key points in the strike, but one that the coal companies vehemently opposed. They had brought in hired gunmen at seven dollars a day to try and prevent the colliers from unionizing.

Matters were made worse in mid-April when the state ran out of money to keep the National Guard on the scene. Fearing an outbreak by the strikers, Governor Elias Ammons left two units in the area and allowed the company's hired henchmen to wear National Guard uniforms and keep the order.

On the morning of April 20, Carmela saw three Guardsmen walking through the camp toward Louis Tikas. She recognized one of them as the stocky Lieutenant Linderfelt. A murmur of whispers passed through the camp, and by the time they got to Tikas, hundreds of striking colliers had slowly came out of their tents and surrounded the Guardsmen. They stood as if posing for a photograph, most of them puffing on cigarettes or pipes. From behind the railroad tracks, over two hundred well-armed men in uniforms stood up and aimed their carbines at the crowd. The armored Death Special suddenly roared across the railroad tracks and took up a position on the road. A Guardsman spun the M1895 machine gun toward the crowd.

"Morning Lieutenant," Tikas said. His demeanor of calm caused the colliers to lower what few weapons they had. The militia did not.

"I have orders to search your compound for Tobias Simmons," Linderfelt said in a high, strained voice. "We have reason to believe he is being held here against his will."

"May I see your court order for the search?" Tikas asked, his own voice still calm.

"No papers are required for a military matter," Linderfelt said.

The colliers slowly began to raise their rifles again.

Linderfelt's nostril's flared, and there was a noticeable quivering of his chubby right cheek.

"Perhaps we should discuss this in private," Tikas said.

Linderfelt's eyes moved back and forth among the angry miners. "You will accompany me to the train station in Ludlow!" he said.

Tikas smiled and began walking toward the railroad tracks. The three Guardsmen quickly fell in behind him. The miners didn't lower their guns again until Tikas and his escort crossed the tracks and entered the building. Most of the militia melted back behind the hill again, though the Death Special remained positioned between the tent city and the train station.

Charlie Costa and half a dozen men gathered for a moment, talking excitedly, then went their separate ways throughout the community, shouting directions. Carmela couldn't find Rolfe as the frenzied, yet orderly crowd began moving about the camp.

"You ladies," Costa yelled to the single-women side of the camp, "gather the children and take cover in the tents that have the deepest trenches. Take all the food and water you can."

"Mister Costa." Carmela grabbed the man's arm with both hands. "Do you know where my husband is?"

"He went with some other men to meet the supply truck," Costa said gruffly, then seemed to catch himself. He gently touched her hand. "Rolfe will be okay, Carmela. I just need you to help these women with the children. Fedelina and our two are already getting our tent ready."

Carmela was on her way to find Fedelina Costa when she saw Mary struggling to herd half-a-dozen children into a tent. She followed her through the opening. The hole filled most of the room and even ran beneath the wooden floorboards. They were able to tuck a dozen children into the space. When the older youngsters began playing hand-puppet games with the smaller ones, Carmela was amazed that none of them were crying. Mary Thomas was a blur of activity as she helped other women and children to safe spots and then brought them all the food and water she could find.

Colliers folded back tents that faced the railroad tracks while dozens of the strikebreakers took cover in their trenches. Her gaze caught a faint movement up on the hill above them. She thought she saw a Guardsman cap. She immediately recognized a flaw in the collier's preparation. While they were all busy in the canyon taking cover, the company thugs could be surrounding them on the hills.

She looked for someone to warn, but before she could there was a loud explosion and someone yelled, *"Tikas is coming back!"*

Carmela saw Louis Tikas racing as fast as he could toward the encampment shouting as he ran. His voice was drowned out by all the other noise in the camp. When he got close enough she heard him yell, "Please, please! Listen to me. They're going to burn us out! They claim they're going to clean this camp out today!"

"Where do we go?" a woman yelled. She ran into her tent and came out with three children on her heels.

Suddenly dozens of women and children were running toward the hill where Carmela had seen movement. She yelled at them, "Stop, stop, you're running toward the Guardsmen!"

As a roar of gunfire erupted from that hill, all those running toward it fell to the ground. Carmela couldn't tell if they were ducking down or if they had been shot. A swarm of bullets buzzed past her. She ran and dove into the tent where Mary Thomas had helped her place the young ones. Women and children who had learned to sleep nightly with the sound of gunfire screamed and ran for cover, begging for the shooting to stop, but it didn't stop, not for minutes or even hours. Carmela lay in the hole, her arms and legs over as many children as she could cover, the gunfire so heavy she dare not even raise her head. The shooting didn't stop even long enough for those in the hole to get a drink of water or eat the food they had brought. It went on all day, and at dusk the thick, acrid smell of gun smoke was replaced with the smell of burning canvas from the tents.

"They'll burn us up inside here!" a woman lying between Carmela and Mary screamed.

"Shut up!" Mary yelled, "Listen! *LISTEN!*"

The women in the foxhole quieted the children as best they could. Above the sounds of gunfire and screaming they heard a train whistle.

"*A train?*" The woman yelled. "How is that going to help us?"

"*Listen to me!*" Mary shouted again. "The train will pass between our camp and the machine guns!"

"It will give us cover for a few moments," Carmela said, understanding immediately. "We can run for the Black Hills and get away."

"But where will we go?" someone asked.

"If we don't leave we will burn to death in these tents!" Mary shouted as another bullet passed through the already shredded canvas above them. "When I yell 'run,' I want you to follow me away from the tracks. Do you understand, Carmela?"

She nodded and watched as Mary Thomas crawled on her hands and knees out of the protective cover and straight on through the tent opening. Carmela grabbed the two smallest children in her arms and instructed an older one to hang onto her skirt. Two of the other women did the same.

The train whistle blew another long, loud blast. Carmela had been in the camp long enough to know how the trains ran, and when she heard it slowing she wondered if the engineer had recognized the situation. Perhaps he intended to try to give the miners cover from the machine guns and the Guardsmen's carbines that were continuing their assault from the far side of the tracks.

"*Run! Run!*" Mary yelled. The gunfire slowed to individual shots instead of the cannon-like explosion of moments before.

Carmela was on her feet and going as fast as she could

through the opening. She turned to run away from the tracks and saw Guardsmen frantically waving at the engineer to move the train.

The scene before her was terrible. As she followed Mary and her two girls she saw that men, women and children lay scattered throughout the camp. She couldn't tell if they were dead, wounded, or just too afraid to move. On the hill to her left a machine gun continued to fire behind a thick cloud of gun smoke. Some of the women and children she had seen running up the hill that morning were crawling back toward camp. Others remained motionless on the ground.

"*Run! Run!*" Mary and Carmela screamed into the tents they passed. Soon there were hundreds taking advantage of the lull in gunfire to get away.

Carmela saw Fedelina Costa looking out of one tent.

"*Come with us!*" Carmela screamed. "You have to get away now!"

"No!" Fedelina shouted back. "Our hole is deep. We're staying here!"

Carmela continued to run, though she wondered if they would be better off staying in the protection of their holes like Fedelina. Her arms were aching from carrying the two children, and the other little ones slowed her by holding onto her skirt. By the time she got to the incline of the Black Hills to the east she was out of breath and didn't think she could climb them.

Just then she heard another loud whistle from the train and a moment later the hill was pounded with bullets. She saw Mary's left foot kick forward and the heel of her shoe flew off. Mary fell to her right knee but didn't drop the two children in her arms. A child that was holding onto her skirt ran forward, picked up the shoe heel and brought it back to Mary, whose foot was bleeding profusely.

"You hang onto it for me, dear," Mary said as a bullet buzzed by her head and kicked up a pile of dirt in front of her. She stood and calmly limped the remainder of the way up the hill.

A few moments later the first wave of women and children were over the ridge. They immediately fell to their knees and lay completely still except for their heavy breathing. Over the next several moments more of the survivors joined them. When a few began to catch their breaths, one woman began vomiting. The sound and smell caused a chain reaction as several others did the same.

"We are still not in a safe place," Mary said as Carmela took off her own sock and used it to bandage the bleeding foot of her friend. "Bullets are passing overhead. After all we've been through, I don't want anyone to die from a stray gunshot."

When the little Italian woman had tied the makeshift bandage as tightly as possible, Mary stood up and shouted. "We need to get these children further away from the fighting! There ain't much cover out here, but I know of a dry well about half-a-mile away!"

"No!" one woman said, "I'm circling back around to town with my children."

Several others began talking about where they would go. Some chose to stay put a little longer. In the end, Mary, Carmela and two other women led twenty-four children to the dry well. Most of the children had lost their mothers during the mad escape to the top of the hill and it was all the women could do to keep them calm. Carmela could still hear the gunfire as she and Mary lowered the last of the little ones into the seven-foot deep hole with the other women.

"I'm going to a ranch where I think the people will help us," Mary announced from the ground level after Carmela dropped down beside the others. "I'll get food, water and blankets."

"I'll go with you," Carmela said.

"No," Mary said firmly. "You'll stay and take care of my girls. When I get back, we'll all go to the ranch. That is if the people say they will help us. I think they will but I don't want these children walking that far in the open if they won't."

Carmela understood strong women and knew this was

not a battle to fight. She settled down on the crowded ground and let the youngest children rest their heads on her. Within moments they were all asleep.

13

Though Mary Thomas was almost a mile away from the fighting, she occasionally saw dirt kicked up from bullets landing near her. She was tired and her injured foot sore, but she scampered the best she could the first quarter mile, then limped slowly the remaining two miles to the ranch house. Old John Powell and his wife Ruth had told her they were union sympathizers but didn't want the company to know it. They had lived on their small ranch for forty years and didn't want any trouble.

Still, they had heard the battle and had been watching the smoke rise in the western sky. When Mary came limping up that dirt road in the dark they both ran outside to meet her. She was happy to have John's shoulder to lean on and he set her down on the porch step while Ruth ran for water.

"We've been listening to the gunshots," John told her. "It sounds just like Vicksburg in sixty-three."

"I've got about two dozen children and a couple of women back at the dry well," Mary said as she took a drink of cool water from Ruth. "They need food, water and blankets for the night. It's too dangerous for them to move 'til the shootin' stops."

"I'll take 'em everything I can," John said. "You stay here and rest."

"No." Mary stood and put weight once more on her foot. "You go to the children. I'd like to take some food to the miners who are fighting. I'll not be arguing with ya."

John made a fast trip to his smoke house and brought out a large slab of ham. He handed it to his wife and she rushed back inside to cut it into slices. By the time John came out of the hen house with two-dozen eggs his wife had two sacks of food. One she wrapped in a blanket for Mary and the other she threw in a basket for her husband. John stacked up a pile of blankets, coats and gunnysacks onto his wagon. While he hitched his horse, Mary took a few bites of ham, washed it down with water, turned and headed back toward the fighting.

<><><><><><>

"I was in Cuba in ninety-eight," one of the miners told Louis Tikas, "but it was nothin' like this."

Tikas rolled onto his back. The barrel of his gun was so hot he had to hold it away from him. Eleven men lay prone along the hill firing at will at the Guardsmen along the railroad track. They were hoping to draw the fire away from the tent colony so those still trapped there could get away. Tikas was starting to reload when he saw Mary Thomas limping up the hill carrying a big, bulging blanket. She stopped at a canvas covering Charlie Costa up to his neck. He had blood on his head and his breathing was shallow. The man kneeling beside him looked at her and shook his head.

"Fedelina?" Charlie said weakly, his eyes lost in a long ago memory.

Mary took his hand and held it to her cheek. She held her ear close to his mouth.

"Sing the Union Song for me, Fedelina." Charlie gasped.

Mary raised her head and sang the chorus as loud and sweet as she could. The gunmen on the hill stopped firing and turned to listen.

"The union forever, hurrah, boys, hurrah!
Down with the Baldwins, up with the law;
For we're coming, Colorado, we're coming all the way,
Shouting the battle cry of union."

With the final words, Mary looked down. Charlie's eyes were still open, still looking to that memory of his wife and two children. He was smiling as he died.

"Oh, no!" Mary cried for the first time. "He was my neighbor and his wife was my friend."

Tikas came over and gently lifted her. The blanket she had been carrying rolled away and the packages of food spilled to the ground. The men had not eaten all day, but they looked to their leader for instructions. Everyone knew there was no time to mourn Charlie Costa. Hundreds of lives in the tent city depended on them drawing the Guardsman away from the camp.

"Every other man," Tikas pointed to the first man at the end of the hill. "Load your weapons and leave it with the man next to you, then fall out, eat quickly, then replace the next man."

He handed Mary his carbine.

"Mary, I need you to load weapons while the men eat," Tikas said. "Rolfe will show you how."

Rolfe Hiler took one bite of ham, reached into the ammunition pouch and pulled out the last two boxes of cartridges.

"I'm going for more ammo," Tikas said. "You're in charge, Rolfe. If I'm not back by the time you run out, get the men out of here."

Tikas pointed at two other men who laid their guns down and followed him down the hill.

"Have you seen my wife?" Rolfe asked Mary as he showed her how to load the rifle.

"Yes, she's fine," Mary said. She took the weapon and began loading as if she had been doing it her whole life. "She's hiding in a dry well with two other women and about a dozen children."

Rolfe began to cry.

<><><><><><>

Tikas never intended to get more ammunition. He planned to go to the National Guard headquarters and negotiate an end to the hostilities. Unfortunately, he and the two men with him had the bad luck of running straight into a dozen Guardsmen led by none other than Lieutenant Linderfelt. The unarmed men immediately raised their hands.

Tikas knew he was in trouble. Linderfelt hated him, and as two Guardsmen pinned his arms behind his back, the Lieutenant hit him so hard in the head with the butt of his rifle the stock shattered. Shocked by their commander's action, the men holding him released their hold on the prisoner. Tikas rolled onto the ground and received a kick in the head. A moment later he heard a gunshot and felt one last jolt of pain as an explosive bullet ripped through the middle of his back and into his stomach. He never felt the two shots that followed.

The leader of the colliers was dead.

<><><><><><>

When the ammunition ran out, Rolfe ordered two men to carry Charlie Costa's body and they withdrew from the hill.

"Mary." He held her shoulders with both hands. "Get back to Carmela and those children. Tell them not to return here. We will send someone to get you when it's over."

Mary nodded her head and started back toward the dry well.

Shooting was still going on but only sporadically. As Rolfe and the men passed in sight of the encampment they saw that every single tent was burnt to the ground. Dropping their guns, they walked into the camp. Wounded men, women and children who had been lying on the ground most of the day were moaning for help. A dozen National Guardsmen defied their commander's orders and were moving about the camp helping where they could. The terrible odor of burnt flesh drew Rolfe and the men to one of the many craters that was still smoldering. A Guardsman came running up with a light and turned its glow into the dark hole. Thirteen blackened bodies stared up at them from the unholy inferno. The only one that Rolfe recognized was the face of Charlie Costa's wife, Fedelina. Her arms were wrapped around two little children.

Suddenly Rolfe heard a machine gun and pieces of the ground around him flew into the air. The Death Special was roaring toward them with Lieutenant Linderfelt manning the machine gun.

"No one is allowed on this site," Linderfelt screamed at the Guardsmen who were trying to help the wounded. "Arrest those men."

Rolfe and those with him were too stunned to move. The rifles of three Guardsmen quickly covered them. Linderfelt immediately ordered his driver to the other side of the compound. When he was gone, one of the militiamen lowered his rifle.

"Get out of here," the Guardsman said. "Fast!"

Rolfe and his men laid Charlie Costa beside his wife and children and ran back up the hill.

<><><><><><>

Because of his medical experience, Rolfe was ushered to a farmhouse where some of the wounded were brought. He learned there were at least two other sites housing the victims. He trusted that Carmela would be able to get to one of them. They could rendezvous later.

While a doctor and a Red Cross nurse took care of the gunshot victims inside the house, Rolfe set up in the yard to help those with less serious injuries. Within an hour of his arrival the yard was filled with over three dozen crying and sometimes screaming children. Several of the men and women with serious wounds insisted on providing care and comfort to the young ones even as they themselves were slowly bleeding to death. Rolfe found himself cleaning and dressing parents' wounds even as they knelt to help their children.

Rolfe was unaware of how many hours had passed until a nurse brought him a cup of water and urged him to go sit on the porch and rest. Only when he did finally sit down on a wooden step and light up a cigarette did he notice that it was midday. The doctor, whose white shirt was covered in blood, was also taking a break.

"I've been watching you," the doctor said as he tried with shaking hands to light his pipe. "How long have you been a doctor?"

"I'm not," Rolfe admitted. "I never took my final exams. Things kept coming up."

"You should finish," the doctor said. "You have a gift."

Looking around at the devastation, Rolfe saw the feet of two victims lying in the back of a wagon, a tired horse still harnessed to the rig.

"Why aren't those two inside?" he asked.

"No need," the doctor said with a sigh. "One died about an hour ago. The other is a woman with a broken neck. Vertebrate is sticking clear through her skin. I'm amazed she's hung on this long."

Hearing a cry from inside the house, the doctor rose quickly and with pipe in mouth went back to work. Rolfe stood and was preparing to do the same when he heard a moan come from the wagon that held the two motionless sets of feet. His heart began to pound. He rushed over to the wagon so quickly he startled the horse, causing it to jerk the wagon. The woman lying on her back opened her eyes just as Rolfe's face appeared between her and the sky.

"Rolfe," Carmela said, her voice so weak he barely heard his name.

"Oh, my God!" Rolfe started to touch his wife's face, then instinctively stopped when the doctor's diagnosis of her condition registered in his brain. Paralyzed with possibly only moments to live.

"I kept hearing your voice." Carmela said softly. "I thought

I was dreaming but it made me want to stay awake and keep listening for it."

"What happened?" he asked as tears he had been holding back for so long suddenly gushed from his eyes.

"They said I fell off the side of an embankment when we were walking through the dark." She smiled. "Can you believe that? After being shot at all day I fell off a hill."

Though he had been trained to deal with seriously ill patients, Rolfe was so overcome with emotion he couldn't speak.

"Darling," Carmela said, her voice growing so weak he had to lower his ear closer to her mouth. "I want you to take your medical exam. You will be such a good doctor. I can see your diploma even now. R.J. Hiler, M.D."

With those final words and a proud smile on her face, Carmela Hiler left the world.

While he labored the rest of the day and into the night caring for the wounded, the face of every woman reminded him of his dear wife.

<><><><><><>

Carmela was buried alongside the Costa family and the other victims of the Ludlow massacre. What few belongings he and Carmela had brought had been destroyed in the fire, so when Rolfe boarded the train the morning after his wife's funeral, he had nothing but the clothes on his back. Telling no one that he was taking the morning train back east, he boarded at the last moment to avoid talking to anyone. The locomotive lurched forward as he reached for his seat.

He gazed out the train window as they passed the devastation of the burnt tent city. The only things standing where each tent had been were stoves and a scattering of tables and chairs. The hundreds of holes that had been dug for protection were like dark, unfilled graves on the landscape still echoing the screams of the women and children dying in the flames.

Rolfe felt with his thumb for the piece of metal still on the ring finger of his left hand. Until he reached their home in Chicago, it would be the only possession he had of his beloved Carmela. He continued looking through the window until the train rose to the top of a hill and then shot into a valley toward the rising sun.

Eight months later Rolfe received a letter from Mary Thomas.

December 21, 1914

My Dear Friend Rolfe,

Merry Christmas! At least I hope this letter finds you by Christmas. All I put was that you were on 35th Street somewhere in Chicago. But just in case you don't get it I'll keep it short.

We went through so much together, I feel I can tell you anything. I know that I always said I had sworn off men but I have been seeing a gentleman named Don O'Neal who I met before Ludlow. In fact, it was when I came over on the boat. I will let you know how that develops.

Well, as you may have already heard, it's over! Yesterday, the United Mine Workers announced they had run out of money and were calling off the strike in Colorado. My heart is so broken. I have given up doing speaking engagements concerning those terrible days at Ludlow. Mother Jones is angry with me, but I told her that maybe someday I'll write my story. But for now I just want to get on with my life.

The girls and I are going to move to a place called Hollywood in California, and we will stay with a woman I know there. I hope to open a dancehall so I can do what I enjoy most, singing.

I have no regrets. I did appreciate President Wilson hearing what the other survivors and I had to say about Ludlow and was happy that he sent Federal troops to disarm both sides. It is probably a good thing that I was in jail for those two weeks after the massacre or I might have got killed myself. Since then I've had people who lived near the jail write me that they enjoyed hearing me singing to my girls at night while we were in that cell. Did you know I was the only woman arrested? I'm thankful though that they let me keep my daughters in the jail with me.

Those weeks after the massacre were so terrible. I think that things got so bad because Linderfelt left the bodies of Louis Tikas and those other men lying by the railroad tracks for three days. He didn't even allow doctors or the Red Cross to help the victims and had his men shoot at those who went into the camp to help the wounded. Pearl Jolly, who you may remember, was shot right through her Red Cross armband when she tried to help the injured.

At least word got out as to what was going on. That helped the colliers get weapons, and though their invasion of those mines during the subsequent months and all the property they destroyed got some people angry, it was nothing compared to the outrage caused when Mother Jones and the rest of us survivors started telling what Linderfelt and his thugs really did. I still can't believe that terrible little man only received a verbal reprimand for murdering Louis.

Well, we may have lost the strike, but much good was accomplished, wasn't it? State and federal lawmakers passed a lot of good legislation that, in the long run, will improve conditions for our boys in the mines. Little by little we are whittling away at injustices and, I believe, we will someday prevail.

My girls say to tell you that they think of our Carmela often!

That's all I will take time to write for now since you may never get this letter.

Yours truly,
Mary

After a second reading, Rolfe laid the letter on the bed. As he rose and went to shut the window curtain, he gave a glance at the certificate framed on the wall. *R.J. Hiler, M.D.* Once back in bed, he read Mary's letter one last time, turned off his light and snuggled tight against his pillow. In the glow of a slow burning candle he took one last look at the photograph of his wife on the table. The horrors of Ludlow were behind her. He knew that God was with her now, and that Carmela's soul was content, knowing he had received his diploma.

14

Felina Harrison had been having bad luck for over a year. It seemed that every bit of mischief she attempted backfired. Amazingly, Filberto and Libero had become her friends, or at least as close to friends as Felina would allow. It seemed that each time something bad happened to her, the two youngest Vacca brothers were there to comfort her.

She had twice been able to prank people she didn't like by tying a rope around their outhouse when they were inside. Her plan was infallible. She would hide across the alley at night until the person came out of their house and into their little building to relieve themselves before bedtime. Then Felina would run up behind the outhouse and wrap the rope around it and through the door handle. By the time the person tried to come back out she would be sitting across the alley. From that vantage point she could enjoy the screams for help that would eventually come from the one trapped inside.

But now it was becoming more difficult for Felina to pull her prank. Word was getting around, and some folks were leaving their outhouse doors open when they performed their necessities. A few even had a family member stand guard for them.

Despite this, Felina felt she had to get revenge on her teacher. Old Lady Foster had made her stand in the corner that day for swapping math papers with Filberto when he wasn't looking and turning his in as her own. That night, when Mrs. Foster went into her little building before bedtime, Felina ran out from her hiding place behind a bush, ran across the alley and fell straight down into the poop pit. Someone had moved the little outhouse forward and not bothered to fill up the old pit. After she crawled out of the shithole and vomited, she saw Mrs. Foster standing over her laughing.

"I figured you was the one tying people up inside their commodes." Mrs. Foster laughed. "Luckily, I took the Vacca boys' advice and had them make me a fresh pit after school today. Too bad for you they didn't have time to fill up the old hole."

Suddenly, Filberto and Libero were standing beside Felina. Instead of laughing, they consoled her and held out towels they happened to have with them. They even walked home with her.

Felina still hated the Vaccas for digging Mrs. Foster's new pit, but she didn't cause them any trouble, since they were being nice to her. And anyway, she had more enemies at the moment than she could keep track of.

A week later, Felina was sitting between Libero and little Angie Eng at the children's table along with the other Vacca boys. She loved having dinner in the Eng house because they had so many small things she could steal by shoving them under her petticoats. In her bedroom at her house, she had a whole drawer full of things she had stolen on other visits to the millionaire's house. Today, she was eyeing a little clock on the fireplace mantle that had angels painted on it. She saw Filberto looking at it, too, and wondered if he also had a treasure drawer of mementos from the Eng family.

After dinner Felina caught Filberto playing with the back of the clock. Afraid that he would steal it before she could, the next time she passed through the room she grabbed it off the mantle and stuck it under her petticoat. She then grabbed a saltshaker off the table and went out on the porch by herself to look for slugs. Felina loved to pour salt on the slimy things and watch them roll around and melt away as they died.

<><><><><><>

Lena Eng was not one to put on airs. Even after Harley insisted that she employ a house cleaner twice a week, Lena liked to pitch in and work alongside the girl. When it was their turn to have the Vaccas and Harrisons over, she used the everyday china and cooked all the food herself. After dinner the talk turned, as it always did, to coal mining.

"We need to make certain that no one forgets the Colorado Coal War," Harley told Antonio and Joe as Lena and Angeline picked up the dishes. "I'm going to talk to some people I know about purchasing the site of the Ludlow massacre and make some sort of commemoration for those who died."

Joe coughed and shook his head. His friends looked at him, waiting for a comment. In the past, Joe had said he agreed with the company's view that most of the deaths at Ludlow had been a terrible accident and not an act of murder by the Guardsmen. He saw Angeline watching him as she collected the silverware. After a long, awkward moment, Joe got up and poured himself another drink.

Myrna yawned from her chair at the table. She hadn't offered to help the other two women clear the table and wash the dishes. "I have a terrible headache," she said. "Joe, I think we need to get Felina to bed."

Joe moved quicker than he did after lighting a fuse in the coal mine. In another moment Felina was standing between her parents at the doorway listening to the adults say their goodbyes. The Vacca brothers stood attentively as their mother had taught them when someone was leaving the room. Little Angie Eng waited patiently between Filberto and Libero, holding their hands.

"Well," Joe stumbled, "thank you for dinner. Next time will be at our house."

Myrna gave him a glare.

Suddenly the room was filled with the sound of musical notes.

"Why is my angel clock chiming now?" Lena looked at the fireplace mantle. "Oh dear! Where did it go?"

Felina put her hand over her dress and the sound became muffled. Everyone looked at her. Joe roughly turned his daughter around, reached beneath her dress and pulled the little clock out. As he held it away from his body, his eyes seemed to grow three sizes as the clock made its last chimes.

"That's Felina's clock," Myrna said. "She has one just like Lena's."

"Of course, dear," Lena said after a moment of awkward silence. "You all have a wonderful evening, now."

With one hand still on his daughter's arm, Joe set the clock down on the table next to the door and led her roughly out onto the porch. Then came the loud slap of a belt on his daughter's backside.

"Oh, my baby girl!" Myrna shouted and ran out the door.

Libero and Filberto smiled at each other.

<><><><><><><>

"I want you to get Bullo a job picking rock," Angeline told her husband a few days after Christmas. She rocked forward in her porch swing so she could better see the boys play with a large group of children taking advantage of the unseasonably mild weather. "You said you didn't want him to work until he turned sixteen," Antonio said.

"He will be sixteen in a few weeks," Angeline said, her jaw set in a firm look. "And he is too handsome to stay in school."

"I've never heard of a boy going to work in a coal mine because he is too handsome." Antonio watched Amelia Mathon walk up behind Bullo and flip off his cap.

"Then our son shall be the first." Angeline folded her arms over her chest. The discussion was over.

Angeline wanted her son away from the girls, at least until she could find a suitable Italian girl for him to marry. She understood the ways of young females and didn't want Bullo to get a girl in trouble. Vinnie was another matter. She would have her hands full just keeping him out of fights. She wished he had inherited his father's quiet personality instead of her own feisty one.

Filberto was the best student among the siblings, and she was already trying to save money in a jar so he might get a good education after high school. She had not yet decided what career she would have him pursue. Libero would always be her bambino and the one she would count on to take care of her and Antonio when they were old.

If only a mother's plans bore the expected fruit.

<><><><><><>

Bullo didn't know that he was handsome. He just thought that girls annoyed him because they were natural pests. So he was happy to go to work to get away from the girls, as well as the schoolwork. Many of the other boys his age had already been working at the picking table. The job of picking rock out of coal was not an exciting job, but with thirty young boys all doing it in close proximity, teenage talk and high-jinx were in abundance, especially after work. Most evenings the boys would go fishing or swimming in warm weather and sledding or hunting rabbits and squirrel in cold.

Because of the war in Europe, the mine remained open into early summer. With the United States supplying materials to both sides in the war, factories worked overtime to keep up with the demand. In the Christian County mines, workers were divided on their loyalties based on how it might affect their homelands. Germans wanted the United States to remain neutral. Irish Catholics were against supporting the British. Some Italians favored neutrality, others wanted America to join the British. Regardless of their political affiliations, all the miners liked the fact that they were getting extra work. Even after giving his mother the bulk of his wages, Bullo still had a little money of his own.

The boss of the rock picking crew was an old miner with a gimpy leg named Harry Filson. Harry loved kids and even helped at the schools when the mine wasn't working. The rock pickers had worked through a mild winter, which turned into a very warm, dry spring. Harry liked to have his boys out to his lake lot for swimming, beer and food. By late May, the water in the lake was already warm enough for swimming.

"Boys will be boys," Harry Filson told his wife, Martha, one evening as he related to her the mischievous goings-on of the boys in his rock-picking crew.

"But pulling another boy's pants down to his knees?" Martha held her hand over her mouth. "What if a woman had seen that?"

"What would a woman be doing on a mine tipple unless the emergency siren sounded?" Filson asked. He loved seeing the shocked look on his wife's face as he related the shenanigans of his young workers. "I think it's about time to have the boys out to our lake lot."

Harry and Martha had never been blessed with children. She loved cooking for her husband's lake parties, primarily because she loved the compliments she received from the polite young men.

"You'd better make them bring blankets so they can stay the night," she warned. "I don't want Mrs. Botts yelling at me again if her son gets a snoot full."

<><><><><><>

"Cold beer." Bernard Phelps sighed and took a long swallow from his brown bottle. "Life doesn't get better than this."

Bullo and Bernard were sitting on the roof of Harry Filson's lake house with six other boys who were all smoking and drinking. A half dozen similarly built cabins stretched out along the shore.

"Hold your beers up while I get your picture!" Filson yelled to them from down on the ground. The boys cheered and waved their beers above their heads as their boss looked down into his Brownie camera and snapped the picture.

"I'm going to my sister's," Martha said to her husband, "before one of them young 'uns comes tumblin' off that roof."

"Doubt if they'd feel it if they did," Harry said with a wave goodbye.

Though Bullo was having a great time, he did feel bad that Vinnie couldn't be there with him. Since he'd started picking rock, their relationship was not as strong, and without his big brother's guidance Vinnie was increasingly in trouble. Bullo decided to put one of his beers under his blanket and give it to Vinnie in the morning.

"Good golly, lookie there," Bernard said when the boys had lowered themselves back to the ground.

Bullo followed his friend's eyes and saw an incredibly full-bodied woman walking toward them. He could tell she was full-bodied because of the blue and white-striped swimming outfit she was wearing. Though her waist had a very wide girdle, her navy blue lapel was open below her neck, allowing for a tantalizing glimpse of shoulder and cleavage. She also wore a blue belt, matching wide-brimmed hat and a skirt that hung down past her knees. Her silk hosiery had fallen to her ankles displaying more female limb than any of the boys had ever seen.

"Ada, fix your suit, woman!" a man carrying a fishing pole and a string of catfish said from behind the voluptuous woman.

"Oh, hush now, Leo," Ada scolded. She studied the young men who were sucking their already flat stomachs in and struggling to not sway too much from their light heads. Her eyes quickly found Bullo. "You may carry my bumbershoot, young man," she said, handing him a large, blue umbrella that matched her bathing suit.

Bullo followed the lady who, when the sun hit it just right, appeared to have unusual, almost completely white hair. His friends made hooting sounds. Her husband, carrying his cane pole and fish, walked quietly behind them and turned into a shed.

Ada went straight into her house, but Bullo stopped and stood at the door.

"Oh, come in, young man," Ada said.

Bullo recognized right away that Mrs. Corso enjoyed scolding and bossing people.

"Do you like my swimming suit?" she asked when he stepped into the cabin. He saw that the building was just one room, with a small, feather bed and a couch in front of a fireplace.

"Your beach hat is very becoming, ma'am," Bullo said, though his eyes had not yet gone that high.

"Huh!" Ada removed a pin from her big hat and flung it onto the couch. "Yer sure a good-looking boy. You ever kissed a girl?"

"Why, no, ma'am," Bullo said, taking a step back. "I'd best be goin' now."

"Oh, fiddle." Ada moved toward him. "Can't you stay on awhile? I just hate being alone all the time."

"Alone?" Bullo said, scratching his head. "Why, your husband's right outside there, ma'am."

"Quit callin' me 'ma'am,'" Ada said. "Why, I ain't much older than you. And besides, my husband will be cleanin' fish for a long while yet."

Without another word, she grabbed Bullo's head and kissed him hard on the mouth. Bullo felt a sensation throughout his body he had never before known. Without any effort his mouth responded, and a moment later he felt his hands on her back.

As the voluptuous woman pulled him closer, Bullo seemed to hear his mother's loud voice yelling at him in Italian. Bullo pulled away from the woman, turned and ran out the door. Years later, when he recalled that moment, he actually believed it had been his mother's voice chastising him over the loose woman with the fisherman husband.

<><><><><><>

"Watch where you're walkin," Vinnie told his brother as the two crossed the street onto the town square.

Abandoning his reverie, Bullo stumbled and sidestepped the big pile of horse dung. During the day he thought about the warm mouth of Ada Corso, and at night he thought about the feel of her firm, full body.

"You thinkin' bout her again?" Vinnie asked.

Bullo was beginning to regret that he had shared so much with his brother. He walked a little faster.

"Nah, just not payin' attention, I reckon," Bullo said, trying to be more careful where he was stepping. Suddenly, someone came out of Barney's Grocery Store and bumped into Vinnie.

"Excuse me, ma'am," Vinnie said and kept walking.

Bullo stopped. The girl had both hands around a big, wooden box full of groceries. A can of beans balancing precariously on top fell off. He caught it midair.

"Oh, thank you," the girl said as he placed it back into the box.

Bullo started to tip his hat when he realized he wasn't wearing one. The girl didn't seem to mind his mistake. She had red hair, green eyes and a clean freshness to her skin.

"My name's Bullo Vacca," he said. "May I help you with that?"

The girl seemed about to say no, but then the fingers on her left hand slid out from under the box. Bullo again came to her rescue, catching it before its contents could spill out.

"Come on, Bullo," Vinnie said.

"You go on, I'm going to help this girl." Bullo began rearranging the food in the box so they'd ride better.

Vinnie muttered something and continued down the street.

"I'm Mary Kate Danaher," the girl said.

"I'm Bullo Vacca," Bullo said before realizing he had already told her his name. "I seem to be having an awkward day."

"Not awkward enough that it prevented ya from saving me twice already," Mary Kate said, a pleasant lilt in her voice.

"You're Irish." Bullo took full possession of the box and began walking beside the girl.

"You're Italian," Mary Kate said and giggled. "Are ya a miner, Bullo?"

"Yes, ma'am."

"My father was a miner." She stopped at a decrepit boarding house. "The top fell on him last winter." She looked away. "Now his mind is almost gone."

"I'm a rock picker above ground," Bullo said. "I guess I'll be soundin' my tops real good when I do go underground."

"I'm glad," she said, taking the box of groceries.

"Does anyone else live with you and your papa?" Bullo asked.

"No," Mary Kate said. "We're all alone. I work in the glove factory."

"I'll be carryin' your groceries from now on," Bullo said, "if you'd let me."

"That would be fine." Mary Kate walked to the house. She turned around and looked at Bullo. "I'll be shopping again next week at the same time."

Bullo Vacca never again had thoughts of Ada Corso's warm mouth or firm and full body. He never again had such thoughts of anyone except Mary Kate Danaher.

<>< ><>< ><>< >

Mary Kate sewed twelve hours a day, six days a week in the glove factory. After work each evening she cleaned houses for another three hours. The Eng house was her favorite because Mrs. Eng worked alongside her and talked like a schoolgirl, especially when she found out Mary Kate had met Bullo.

"Oh, Bullo is such a nice Italian boy," Lena told her.

"But does that mean he wouldn't like an Irish lassie?" Mary Kate said. She was worried her future happiness could be ruined simply because her family was from the wrong side of Europe.

"Oh, no," Lena assured her as they mopped the kitchen floor. "That won't bother Bullo. But his mother is another matter. I'll tell you what, though. If the two of you decide to get together, tell me before you tell his mother. I think I can handle Angeline Vacca."

15

Vinnie was excited. The United States had finally entered the war in Europe. He would run away and join the Army. Last fall he had tried to follow the circus when they left town. His mother got wind of it and locked him in his room for almost a week. He was fifteen now and knew that, being taller than even his father, he could pass for eighteen. This time she would not succeed. She would not be able to lock him in his room until the war was over.

He was standing in front of his bed throwing his clothes into a duffle bag when his youngest brother entered. Libero was eleven years old and the proverbial apple of his mother's eye.

"I'm gonna tell Mama if you walk out that door," Libero said in a low voice, "and she'll beat your butt, but good."

"I'm not a baby like you," Vinnie hissed back, "and I'll pound your butt but good if you get in my way."

"Vinnie?" their mother called from the kitchen. "Could you bring me the washboard? It's on the porch."

"Ohhh," Libero smirked, "you're in for it now."

"She's not going to beat me with a washboard, bambino." Vinnie said. He tucked the duffle bag behind the pillow of the top bunk. "I suppose it wouldn't hurt to do one last thing for the old lady before I vamoose."

Vinnie fetched the washboard off the porch. After all, she was a good mother, he decided, even if she did beat him with a hickory switch just about twice a month.

When he entered the kitchen, he saw his portly little mother standing as usual at the washbasin. He wondered if she had even heard that their country had just declared war on Germany.

"Here you are, Mama." Vinnie set the washboard on the counter beside her.

Tears dampened her eyes. "Thank you, dear," she said.

It upset him that she was crying. Had she heard about the war? Did she know he was running off to fight the Germans? Was she peeling onions? He didn't see any onions.

"Why are you crying, Mama?" Vinnie wanted to put his hand on her shoulder, but he had been avoiding displays of affection for the past few years. He was an adult now, and men didn't do such things. His father did, but that was different, he was her husband. Vinnie didn't know if he would want to be that kind of husband.

"It's okay, dear," his mother said. "It's nothing for you to worry about."

Vinnie turned to go, but when he heard her sniff, he stopped and came back. "What's nothing, Mama?"

"You just don't worry about it," his mother said. She pulled her shoulders back. "Your father and I will always take care of you boys."

"Of course you will, Mama," Vinnie said. He didn't think she knew anything about the war or his leaving. So why was she upset? "Do you need money, Mama? If you do, I could go to work picking rock. Bullo picked rock when he was fifteen."

His mother's arms were around him before he could stop her. He felt her wet tears on his shoulder.

"Oh, Vinnie," she said between sobs, "you are just the best son. Would you really go to work to help us?"

"Of course, Mama," Vinnie said, relief in his voice. "I'll go right now and talk to Mr. Filson. I'll bet I can start tomorrow."

As he left the kitchen he thought he smelled onion on the shoulder of his shirt, but he had not seen an onion. He also didn't see his mother quit crying the second he was out the door, or the piece of onion she had tucked into her apron pocket.

<>< ><>< ><>< >

That night Angeline gave her husband a pleasure he had not asked for. Later, they lay listening to Filberto snore. Because of his broken nose, he was the only one of their sons to snore, and he was louder than even his father.

"I thought Vinnie would want to run off and fight the war," Antonio told his wife, "but Harry Filson said he came in today and asked for a job picking rock."

"Oh, did he?" Angeline looked surprised. "He's a good boy, our Vinnie."

"Did you say something to him?" Antonio closed his eyes.

"Me? No, *il mio amante*," she said as she stroked her man's temple with a finger. "But do not be quick to spend money until this war is over."

<>< ><>< ><>< >

Angeline thought this was as good a war as one could be. Her sons were too young to fight and her husband too old. Men twenty-one to thirty-one years of age were required to register for the Selective Service. Antonio was thirty-eight. Besides that, coal miners were exempt because their jobs were considered critical to the nation.

The night after Vinnie's first day of work, she snuck into the boys' room. One at a time, she pulled the quilt snuggly against each son's neck and kissed him. She wasn't worried about waking them. They were used to this middle-of-the-night ritual. When she came to Vinnie, she rubbed his feet for several moments, just as she did his father's after a hard day's work. Vinnie was so tired he lay with his mouth open and didn't move.

Angeline Vacca wasn't so worried about any of her

sons except Vinnie. He was the fighter. He was the one she understood best because he was just like her.

<><><><><><>

Lena had been watching her husband all day. Harley sat silently in the leather chair of his den staring at the hundreds of leather-bound books that were neatly organized by subject on the shelves. She knew he had read them all, some more than once. It was as if he were rereading them in his mind.

When he finally did move, it was to lean forward and take one off the shelf. He was thumbing through it when she walked behind him with the pretext of cleaning the shelves with a feather duster. *The Red Badge of Courage* by Stephen Crane. She knew it. He had been silent since hearing that the United States had entered the war. She felt suddenly sick to her stomach and hurried out of the room.

She knew her man. She knew what he was thinking, and it scared her to death. But she also knew what her man secretly craved, what he desperately needed. He had come to hate being looked upon with disdain because he had money. Jonathan Eng did not fit in with the other wealthy members of the community, and as hard as he tried, he did not fit in with the workingman. Because of her relationship with Angeline, Antonio Vacca was the closest thing he had to a close friend, but even the friendly Italian seemed to run out of conversation after so long.

Lena wanted to cry. Would Angeline cry in this situation? Lena envied her friend's spunk and courage.

Later that evening, Angie was playing with her dollhouse when her father finally came out of the den. Lena looked up at him from her sewing, knowing what he was about to say.

"I have to go," Harley told his wife. He seemed unable to say more.

Lena put down her sewing, stood and walked over to her

husband. "Then," she said, putting her arms around his waist, "those Germans had better watch out, 'cause my man is coming after 'em."

<><><><><><>

"I guess enough men have enlisted they need more company employees," Joe told Antonio while walking to work.

"You going to take it?" Antonio asked. He stopped outside the gate to the mine yard.

"I'd be a fool not too, wouldn't I?" Joe was irritated that his friend would even ask. Being face boss would mean he'd be the top paid workingman. "Besides, you'll be taking Bullo on as a partner."

As usual, Antonio said nothing, a silence Joe knew meant he didn't approve. Since the events at Ludlow, many miners had become skeptical of anything the company did.

"You and I are not going to agree on this, so why are we talking?" Joe said.

"I'm not talking," Antonio said.

"You *were* talking, dago." Joe said. "Not with your mouth or even those damned dago hands of yours, but I still heard you loud and clear."

Joe turned and walked straight into the mine office. The next day he began his new job, and Bullo went down in the hole for the first time.

<><><><><><>

Mary Kate was excited yet concerned by Bullo's news.

"Ya will be careful like ya promised," she told him. Though she had never met Angeline Vacca, Lena spoke highly of the little Italian woman's strength of character. She knew that Bullo would expect no less from his girlfriend.

"I'm a sounder like me old man," he said, putting his arms

around her and teasing her with an Irish lilt he had been practicing. "I'll be sounding roofs till the top o' the morn, b'gosh, I will!"

Mary Kate smiled and ran her hands up her man's arms. They were full and strong, like her father's used to be.

"You'll be a fine miner, you will," she said. Across the grassy field where they stood, she saw the mine tipple. Somewhere down that hole her father had nearly lost his life and did lose most of his mind. She couldn't bear the thought of losing anyone else, but she knew she had to be strong and show a brave face for her Bullo, just as his mother would do.

<><><><><><>

Lena sat in her living room rocker and began reading Harley's letter for the third time:

June 3, 1917

My Darling Lena,

I am so happy! A brother or sister for our sweet Angie will be like a dream come true. I want to be there with you when the baby comes, but since I have already requested transfer to Europe, I don't really know where I'll be. At least staying in Ft. Sheridan will be more bearable, knowing I will be close to you when your time comes.

You know how much you and our little ones mean to me, but I know you also understand my need to serve my country. I have stood on the sideline of life watching the suffering of my fellow man long enough. This is my chance to do something useful.

That sounds so selfish when I think about you and Angie and now the baby. Loving the three of you should be enough, but I keep remembering those men at Cherry and that seventh cage. It comforts me to know that my family will be taken care of financially. Just in case this war does something to my investments, I have taken out a $20,000 life insurance policy.

Lena set the rest of the letter down on the coffee table. She knew those pages already by heart. Her husband's love for her was unconditional, and if she asked him to he would desert his duties to his country and flee with his family to the mountains or Canada. But making such a request would only leave her half a husband. The other half would always remain with those miners from 1909. The ones in the seventh cage.

16

By the beginning of 1918, the war in Europe was in full swing. The mine was producing faster and more efficiently than ever. Wages were up, and the miners had as much work as they could handle. When Antonio had a day off, he liked to take full advantage and relax body and mind. But one Sunday morning as he sat at the kitchen table reading the morning paper and smoking a cigarette, he became apprehensive. His wife had not said a word all morning. Her right eyebrow was also higher than the left, a clear sign that she was deep in thought.

"It is time for me to choose a bride for Bullo," she mumbled as she stood over the stove, turning bacon in a large skillet.

Antonio thought she had spoken so softly he might have a chance to sneak out of the room. When she turned back to the coffee pot, he quietly set his paper down on the table and stepped slowly toward the door.

"Antonio, sit!" Angeline said, without looking toward him.

Antonio sat back down.

"I think we should meet with the Demuzio family," Angeline said. "They have two nice daughters who are soon coming of age."

"Angeline, we are in America, the land of freedom," Antonio said. He tried to control his hands. "Young people choose for themselves who they want to marry."

"Hah!" Angeline said as she poured her husband more coffee. "You would have your sons marry for flesh, I suppose? *Perché parli così sciocco?*"

"I do not speak foolish!" Antonio shouted. "And I will not talk to the Demuzios!"

He got up and headed toward the door.

"We will meet with the Demuzios next Sunday after church," Angeline said firmly.

"Make it after dinner," Antonio said over his shoulder. "I am busy in the afternoon."

<><><><><><>

When Bullo heard what his mother was up to, he went straight to Vinnie. He found his brother behind the church pitching pennies with a group of boys.

"I need you to take this to Mary Kate Danaher," he said, handing over a sealed envelope. "Wait for an answer."

"What is it?"

"It's a *masciata*."

"What?" Vinnie said, shaking his head. "You speak Italian now?"

"Mama is more likely to go along with this if we do it the old-country way," Bullo said, with urgency in his voice. "You are my matchmaker, and this is a marriage proposal."

<><><><><><>

"I told you to let me talk to Angeline first!" Lena shouted first in Italian, then English. Mary Kate had shown up at her doorstep frantic and out of breath.

"I know," Mary Kate said, tears running down her face, "but Bullo said he had to tell her because she was trying to arrange a marriage for him with someone else."

"That *woman!*" Lena said. "She hasn't even met you yet. Oh well, what you need right now is an Italian temper as bad as Angeline Vacca's. Run next door and see if Mrs. Cummings can watch the girls."

Ten minutes later, Lena burst into the Vacca home without knocking. Filberto and Libero heard the two women screaming at one another in Italian and ran outside. Mary Kate was sitting in the Eng's Model-T Ford when the boys hurried past.

"Tell our mother we have gone fishing and won't be back until dark," Libero told her.

"And if she's still yelling at dark," Filberto added, "we won't be back until morning!"

After five minutes of both women screaming at the same time, it slowed to one woman yelling followed immediately by the other. After another five minutes, Mary Kate heard a smattering of English. A few minutes after that, Lena came out the door, followed by the plump, little mother. Angeline rushed to the automobile, opened the car door and almost lifted Mary Kate out of it. Suddenly the young girl was being smothered in kisses.

Her future mother-in-law then took her by the hand and walked her to an area a dozen yards from her house. "We will build you a home right here between the oak trees that Antonio planted near twenty years ago. And when you and Bullo need your kissing time, you can send your bambinos over to Grandmama's house."

When Antonio got home he found his wife teaching a red-haired girl how to make tortellinis.

"I would love to marry Bullo in an Italian wedding," the girl was telling Angeline. "I have no family except for my father. Because of his head injury I don't think he understands that I'm getting married."

"Don't worry, dear," Angeline told her. "We will take care of him like one of our own. Antonio will build you a house with three bedrooms so your father will always have a place to live."

This was how Antonio Vacca learned his oldest son was getting married.

<><><><><><>

Two nights later as Antonio placed his hand on the outside

doorknob to his house he heard the breaking of glass. When he entered, he saw Angeline standing in front of the fireplace with a wine glass in her hand. Not seeing him, she threw it at the stone fireplace and quickly got down on the ground to count the pieces.

"What are you doing?" Antonio yelled.

"I'm testing different glasses," Angeline said without looking at him, "to see which one breaks into the most pieces."

The little mother pulled out a pencil and paper and wrote a number. "This one will do." She held up a pair of wine glasses. "When our son and his bride break these after the wedding toast, they will have many years of happiness."

Antonio would find this was just the beginning of his wife's determination to give her daughter-in-law a proper Italian wedding. Angeline and Lena spent countless hours over the next few days getting ready for the Sunday wedding. Mary Kate was completely overwhelmed with the motherly attention, but she loved every moment of it. Angeline convinced her to quit her job in the glove factory, but encouraged her to continue cleaning houses.

"Remember, dear, that your husband's income is also yours, and whatever money you make. . ." Angeline thought for a moment. "Well, that's yours, too."

Since there was still an unusually high demand for coal because of the war, Bullo worked all week in the mine with his father. The young couple's new home was not built as quickly as Antonio and Angeline's had been eighteen years before. It took longer because it was a workweek and the men had to build on it in the evenings. Still, Angeline had dictated that it be completed by the wedding day, and so it was. The new home not only had the extra room Angeline had promised for Mary Kate's father, it had a basement for the children to play in during bad weather. Angeline had made it clear that a bambino would be coming before the end of the year.

<>‹›‹›‹›‹›

On her wedding morning, Mary Kate kissed her father, thanked Missy Weir again for watching him, and walked out of the boarding house ahead of Lena. When she opened the door she found that someone had tied a white ribbon over her front entrance.

"Oh, that Angeline!" Lena said from behind her. "Don't move."

She hurried back into the kitchen and returned with a pair of scissors, which she handed to the bride.

"You must cut the ribbon to symbolize the beginning of your new life with Bullo," she told her.

Mary Kate could not help laughing with joy. Bullo had said she would encounter many traditions that would be explained throughout the day. A few she had already experienced, such as the green instead of white wedding dress that Angeline said would ensure fertility.

Just then, Joe Harrison drove up in the Eng's big automobile. He jumped out and hurried around to open the car door for the bride. He was dressed in a handsome, three-piece suit. Mary Kate thought it must be a mighty rare thing indeed to go to the chapel in the chauffeured car of a millionaire.

When she got out of the vehicle at the church, the young bride saw that Angeline had tied another white ribbon around that door also.

"You don't cut this one," Lena told her as they went inside. "It's just to announce the wedding."

Angeline came bustling up to her, filled with excitement. After a tearful hug, she hurried her into the bridal room. Father Marco was beginning the nuptial mass, and Bullo and his best man, Vinnie, were already sitting in the front of the church.

In the bridal room, Angeline placed a pretty, green veil on Mary Kate's head, then tore it down the middle. "That's for luck," she said, giving the bride another hug.

The three women did some last minute adjustments to the bridal dress, then they heard the processional music. Mary Kate followed her flower girl, seven-year old Angie Eng, down the aisle alone, knowing that by marrying into the Vacca family, she would never be alone again.

<><><><><><>

Bullo held his wife's hand as they walked out of the church after the ceremony. The weather had cooperated with a mild January day. The couple ducked through the shower of rice thrown by the many guests and began walking toward the town square.

"Where are we going?" Mary Kate asked her husband.

"You will see."

Before they had gone half a block, Mary Kate bent down to pick up a broom someone had dropped in the road. She heard a loud cheer from the people behind them who were watching from the church stairs.

"See," Angeline said, when the ovation stopped, "I told you she would keep a clean house."

Mary Kate and Bullo laughed and continued walking.

"Is everything going to be a test?"

"Well, not that dead squirrel," Bullo said, pointing to some road-kill on the street, "but it would be wise to stay alert."

After a few more blocks, only a few from the church still followed them, some in cars and others in horse-drawn buggies.

"The rest, including Mother, have gone into the grand hall to prepare for the reception," Bullo said.

When they reached the town square, they saw a sawhorse, a thick log, and a double-handled ripsaw.

"This will be the last obstacle," Bullo said. "But I'm not sure what it means."

"You must work together to saw the log in half," Mrs. Borgononi said from the back of the first buggy. "It represents the cooperation it takes to have a successful marriage."

"Oh, no," Bullo said, shaking his head.

"Come on, love," Mary Kate said in her finest Irish lilt. "I want to see if my mate is a team player." She spit on her hands, and when she grabbed one end of the saw, a cheer arose, even from pedestrians who had not been at the wedding. People began to come out of buildings to watch the couple.

Bullo was embarrassed by the attention, but Mary Kate's Irish blood seemed up for the challenge. It took the newlyweds nearly ten minutes to saw the log all the way through, but they did it without stopping. When the wood dropped to the ground, the crowd gave another long cheer. Suddenly the bride and groom were surrounded by well-wishers. Someone handed them each a glass of wine and others offered them money.

"Here, darling." Mrs. Borgononi said. She tied a small, satin bag around Mary Kate's left wrist. "Your mother-in-law told me to give this to you. It's the la borsa for people to put money in during the reception."

<><><><><><>

From inside her head, Angeline ran off an explosion of expletives as she watched her son, Vinnie. Standing in front of the wedding table beneath a cloud of cigarette smoke, the best man was fumbling miserably over the Italian toast she had taught him.

"*Ci siamo riuniti oggi,*" Vinnie said, starting the speech again for the third time. His face went red and he looked guiltily at his mother. Finally, he simply held up his glass and shouted, "*Per cent'anni!*"

The audience erupted in cheers.

"*Evviva gli sposi!*"

"*Auguri!*"

"*Evviva gli sposi*"

"*What did they say?*" Mary Kate shouted over the cheers to

her husband.

"Vinnie said, 'one hundred years!'" Bullo said, "And the others are saying, 'best wishes' and 'hooray for the newlyweds!'"

"I guess I'm going to have to learn Italian," Mary Kate said and kissed her husband.

Suddenly Vinnie grabbed Bullo by the necktie. With a quick snip of the scissors he clipped it off the groom's neck.

"Who wants to buy a piece of my brother's tie?" He yelled. A dozen men shouted and stepped forward, holding out money.

"My la borsa is almost full now," Mary Kate said.

"Take some of it out," Bullo told her. "Since we don't have any grandmamas here, give it to one of the oldest woman in the room to hold for safe keeping."

Mary Kate found Mrs. Borgononi sitting with a group of elderly ladies. She walked across the room, held a handful of money out to her and kissed her cheek.

"I am honored," Mrs. Borgononi said. Her eyes became misty.

Angeline cupped her hands over her heart and smiled.

The accordion player began slowly playing *"La Tarantella."* Everyone stood up, joined hands, and began slowly dancing clockwise. After a few moments, the music became a little faster and the dance went in the opposite direction. Moments later, it sped up again, as did the dancers, and they again changed direction. Back and forth the dancers went each time the music sped up. Soon it was a frenzy of movement one way, then another, faster and faster, until finally one of the guests fell down laughing, followed by everyone else.

Later, when the couple toasted each other and threw their wine glasses into the fireplace, Mrs. Borgononi had the honor of counting the sixty-six pieces of glass. Angeline looked at her husband and gave him a knowing smile.

The reception carried on until the wee hours of the next morning.

Kevin Corley

<><><><><><>

Because of his head injury from the mine, Will Danaher didn't understand what was happening when his daughter and a man he didn't know dressed him in warm clothes and took him out of his house and into a waiting carriage. As the buggy pulled out into the street, several other men went into his home. After a long and pleasant ride through the country, he was brought to a different house and into a different room. His bed and other belongings had magically appeared in this room, so he went straight to sleep.

When he awoke, he had no memory that he had ever lived anywhere else. The short, pudgy woman who sometimes came in to care for him reminded him of a nice Italian lady he had known when he was a child in Ireland.

Will Danaher lived in the house for nine months with his daughter and a man who was also kind to him. One night he dreamed he heard a baby cry. It reminded him of the evening his daughter was born. He was thinking about that happy moment when his heart stopped.

Mary Kate and Bullo named their newborn son William.

17

Harley Eng's frustration at being stuck for over a year in Ft. Sheridan, Illinois, was complicated even further the second week in June when he came down with a terrible case of the flu. He lay in the medical ward at the Great Lakes Naval Training Station for nearly a week. His only real company during this time was Dr. Rolfe J. Hiler, who preferred to be called RJ.

"I don't like this flu," RJ told Harley as they played a game of chess on his bed. "I had it myself last month, and it's like nothing I've seen before. They lost almost fifty soldiers out in Kansas."

"I doubt it kills as many men as the war will," said Harley. He had learned to like and respect the doctor who, though almost completely bald, was not much older than he was. "If I could get out of this damned bed, maybe I could get over there and do something useful."

"To put a gun in the hands of a man with your intelligence would be a great waste," RJ said as he castled to his right. "But I understand how you feel. It took someone I cared about to convince me to become a doctor."

"I'm not doing much good here though, am I?" Harley took the physician's rook with his knight. "Check."

RJ shook his head when he saw the predicament his white pieces were in. He moved his king to the corner, his only move, and then watched his opponent take his knight's pawn with a black queen.

"Checkmate, Doc." Harley lay back in his bed.

"Why don't you join my staff?" RJ said.

"What do I know about medicine?" Harley was caught off

143

guard by the suggestion.

"Probably more than you do about killing people." RJ stood, walked to the door, and then turned around. "They are not going to send a millionaire into battle to be killed, Harley. You might as well accept that and find a way to make yourself useful while you're here."

Harley did know that. He had been requesting combat duty for over a year. He looked at the doctor.

"Checkmate, my friend," RJ said as he turned and walked back to work.

The next day, Harley Eng, millionaire, began cleaning bedpans.

<><><><><><>

The first big wave of flu victims came into the ward on September 11. Within a week, the hospital had almost three thousand patients. Before the end of the month, there were close to two hundred deaths in the Chicago area.

"I can't guarantee it," RJ told Harley as they hurried through the hospital hallway, "but I think you and I are immune to this strand of influenza because we had it last spring."

Fatigue, fever and headache were the first symptoms of the deadly disease, followed by the skin turning blue. Then patients would cough so hard they tore their abdominal muscles and had severe bleeding from the mouth, nose and even ears. Many of those who didn't vomit became incontinent.

Harley found himself carrying bodies just as he had at the Cherry Mine Disaster in 1909. Each day as the body count increased, so did the panic. At first there was an attempt to cover up the seriousness of the pandemic.

"We have to quarantine," Dr. Hiler told his colleagues during a conference in the hospital cafeteria. Harley sat beside his friend, taking notes. "This war is the worst thing that could happen during a pandemic. Sending these soldiers out across the country and on to Europe will only spread the disease further."

"Do you expect the governments to stop the war so you can treat your patients?" An Ivy League doctor named Isaac Burns smirked at Hiler.

"I am just a country doctor," Hiler told the staff. "But if I make a house call and find a disease like this, I can contain it in the house, maybe even a bedroom. When our soldiers contract the flu in the trenches, they are taken back to the hospitals where they spread it to others."

"What can we do, then?" a nurse asked. "It will spread everywhere."

"Isolate people until this passes," Hiler said. He dismissed the staff back into the medical ward.

Harley immediately found a telephone and called Lena.

"How much food do you have in the house?" he shouted into the wall speaker when he heard her voice. He had a bad connection and had to hold the handheld receiver tightly to his ear.

He barely heard her say something about what was in the fruit cellar.

He shouted slowly and clearly. *"Lena, listen to me and do exactly what I say. This flu is very dangerous. Make one trip to the store. Buy enough food for a month. Lock yourself in the house with the girls. Don't let anyone in and don't leave until this disease passes."* He heard Lena say she understood, then the line went dead.

Harley rushed back into the medical ward. Orderlies were bringing in patients so fast there were no more beds. They began laying the sick along the hallway floor. Within the hour, even that room was full of coughing, sniffing, crying and moaning patients. People vomited on the floor when they were too weak to hold sacks to their faces. The smell of sick permeated the room.

"Open those windows!" Hiler barked to an orderly who was

rushing around in a panic. "Sergeant, these people would be better off outside where the air is fresh. See if you can screen in the breezeway."

"Go get military bunks from the barracks," Hiler said to a nurse. "The soldiers can sleep on the floor. You, soldier, quit crying and take these information sheets to the newspaper offices. Have them put out special editions right away."

Hiler saw a woman squatting over two teenage boys lying on the floor. Their faces were too blue to even tell the color of their skin.

"How long have these boys been sick?" he asked.

"Only a few hours," the mother said, her hands shaking. "I don't understand. They never get sick. They have never even had a bad cold before."

While the doctor inspected the larger of the boys, Harley checked the pulse of the smaller one. He slipped a small mirror under his nose and looked at RJ.

"Take this woman to the waiting area," Hiler said to an orderly in a commanding voice. The woman stood and moved in a daze toward the entrance.

"Harley," Hiler whispered when she was out of hearing range, "give her ten minutes, then tell her that both boys are gone."

<><><><><><>

"The healthier the patient, the more severely they are affected by the virus," Hiler told Health Commissioner John Robertson during a staff meeting the next day. A dozen doctors sat around the big table with weary looks on their faces.

"That makes no sense," Dr. Burns said, rolling his eyes.

"Most of the deaths have been healthy young adults who've had a history of strong immune systems," Hiler said. "Flu viruses we have seen in the past are fatal to babies and older people."

"How have you had time to do a controlled research?" Burns asked.

"I did it while you were taking your hourly cigar breaks," Hiler said. He was growing weary of his colleague. "How many of these victims have *you* talked to, Isaac?"

"Easy, gentleman. We are all tired and cranky," Commissioner Robertson said.

"What's going on in the city?" Hiler asked.

"I've had signs posted advising against spitting, sneezing and coughing in public," Robertson said. "All non-essential social settings have been ordered cancelled or postponed. That includes theatres, sporting events, saloons, and so on."

"What about churches and schools?" Hiler asked.

"I recommend we keep them open," Burns said. "We don't want to cause a panic. There is enough anxiety due to the war. I have also recommended that everyone going out in public be required to wear a facemask."

"A facemask?" Hiler said, shaking his head. "We can barely see the bacteria through a high-powered microscope. You'd have better luck catching a mosquito with a fishnet."

"I'm also limiting funerals to ten mourners at a time," Robertson added. "And I've asked businesses to operate every other day so there will be fewer people on the street."

"I think that will be enough," Burns said, looking smugly at Hiler. "I have over forty years' experience in medicine, and I can guarantee there will be no escalation of this epidemic after these precautions are enforced."

The following week there were over 6,000 new cases of influenza and more than 600 deaths in the Chicago area. Harley Eng seldom got more than three hours sleep a night. Despite everything the doctors attempted, there was nothing they could do to keep patients from dying. They made them as comfortable as possible and tried to prevent pneumonia from developing. Day after day passed with no break in the number of sick. By the middle of October, the death toll in Chicago climbed to over 2,000.

Though he tried several times a day, Harley was unable to get a call through to Lena. He was afraid to send her a letter for fear it would carry the virus. Neither did he receive any letters. When he tried the telegraph office, he was told that only pertinent military messages were being allowed.

On October 15, Harley walked wearily to his cot, where he saw RJ sitting on the floor crying, a paper in his hand. Dozens of other cots were jammed in the room, with medical personnel sleeping soundly.

He helped the doctor into a sitting position on his cot.

"Do you believe in God, Harley?" RJ said, handing him the paper.

"Yes." Harley took the paper and read it. The names of Illinois cities and towns along with their population and the number of infected was written in long rows. He scanned quickly to find Taylorville, but only found communities near it.

He saw that Nokomis, just to the south of Hewittville, had 1,973 residents of which over 600 were sick. There was a side note stating they had no medical facilities. Assumption, which was a few miles east of Taylorville, had a population of 1,918 and over 500 cases. They were sending out distress messages asking for doctors and nurses.

The paper did not state the number of deaths, but Harley knew that was just to prevent further panic. He had helped victims long enough to know that between ten and twenty percent of those infected would die.

The notation at the bottom of the paper said, "The state influenza commission states that although the situation in the down state communities is bad, it will get worse before it gets better." All Harley could think about was Lena and Angie and his baby daughter, Margaret, whom he had yet to hold.

"This must be the unveiling that is talked about in Revelations," RJ said, lying back with a forearm over his eyes.

"No," Harley said. "God wouldn't be this cruel. This is just a terrible disease. One which we will survive."

Two days later, Harley wondered if RJ was right about the end of the world. That day became known as Black Thursday. In Chicago alone, 1,200 new cases were contracted and 381 people died. The city ran out of hearses and had to use street trolleys draped in black to carry the dead. Terror gripped the city as nothing had since the great Chicago fire of 1871. A man driven insane by fear locked his wife and four children in his apartment and cut their throats. "I cured 'em my way," he shouted when the police came for him.

The second half of the month passed as slowly and miserably as the first. Then in November, for no apparent reason, the number of newly inflicted victims began to slow. Dr. Burns claimed it was because he had learned to slow the advance of pneumonia. Harley wondered if it was because word was being spread that the war in Europe might be coming to an end.

"Could the good news about the war ending improve spirits and cause fewer people to get sick?" Harley asked RJ one day as they watched soldiers removing cots from the hallway.

"Not likely," RJ said. "I don't think this influenza has anything to do with positive attitudes. In fact, I wouldn't be surprised if the war is coming to an end *because* of the flu."

"What do you mean?" Harley asked.

"Millions of people across the planet have died from this pandemic. Maybe more than from the Black Death of the fourteenth century. It's possible that the loss of so many lives in every country gave governments an added reason to make peace."

When Dr. Hiler saw the celebrations in the streets of Chicago on Armistice Day, November 11, he ordered the soldiers to start bringing the cots back in. The next morning, a hung-over Dr. Burns ran down the hall and screamed at his colleague, "What are you doing ordering those beds?"

"Over one million people just broke quarantine, Doctor!" Hiler shouted back. A dozen heads popped out of doorways looking at the two men standing toe-to-toe. Harley walked up and stood behind his friend, his arms crossed.

"You think you know so much, do you?" Burns said, swaying as he spoke. "Well, just you see. You'll see."

Within forty-eight hours, the ward was again full of seriously ill patients. Although this wave of the disease was not as deadly as the one before, it did add dozens more deaths to the count. In the end, 8,500 people died from the flu in Chicago alone.

A month later, Harley Eng received an honorable discharge from the United States Army. He was not honored with a ticker tape parade, as many of the returning war heroes from Europe received. The only person seeing him off at Chicago's Union Depot was Dr. Rolfe Hiler.

"Thanks for riding with me to the station, RJ," Harley said, offering his hand to the doctor. "This is not exactly the way I expected to be going home."

"No medals for bravery this time." RJ smiled as he returned the heartfelt handshake.

"It was an honor to work with you." Harley stepped on the narrow platform of the train.

"Harley, you do understand what you accomplished these last three months, don't you?"

"Sure, Doc," Harley said, though he couldn't imagine what his friend was talking about. "Cleaning bedpans and taking care of sick people was quite an accomplishment."

"The point is, you didn't *have* to do those things," RJ said as the train began moving. "You could have stayed home and enjoyed your fortune."

Harley waved as the good doctor disappeared in a burst of steam from the train. He took his seat beside a sad looking old man who wore a black armband. When he studied the others on the train, he realized that everyone but he was wearing the black armband. The realization that in just a few hours his own arm might be cloaked with that dark symbol of mourning caused him to lower his head. Trying to stifle a sob, he felt a hand on his forearm. It belonged to the old man with the sad eyes. The two sat that way until the train stopped in Bloomington, where the old man got off.

<><><><><><>

Harley hadn't tried to let Lena know he was coming home. Each time he started a letter or telegraph, he hesitated. Fear gripped him in a way he had never known. He convinced himself that his wife and daughters were fine, that the pandemic hadn't even touched their community. Wearing his uniform with the broad, flat military hat, he hoisted his duffle bag over his shoulder and walked from the train station in Taylorville to his home.

Nothing looked different, although he saw few people on the streets. That could be normal, he told himself. It was a cold, wet afternoon, after all. When he came to the door to his house, he tried the doorknob and was surprised to find it unlocked. Mrs. Cummings jumped when she saw him walk in.

"Oh my, you scared me to death, Mr. Eng."

"Where's my wife?"

"I thought you knew," Mrs. Cummings said, putting a wrinkled hand on her throat.

"Where is she?" Harley shouted.

"Why, I suppose she'd be at Oak Hill Cemetery about now."

Harley couldn't think. The strain from the past few months seemed to hit him all at once. He ran out of the house and sprinted the six blocks to the cemetery. His mind raced over all the possible explanations why Lena would be at the Oak Hill Cemetery. It was possible she was simply visiting the graves of some friends and family interred there. But he knew this wasn't the case.

When he came up the hill into the cemetery, he saw hundreds of miners and their families gathered in a circle around a tent. He pushed through the multitude, causing a stir of surprised gasps and murmurs. Father Marco stopped mid-prayer when the shouting of the crowd drowned out his words. Breathing heavy, Harley stepped in front of the little canvas pavilion.

He looked inside and saw Angeline sitting in the mourner's row between Antonio and Lena. He thought his heart would stop as he looked at the casket resting on poles above the open grave. The coffin was too big for his baby Margaret, so it had to be little Angie. Harley began to cry. Suddenly Lena was in his arms, and a moment later, Angeline. Antonio came to his side with a hand on Harley's shoulder.

"We didn't know if you had received our messages," Antonio said. "I'm glad you're here. It means a lot to us."

It took a moment for the words to sink in. Harley looked back in the tent and saw Angie sleeping on Bullo's lap. Mary Kate sat next to him holding a very tiny baby. Then he saw Vinnie but no one else.

"Where? Who?" Harley was almost too emotional to speak. He suddenly felt weak.

Angeline pulled him gently by the arm and walked him to the casket.

"It's our Filberto, Harley." Angeline said. "He's gone to join his brother, Libero, who passed the day after Thanksgiving."

Harley looked at Angeline. Her face was full of sadness, but also great strength. She pulled the soldier's head all the way down to her shoulder. He felt like a child in his mother's arms.

18

Since healthy young people were the ones most affected by the devastation of the flu, the true effect of the disease became lost in the obituary pages alongside deaths from the war. In their mourning, the Vacca family found new ways to love one another, as well as their friends. The healing process was slow, but there were so many other families in the community experiencing similar pain, they always had others to comfort them.

By the following summer, life was returning to normal. It was the Engs who finally coaxed Angeline and Antonio out of their house. The two families were becoming closer than ever, and seldom a week went by that the couples didn't do something together.

"Father Marco has sent money to a priest in Cuomo so that Sonny Berlusconi's mother can come to America," Lena told Angeline one afternoon as they played bocce ball with their husbands. The game had progressed through most of the yards in Hewittville and had crossed paths with games played by several of the other Italian couples.

Holding a glass of wine in one hand, Antonio tossed the grapefruit-sized, wooden, bocce ball toward the smaller, metal pallino ball.

"*Merda!*" Antonio swore when his throw got caught on a downgrade and rolled away from the other balls.

"Antonio!" Angeline scolded.

"Well, Lena had to bring up that infernal priest's name," Antonio said. He watched as his wife expertly threw her bocce so that it landed inches from the pallino.

While the mining communities grew, Father Marco did a thriving business in his church, not just from the tithes that he adamantly enforced, but also as an agent for helping the vast Italian population send for their relatives in their home country.

"Maybe you'd play better if you put down that glass of wine," Harley told his friend.

"You would tell an *Italian* that?" Antonio said, staggering slightly. "God gave you two hands for a reason. One for the bocce ball and one for the glass of wine."

"What are you going to do next year when Prohibition goes into effect?" Harley asked.

Antonio waved his glass. "Ah, they will never be able to enforce such a law."

"Well," Lena said as she threw her bocce ball, knocking Angeline's away from the pallino, "I think it is wonderful that Father Marco is helping Sonny."

"We shall see," Antonio said. He threw his last ball and smiled broadly when it knocked Lena's away to take the point. *"Eccellente!"*

<><><><><><>

"It has been six months!" Sonny Berlusconi shouted as he made a feeble attempt to pull away from his wife's firm grip on his arm. "My mother writes that the counsel in Cuomo has still not received the money I gave you so she could come to America." Though young Berlusconi was short, he had forearms as thick as a normal man's thigh and could lift coal into a car with a number two banjo shovel in each hand.

Father Marco was six-foot, four-inches tall but thin as a rail. He had a huge Adam's apple that quivered when he was upset. "I won't have you insulting this cloth by implying a priest would betray his sacred oath."

"How did a priest with your income buy one of those new

Model Ts that no one else in town could afford?" Sonny asked.

"That is not for you to know!" shouted the priest, his Adam's apple quivering.

Sophia tried to calm her fiancé. "It is all right, Sonny. We will wait until your mother is here before we marry."

"*No*," Sonny said, his eyes blazing with hatred for the priest. "It took me two years to save that money to send for my mother. We will wed next month as planned, but we will have a different priest marry us. And I will get my money back!" He spat at the shoes of Father Marco as the couple left.

Father Marco went straight to his office and sat at the desk. He wrote a hasty letter and put it in an envelope. As he sealed it, his Adam's apple quivered furiously.

<><><><><><>

After returning home from their honeymoon in St. Louis, Sonny and his wife Sophia couldn't wait to get to bed, but they knew sleep would have to wait. They expected the traditional shivaree. So when they turned out the lights in their bedroom they were not surprised to instantly hear dozens of pots and pans clanging loudly outside their window. The couple dressed hurriedly, and by the time they opened the front door, it seemed the entire mining community of Langley had come out of their homes and hiding places to join in celebration.

Several trays of warm bagna cauda and fresh vegetables appeared on tables around the home, and throughout the night, the guests dipped a vegetable into the greasy, Italian dip and washed it down with a beer.

Vinnie Vacca organized a friendly wrestling match and was soon rolling across the lawn with a man twice his size. The children ran throughout the dark neighborhood playing spook tag. Later that evening, Lena and Angeline were setting up more food and drinks in the kitchen when Mary Kate interrupted them.

"Mama," Mary Kate said and motioned for her mother-in-law to join her on the porch. "I am afraid our husbands are up to no good. I heard them talking about getting even with Sonny for a prank he played on them in the coal mine."

"My husband had better not ruin Sophia's shivaree." Angeline balled her tiny fists.

At that moment Antonio and Bullo came out of the house, their arms around the groom.

"Che male vi sono fino a, mio marito?" Angeline yelled as she grabbed her husband by the top of his shirt.

"Unhand me, woman!" Antonio shouted back. He then held his fingers together as he made his defense with wild gestures. "Why do you say I am up to mischief? Am I not giving my good friend, Sonny Berlusconi, my best wine so that he may be strong on his first night home with his bride?"

"I know you, Antonio Vacca!" Angeline said as her husband continued to lead the staggering newlywed into the yard. "You want to get him drunk so that he will not be able to please his new wife."

"This night you will sleep in the spare room!" Mary Kate shouted at her own husband, who turned his back on her and followed his father. "And if you do this, you can sleep there from now on, because you will see no more bambinos from me, Bullo Vacca."

The party continued until late into the night. When even the neighborhood dogs had tired of barking, people began to go home. The Vaccas were the last to leave. After Antonio and Bullo deposited their wives in their buggies they turned and ran quickly back to the Berlusconi house.

"I *knew* they were up to no good," Angeline said as she and Mary Kate jumped out of their seats and ran after their husbands.

As the two women came around the corner to the back of the house they saw their men crouching outside the bedroom window. Mary Kate grabbed a big rock and flung it just as she heard a harmony begin that she could not believe was coming from the two burly men. Bullo never missed a chord as he rubbed the spot on his head where the rock had hit.

Let me call you Sweetheart, I'm in love . . . with . . . you.
Let me hear you whisper that you love . . . me . . . too.
Keep the love-light glowing in your eyes so true.
Let me call you Sweetheart, I'm in love . . . with . . . you.

"Why is it that you never told me that you could sing?" Mary Kate asked her husband later as their horse trotted unhurriedly down the moonlit road toward Hewittville.

"Why is it that you never told me you could pitch?" Bullo said as he rubbed the big knot on the back of his head.

That night the Vacca family grew by one more bambino.

<><><><><><>

The next morning, Mary Kate was humming "Let Me Call You Sweetheart" when Bullo and his father appeared in the kitchen. She stopped when she saw their sullen faces. A moment later, a crying Angeline rushed past them and wrapped her arms around her daughter-in-law.

"Who?" Mary Kate asked.

"Sonny and Sophia," Angeline sobbed. "Oh, Mary Kate, they're dead."

<><><><><><>

Most of the miners in the community attended the burial at Oak Hill Cemetery. Many of them had worked at the Cherry Hill mines. Even ten years after the tragedy, they were still experienced mourners. They put their hearts and souls into the songs sung around the two graves and clearly knew all the words to each. Antonio was unable to use the clear baritone voice Angeline had heard just three nights before. Father Fitzgibbons presided over the services, since Father Marco was conspicuously unavailable.

Later that evening, Joe Harrison was sitting alone on the Vacca porch when the Engs arrived. They quietly took seats next to him and an awkward silence followed.

"Sonny and Sophia didn't have a chance, did they?" Harley Eng finally said quietly. "Does anyone know what happened?"

"Where's Myrna?" Lena asked when Joe didn't comment.

"Home with one of her headaches," Joe said as if his wife's absence was of little consequence. "The sheriff thinks that two men broke into the Berlusconi house around four o'clock this morning, took them down in the basement and tied them up. Sonny had used the basement to teach men how to mine and there were lots of picks and—" Joe couldn't go on.

"*Why?*" Harley shook his head.

"Because Sonny wanted his money back from the priest," Antonio said as he walked out of the house. "The scoundrel had taken pay to bring Sonny's mother to America and had not delivered."

"Where's Angeline?" Lena asked, ignoring the comment.

"Lying down," Antonio said. "You can go to her."

When Lena was inside, Joe said, "Antonio, you can't be accusing people. Especially not a priest."

Antonio sat on the top step of the porch and buried his head in his powerful hands.

<><><><><><>

That following Saturday, Father Marco put his shiny, new Model-T Ford Tourabout into second gear and pushed it to its maximum speed of forty-five miles per hour. He loved the feel of the wind on his face and the sound of the twenty-horsepower engine whining softly beneath him. He had paid nine hundred, sixty dollars for the Tin Lizzie. That was every penny he could come up with. The church roof would have to wait.

Seeing that the ten-gallon fuel tank was getting low, he reluctantly turned back toward town. When he arrived at the parish, he pulled the vehicle into the carriage house, and then spent an hour polishing the extensive brass fixtures. The grill on the front was still full of bugs, but it was getting dark, so he gave up and went into the church. The priest sighed when he saw a parishioner kneeling in the front pew. Father Marco hastily genuflected, crossed himself and hurried to the confessional. A moment later the man crossed himself, rose and walked into the booth next to him.

Father Marco opened the grille. "God be with you, brother. When did you make your last confession?"

"In about eighteen-ninety-eight, I guess."

"And what brings you to finally seek God today?"

"I killed two men in nineteen hundred."

Father Marco looked again through the grill at the man whose head was down. Only the shadowed outline of a face was visible. He had a pointy nose and practically no chin.

"And in nineteen oh-three I killed another man." The man paused. "Three years ago, I killed a boy and his dog."

The priest heard a sound from the back of the church. A second man, wearing a black hat and topcoat, locked the two big doors. The man walked with a gimp in his left leg as he slowly approached the confessional.

"Then three nights ago," the man in the confessional said, his voice growing louder, "I killed a man and woman who just got married."

Father Marco set his Bible down next to him on the bench.

"Now," the man said, his voice growing cold, "I'm told the contract for that last killing hasn't been paid."

"I told him I'd pay it after Christmas," Father Marco said quickly, his voice high and weak. He saw the man in the rear of the church standing nearby with his back to the doors, his head down and hands grasped in front of him as if he were praying.

"We always get a lot of tithes at Christmas." The priest's voice shook. "When the miners are back to work."

"Then I saw you today in that nice automobile," the pointy-nosed man said, "and I says to my associate, 'Wouldn't you like to drive back to Cicero in that pretty Tourabout'?"

Father Marco felt a sharp pain as the bullet passed through his throat and severed his spinal column. He remained conscious while being dragged by his feet out of the confessional. Then he heard voices above him, though all he saw was a glass-stained window with a rendition of Saint Mary.

"I told you to shoot him in the stomach so he'd live longer," said a deep, raspy voice.

"I saw that big Adam's apple bouncing around and thought it would be more poetic to shoot him in the throat. Get it? Adam's apple . . . Priest . . . Bible?"

"I don't get it, Vito," the first man said.

"Never mind. I'll explain later."

Father Marco watched as the shadow of the men's faces appeared over him. Then they began to slowly fade. His last thought was he should have cleaned the bugs off that grill on the Model-T.

19

The Clubhouse was a brick farmhouse a few miles north of Taylorville, where women and bootleg whiskey were the pleasures of the day. Despite its lurid purpose, the décor in the home was pleasant, with a simple couch and chairs in front of a brick fireplace.

"Prohibition means nothing to an Italian," Leo Corso told his guests as they lounged on the comfortable furniture smoking cigars. "Where you find Italians, you will find wine."

A young, round-faced man with a scar on the left side of his face took a small sip from the Ball blue jar Corso handed him.

"This ain't wine!" He gasped and spit the water-colored drink onto the wooden floor.

"In a pinch, we improvise," Corso said with a smile.

"What's your recipe?" the man with the scar asked as he placed the glass to his nose and sniffed.

"Juniper berry juice, glycerin and moonshine," Corso said.

"White lightning?" The scar-faced man laughed and turned to his traveling companion. "Can you believe this, Vito? I come all the way from Cicero to be poisoned."

"Hey, that's funny!" Corso said. "That's what they call me down in the mine. *Poison.* That's my nickname. If you mix the stuff with something it really ain't too bad."

The round-faced man lost his smile.

"You want me to throw it away, Snorky?" Vito asked, holding out his hand for the glass.

"Snorky?" Corso laughed. "Is that your nickname? I figured it would be Scarface."

Wincing, Vito moved his hand inside his suit jacket. The

one called Snorky waved at Vito, who withdrew his hand. The laughter left Corso's face.

"You can call me Al," the man with the scar said, "or Mister Capone if you prefer."

"Yes, Mr. Capone," Corso said. Though he had never heard of Al Capone or his friend Vito Cambruzzi, Corso knew they were from Chicago. They had also indicated they were interested in buying large quantities of the homebrew that many people in the community sold. Since Prohibition had been enacted the year before, many rural residents thought the enterprise would be a lucrative way to supplement their income, especially during the summer when the coal mines were down.

"You think this would be a little strong for use in your speakeasies, Mr. Capone?" Corso said. He wanted to please the man, not just because he was a customer, but because he had suddenly recognized the element of danger surrounding the two men.

"Speakeasy?" Capone looked at Vito.

"Well, boss," Vito said, "I think he means those places in the city where people go to drink alcohol illegally."

Capone rose and stood face to face with Corso. Smiling, he gave the man a hard slap on the face with his palm. Leaving his hand on the man's cheek, he added a firm Dutch rub.

"Ah, Mr. Poison. Is that what you said they call you?" Capone sighed. "We need this alcohol for the hospitals for medicinal purposes. I'm sure you understand that. Capito?"

"I understand." Corso looked at Capone's hand as if it were a pistol held to his head.

The tension in the room was abruptly interrupted when Vinnie Vacca walked in the front door, a cigarette hanging from the corner of his mouth. Capone slowly removed his hand from Corso's cheek.

"I told you to wait outside!" Corso growled. He regretted asking the boy to come, but if the deal worked out he would need to send messages to the bootleggers.

Kevin Corley

Saying nothing, Vinnie flipped his cigarette out an open window and continued to strut toward the three men. He was eighteen years old, not much younger than the man with the scar.

Corso didn't like the determined look on the boy's face.

"I was on the porch and couldn't help overhearing," Vinnie said.

"You were eavesdropping," Capone said, clearly impressed.

"What of it?" Vinnie stood less than a foot from Vito Cambruzzi, who was middle-aged and heavy.

"I like this kid," Capone said, smiling. "He reminds me of me."

For the second time in just over a minute, the sudden opening of a door interrupted the tension in the room. A beautiful woman with bleach-blond hair entered from the kitchen. She was visibly startled when all four men turned quickly toward her.

"Th . . . this is my wife, Ada, Mr. Capone," Corso said. He resisted the temptation to put his own hand to his red cheek that still stung from the slap.

"Well, well." Capone smiled and took several steps toward the woman. He took in her well-shaped figure only partially hidden beneath a red, lacy dress. "It seems we have underestimated you, Mr. Corso."

Ada Corso displayed no fear. Instead, she pulled her shoulders back and assumed the pose of a Sears and Roebuck catalogue model, the roundness of her ample breasts protruding noticeably above a low neckline.

While most of the women in the clubhouse were available for the right price, Corso did not like the idea of Ada being among them. He had only brought her along because she was the experienced one when it came to making the homebrew.

"Now, Ada." Corso touched his wife's arm. "Why don't you go on back to the kitchen and let the men do the haggling?"

Glaring at her husband, Ada pulled her arm free and moved

163

away from him. Corso was a little embarrassed that Vinnie Vacca took a long step and stood between his wife and the men from Chicago.

"Oh, now," Capone said, "let's not have any marital strife. Why, I'm a newlywed myself." He took a cigar from his breast pocket and handed it to Corso. His demeanor was suddenly very friendly. "Do you have children? Myself, I have a little boy named Albert, but we call him Sonny."

Corso took the cigar. After licking it, he accepted a light from Capone. "No children," he said, taking a puff and slowly exhaling the bluish smoke. Hearing about the man's wife and son made the gangster look less dangerous. Besides, Corso knew that if he became the middlemen between Capone and the local bootleggers, he could make a fortune. Leo Corso loved his beautiful wife dearly, but she required, no, she demanded much from her coal miner husband.

Reaching into the same breast pocket where he had extracted the cigars, Capone, brought out and opened a wallet. He took several bills and handed them to Corso. "Go get me a truck and a driver. Load it with all the wine, bootleg whiskey, and," he picked up the glass full of the white substance, "when you run out of good stuff, finish loading it with this."

Corso was excited. "Let's go, Vinnie. Ada."

"The broad stays here," Capone said, the pleasant demeanor gone. "Vito, you go with them."

Corso looked at his wife, who showed no emotion. She didn't even turn her head away from Capone's gaze.

Capone said coldly, "She's my insurance so you don't talk too much."

Corso hesitated, looking again from Capone to his wife.

"No deal," Vinnie said. "She goes with us."

Ada touched Vinnie's arm and ran her hand up under his shirtsleeve. "It's okay, Vinnie, I want to stay. Now you go along with Poison."

After a long, silent moment, Vinnie turned and walked out

the front door, followed by Leo Corso and Vito Cambruzzi.

When she heard her husband's flivver grind to its usual slow start and begin backfiring as it moved away from the house, Ada took the glass from Capone. "Now," she said with a wicked smile, "what else can I give you?"

Capone reached out and ripped the front of her dress down to her waist. "I'm the boss," he said, turning her around and bending her over the arm of the couch. "Keep your mouth shut unless I give you something to put in it."

<><><><><><>

Angeline understood Vinnie. While he and his older brother had been close during their youth, the distance between the two widened when Bullo went to work picking rock. Then his brother married. As much as Vinnie loved Mary Kate and his nephews, his mother knew he felt he was just the uncle. Often he took care of the children while his parents did "couple things" with Bullo and Mary Kate. He even sat at the little kids' table during meals while the married folk took the big table.

Angeline had put on a strong front in front of her family in the months following the deaths of Filberto and Libero. She did her crying when she was alone, or sometimes with Mary Kate or Lena, but never in front of her men. When Antonio cried, she comforted him and spoke of God and Heaven and read passages from the Bible to him.

Though she knew he missed Filberto and Libero perhaps more than anyone, Vinnie would never speak about how he felt. Angeline had decided that marriage was out of the question for him at this time and didn't pursue the subject. He needed to "find himself." When he began going to The Clubhouse, hanging out with Poison Corso and getting in fights, she decided the time had come to take action.

One day as Vinnie helped Angeline till her garden, she said, "Your Uncle Vincent is struggling to feed his family on account of the coal mine strike in West Virginia. Bullo and Papa are doing well as partners in the mine. I was thinking we might send Vincent some money, if we can spare it."

"We can spare it, Mama." Vinnie said. "I'm ready to go down in the mine. I could help send Uncle Vincent money."

"Bless you, Vinnie," Angeline said. She didn't think the garden was the right place to hug her proud son. One of his passing friends might see. "Oh, I wish your Uncle Vincent had someone like you to be there for him during this terrible time. Those miners out there are trying to join the United Mine Workers. While our Illinois miners got a raise of twenty-seven cents last year during our strike, the West Virginia miners got nothing. The company even pays them with scrip. They can only use it in the company stores."

Vinnie's face turned red with anger. He hated injustice. In fact, he loved picking on bullies who picked on the weak. At least, that was always his excuse for fighting.

"Mama, I'll go to West Virginia to help Uncle Vincent."

Acting like the thought had never occurred to her, Angeline said, "Why, Vinnie, that's a great idea! But you know if you get a job, you'll have to give Aunt Eunice all your income for your room and board."

Vinnie winced.

She might have overplayed her cards. But it was important that Vinnie not have money for frolicking.

"I'll do it!" Vinnie said, the excitement of the challenge all over his face. "I'll run to the train station and get my ticket right now. What's the name of the town where Uncle Vincent lives, Mama?"

"Matewan."

As Angeline watched him run back to the house to get his money, she had a wonderful sense of happiness knowing that her son would have something constructive to do to keep him out of trouble. Antonio would, of course, say that West Virginia was too dangerous with the United Mine Workers trying to unionize the workers. But he didn't know the man their Vinnie was named after as well as she did. Her brother Vincent was a kind, intelligent man who would know how to deal with a hot-blooded youth like Vinnie. Yes, Vinnie would have a wonderful time frolicking in the backwoods of the Appalachian Mountains hunting and fishing. She wished she could go with him.

20

The Norfolk Western Railroad wound through the beautiful Tug River Valley to the town of Matewan, West Virginia. Vinnie, who had never been out of Illinois, couldn't believe the steep, rolling hills and deep valleys. He had always enjoyed hunting and fishing, and this land seemed abundant for both. Toward evening, the train came around a sharp curve and stopped right in front of the town's main street. A dirt road ran between the railroad tracks and the buildings.

Uncle Vincent and Aunt Eunice met him at the station. He had remembered his mother's brother as being a big man, but when he shook his hand, he realized he was only about five and a half feet tall.

"My, how you've grown," Aunt Eunice said as they followed Uncle Vincent out of the station house. When she refrained from kissing him, Vinnie sensed that his mother had written them with some suggestions. Eunice was half-a-head taller than her husband and had hands as big as Vinnie's.

"It's not a good idea to stand here in the road gabbing," Uncle Vincent said when they approached the street. "Load your grip in the buggy and let's get on home."

As Vinnie threw his black leather satchel onto the seat, he saw that the sidewalks were full of men standing around talking. Many of the conversations looked like they were getting heated.

"The Baldwin-Felts thugs came to town this morning," Uncle Vincent told him. "Things are going to get complicated, I suspect. Most of the scabs are Italians or colored, so we need to keep a low profile."

Vinnie sat in the back seat as his uncle shook the reins at his mule to get moving. His father had told him about the Baldwin-Felts' role in Kentucky. In his mind, he saw them as bullies that he would take great pleasure in fighting. His confidence as a boxer was limitless, though he only weighed a lean one hundred sixty pounds.

Three men sat on a second floor balcony at the Urias Hotel. As he stared at the men, one of them raised a pistol, smiled and aimed it at him.

"Don't be gawkin', boy," Uncle Vincent said over his shoulder.

Ignoring the warning, Vinnie smiled back at the man on the balcony and tipped his hat. The largest crowd of men was gathered in front of the Chambers' Hardware Store. As they passed, a gray-haired lady who was even shorter than his mother pointed at one of the men's chest with her finger as she talked. She turned her head toward their buggy and followed it with intense eyes as it turned the corner onto a dark street.

Halfway down the block, a man stepped out of the shadows and stood directly in front of the buggy, a shotgun resting across one arm. Uncle Vincent reined his mule to a stop. The man had a black patch over one eye. He walked around to Vinnie's side of the wagon.

"Get down," the man told him.

Vinnie was glad to oblige. He hopped out of his seat and stood directly in front of the man, smiling.

"You a union boy?" the man said "If you is a union boy, you ain't stayin' in no company house."

Vinnie looked at the man and laughed.

Uncle Vincent told him to hush.

"What's so funny, kid?" the man said.

"I ain't never seen an eye patch before," Vinnie said. "It looks kinda stupid on you."

The man started his gun butt toward Vinnie's head but the young boy was quicker. He smashed his fist across the man's jaw and then caught the weapon with both hands before it could follow its owner to the ground.

Vinnie spun around as he heard footsteps running up behind him.

"What did you do here, boy?" the old lady he had seen on the streets said as she leaned over the unconscious man. He saw fire in her eyes like he had never seen from anyone except his mother.

"You trying to git my boys kilt, young 'un?" the woman said. She ripped the shotgun out of his hands, turned and tossed it to one of the men. "Hold that hog leg, Frank." She spun back to Vinnie and waved a hand at him. "Now get on outta here before I let those thugs do what they will with ya."

"Yes, ma'am," Vinnie said and climbed back on the buggy.

"You men there," the woman said. "Pick up that varmint and dump him in the ditch outside of town. Throw a shot of whiskey down his throat and soak his shirt good in it. And don't be samplin' none of the stuff yerself. Understand?"

"Yes, ma'am," several men said as one. Four of them grabbed the man and carried him on down the street.

"I told you to get that boy outta here!" the woman yelled at Uncle Vincent. "Now strike up that mule."

Uncle Vincent shook the reins hard and the mule leapt into a trot. No one spoke until they neared the Stone Mountain Company houses, which looked very much like the ones he had seen in Jeiseyville back home, except these were built half way up a steep hill and seemed in much poorer condition.

"Who was that old bat?" Vincent finally asked to break the silence.

"That was the miner's angel, son," Aunt Eunice said over her shoulder. "We call her Mother Jones."

<><><><><><>

Vinnie thought he was going to get a good scolding from his uncle when they arrived at the tiny company house. When the little man took his nephew out to the woodshed, Vinnie thought his uncle was going to try and give him a beating, which Vinnie would not tolerate. Instead, Uncle Vincent talked to him in a calm, clear voice.

"Vinnie, there are three thousand miners and their families in the Tug River Valley who are armed and itchy-fingered. Do you want to walk in here without really knowing what's going on and be the one responsible for starting a gunfight?"

"No, sir," Vinnie said. He looked in his uncle's eyes as his mother taught him. "I understand, sir."

Uncle Vincent took his nephew's hand and examined the scrapped knuckles. "Can you show me how you used that right cross, sometime?"

Vinnie grinned. "Yes, sir."

Vinnie's four young cousins, all girls under ten years of age, were lined up by size in front of the door when he and their father came in the house. It was a three-room home with two bedrooms and a front room that served as both a living quarters and a kitchen. A pile of blankets on the floor next to the couch told him where he would be sleeping.

"You remember the girls, Vinnie," Aunt Eunice said. "Annabelle, Betsy, Catherine and Delores. Easy to remember if you know your alphabet."

"The next one'll be Esther," Catherine said, then looked quickly away.

"Or maybe Edward," Uncle Vincent added hopefully.

<><><><><><>

"Your name Samantha?" Vinnie asked the girl who walked up to him as he was cutting firewood the next morning. She fit the description of the mountain gal his aunt said lived next door.

"Nope, just Sam," the girl told him.

Vinnie had noticed girls before, but had always kept it

to himself. Even when the other boys picking rock with him talked about females, he avoided joining in. He knew his mother would whoop him good if she ever found out he had talked about girls the way some of the other boys did. She could tolerate fighting but not disrespect.

This girl, though, was hardly a girl at all. She wore a work shirt and blue bib overalls with suspenders, though the curve of her hips made the suspenders unnecessary. She only wore one strap over a shoulder, and like many of the other miners in the area, she sported a red bandana around her neck. Her blond hair was cut short, especially around her ears. Still, she had a feminine face that Vinnie found appealing.

"Whoo!" Vinnie caught a whiff of a couple of pigs rooting beneath a porch nearby. "Don't that stink bother you?"

The girl raised her nose to the air.

"Smells like money to me," she told him. "Ever been frog giggin'?"

"Not much. Mostly we fish." He loaded one arm with as much firewood as he could carry and picked up his axe with the other. "We gigged some once in a cornfield when the creek overflowed."

"I like fried frog legs better than fried chicken," Sam said, picking up a load of wood and following him toward the house. "Hey, there, set that axe down! Don't you know it's bad luck to carry an axe into a house?"

Vinnie dropped the axe on the porch, which he had intended to do anyway, not because of superstition, but so that he could open the door.

Without even paying the neighbor girl a good morning, Aunt Eunice set an extra plate on the table. Sam got down on a rug and rolled marbles with Annabelle and Betsy. Vinnie made two more trips for firewood, then washed up for breakfast. Sam took a place at the table and said grace without being asked.

"I want you all to pack the valuables," Uncle Vincent instructed the family after they had all filled their plates.

"Vinnie will take them down to the church this afternoon. The Baldwin thugs are threatening to evict all of those who joined the union. If they pick on our house I doubt they'll be too careful with Grandma's china."

"Pa says they probably won't throw y'all out cause you're wops," Sam said, "and the company don't wanna piss off the dago scabs."

"Oh piddle, Sam," Aunt Eunice said, "don't be sayin' words like piss at the dinner table."

"Well, piddle's just a puddle of piss, ain't it?" Sam spooned a mouthful of grits. "They threw the Petersen clan out last night. They broke Emma's organ stool, and it had been all the way to Oregon and back."

"Ol' Sam," Aunt Eunice said, laughing, and slapped the young mountain girl on the back. "You know all the gossip, don't ya? You'll need to marry this gal, Vinnie. She can do a man's worth of work. Why, she even went down in the mine for a bit and chucked coal with her pa. Remember doin' that, Sam, when your pa's pard went to fight over yonder in France?"

Sam's face flushed. She scooped another mouthful of grits and grinned.

That afternoon, Vinnie loaded wooden boxes of breakables and other valuables and drove the buggy to the Matewan Community Church. Two armed miners came off the porch and helped carry the containers into the foyer. A stocky little man who introduced himself as C.E. Lively labeled the boxes.

"You union?" Lively asked as he stacked them next to dozens of other miners' heirlooms.

"Sure am," Vinnie said, "and proud of it."

"I own the restaurant down the street," Lively told him in a low voice, his eyes on the two gunmen. "Union men are always welcome. Let me know if you hear anything that don't seem right. Them company thugs are always trying to stir things up around here."

Vinnie had an uneasy feeling as he shook the man's hand.

C.E. Lively's enthusiasm seemed to be a little overboard for a local businessman.

That evening, Vinnie sat on a log around a fire with a group of miners when ten heavily armed Baldwin-Felts thugs came up the hill toward them.

"Those are Thompson machine guns they's a totin'," a miner named Hawthorne said. "Don't nobody do nothin' stupid."

At that moment Sam walked out of her house and wiped her hands on her overalls. She lived with her father and her ten-year-old twin sisters. Like the other men, Vinnie kept his head down as the thugs walked past the campfire and stopped in front of Sam.

"You one of the Wiggins clan who's livin' in this house?" a man with a black eye-patch asked. Vinnie saw it was the man he had knocked out the night before.

Though Sam didn't respond, she showed no fear.

"My name's Leroy Crawford," the one-eyed man continued, "and these men and I are duly authorized to evict the Wiggins family from these premises."

Sam continued to stare at the men in silence.

"You a girl or just a girly boy?" Crawford asked, getting a few chuckles from his men.

Not all the thugs seemed amused. Some even had impatient looks on their faces.

"Let's just see if you've got any bumps inside that shirt." Crawford ripped the front of Sam's shirt. The man shot several feet backwards.

The mountain girl had kicked the man so powerfully between the legs, both his feet came off the ground.

There was immediate silence in the camp. Vinnie thought with certainty the thugs would react with violence. Crawford doubled forward, his one eye staring into space as he came down like a slow-falling tree straight onto his face.

After a long moment, one of the Baldwin-Felts thugs began to laugh. His colleagues quickly followed suit. The miners were careful not to laugh, though a few hid smiles with a hand.

"Do ya think I kilt him?" Sam asked, one hand over her mouth and the other holding her shirt together.

"Well, I dunno," the miner named Hawthorne said as he walked up beside her and looked down at Crawford. "But if he does die, I'd s'pect he might be the first man kilt by a kick to the groin."

Two of the agents looked disgusted as they lifted the unconscious man by the arms and legs and carried him none-too-gently down the hill. The other thugs followed.

When they were out of sight, men and women quickly surrounded Sam, giving her hugs and slaps on the back.

"Where'd you learn to kick like that?" Vinnie asked.

"She's always buckdancin'," a stout looking woman said. "Remember when them high kickin' gals came from out east? You saw 'em, didn't ya, Sam? I betcha that had something to do with her havin' a hard kick."

A few moments later, an old, gray haired woman came bustling up the hill.

"Where's that lassie?" Mother Jones shouted. "I wanna meet the lassie that mule-kicked that one-eyed varmint!"

The old woman followed the pointing crowd to the young girl in the bib overalls. Vinnie thought she'd hug Sam, but instead she gave her a slap on the back that nearly dropped her.

"Well, missy," Mother Jones said in a voice that echoed through the valley. "We'll just have to have you take care of the rest of those varmints for us. At least if you do, we'll be sure they won't be makin' no more young 'uns."

The crowd roared with laughter. Mother Jones spotted Vinnie, who was walking up to get a better look at the famous woman.

"Is this your sister, laddie?" Mother Jones asked him.

"No, ma'am," Vinnie said, "I just met her."

"Then you best be marrying her," Mother Jones said, "'cause if the two of you fighters have ten or twelve young 'uns, we'll have an un-stoppable army."

As everyone again laughed, Mother Jones looked down at Sam's heavily soiled boots. "Somebody get this lassie a new pair of shoes tomorrow and bring me her old ones," Mother Jones said. "I want to keep them as a souvenir."

21

The next morning, more Baldwin-Felts agents arrived on the Number 29 train. Word spread quickly through the mining camp that brothers Albert and Lee Felts were among them. Men began checking and cleaning their guns.

"Police Chief Sid Hatfield and Mayor Cabell Testerman met the agents as they got off the train," Sam told Vinnie and his family over lunch. Using deep voices to impersonate the two men, she launched into a re-creation of the conversation that took place at the train station. "They tried to talk 'em outta evictin' anymore miners, but Al Felts told them the coal company sent them down to put the miners out of the houses, and that is what they were goin' to do."

"What did Chief Hatfield say?" asked Vinnie.

"Sid Hatfield told them it was gonna lead to trouble, but ol' Feltsy said his men was trained t' take care of any trouble and the police would be wise not to interfere with the Baldwin-Felts detectives."

Vinnie listened to Sam's impersonations with a feeling of wonderment. He was increasingly appreciating her clear-skinned face and tanned arms. Sam Wiggins was the only girl he ever met that didn't need to act like a girl to be pretty.

That evening, Uncle Vincent went with a group of miners to guard the belongings at the church. Vinnie and Sam sat alone by the fire between their homes and watched the Baldwin-Felts thugs down the way as they moved miners out of company houses. As his uncle had predicted, they were none-too-gentle with the belongings as they threw chairs, tables and other household items out on the road. Women and children stood and watched, knowing they would be spending the night in a union tent on Stone Mountain.

At another campfire, a group of men began playing music to keep spirits up. A mandolin, guitar, banjo, fiddle and upright bass played mountain music with an old timer keeping time by blowing into a half-filled jug of mountain dew. A few of the men and women got up and began dancing a jig around the blazing fire.

"Let's go into town," Vinnie said to Sam when he realized the thugs would not get to their hill that night.

Sam thought a moment, then nodded and jumped up off the log. When they reached Mate Street, they saw the usual congregation of miners standing in front of Chamber's Hardware Store. It began to drizzle, but seeing that Sam paid it no mind, Vinnie didn't either.

"That there's Sheriff Sid Hatfield," Sam told Vinnie and pointed.

Vinnie saw a man in his mid-twenties wearing a black suit with an extremely big badge pinned to it. Hatfield walked past them and on toward Chamber's.

"What's doing, Chief?" Sam asked in a deep voice that could have passed as a young man's.

"I aim to arrest Albert Felt and those damned company thugs," Hatfield said, a determined look on his face.

A group of miners began following the lawman, many armed with pistols poorly hidden under belts or with rifles tucked beneath long overcoats.

Women ran after children. "Get on home, young 'uns, *now!*" the women yelled. The children scurried up the hill.

Seeing one-eyed Leroy Crawford looking at him from across the street, Vinnie realized he and Sam were unarmed.

"Let's get between these buildings where we can watch the goin' ons," Vinnie said, not wanting to frighten Sam.

They found a spot where two buildings formed a little nook and huddled on a step going into a doctor's office. From that vantage point, they could see above the heads in the street. Vinnie became uneasy when he lost sight of Crawford.

"That's Mayor Testerman standing beside Hatfield," Sam said, "and I'll bet that fella walkin' toward them in the rain coat is one of the Felts brothers."

A large contingent of company thugs followed Felts. A few carried satchels that looked big enough to hold large guns. The town was suddenly still as the men faced off.

"I don't like that Felts fella having his hands under his raincoat," Vinnie whispered to Sam. He had plenty of experience on both sides of sucker punches.

"Felts," Hatfield said in a clear, cool voice, "I'm arresting you and your men for conducting evictions without proper Matewan authority."

"Why, hell, Sid," Felts said and laughed, "I've got a warrant for you, too. I'm going to take you with me to Bluefield."

"Let's see it," Mayor Testerman said. The fat mayor was the only one who didn't act like the whole thing was great fun.

Felts handed him a paper. Hatfield had a broad smile on his face as he and the mayor backed up into the hardware store so they could have more light. A moment later, Testerman stepped out and handed the paper back to Felts.

"It's bogus," Testerman said.

One of the miners in the crowd shouted, "It might as well be written on gingerbread."

Vinnie watched the men carefully. Hatfield was still just out of sight inside the entrance to the store. Felts' raincoat moved. Vinnie would swear later that the first two gunshots were almost simultaneous. He was sure that one shot came from Hatfield's gun inside the store. The other came from beneath the billowing raincoat of the Baldwin detective. The mayor staggered backwards before falling and Felts, also hit, dropped to one knee. The next shots came in a roar as the sound of screams and relentless gunfire filled the night. Some men ran from the fight; others, toward it. Even the Baldwin men jumped for protection behind trees and fences. Hatfield emerged from the building, the gun in each hand blazing.

Vinnie pulled Sam down on the step and covered her with his body just as bullets slammed into the building close to his head. He looked to the street. Men continued to scatter as they fired guns and tried to gain an advantage on their opponent. Blood splattered away from one man's face as his head twisted sideways in a ghastly manner. Both miners and company men struggled to keep their feet and maintain a shooting position.

One man yelled, "Oh Lord, I'm shot!"

When Sam tried to raise her head, Vinnie fell down hard on her a second time as another bullet just missed them. He looked into the street and saw Crawford staring at them with his one good eye, a smoking pistol in his hand.

"Into the building!" Vinnie yelled.

He kicked the door next to him open and jerked Sam inside. Another bullet followed them into the room and shattered the glass in a cabinet. Sam grabbed his arm and pulled him down behind an oak table. Two more bullets bored their way through the thick wood. Vinnie felt a sting on his arm as if a yellow jacket had stung him.

They were trapped. When he glanced over the table, Crawford zigzagged through the street toward the office, clearly targeting only them. Vinnie reached into the cabinet near the table and fumbled with several bottles until he found one in a heavy, glass container.

"When I move," he said to Sam above the shooting and screams, "skedaddle out the door and get someplace safe."

She started to protest, but when Vinnie heard footsteps enter the office, he charged out from behind the desk wielding the bottle like a tomahawk. Sam was quicker, though, and Crawford turned his gun toward her. The black eye patch of the man was now to Vinnie's side of the room. The bottle crashed hard against his temple. His gun exploded one last time. An angry, white cloud burst from the shattered bottle along with the liquid.

Vinnie inhaled the vapor, staggered a moment, and collapsed hard against the floor.

<><><><><><>

When Vinnie awoke, he was lying on a cot in the doctor's office. Injured men lay across every inch of the room.

"Get this boy outta here!" a man wearing a bloody white apron yelled. "We need this cot."

Someone helped Vinnie stand and held his arm as he staggered toward the open door. Men carrying more wounded bumped into him.

"And young man!" the doctor yelled from behind him, waving his bloody hands. "The next time you decide to kill someone, don't use my last bottle of *chloroform!* I don't know how I'm going to operate on all these men without it!"

Vinnie's lungs burned when he breathed in the cool, outside air. He looked down Mate Street. People lay or sat on the ground everywhere. Along the sidewalk, men lined up the corpses of the dead. He looked to see if there were any young girls among them.

Suddenly he heard a stifled cry and saw Sam run across the crowded street toward him. Her forehead had blood on it but otherwise she seemed fine. The one-eyed man had missed with his last shot. She stopped just short of hugging him, which he judged a good thing, since some of those watching might have taken her for a boy.

"That's Crawford," Sam said, pointing to a man lying among the dead.

Vinnie hadn't recognized him because his eye patch was missing.

"Where's his—"

Sam held up the black patch. "This one's my souvenir."

She led him down the hill toward the Tug River. As they

walked, she told him that dozens of people had panicked when the shooting started and tried to get away by swimming across the river into Kentucky. She found a fallen tree and straddled it, facing him. He did the same, facing her.

"It was Albert Felts who Hatfield fired that second shot at," Sam said. "The yellow thug high-tailed it into the post office. After the first round of shooting, the miners surrounded the building, and Hatfield told him to come out and shoot it out like a man. Felts yelled back, 'If you want me, come and get me.' Hatfield started walkin' toward the building and Felts suddenly came out with his gun a blazin'. Ol' Sid shot him dead."

"How many died?" Vinnie asked.

"At least seven of the Baldwin thugs, including Albert and Lee Felts. We lost two or three miners, and Mayor Testerman was dying last I heard. They're saying that's more people killed than at the OK Corral fight between the Earps and the Clantons."

Vinnie wiped away a trickle of blood running down Sam's face. She reached out and touched the wound on his arm, which he had forgotten about.

She looked at the wound. "You have a piece of wood in there."

Vinnie felt her fingers working the splinter out, and then her mouth was suddenly on his arm. She pulled an inch-long piece of wood out with her teeth and dropped it into her hand. "Another souvenir," she said.

As the drizzling rain returned, the two young fighters walked home.

<><><><><><>

The invincible Baldwin thugs had been defeated. Sid Hatfield was not just a national hero to coal miners, he was a living legend. Governor Cornwell ordered the State Police to take over the town of Matewan. The miners complied by turning their guns into a holding area in the hardware store. As news of the victory spread, miners across the country signed up with the United Mine Workers.

The summer passed quickly. Hatfield married Mayor Testerman's widow, Jessie, just two weeks after her husband died, causing a stir of gossip.

Vinnie got into a fistfight with one man who tried to say that it was not Felts who killed the mayor but Hatfield because he wanted his wife.

Hatfield also turned Testerman Jewelry Store into a gun shop. This infuriated The Stone Mountain Coal Company and the Baldwin-Felts Detectives, since it gave the miners quick access to weapons.

In the meantime, Vinnie helped feed Uncle Vincent's family by hunting and fishing, and sometimes even frog gigging with Sam. He spent nearly every day with the mountain girl. The two were tied by the dangers they had faced as well as by the need to provide for their families. With no jobs available, salvaging for food was a full-time occupation. Sam carried an Enfield rifle musket that her grandfather had used in the War Between the States. She was proficient enough with the weapon to bark a squirrel from one hundred yards. But with near everyone hunting, game was scarce. The two often hiked as far as Blair Mountain and at other times across the Tug River deep into Kentucky.

The only book that Vinnie had ever read all the way through was a biography of Daniel Boone. Now he felt he was living that frontiersman life alongside a sharpshooting Annie Oakley with a gun that was made only thirty years after Boone died.

When Vinnie told Sam about the book he had read, she told him stories about their own local heroes, like Simon Kenton who once saved Daniel Boone's life. She also told him that the Hatfields and McCoys, who had been feuding since the Civil War, lived on either side of the Tug River and still hated one another.

Vinnie became something of a hero as the boy who killed a thug with a jug of chloroform. He avoided the praise whenever he could, partly because the doctor gave him dirty looks every time he saw him and Vinnie feared the doc might sue him for the cost of the chloroform. He also didn't want his mother to find out what happened, because she would most certainly have ordered him home, and nothing could tear him away from Sam Wiggins. Not even his mother.

The country girl had filled the empty place made when his younger brothers died and Bullo married. The only hesitation Vinnie had about Sam was the feeling he got when the two accidentally touched, or when she would roll up the sleeves or loosen the top buttons on her work shirt. He was slow and backward when it came to talking with girls. Luckily, Sam showed even less knowledge toward romance, so their bond of friendship grew at a slow, steady pace they could both deal with.

Unfortunately, the events in West Virginia would be anything but slow and steady.

22

In January, Tom Felts, the sole surviving Felts brother, did everything he could to get Sid Hatfield and twenty-two of his cohorts charged with the murder of his brothers and the other five detectives. Felts was furious when a jury acquitted all the defendants. C.E. Lively proved Vinnie's instincts correct by testifying that Hatfield and the other striking miners told him how they intentionally murdered the Baldwin men. Lively testified that Hatfield confessed to being in love with Mayor Testerman's wife, and that Sid killed the mayor so he could have his wife. Despite the perjured testimony, the jury, made up of several coal miners, found for the defense.

That started another series of fighting between the striking miners and the Baldwin men. Rarely a night went by that Vinnie didn't hear gunshots as company snipers fired into the tent city on Stone Mountain, often killing or wounding someone. Since his family was Italian, as were many of the strikebreakers, they were able to stay in the company house. Vinnie didn't like being associated with scabs, even if the union men knew it wasn't true, but neither was he willing to move to the tent city away from Sam. The word around the mining camp was that the Wiggins family kept their house because of the Baldwin thug's respect for the mountain girl's hard-kicking abilities.

One day in late spring, Sam came bursting into Uncle Vincent's house.

"Grab your guns," she yelled, "the miners is a marchin' on Merrimac."

By the time Uncle Vincent, Vinnie and Sam got to the town of Merrimac, it was under full-scale siege from over one thousand miners.

"Listen for the cow horn," a miner nicknamed Flatnose told them when they arrived on a hill overlooking the town and the mine yard. "One blast means start shootin'. Three blasts mean cease fire."

"What'll we shoot at?" Vinnie asked. The town seemed vacant of human life.

"I been trying to bring down that house next to the post office," Flatnose said. "I figure a couple of hundred more shots and this whole side should cave in."

The cow horn sounded. Sam promptly took aim and shattered the little glass window of the house.

"I been shootin' at that window all day and couldn't hit it," Flatnose said with wide eyes.

That evening Vinnie and Sam joined a band of fifty miners walking to intercept state troopers who were coming to the scene in a caravan of brand new automobiles. The miners arrived at a muddy road running alongside the railroad track and hid behind trees with the others, waiting.

Within the hour, a long string of cars came sliding down the road toward them. When the vehicles reached the pass, the lead car bogged down in the mud so badly the troopers had to get out through the windows. Though the troopers were out of firing range, the union men enjoyed watching the keystone cops slip, slide and fall in the mud as they tried to push the vehicles forward. Finally giving up, the troopers wiped themselves clean the best they could, grabbed their firearms, and began walking.

This was the moment Vinnie had dreaded. The ambush was about to commence and even he would be a good enough shot to bring down at least one of the fifty or so uniformed men walking past. Vinnie was certain Sam could see the barrel of his Winchester shaking.

"Aim at their heels," Sam whispered.

She apparently wasn't the only one thinking that way. One of the miners suddenly yelled, "Make 'em dance boys!"

Fifty rifles exploded as one. When the ground around them kicked up like tiny geysers, the state troopers jumped as one and ran as fast as they could for the cover of the woods. The miners kept up the assault for nearly five hours until a passing train provided cover for the troopers to make a getaway.

"They shoulda stuck with mules instead of those fancy new machines," an old miner said. "Much more reliable, them mules."

The attack on Merrimac became known as the Three Days Battle. As many as twenty men were killed on both sides. Vinnie knew those numbers could have been much higher had the miners chosen to shoot to kill.

On May 19, the first anniversary of the Battle of Matewan, Governor Morgan declared martial law in West Virginia. Freedoms of speech, press and assembly were taken away from the striking miners and charges brought against dozens, including several new charges against their hero, Sid Hatfield.

All this made for a peaceful summer for Mother Jones' favorite young fighters, Vinnie Vacca and Sam Wiggins.

<><><><><><>

"You ever kissed a gal?" Sam asked Vinnie. The legs of her overalls were rolled up to her knees and her feet dangled into the Tug River from the tree stump on which she sat.

Vinnie stood nearby and tried not to look at her bare limbs; they made it hard for him to concentrate. When the cork bobbed violently on the line at the end of his cane pole, he wasn't able to comprehend its meaning.

"No," Vinnie answered, blushing. He decided he'd give it right back to her. "You ever kissed a fella?"

"Aw, heck, no," Sam said, matching his blush. "Who'd wanna kiss me?"

Vinnie tried to take his mind off Sam's lips and the smooth skin running from her knees down to her dirty, little feet.

Feeling his line snag on the bottom, he jerked it so hard the hook flipped up into the tree branch above him.

"Oh," Vinnie said, growing more frustrated by the second. "I suppose I'd kiss ya."

Sam looked up at him. It seemed to Vinnie that every day he found something else attractive about her that he'd have to learn to ignore. For some reason, at this moment her eyes didn't look like they had for the past year. Her eyelashes were long and black, and the color beneath them was like looking through a thin, green leaf at a bright, blue sky. She didn't invite him to get closer, but neither did she look away.

Vinnie had all this he could take. He reached down, lifted the mountain girl off the ground and pulled her body tightly against his. Neither of them cared that Sam had dropped her favorite cane pole. They kissed with a passion that had grown for fifteen months of shared hunger, sacrifice and danger.

When the kiss ended the two took a long look into each other's eyes.

"I s'pect I'd best talk to your papa," Vinnie said.

Sam nodded.

The two grabbed their fishing equipment and ran home.

<><><><><><>

Vinnie and Sam decided it would be foolish to try and have a nice wedding when no one they knew could afford even a good, old-fashioned shivaree. Preferring to maintain their privacy, they eloped on Uncle Vincent's mule to the town of Welch, enjoying the beauty of the West Virginia hills and valleys during their leisurely journey.

Mr. Wiggins said little about losing his oldest daughter. His twin girls were getting old enough to do the chores, and he had one less mouth to feed. Besides, Wiggins was glad to no longer have Sam always pestering him about getting sloshed on his mountain dew.

Vinnie and Sam arrived in Welsh on the first day in August and rode straight through the busy town. The McDowell County Courthouse was a beautiful Romanesque revival building resting on the side of a hill with two sets of broad stone steps leading to the entrance.

"I saw this building when I was a young 'un," Sam told Vinnie. She slid off the rear of the mule and tied the reins to the hitching post. "I never dreamt I'd be a gettin' betrothed here."

The couple walked up the steep steps to the first landing. It was a beautiful, sunny day with just a few storm clouds threatening in the distance.

A half dozen well-dressed men exited the building. Vinnie and Sam stood next to the flagpole and let the solemn-looking men pass. As the young couple continued on up the steps, one of the men smirked at them, but Vinnie ignored him. He didn't want to start something on his marrying day. Sam stood for a moment looking in amazement at the rich beauty of the foyer.

"Those three sure do look familiar," Vinnie said. He felt his brain was even more sluggish than when he'd delivered the toast at Bullo's wedding. "Wasn't that one fella with Felts that day in Matewan?"

"I think we need to go up them stairs," Sam said, intent on their mission.

They found the Justice of the Peace office on the second floor.

"We'll have to make this a quick ceremony," the elderly man said when Vinnie explained their wish to be married. "Sid Hatfield is being charged today with dynamiting a coal tipple."

"*Hatfield*?" Vinnie looked at Sam. "Those men on the steps are the thugs that were at Matewan. One of them's that smirky turncoat fella, C.E. Lively, that testified against Hatfield and the others in the trial."

"They must be waitin' for this here new trial," the justice said. "Are you sure you want to get married today?"

"Yes, we do," Sam said quickly.

With a sigh, the old man pulled a well-worn Bible out of a drawer. Vinnie hadn't really listened at the service when Bullo got married, but he was sure there were a lot more words than he heard over the next minute and a half. Suddenly a piece of paper and a pen were shoved in front of him and he found himself signing his name. Then Sam signed her name, folded the paper and stuck it down the front of the dress she had borrowed for the ceremony. The next thing Vinnie knew, he was walking with his bride out of the building, a married man.

"Weren't we supposed to kiss or something?" Vinnie asked as they passed the three Baldwin thugs who were still standing on the top landing smoking cigarettes.

"We'll be doin' plenty of that soon as we get our camp made," Sam said.

Vinnie unhitched the mule, swung on and then gave a hand up to Sam. When they were a block away, three well-dressed men and two women walked toward the courthouse.

"Why, that's ol' Sid," Vinnie said and reined the mule into a tight turn.

The two watched as Sid Hatfield and his wife, Jessie, followed another couple across the street. The second woman was carrying an umbrella. A third man walking behind them, Vinnie guessed to be a bodyguard.

"I think that couple in front is Ed and Sally Chambers," Sam said. "I've seen them sitting on the porch at the Hatfields'."

The two couples and the man ascended the stone steps. When they got to the first landing, the three men near the entrance pulled pistols out of their suits and started firing. The explosive sound of gunshots made the mule rear. Sam fell backwards onto the ground. Vinnie jumped off the animal, which continued bucking and kicking its way down the street away from the courthouse. Vinnie ran to Sam and threw his body on top of her just as he had at Matewan.

The firing stopped as quickly as it had started. The bodyguard who had been walking behind the two couples ran for cover along with other pedestrians. At the same time, C.E. Lively pushed past a screaming Sally Chambers. The brave woman made a failed grab at the assassin. Her husband was rolling down the stairs and looked dead by the time he careened to a stop.

Lively wasn't deterred by the man's lifelessness. He stuck his gun behind Chamber's right ear and shot him one more time.

Vinnie wanted to rush into the fight, but Sam wrapped her arms around his neck and held him tight. There were now four armed men on the scene.

With a piercing cry, Jessie Hatfield ran down the stairs on the far side and continued running and screaming when she hit the street. Sally Chambers screamed too, but hers was more like a roar of anger. She attacked Lively and beat him viciously in the head with her umbrella.

The man swore and grabbed it out of her hands.

Then she threw herself on her bloody husband, opened his jacket and pulled the linings out of his pockets.

"See, he has no gun! He was defenseless!" she screamed. "Why did you do this? We didn't come up here for this."

"Well, that's all right," one of the other gunmen said as he walked down the stairs toward her. "We didn't come down to Matewan on the nineteenth of May for this neither."

A fourth man came from the opposite side of the stairwell, took Sally Chambers roughly by the arm and led her away from the scene. As they left, he dropped a smoking pistol next to the dead man's hand.

Dozens of townsfolk came hesitantly from behind cover and out of buildings toward the courthouse stairs. Vinnie and Sam had seen death before. Rushing first to the body of Ed Chambers, they saw from the wound on his head he was beyond hope. Vinnie continued on up the steps. He saw four round blotches of blood on the chest and stomach of Sid Hatfield's shirt. There was no doubt. The hero of Matewan was dead.

<><><><><><>

Because they were witnesses to the shooting, the city paid for Sam and Vinnie to stay the night. They spent their honeymoon in a hotel, a first for both of them. The couple was too shaken for romance. With their backs to one another they quickly got ready for bed. Glancing over her shoulder, Sam removed her dress and pulled on the white nightgown her mother had once worn. Then she tucked her short hair under a matching nightcap and jumped under the quilt.

Having become used to sleeping in his trousers in his Uncle Vincent's house, for a moment Vinnie considered leaving them on. After some complicated thought, he finally sat on the edge of the bed, pulled his britches off and threw them on the chair. He swung his legs immediately under the blanket so Sam wouldn't see the holes in the knees of his long johns. He did, however, feel comfortable going shirtless in front of Sam, as he had done many times during the hot days of summer, so his shirt quickly followed his pants onto the chair. The two lay on the bed and looked up at the ceiling the entire night. Vinnie was certain that neither of them got any sleep.

Early the next morning, Vinnie answered a knock on the door to find a deputy sheriff standing with a carbine resting across his arm.

"They decided that since you were at the Matewan shooting, your testimony would be prejudiced," the officer told him without introduction. When the deputy saw the young mountain girl walk up behind Vinnie wearing her wedding dress, he blushed and set the rifle against the wall. "They want you to leave town immediately."

"Can't we at least eat something first?" Sam asked.

The deputy's hard demeanor seemed to melt when he saw the innocent look on her face. "I guess that's all right," he said. "In fact, breakfast will be on the city."

"Well," Sam said, "in that case, I'll take one of everything on the menu."

And she did just that.

23

When Angeline received word that Vinnie was married, she immediately sent money for their trip home. The little Italian mother was not going to tolerate a daughter-in-law she had never met. By the time the train pulled up to the station in Taylorville, she was ready to cry. Her two boys had found love without her help, and while she was happy with the choice Bullo made, she had less faith in Vinnie.

She was also sad that Filberto and Libero would not get to meet their sister-in-law. She decided that when the right time came, she would take Vinnie's new wife to where his brothers rested and tell her about them. It was important that she understood what the Vacca family stood for.

Vinnie long displayed an inability to understand family ties. In her letter, she asked the name of his wife and what she looked like. He had avoided the question, instead replying that everything would be answered when they came for a visit. That word "visit" bothered her too. How could the family stay strong if Vinnie planned on going back to West Virginia?

When the train came to a squealing, steamy stop, passengers began slowly disembarking onto the station landing. Finally, Angeline saw her Vinnie step out carrying a well-worn grip. She leapt into her boy's arms and smothered him with kisses. She was surprised that he returned her hug and even gave her a little kiss on the cheek. Then he shook his father's hand.

"Mama, Papa," Vinnie said, followed by a deep breath, "this is Sam."

Taking a closer look at the person she had thought was a man standing next to her son, Angeline saw it was a woman wearing a work shirt with a red bandana around her neck and blue, bib overalls.

"Everything happened so fast we haven't had the time or money to buy new clothes," Vinnie said, his face flush.

"Don't you worry, we'll take care of that this afternoon," Antonio said as he hugged his daughter-in-law. "Mary Kate went with Bullo to a union meeting in Virden, but they will be home this evening."

For a long moment no one else said anything. Sam just looked down at the shoes that Mother Jones had bought her. Vinnie glanced hopefully at his little mother.

"Samantha," Angeline suddenly cried out. She grabbed the mountain girl and hugged her.

"Just Sam, ma'am," Sam said, her hands at her side.

"You call me *Mama*," Angeline said.

"Yes, ma'am." Sam looked back down at her shoes.

"Well, now that we have everyone's handle worked out—" Antonio seemed on the verge of laughing. He took Vinnie's bag from him. "Let's get these two on home."

The silence returned as they walked to the buggy and climbed in. Vinnie and Sam sat on the backseat.

"Did you enjoy school when you were young?" Angeline asked when they were moving.

"I did the first two years," Sam said, "but the third year we got a new teacher who was mean. Anyway, Ma was sick after the twins were borned, so Pa made me stay home and do chores."

Angeline remained quiet for the remainder of the ride. When they came to their house, they rode right past it and then passed Bullo's house, stopping in front of a brand new two-story home built between two of Antonio's twenty-two year old oak trees.

Vinnie's wide eyes went from the building to his parents.

"Papa and Bullo built it for you and your new bride," Angeline said, still avoiding the use of her daughter-in-law's name.

Antonio pulled the brake on the buggy, tied the reins and jumped to the ground. Angeline knew he was bursting with pride in the new home and couldn't wait to show it off. She also noted Sam's surprise when Antonio offered his daughter-in-law his hand to help her down from the buggy step. Angeline waited for a similar gesture from her husband, and with more grace and elegance than she had ever displayed, stepped to the ground.

Without a word, Vinnie followed his father and Sam up the porch steps and into the new house.

"We put a water pump right in the kitchen so you won't need to go outside for water." Antonio said proudly.

"A water pump?" Sam said in amazement. "*Inside* the house?"

"Inside the house," Antonio repeated.

They walked through the unfurnished living room into the kitchen. Antonio went straight to the water pump and primed it with a glass of water sitting on the counter. After three pumps, clear, cool water gushed into the basin.

"Look, Vinnie," Sam said loudly. "There's an icebox in here, too."

Sam's eyes showed amazement, but Vinnie kept his stone face.

"The ice truck comes by on Monday and Thursday," Antonio announced.

They went into another small room on the ground floor. "We figured this can be your and Vinnie's room," Antonio said. He opened another door. "And this can be a nursery, or maybe a sewing room when the kids are grown up enough to sleep upstairs."

"Do you sew?" Angeline asked.

"Oh, yes, ma'am," Sam said. "Papa had the Widow Douglas learn me."

Angeline stayed downstairs as Antonio and Sam negotiated the steep, narrow staircase to the second floor. Vinnie stayed with his mother who, he felt, was staring a hole through his head.

"Oh, Vinnie!" Angeline said, shaking her head.

"We're not staying," Vinnie said, a vein in his forehead pulsing. "We'll be heading back to West Virginia in the morning."

Before Angeline could respond, Sam came running down the steps, her face aglow with excitement.

"Vinnie, there's a little room up here for toiletries," she said. "And a little chair with a big hole in it. Your Pa says we can put a pot under it and take it outside and clean it each morning." She started back up the stairs, then turned around. "Is it civilized to do your necessities inside like that?"

Antonio came back down the stairs, took his wife gently but firmly by the arm, and walked her out the front door. Once they were outside, she jerked her arm free.

"We must leave them alone for a few moments," Antonio said with a firmer tone than he had ever used with his wife.

"*You.*" Angeline tried to talk but was so angry she was ready to cry.

"Mama," Antonio said in a calmer voice, "this is one time you need to listen to your husband." He held up a hand when she started to speak. "And you are going to stay quiet and let our son and his bride make their own decisions."

Angeline's mother had taught her that when a man put his foot down it was good to let him have his way. Then when he found out he was wrong he would listen to her better the next time. She turned, raised her head defiantly and walked to her house. After entering she slammed the door so hard, the coal bucket that miners put money in to pay for her vegetables bounced off the porch.

<><><><><><>

"I want to live in this house for the rest of my life," Sam said to Vinnie when he came up the stairs.

"*What?*" Vinnie could not believe his ears. "You want to leave those beautiful hills and valleys to live in a land that is *flat?*"

"No, I don't," Sam said, "but you're a coal miner. Since Hatfield died, the men back home are yellow-dogging right back to the mines. You've got the union here to protect you. Back in West Virginy, there's nothing but dying from either fighting or tops fallin' on ya."

"What about your papa and the twins?" Vinnie asked.

"The twins have always preferred each other, and Pa's got his jug." Since Sam wasn't usually a touchy person, when she put her hand on her husband's shoulder, he listened. "Besides, Pa told me that if I ever got a chance to see the elephant, I should do it."

Vinnie didn't understand.

"You've got somethin' here I want," Sam added.

"What's that?" Vinnie asked.

"Family."

The discussion was over.

24

When Joe Harrison heard that Vinnie was back in town, he immediately called the Vacca boys into his office. He set behind his desk, looking every bit a company man. One wall of the room was lined with the new masks that had been developed during the war to combat the use of nerve gas.

"We're going to try a cutting machine," Joe Harrison told Vinnie and Bullo. "We need young men who are willing to learn how to run it."

"What are you going to do about the air problem?" Vinnie asked. "Machines cause a lot more dust than mining by hand. You gonna make everyone wear one of those big, heavy masks all day long?"

"Harley Eng bought us those masks. In fact, he bought us a whole shed full of rescue equipment," Joe said, irritated. "But the bad air is why we need young men running the new equipment," Joe continued. "You will be able to handle the dust because you are healthier. Also, you can learn machines faster than old timers like me and your pa. It will be your responsibility to come up with ideas to cut down on dust and maintain your safety. Not much different than being responsible for sounding your own tops, is it?" Seeing Vinnie's skeptical look, Joe said, "You talk like your father. You think the mine owners are Satan?"

"Nah," Vinnie said, "they're just sleek, dignified church-going gentlemen who would rather pay fabulous sums to kill men for wanting to join a union than pay those same men for delving into the subterranean depths of the earth and producing their wealth for them."

"You a writer now, Vinnie?" Joe asked.

"Nah, just something I heard someone say at Sid Hatfield's funeral." Vinnie stood up. "I'll stay with Papa."

Bullo watched his brother walk out of the room. He knew their father was against mechanization of the mine, not only because it would replace workers, but because of the dangers to worker's health and safety. Still, he had a wife and two children to support.

"How much will it pay?" Bullo asked.

"Machine operators will be the top paid men in the mine." Joe told him. "You'll make as much as me, seven-ninety a day."

"I'll take the training for cutting machine operator," Bullo said. He realized that by saying those words he was creating a rift between himself and his father and brother. Sides were being chosen. He prayed that his decision was the correct one.

<><><><><><>

Home less than a week, Vinnie felt he had done nothing but deal with problems. He didn't blame Bullo for taking the job, but he didn't respect him for it, either. When he walked into his house, Sam met him at the door holding a newspaper.

"It says somethin' in here 'bout Blair Mountain." With less than a third grade education, she didn't read very well.

Vinnie took the paper and sat on a wooden chair, one of the two pieces of furniture in the room. Sam squatted at his feet, listening intently as her husband read aloud.

Logan, West Virginia September 2, 1921

REGULARS ARE ORDERED INTO COAL FIELDS
The fighting zone blazed afresh today. Late reports to the county headquarters stated the entire twenty-five mile front underwent the heaviest shelling since hostilities began.

At that time, 10,000 West Virginia coal workers marched against mine owners. The miners continue to fight deputies, state police, and makeshift militia.

State forces are said to be holding their ground on Blair Mountain and near Mill Creek. Reports that more airplanes dropped bombs on the homes and gathering places of the miners on the Hewitt and Crooked Creek sections reached here today. The reports did not make clear what casualties or whose planes were involved.

Estimates were of 50-100 miners have already been killed along with 10-30 of the state force.

Fighting is expected to cease upon the arrival of the federal troops. The miners announced their intentions of going home peacefully when the troops arrived.

Air scouts late today reported that at least five miners had been killed in the latest engagements. Reports to Sheriff Chapin were that one defender had been wounded.

Sam put her hand under her chin. Vinnie stopped reading and slid out of the chair to squat on the floor beside her. Though they rarely touched physically, he felt their hearts were totally connected.

"Are you worried about your papa?" he asked.

"Pa?" Sam shook her head. "Nah, he's probably still sleeping off the hangover he got from celebratin' gettin' rid of me. I was just thinkin' about what this is gonna do to the union effort. They tell me there's a piece a paper called the U.S. Constitution that's supposed to protect our rights to get together and talk to each other and a bunch of other things. I guess those laws just ain't as powerful as bombs and machine guns."

Vinnie and Sam lay back on the floor and stared up at the ceiling. He thought of the thin, hungry children they had seen in the union tent cities of West Virginia. It would be only a matter of time before miners, desperate for work, would be forced by the mine companies to sign contracts stating they would not join a union.

Sam was right. Machine guns were stronger than the Constitution.

<><><><><><>

The next day, three hundred feet below the surface of the earth, Antonio watched Bullo working with several other men to move the big, cutting machine through the main west roadway away from the main shaft. The jaws on the front of the machine looked menacing and dangerous to old timers like Antonio.

Shaking his head, he picked up two freshly sharpened picks and walked with Vinnie to the end of the gallery and on to the second north entry. They would be working over a mile from the main shaft, deeper into the mine than anyone in the third vein.

The morning was spent teaching Vinnie the art of coal mining: timbering, laying track and undercutting the coal. Antonio was pleased his son was a fast learner. By mid-afternoon they had blasted two compartments and loaded and sent to the tipple over ten tons of coal. The veteran miner wondered if the check-weigh men would be as lenient with their calculations as they had been before Vinnie turned down the machinist job. He decided to blast one more compartment before going home.

After drilling into the face, Antonio was placing his shots when he heard someone shouting something from an entry branching off from the road. He and Vinnie set down their equipment and walked out of the compartment. Lights approached from the entry. Antonio recognized fellow miners Cuthbert Hardin and his brother Forrest. The looks on their blackened faces said that something was wrong.

"Cave-in down at the second north entry," Cuthbert said in a flat voice.

The news brought Antonio's senses to full alert. While the Hardin brothers, both pushing sixty years old, had been in tough situations before, Antonio doubted the two had ever been trapped at the furthest point from the main entry with the air circulation from the fans cut off; conditions that were perfect for a miner's worst fear—the black damp.

<><><><><><>

The most terrible sound a coal miner's wife could hear was the disaster siren. In her nightmares, Angeline had listened to the sound a thousand times. When she heard it as she was washing Antonio's spare long johns, she surprised herself by calmly setting the washboard on the floor, shaking water off her hands, and walking outside. It was only when she saw Mary Kate and Sam's faces as they ran up to her porch that her heart beat faster. She noticed that Vinnie's wife was dressed in her dang overalls, red bandana and work shirt again. She forced her mind to slow down and get calm.

"Mary Kate," she said, "fetch Mrs. Borgononi to watch the boys." She turned toward Sam. "You go grab as many blankets as you can carry."

The young girls ran to do as they were told. Angeline went back in her house and filled her husband's old dinner bucket half way up with water. She then put the metal spacer into the bucket and loaded some roast beef and sweet bread on top. Finally, she grabbed the medical bag that she used when helping to deliver babies.

Once outside, she saw women running empty-handed toward the mine. Angeline had listened to Harley Eng talking about the Cherry Mine Disaster, so she knew that if this was really a catastrophe, it would be more important to arrive at the mine yard prepared to deal with the injured. She noted that it was late afternoon, so her men might have already left the mine, though Bullo had just begun work on the cutting machine that day and might have stayed late to clean the equipment.

Mary Kate and Sam joined their mother-in-law and dozens of other women on the road scrambling to the mine yard. When they arrived, Angeline saw Joe Harrison standing on the cage directing men wearing rescue equipment and carrying gas masks. When he signaled the engineer, the cage began its descent. For the next two hours, the Vacca women stood in the same spot and watched as the cage came up and went back down for more miners. Each time an elevator unloaded, they struggled to look through the dirty faces for one of their men. Angeline was envious of the women who would scream and run into the arms of a loved one.

At first the men coming up were calm. There seemed no signs of distress. The last two cages brought up fewer miners, and they seemed weaker. A few even needed to be supported.

Mary Kate and Angeline held hands, hugged and rubbed one another's backs. Sam paced like a wild animal, asking questions of miners as they came up. Angeline didn't like it that her new daughter-in-law showed no tears. Then Lena Eng pushed her way through the crowd and ran into Angeline's arms.

"Harley is in the mine office talking to Joe," Lena said. "Have the boys come up yet?"

Angeline shook her head. Her mind was so muffled it didn't really register when Vinnie's wife turned away from the women and hurried through the crowd toward the mine office.

<><><><><><>

Perhaps because of the way she was dressed, no one paid attention to Sam Vacca as she came into the room that was crowded with men standing around a table looking at a map.

"We opened a small area between the room neck and the second north entry," Joe said, pointing at the map. "It's too small for a man to fit through and the top's too unstable, so they're cutting through from an adjacent compartment deep in the mine where we think they may be trapped."

"How many men are in there?" Harley Eng asked.

"At least two," Joe said. "Bullo Vacca says that he and his father were working that territory before he took the new job on the cutting machine. Today was Vinnie's first day."

"How is the air back in there?" one old miner asked.

"Not good. We recognized black damp coming from the hole." Joe's voice had grown weak. "We put a fan near the opening to pump fresh air into that entry."

"With a mine over twenty years old," a man wearing an orange rescue jacket said, "it would take dumb luck if they found their way out through that maze of entryways."

"Then they're goners," the old miner said and spit a chaw into a cup.

Men hung their heads and began filing out of the room until there was just Sam, Joe Harrison and Harley Eng.

Joe spotted the girl. "What are you doing here?" he asked.

Harley turned toward Sam. "You don't need to be saying anything to the other women yet."

"What would *you* do if you was trapped down there with the black damp a creepin' up on ya?" Sam asked, looking at Joe. "You'd seal yourself into a chamber to give yourself a chance to live, wouldn't ya?"

"Most men would rather die from the black damp," Joe said, "than hole themselves up and die slow."

"My man ain't most men," Sam said. "He and his pa are holed up down there in one of them chambers waitin' for me and you to lead them to a chamber with fresh air, and you know it."

Joe looked at Harley.

"Sam, we can't get through," Joe said. "I understand how

you feel, but the hole is over thirty feet long and too narrow for even a small man to squeeze through. Besides, you've never been in a mine before."

"I have so been in a mine before and a three-foot mine at that!" she said, her face defiant. "A lot of us women folk worked the mine in West Virginy durin' The Great War. I shoveled coal on my hands and knees. You ever worked a three-foot vein before, Mr. Harrison? I can squeeze myself as small as a mouse goin' through a crack in a wall." Sam's face was full of grit and determination. She took one of the gas masks hanging on a hook. "Now show me how to use this here contraption."

<><><><><><>

Angeline felt someone pushing forward between her and Lena.

"S'cuse, ma'am," a deep voice said.

A thin miner wearing a rescue outfit that was too big for him pulled his canvas cap low on his forehead and squeezed past her. Joe Harrison, not noticing Angeline standing beside his own wife, followed him. He looked tired and upset as he and the thin miner took the last spots on the elevator. As the cage started its descent, Angeline looked into the familiar bluish-green eyes of the thin miner. The matriarch of the Vacca family turned and looked through the crowd for Vinnie's wife, but the thin mountain girl with the bluish-green eyes was nowhere to be found.

25

Antonio knew the deepest place in the mine would be the safest until the rescuer's arrived. The black damp was a slow-moving, odorless gas that would creep toward them with the stealth of the grim reaper. It formed rapidly in mines when air wasn't continually entering. Because of the cave-in, the fumes were probably already metamorphosing from the coal beds in the chambers behind them. Their only chance would be to stay alive until a rescue party could fan fresh air into the entries one at a time until they found them. He remembered that at the Cherry Mine Disaster in 1909 twenty-one men had survived for eight days until rescued.

Though he felt lucky to be holed in with veteran miners like the Hardin brothers who knew what needed to be done to survive, he questioned whether they would be willing to face the terrible suffering in store for them until their last breath.

"Why can't these things happen at the beginning of the day when we've got a full supply of water?" Antonio asked as they consolidated water from their dinner buckets into one. "How long you figure we got?"

"That cave-in couldn't have happened in a worse spot," Cuthbert told him, and then coughed into his glove. He gave the half-full bucket to Vinnie to carry and picked up his shovel and pick. "Without any air-circulation, we'll be feeling the effects of the black damp come morning."

The four men began walking, each still carrying a pick and shovel. The end of the gallery came far too quickly. The three younger miners stopped and looked at Cuthbert, who was the oldest.

"Do you want to start walling now, there's only four of us?" Antonio asked. He saw the brothers look at each other.

"We'll help you get the wall started," Cuthbert said. "We'll decide later how we want to use it."

Antonio was proud that Vinnie never asked questions. When the other three men stopped and used their number two banjos to shovel rocks and dirt into the walkway, his son joined right in. It took most of the night, with short intervals to stop and rest. During these breaks, the men crawled on the ground looking for sources of moisture. Forrest found a small trickle of water oozing slowly from between two rocks. He and his brother began digging out a space for the precious liquid to pool, then went back to work building the barricade.

After more than seven hours of labor, they had a wall of dirt and rock almost to the ceiling. Cuthbert threw his shovel through to the other side.

"We'll help wall you in from over there," he said to Antonio and Vinnie.

Antonio knew what that meant. The Hardin brothers would rather go to sleep from the approaching gas than suffocate with the Vaccas.

"I won't argue with you, Cuthbert," Antonio said. "My main concern is the boy." He looked at Vinnie. "He just got married. I figure he deserves a chance to go on."

The three older men looked at Vinnie, whose eyes looked sleepy. Antonio took a quick inventory of his own senses and realized he felt as though a heavy weight was crushing his chest. He was lightheaded and a suffocating sensation crept through his body.

He knew the Hardins must have felt the same because they immediately began filling up the rest of the wall with rocks, dirt, and clay. Antonio shoveled feverishly, inspired by the realization he was fighting for his boy's life. Out of the corner of his eye he saw Vinnie fall forward on his face. He kicked his son's carbide lamp off his head and away from him as he continued to shovel. As soon as the wall was completely sealed, he felt the air improve. He sat down next to Vinnie and rolled him over on his back. The boy's breathing was still shallow but seemed steadier.

"I thank you for that," Antonio said to the brothers, who sat next to him. He knew the gas lingering outside was a solid mass, waiting for the inevitable opportunity to penetrate or to form anew inside their tomb.

"You got a good boy there," Cuthbert said, wiping his brow. "We'll give him every chance to get out of this. Let's put out all our lights except one to save on air."

Used to the cold and damp of the mine, Antonio knew that staying warm would require being on his feet to keep up the circulation. Deciding to let his son sleep for a bit, he removed his own shirt and placed it under Vinnie's head for protection from the cold ground.

There was nothing to do now but wait.

<><><><><><>

"You sure you want to do this, Sam?" Joe asked when they reached the spot of the cave-in. "Any of us men here would try it ourselves if we was small enough."

"I know you'd try, Mr. Harrison," Sam said as she tucked the laces of her boots so they wouldn't snag on a rock. "But tryin' ain't good enough. My men are in there and I'm willin' to die tryin.'"

"We're going to tie a rope around one of your feet so we can pull you back if we need to."

"Nope." Sam put the gas mask on her face and tightened it securely to her head. "It might get hung up on a rock. Besides, I ain't coming back alone."

"Okay, we won't pull you back," Joe said. "Tell the men to come back to this wall and we'll keep fresh air piped through. They can seal themselves along this wall until we cut through to them from another entry."

Sam allowed the man to check her gas mask one last time.

"Remember," Joe said, "the gas mask will only last—"

"'Bout two hours," Sam finished for him. "Just have those extra masks and canisters ready when I bring the boys back."

She crawled up the rocks and into the hole. The only light she had was from the men behind her, so she felt in front of her with gloved hands. The first ten feet were easy, but then the hole narrowed rapidly. At that point Sam had to almost dislocate a shoulder to get around a small but sharp change of direction. She remained wedged that way for ten minutes before finding a handhold and pulling herself half an inch at a time through the opening. Then the right shirtsleeve of her uniform tore off at the shoulder. When it caught on a jagged rock, she had to remove her gas mask and use her teeth to further rip it so it would come free. By the time her legs negotiated the turn, she was so tired she had to stop moving and rest.

The men behind her coughed.

"You okay?" Joe yelled through the hole.

"I'm okay!" Sam replied. "Just restin'!"

"Is it pretty much like your mines in West Virginia?"

He was trying to keep her spirits up, but Sam's mind was focused on just one thing. Though she had only gone about twenty feet, there was no going back. It was hard enough to negotiate the turn she had just gone through headfirst. Backwards would be impossible. Even if a rope had been tied around her foot, the men would have had to pull her body in half to get her out.

<><><><><><>

"Have you seen my daughter-in-law?" Angeline asked Harley Eng. "She's not good for much, but I guess she needs to be here when Vinnie comes up."

As much as Harley loved Angeline, at that moment he didn't

like her very much. He surprised his own wife by grabbing the plump little woman by the arm and pulling her away from the others.

"Harley?" Lena said, following them into the mine office, Mary Kate behind her.

"Let me tell you where your worthless daughter-in-law is," Harley said. He slammed the door shut with the ferocity of an angry Italian papa.

<><><><><><>

Sam's hands were numb with pain from pulling her body. She tried to use her feet to push herself forward, but realized her fingers would just have to wake up and do the work. After being in the hole for thirty minutes, she was in total darkness. At this pace, the air canister on her mask would run out before she made it through. Pulling with all her might, she moved another inch forward.

For the first time, Sam Vacca began to despair. The earth seemed to be pushing in from all around her, smashing against her chest, suffocating her. She pulled harder with her hands, but seemed to only move a fraction of an inch. Again and again she pulled. Suddenly she couldn't find a rock to grasp and she felt around with her hand. There was nothing there. She was almost through the hole.

Taking one more long rest, she once again heard the words of encouragement coming from the men behind her. The only encouragement she needed was the thought of her Vinnie, the man who had thrown his body over her twice to protect her from bullets. She squirmed like a worm, using every bit of her strength as she struggled to pull her body up and out of that eternal grave. Suddenly, she was falling. Falling and rolling.

She landed hard on the sharp rocks of the roadway. She felt the iron of a mine car track against her back. She had made it. Now, all she had to do was find her way through the dark maze of tunnels to the very end of the third vein and bring her man home.

<><><><><><>

Antonio watched the carbide lamp. It seemed to have been dimming for days, though it could only have been a couple of hours. They don't keep that kind of time in watches anyway, he thought. Smaller and smaller burned the tiny flame, until it finally began to sputter as if coal dust had been thrown on it. Vinnie was taking his turn at banging a shovel against a big rock; his eyes closed as he beat out the rhythm that would tell rescuers where they were. The sound echoed through the chamber in an eerie, haunting way.

Antonio closed his eyes and thought of his plump little wife in her blue, flour-covered apron that was older than her children. She stood in the middle of her beautiful garden. The big oak trees he had planted at the end of the last century were fully grown now. Four young boys holding hands played ring-around-the-mama. Angeline stood inside the circle, laughing and yelling at the boys, swiping at them with her broom.

Hearing a steady, far-away banging, he shook himself awake. Vinnie had stopped beating his shovel and was asleep or unconscious. Or was he . . .

Antonio pulled himself into a sitting position. The pain in his chest was excruciating and hurt worse when he coughed. The air was so thin, he was light-headed. The Hardin brothers also lay as still as death. Again he heard the rhythmic echo of a shovel against rock and thought he must still be asleep. He was about to close his eyes for one last time when he was startled by a muffled shout that seemed far away. He managed to get his legs in the right position so he could slide over next to Vinnie. He took the dropped shovel and banged it as hard as he could against the rock.

Cuthbert stirred and slowly crawled over next to him. A

shovel outside their airless tomb sounded again, louder and closer. The two men crawled to the top of the wall they had built and began pulling rocks and dirt away. Hearing someone on the other side doing the same, Antonio worked faster. Suddenly, there was an opening, and he saw light. He tried not to breathe in the foul air, expecting black damp. Giving up the effort, he took a breath and realized it was fresh air. Filling his lungs, he felt immediately weak and faint, and realized his body was so used to the stale air of the developing black damp that the fresh air now felt like poison to his lungs. He knew that the fresh air meant the fans were blowing again.

He and Cuthbert slid back down next to Vinnie and Forrest. Vinnie stirred, then somehow was able to stand on his feet. Antonio lay on his back as someone broke through the wall and slid head first down beside him. He dozed in and out, dreaming again of his family. When he awoke, he was still in the chamber but wrapped in a warm blanket. He thought he was still dreaming as he looked up into the bluish-green eyes of his daughter-in-law.

"What's doing, Sam?" Antonio said slowly. Then he saw Bullo leaning over her shoulder looking down at him. "Bullo? But, how...?"

Sam wrapped a second blanket around him. "Bullo found a way to make the cutting machine work faster," said Sam. She gave Antonio a small drink of water.

"No more, Mister. Vacca," Sam said when he tried to guzzle the water.

"Call me *Papa*," Antonio managed to say.

"Si, Papa," she said.

<>< ><>< ><>< >

Rosary in hand, Angeline Vacca had been praying nonstop ever since Harley told him what Sam had done. Guilt plagued her. Never in her life had she felt so betrayed by her own nature.

Never had she disliked herself so much.

She was still kneeling on the ground when the cage came up. Joe Harrison was supporting her husband and Vinnie was leaning on the shoulders of Bullo and her daughter-in-law. Angeline wanted to stand and rush over to them but she couldn't. She was so weak from anguish she fell to the ground and cried. She felt so ashamed and too weak to even stand. She was lying like that when a gentle but strong hand reached down and lifted her to her feet. Bullo held his mother with her face buried in his chest. Joe Harrison supported Antonio as the little woman finally moved away from her son and kissed her husband's blackened face.

"Nobody died, Mama," Antonio said weakly. "Bullo's men got through and found Sam. She had crawled through hell to get to us. Then they found us."

Then Angeline stumbled slowly toward Vinnie. He stood with his arm lying heavily across Sam's shoulder. With very little effort the thin, little wife was holding her man up. The right sleeve of the young girl's rescue uniform was torn completely off and the skin on her arm was black with dark-red streaks of blood. Angeline wrapped her short, little arms around them both and cried again.

"It's all right, Mama," Sam said. "Your men are home."

"And my Sam," Angeline said, touching her daughter-in-law's cheek. "You're back too."

26

The winter of 1921-22 was a good one for the Vacca and Eng families. Bullo became top man on the machines. He came up with several innovations the company boss patented and made a fast buck money on. Even with all the new technology, the machines still had trouble competing with Antonio and Vinnie, who brought up a record tonnage of coal for a hand-loading team. Harley Eng even gained some respect from the miners who, after the near fatal mine collapse in September, came to appreciate his efforts at providing mine safety equipment.

The only unhappy person among their social circle was Joe Harrison, who was depressed about his job, his wife and his life. On mornings when he had no work, he lay in bed all day and stared at the ceiling. As spring brought in flowers and insects, he began having nightmares about hoards of grasshoppers attacking him, knocking him down and feeding on his cheeks and eyes. They would eat away his skin, leaving a new face as black as coal. A burst of dark blood would gush from his mouth and nose until he couldn't breathe. He would wake up, his entire body shaking and soaked in sweat.

One summer morning when he'd gone for several nights without such nightmares, he awoke feeling unusually cheerful. Even amorous. The mood was short lived.

"I need to get away from Taylorville," Myrna told Joe when he leaned across the bed to kiss her neck. "Why don't you ever take me anywhere?"

"We can't afford to go anywhere 'cause you spent all our savings on that brand new automobile," Joe said, dropping back into bed.

"Lena has a nice automobile. I'm prettier than her and deserve to have pretty things around me. Why should I have to ride around in an ugly old flivver?"

"Because we're not millionaires and you won't even learn how to drive." Joe threw the blanket off, got out of bed and began dressing.

"We could go to your Uncle George's farm," Myrna said. "Didn't you say he invited us?"

Joe looked at his wife. That was the first good idea he'd heard come out of her mouth in years. The United Mine Workers was planning a nationwide strike during the slow summer months. Union membership had began declining following the murder of Sid Hatfield and the devastating loss on Blair Mountain, while the Red Scare and the Palmer Raids of the 1920s made it so anyone contemplating a union was considered a communist.

"I'll write Uncle George," Joe said. "You sure going to a farm in southern Illinois will be enough of a vacation for you?"

"Well, if that's all you can afford." Myrna pulled a black mask down over her eyes. A moment later she was fast asleep.

<><><><><><>

At eighteen years of age, Felina Harrison hated her parents. Sitting in the backseat of the automobile for one hundred and forty miles was torture enough, but her mother getting constantly carsick and forcing Joe to stop every half hour until her dizziness passed made matters worse. Everything was so *boring*. Why couldn't her father have a lot of money like Harley Eng? One thing was for certain, the man *she* married would be able to take her someplace other than a smelly old farm.

The only problem with her marriage plans was that she loved boys who lived recklessly, even though she knew that made them less prone to have good incomes. She wanted to find a man with both money and excitement, like the actress Olive Thomas had found in her husband Jack Pickford. Now *that* was a perfect marriage, with plenty of drinking, smoking, dancing and lots of Barney-mugging.

Her own mother acted like sex was a necessary evil to a marriage. She would probably have been happier if Joe went to The Clubhouse for his pleasures. Felina, on the other hand, planned on going to speakeasies every night once she was married, once she found a man like Jack Pickford to party with.

Olive Thomas was her idol. Olive had escaped a steel mill town in Pennsylvania to become a famous actress and had helped to give a moniker to young girls like Felina who wanted to live their lives to the fullest. The Flapper was one of the last films Olive made before accidentally drinking poison and dying two years ago. Seeing the picture twice, Felina, along with many other girls across America, aspired to live the carefree lifestyle of a flapper.

Her parents fought every aspect of Felina's attempts at transformation, from bobbing her hair short and putting blush on her cheeks, to wearing dresses that displayed more limb than they thought acceptable. They didn't know about her smoking, drinking and petting the boys she called "snuggle pups" at necking parties. She had never done any real Barney-mugging, just enough petting to achieve a reputation as not only the prettiest girl in town, but also as a full-fledged flapper.

Now as they drove across the Illinois prairie, she yelled at her father to drive faster. She thought it funny that he pulled the automobile to the side of the road before turning around in his seat to tell her to keep her mouth shut. Seeing her mother dozing off five minutes later, Felina screamed a second time. She laughed wickedly when Joe pulled the vehicle off the road and made Myrna switch places with her. The last stint of the road trip was without incident, and her mother was asleep when they drove down Uncle George and Aunt Dee's lane. When her father honked the air horn several times, Felina rolled her eyes at his attempt to act like a big cheese.

Their cousin Fred came running out of the barn to greet

them. Fred was a strapping young college man who attended the University of Illinois. Felina perked up immediately when she saw his lean, chiseled features.

She watched her father shake Fred's hand and thought it amusing that her mother walked past the youth without a word or a smile.

"I hope you can do something about that odor," her mother said. "What is that smell?"

"Like they say, it smells like money to me," Fred said, taking a grip from the back of the car.

"You still studying to be a vet?" Joe asked.

"Yep," Fred said. "I graduate next year."

A squeaky screen door slammed. Uncle George and Aunt Dee walked toward them with big smiles on their faces.

Felina cringed when her aunt and uncle hugged the others. When they came to her, she kept her hands to her sides and tried to show she didn't like them touching her.

While Aunt Dee warmed up the food and put it on the kitchen table, Fred led Felina into a bedroom to hang up her clothes. Felina was not happy that she would be sleeping in a room with hunting and fishing pictures on the walls.

"This is my room," Fred said as he hefted her luggage onto a chair.

"Where are you sleeping?" Felina thought the room would be more exciting if he were lying next to her.

"In the barn. We have a mare about ready to give birth that's not doing well. I'm afraid we'll lose either her or the foal."

"Is there a town very near here?" Felina asked, indifferent to the struggling of the animals. "I need to see a man about a dog."

"What?" Fred asked.

"I need some hooch," Felina said with a sly smile. "You know, booze?"

"Well, Herrin is a few miles away. But I'd stay close to the farm if I were you," Fred said, backing into the hallway. "There's been some trouble down at the coal mine."

"What kinda trouble?" asked her father, who had just come out of the other bedroom. "They have a strip mine, don't they?"

"Yep. A man named W.J. Lester is the owner." Fred turned his back on Felina, something she wasn't used to from men. "Lester brought a pack o' scabs in from Chicago to work the mine during the strike. And he's got thugs bullying and searching anyone passing near the mine. Looks like there's gonna be trouble."

"There usually is where coal mines are concerned," her father said. He smiled and slapped his cousin on the back. "But I'm just a farmer this week, huh, cuz?"

At the dinner table in the kitchen, Felina looked at the plate of liver and onions and the old, scratched pinewood table. Raising her head, she scrutinized the faded wallpaper tearing loose in several spots. Dinted and discolored pots and pans hung from hooks above a deep kitchen sink. The paint on the cabinets had peeled away, exposing bare wood. Though it was generally clean, the sad condition of the house made her depressed. Felina barely touched her plate.

"Why, Felina, you haven't even touched your dinner," Aunt Dee said. "You're going to wilt away to nothing if you don't eat."

Felina shook her head. She was struggling to lose weight. Besides, how could this dumb, country bumpkin know she was wearing one of the new bust bodices to hold her ample bosom tight against her chest? Flappers liked the boyish, straight-bodied look. Big breasted women like her mother and Aunt Dee were considered unsophisticated. Felina had always envied Sam Vacca for having the perfect flat-chested body. It was too bad Sam was just a stupid hillbilly.

When her parents took Uncle George and Aunt Dee for a ride in their new automobile after dinner, Felina decided to look for Fred, thinking it would be fun to tease the backward, country hick.

The barn smelled of wet straw and horse dung. It was longer than it was wide, with a walkway along the middle big enough to drive a buggy through. Above and to either side of the walkway ran two lofts stacked with bales of hay and straw. She found Fred in a stall, squatting beside a horse who lay on its side. The animal, massive next to the young man, struggled to breathe.

"Well, is it going to live or die?" Felina asked indifferently.

Fred wiped his eyes with the back of his hand.

"I'm going to have to put her down," Fred said. He nodded toward the pistol on the stool next to him. "The foal's already dead."

Felina found herself strangely excited. The idea of a living thing so enormous taking its last breath seemed fascinating.

"I need to go tell the folks," he said. "With all the trouble down at the coal mine, I don't want the gunshot to startle them." Fred patted the horse on the side, stood and walked past her.

When he was out of the barn, Felina looked from the heavily breathing horse to the gun on the stool. The mare's eyes were so big Felina could see her own reflection in them. Looking again at the pistol, she realized she was taking heavy breaths in unison with the horse. She touched its massive side and felt the beat of the heart. It would be so simple to make it stop. She had the power on the stool right in front of her.

Once when she was sixteen, she stood on a bridge and thought about jumping. That had been exciting, too. She put her hand on the gun and lifted it slowly to her own temple. She thought about where her brain was and moved it to different positions and angles. She even put the barrel in her mouth. The iron felt cold on her wet tongue. When her finger started pulling the trigger back she became scared and pushed the gun away. She aimed it at the horse's eye. In the reflection of the black orb she watched the gun barrel moving closer. Having the power of life and death, she had never felt so alive.

The explosion of the gun was followed immediately by a scream from the big animal. As the horse tried to raise its head she fired again and then again. Each bullet sent blood splattering against the wall and back into her face. She tasted the warm wet blood on her mouth and heard herself laughing as she fired one more time. Still the horse kicked.

Suddenly, she felt Fred rip the gun out of her hand. He quickly placed it directly behind the struggling animal's ear and pulled the trigger.

Even though she knew this bullet had passed through its brain, she was amazed the animal continued to shake for almost a full minute before it finally lay still. Felina realized that her own body had also been shuddering.

She put both hands on her bloody face and let them slide down her neck and beneath her blouse. For one long, sensual moment, she stood like that, then her senses came awake. She looked at her cousin, who stood staring at her with an open mouth.

"You knew no one was in the house," Fred said, his words slow and his breathing heavy. "You didn't tell me because you wanted to do that."

Felina moved toward him. She wanted him.

Fred stepped backwards and tripped over a bucket, not taking his eyes off the crazy girl with blood streaking her face. He turned and ran toward the house. Felina lay down next to the mare and rested her head on its back. She stayed there until all the warmth had left the animal's body.

Wow, she thought, that was the cat's meow!

<><><><><><>

"I was at Blair Mountain," Keiran Phelan told the miners sitting around the picket fire near Herrin, Illinois. They were camped behind a hill of dirt outside the Southern Illinois Coal Mine. "It was good and hot, I tell you. You should never live through somethin' like that. It was terrible. They shot women and children just to scare us into givin' up. Fifteen thousand of us there were, the biggest army on American soil since The War

225

of Succession. Those dirty scabs wouldn't have been so bold if they hadn't had hired gunmen backing 'em up with machine guns."

"Did you kill any of 'em?" a black man named Lofton asked. Phelan hated colored, but Lofton seemed to have a blood lust equal to his own.

"I kilt my share, I suppose," Phelan said. He stood and stretched so it wouldn't be interpreted that he favored association with the Negro. Phelan had been working the miners for the past several months to gain their confidence. If there was trouble, he wanted to be at the center of it calling the shots. He was certain if he had been in charge in West Virginia, the striking miners would have won.

Phelan was a short, burly man with dark skin that always looked dirty. His appearance worked against him in that people feared him and wanted him on their side.

"Oh, hell," a skinny, young miner said. "Weren't that many of the company men kilt at Blair Mountain."

Phelan, who had never lost a fight in his life, hit the young miner hard in the mouth, knocked him down and kicked him in the gut. It took three strong men to pull Phelan off the boy, who rolled to his side and spit teeth from his bloody mouth. The small, dark man quickly regained his composure.

"Won't tolerate being called a liar," Phelan said when the men released him.

"Well," a gray-haired miner said, "I'd s'pect you're the fella I'd want next to me in a foxhole."

27

In their third morning on the farm, Joe and Uncle George went into Herrin to buy supplies. Felina begged to go, but her father put his foot down. With all the mine troubles and his daughter's ability to stir things up, it would be better if she remained safe at the farm. Joe had already caught Cousin Fred whispering to his father about keeping her away from the farm animals.

He let George drive the car, causing quite a stir when they pulled up in front of the general store. Several town folk came out to look at the sleek vehicle.

"Grain prices must be mighty good, George," a man in bib overhauls said, then spat a blackened chaw on the street.

"I'd like to tell you it's mine, but I can't lie," George said. "Belongs to my nephew Joe here."

"It's one of them locomotives built by assembly, ain't it?" a man wearing suspenders and no shirt said. "Another way to take an honest dollar from the workin' man."

Joe ignored the comments. Southern Illinois was a breeding ground for communists and socialists. They were in constant conflict with the farmers, who stood by those who paid good money for the products they grew. He followed his uncle into the store and proceeded to load the goods as the grocer wrote down their purchases.

"George Harrison," a voice behind them said. Joe and his uncle turned to see a man with a broad smile walking toward them.

"Lucas." George shook the man's hand warmly. "This is my nephew, Joe Harrison. Joe, this is Lucas Hunter. He's a colonel in the National Guard."

Joe shook the man's hand, noting Colonel Hunter was dressed in a civilian suit and sported a broad-brimmed hat.

"You picked a good time to stock up," Hunter said. "Looks like things are heatin' up at the mine."

"I hate to hear that," George said. "You think you can calm things?"

"We got a citizen's group meeting at the Chamber of Commerce office at noon to try and avoid trouble," Hunter said, then appeared to have a thought. "Say, I'd sure like you to come along if you can spare some time."

"Well, I would, Lucas, but I'm not going to leave Joe to run loose by himself in Herrin."

"Bring him along." Hunter slapped Joe on the back. "I always like to have outside perspectives on matters like this."

After finishing their shopping, George and Joe had a coffee and sandwich at a diner. "Why don't we go to that meeting?" George said when they had finished their lunch and were enjoying a smoke. "I'd like to know what's going on. The mine yard is so close to my house."

Joe hid his apprehension. He had brought his family here for the relaxing rural life and to get away from the coal mines. Being a guest, he didn't want to seem disagreeable, so he followed his uncle silently to the meeting. Seven men sat around the big Chamber of Commerce conference table when they walked in.

"Where the hell's Sheriff Thaxton?" Hunter said after introductions had been made.

"Nobody answers in his office," the receptionist said, the phone still in her hand.

"If Thaxton doesn't get rid of those non-union workers and mine guards, somebody is gonna get killed," said Oldham Paisley, a reporter for the Marion Republican.

A deputy walked into the office. "Sheriff Thaxton and the state's attorney went to investigate a report that a truck carrying strikebreakers has been ambushed between here and

Carbondale." The deputy took a deep breath before continuing. "I heard two or three of the scabs were shot and a bunch more are being chased through the woods."

"Damn!" Hunter said.

"That ain't all, Colonel," the deputy went on. "Hundreds of miners are gathered at the cemetery. Someone read a telegram from John L. Lewis saying the workers being brought in are outlaws and should be treated as such."

Before anyone could react, shouting came from the street. A woman rushed into the room. "They're riotin', Colonel!" she shouted. "The miners are breaking into the hardware store and taking the guns."

The men in the room jumped out of their seats and ran to the window. Joe stayed in his chair, picked up a pencil and snapped it in half. He didn't need to go to the window. He already knew what the faces of angry miners look like.

<><><><><><><>

Everything was going the way Phelan wanted. The John L. Lewis letter read aloud at the cemetery had been enough to get everyone's blood up. Hundreds of men, women and children were screaming bloody murder.

"Too many men at Blair Mountain just wanted to scare the scabs!" Phelan screamed at the frenzied crowd. "They aimed at the feet of the varmints instead of shootin' to kill. Is that what you're gonna do to these filthy scum?"

"*No!*" the crowd yelled

"The company thugs killed our women and children without battin' an eye!" Phelan shouted. "I saw babies with their heads blown off and scabs laughing as they killed the mothers, too."

"*Kill the scabs!*" screamed the crowd as they rushed into the town. "*Kill the scabs!*"

Phelan took the lead and ran straight to the hardware store. He picked up a wooden chair from the sidewalk and threw it through the glass window. The crowd knocked down the old storekeeper and his wife and broke into cabinets to loot all the guns, ammunition and knives they could find.

Other businesses were treated the same. The mob came away with plenty of food for their union boys picketing the coal mine. Phelan rode on the running board of a Model T and waved for the crowd to follow him to the mine.

An hour later, the army of vigilantes were in position around the hills outside the mine. Phelan got the show going by firing his rifle at a man walking in the mine yard. An explosion of gunfire followed from the strikers. The scabs and guards trapped in the mine yard ducked for cover and returned fire. Two of the picketers were shot and killed by the more expert Chicago gunmen. The shooting began at 3:30 in the afternoon and continued throughout the day, filling the air with the smell of gun powder.

<><><><><><>

At the Chamber of Commerce room Joe watched Colonel Hunter make a series of phone calls, first to the mine superintendent named C.K. McDowell to warn him an armed mob was on their way, then a series of calls to hardware stores in Marion and the surrounding communities warning them to hide all guns and ammunition. When he called the Sheriff's Office he was told that the sheriff was still out. The deputies refused to go to the mine without him. Thirty minutes later Hunter called again and there was no answer. A runner was sent to the sheriff's office and came back fifteen minutes later saying the doors were all locked and the deputies wouldn't answer.

Hunter called his superior in Springfield and asked that the National Guard be readied. The supervisor said the Guard could be there in three hours if needed. But then the owner of the mine, W.J. Lester, was finally located in Chicago and told of the situation. Lester called McDowell at the mine and told him to cease operations until the strike was over. In the meantime, Colonel Hunter called the United Mine Worker's office and talked to Fox Hughes, who promised to go to the mine himself and put out a white flag if the strikebreakers would do the same.

Hunter immediately called the mine with the good news of the truce. The men under siege in the mine yard immediately ran a sheet up a telephone wire. A half hour later, McDowell called back to say the shooting had slowed but that the strikers surrounding the mine had not shown a flag yet. Hunter called Fox Hughes back and learned that he had not yet left the office but would go right away. The colonel then called Springfield and said the guard would not be needed but to keep them at the ready. His next objective was to get the strikebreakers out of the county and on their way back home to Chicago.

When Joe heard this he was not so optimistic. He thought about the fifty strikebreakers huddled inside the mine yard trying to not get shot. If a sacrificial lamb was going to be offered it would be them.

<><><><><><>

When Felina heard the gunshots from the mine she ran outside. Her first instinct was to rush to the scene and watch the bloodbath. Anticipating this, Fred came running out, grabbed her arm and pulled her back in the house.

"Bullets from a machine gun can travel up to a mile," Fred said. He closed shutters on the windows that faced the fighting.

"It's the middle of summer," Felina complained. "I'm not going to stay cooped up in here."

"You will if you want to stay alive."

Aunt Dee sat in her rocker nervously knitting. Whenever there was a long series of gunshots she looked up and said, "Oh, Georgie!"

Myrna lay across the davenport with her forearm over the

top of her head. "I hope Joe remembers my laudanum. All that noise is giving me such a headache."

28

Seeing the white flag go up inside the mine yard, Phelan was beside himself with anger. He urged his comrades to keep firing, but the strain of having two men dead and several wounded was causing the picketers to lose their resolve. Gradually, the men backed off the hill and went down to the campfires to eat their dinner. Phelan held his position, firing an occasional shot into the buildings to keep the pot boiling, his hunger for action intense.

When a union representative named Hugh Willis finally came into the camp, Phelan went down to hear him speak.

"God damn them," Willis said. "Those scabs oughta have known better than to come down here from Chicago, but now that they're here, let them take what's comin' to 'em."

With that the man got back in his car and drove away.

"You heard him, men," Phelan said, raising his gun. "Let's give 'em what fer."

With a loud *whoop*, the men rushed back up the hill and started firing again. Within moments, someone in the mine yard waved a white cook's apron on a broomstick.

Phelan raised his gun and yelled at the men to stop firing.

"My name's Bernard Jones," the man with the white flag shouted. "I want to talk to your leader."

"What do you want?" Phelan said before anyone else could assume command.

"The men inside will surrender if they can come out and not be harmed!" Jones yelled back.

"Come on out and we'll get you out of the county!" Phelan shouted. Under his breath he said, "and straight to hell."

Men slowly came out from under heavy equipment and from behind buildings. They threw guns down and put their hands over their heads.

"Round 'em up boys," Phelan said.

Hundreds of miners ran through the mine gate and surrounded the fifty strikebreakers. One of the scabs was carrying a piece of luggage.

"You won't need that where you're going," Phelan told the man and kicked the grip out of his hand.

"We got the scabs!" the black man named Lofton yelled and danced around the prisoners. "We got the scabs!"

"See these white sons 'a bitches?" Phelan said as he patted Lofton's head. "Why, we don't think as much of them as we do you, colored boy."

Lofton began beating the unarmed captives with the butt of a shotgun. Several others joined in. Minutes later, most of the fifty men lay on the ground bleeding. A few striking miners began to a mumble of discontent about the brutal treatment and two even threw their guns over their shoulders and started back toward town. For a moment, Phelan thought he might lose the support of the mob, but just then someone fired a shotgun blast into the air and shouted, "Let's march 'em to Herrin."

Suddenly people pulled the scabs to their feet and began walking them two abreast out of the mine yard. Recognizing he had temporarily lost control of the situation, Phelan ran to the front of the line to let everyone know that it was he who was still in command. When they had walked along the railroad tracks about a mile, he held up his hand and everyone stopped.

"What do we do with 'em now?" Lofton said, his eyes red as fire.

"The only way to free the county of strikebreakers," Phelan said slowly and loudly, "is to kill 'em off and stop the breed."

Most of the union men lowered their guns and moved back and forth from one foot to another. A few others cocked their pieces and stepped closer.

"Listen, buddy, don't rush things," one of the younger miners said. "Don't go too fast. We have them out of the mine now. Let it go at that."

"Hell, you don't know nothin'," Phelan said. "You've only been here a day or so. I've been here almost a year, and I saw bastards like these killing women and children at Blair Mountain. I've lost sleep four or five nights watchin' these scab sons-of-bitches and I'm gonna see them taken care of."

Phelan looked over the ranks. One of the captives was the mine superintendent C.K. McDowell. The man's head was down and he was bleeding profusely from his nose and ears.

"Ol' peg-legged McDowell." Phelan grabbed him and pulled him in front of the crowd. "How many of you men remember what this bastard said when the strike started?"

"I do." A miner with long, gray hair stepped forward. "He said that he was going to work this mine with miner's blood if he had to, union or no union."

"That's right!" another miner yelled. "And he said for all us union men to stay away if we didn't want trouble."

Phelan kicked McDowell's cork leg out from under him. "We oughta hang that peg-legged, son-of-a-bitch!"

"I can't walk no more!" McDowell cried out, seeing his artificial leg was gone.

"You bastard!" Phelan shouted. "I'm gonna kill you and use you for bait to catch the other scabs."

The crowd yelled its approval.

"Let me do it!" Lofton shouted. He grabbed McDowell's arm and pulled him off into the woods. The miner with the long, gray hair followed him.

Phelan started the crowd moving again. He wanted the blood lust to build in them as it was building in him. When they had gone a hundred yards, they heard a shot from the woods behind them.

"There goes your God-damned superintendent!" Phelan boasted to the scabs. "That's what we're gonna do to you fellows, too."

Phelan was weighing his options as they walked. He knew the miners had hated McDowell for his arrogance and his cheating them in their pay. Now they had a taste of death. The scabs were too bloody and scared to put up any kind of resistance. Not that they could with five hundred men and women all around them.

"We'll take four scabs down the road, kill 'em, and come back, get four more and kill them, too," Phelan said to those men closest to him.

Suddenly an automobile raced along the road that ran parallel to the railroad tracks. When it stopped, three men opened the doors, stepped out and walked casually toward the crowd.

"Hugh Willis is back!" someone shouted. "Let him through! He's the union president!"

Stepping in front of the crowd with his union officers beside him, Willis said, "Listen, don't go killin' these fellows on a public highway! There're too many women and children around to do that. Take them over in Harrison's woods and give it to 'em. Kill all you can."

As the three men turned and walked back to their car, Phelan felt like he had just received a blessing from the Pope.

"Here's where you run the gauntlet," Phelan said to the scabs after they had walked to the edge of the woods. "Now, damn you, let's see how fast you can run between here and Chicago, you damned gutter-bums!"

He pulled his rifle up and shot the nearest strikebreaker straight through the mouth. The captives turned and ran as dozens of bullets mowed down the ones closest. Hundreds of miners chased after the men firing at the slowest or those that stumbled. The man Phelan had shot rolled over on his back and moaned.

"The son-of-a-bitch is still breathin'," Phelan said. He ran up to him and kicked him in the side. "Anybody got a shell?"

Lofton appeared from behind him and shot the man through the temple with a pistol. Sporadic shooting echoed through Harrison's woods as hundreds of miners chased and shot at strikebreakers. Phelan had accomplished what he wanted. With Lofton following in his footsteps, they walked up to each body and checked it for life by kicking it. At a big maple tree they found a giant of a man leaning against it as miners took turns beating him.

"You big son-of-a-bitch, we gonna kill you!" one of the miners said, then drew a pistol and shot him in the face.

"By God! Some of them are still breathin'!" Phelan laughed as he kicked a body lying on the ground, then shot him for good measure. "They're hell to kill, ain't they?"

<><><><><><>

Felina lay awake all night listening to the gunshots getting closer to the house. At first light she dressed and went out on the front porch. She saw her father with Uncle George and Fred hurrying across the yard, so she hid behind the car parked in front of the carriage house.

A man ran out of the woods toward them, followed by over a dozen men with guns. The Harrison men scattered when the pursuers stopped, took aim at the fugitive and fired. The fleeing man went down like a deer shot in mid-stride. The men ran up to the body, grabbed him by the arms and legs and dragged him back into the woods.

On the other side of the yard, Felina saw a group leading two men at gunpoint into the woods. She waited about five minutes, then followed them into the trees. Within a hundred yards she found the captives hanging dead from a tree. In the distance, she saw their executioners looking for more strikebreakers. She followed them until they came to a road and caught a ride in an automobile.

When the car pulled away, a man ran across the road and

toward a farmhouse. Felina watched as he jumped on the ground and rolled under the porch. She saw men coming up behind her carrying guns. The leader was a short, dangerous looking man with dark skin. A Negro and two other men strolled along behind him.

"There's a man just ducked under that porch up there," Felina said.

"Thank you, pretty lady," the dark man said. "You'd best be going home now. You'll not want to see what's going to happen."

"I do want to see," Felina said. "I hate those filthy scabs. Are you fellas miners?"

"I'm Keiran Phelan," the man said as if reciting a royal title.

"Felina Harrison." Felina made a tiny curtsy. "Pleased to make your acquaintance."

When Phelan and his men rousted the fugitive from under the porch, they hit him with their guns for a while. The dark little leader liked showing off for the pretty, blond girl and appreciated the fact that she enjoyed watching the beating.

"Should we shoot him, hang him or just beat him to death?" Phelan asked Felina.

"Cut his throat!" Felina shouted.

Phelan and Lofton laughed; the other men just stared at her with disbelieving eyes.

Suddenly a truck came up the road and stopped in front of them.

"They caught five more down at the schoolhouse," the driver said. "Hop in the back and we'll take this one to join the other vermin."

Phelan gave Felina a hand onto the flatbed. With their legs dangling from the side as if on a church hayride, they rode to the school. When they got there, they saw several hundred men, women and even children gathered around the scabs. They had removed the prisoner's shoes and socks and were tying the men together with a long rope.

"Here's another one for you!" Lofton pushed the captive on

the ground.

Four men rushed over to the man and proceeded to remove his shoes and tie him in with the others. The women and children beat the scabs with sticks and made them crawl toward the Herrin cemetery. Phelan noticed that the pretty Harrison girl followed him wherever he went, so he put on a show of authority by ordering the captives to stand up and walk.

Just as they arrived at the cemetery, someone yelled, "The sheriff's in town! We need to get this over with!"

"God damn, if you've never prayed before, you'd best be doin' it now," Phelan said to the six men. "Nearer my God to thee!" He took a pistol from one of the men and shot the biggest of the prisoners in the stomach. "I want you to die slow, you son-of-a-bitch!"

The others were pulled to the ground as the big man fell. Dozens of men started shooting the tightly bound men in the arms and legs to ensure a slow death. The crowd cheered when the shooting stopped, then stood in silence for a moment looking at the dead and dying. One of the men stirred. Phelan took a knife and squatted down next to him.

"This one's for you," he said, looking at Felina. He cut the man's throat, then went around cutting the throats of two other men he thought might not be quite dead enough. When he was done, the crowd cheered again. Some of them spit on the men as they left the cemetery and headed for home.

When there were about a dozen observers left, two little boys unbuttoned their trousers and peed on the faces of the scabs. The warm water awakened one that was not quite gone and he begged for a drink. A man with a tag on his jacket that said he worked for a Chicago newspaper pulled out a flask and went toward the dying man.

"Keep away, God damn you!" Felina told the man. She turned to the man who lay bleeding. "I'll see you in hell before you get any water!"

The man who lay on the ground dying was an Irishman

named Patrick O'Rourke. The last thing he saw before he took his final breath was a beautiful blonde leaning down and passionately kissing a bloody, short, dark-skinned man.

<><><><><><>

When Felina didn't come back to the farm that night, Joe Harrison was certain something bad had happened to her. He, George and Fred searched everywhere, returning to the farmhouse well after midnight. Early the next morning, they started making inquiries in town.

The sheriff told them he was too busy looking for bodies in Harrison's woods to help them. By midday, he and his deputies had found nineteen in all. With the two miners killed in the mine siege, the morgue couldn't handle all the dead, so they only accepted the union men. Joe rushed to a vacant storeroom where the nineteen strikebreakers were laid out. When he saw the crowd gathered, he pushed his way through and checked each corpse until he was certain his daughter was not among them. At the back door, he watched the citizens of Herrin file through the room and spit on the bodies. Recalling that terrible day on Williamsburg Hill when the strikers shot the Negro scabs, he shuddered when he saw a woman holding a young child in her arms point at the dead and tell her daughter, "Look at the dirty bums who tried to take bread out of our mouths!"

A ghostly voice echoed through Joe's head. "Just shoot the grasshopper, son." He ran out of the building, found an empty alley and vomited.

"How can humans be so cruel?" Joe said when he felt his uncle and Fred's hands on his shoulders.

"Not everyone, son." George said. "Most union people in town were against this. Many tried to stop it."

That evening, the Harrison men came back to the farm after searching all day for Felina. Seeing an automobile sitting in front of the house, Joe ran inside to find his daughter standing in the arms of a short, dark-skinned man. Myrna was on the davenport crying.

"Daddy," Felina said proudly, "this is my husband, Keiran Phelan."

29

"Don't you ever say anything bad about my Sam," Angeline told Keiran Phelan during the Taylorville Fourth of July parade. She said it quietly so the others gathered along the street wouldn't hear. It was bad enough the dark little man didn't stand when the American flag went by, but he was not going to get away with calling her daughter-in-law a hillbilly.

"Why no offense meant, Mrs. Vacca," Phelan said. "It's just that back in Virginy folks who dress and talk any old way they want are called hillbillies. They like moonshine, whooping and shooting off their guns just to hear the sound of it. Doesn't that sound like Sam?"

At that moment Sam pulled a popgun out of her overalls and whooped with joy as she fired it into the air. Felina Harrison— now, Felina Phelan—gave Angeline a told-you-so smirk.

"Then when you call her that," Angeline said, paraphrasing a line from Owen Wister's *The Virginian*, one of her favorite novels, "you'd better be smiling."

After the parade, the Vacca, Harrison and Eng clans walked back to the park. By the time they got there, it was full of picnics, games, music and a small carnival. Felina walked far ahead of the others, her arm linked with her husband. The pretty blonde had made it obvious since coming home for a visit that she was above the mundane lives of the local yokels. Her style of clothing made Angeline appreciate even the boyish farmer johns that Sam liked to wear. Felina proudly flaunted the flapper's dress-on-a-coat-hanger look. The young girl also flashed a cigarette at the end of a long stick to everyone she saw. Her bobbed hair and heavy makeup seemed a caricature of something that hid a darker nature that frightened Angeline.

Even with a dark cloud to the west threatening rain, it was a beautiful day for the celebration. Bullo and Mary Kate's boys were on either side of Sam, holding her hands. William and Tony, now five and three years old, looked forward to fishing in the park pond with their adored aunt.

Lena's daughters, Angie and Margaret, were twelve and four years old, and they clung to Mary Kate's hands. As the happy group walked toward the picnic area, Angeline thought of Filberto and Libero. She wondered what pranks they would have created for Felina and her new husband. She was certain they would have had no use for Keiran Phelan. She still laughed when she thought about how they had tricked Felina by moving the outhouse, and how Filberto had set the angel clock to chime twelve o'clock at just the right time. They died unaware their mother knew of these things and had given them many kisses at night when they were asleep.

She looked at Lena walking arm in arm with Harley. Her best friend only needed to take one glance to know the little mother needed a good cry.

"Angeline," Lena said, "would you help me get the food out of the car?"

Antonio watched as the two Italian women scurried away from the group and disappeared over a little hill. He had felt his wife's energy wane as he held her hand. He, too, missed Filberto and Libero.

<> <> <> <>

"Did you know the men who assassinated Presidents Lincoln, Garfield and McKinley were all Roman Catholic?" Phelan said to Harley Eng as the two men sat on a park bench away from the others.

"And that is relevant because...?" Harley had gone to sit and enjoy his cigar away from Lena, who hated the smell of tobacco. Having a political discussion with this unlikable man was not what he wanted.

"Foreigners are destroying America," Phelan said, smiling broadly. "We've got an organization in Williamson County that is going to run these types back to where they came from."

"What organization is that?" Harley said, puffing his cigar faster to finish it as quickly as possible. "You don't look like an Indian."

"The Knights of the Ku Klux Klan," Phelan said proudly. "We are already thousands strong. Don't get me wrong. We represent law and order. Our intention is to enforce the Prohibition laws that our government doesn't have the manpower to deal with. We are ridding our county of alcohol, gambling and prostitution. We have the full support of all Christian churches in the downstate communities."

"I never took you for a teetotaler," Harley said, amused by the hypocrisy of the man. He watched as Mary Kate played ring-around-the-rosie with his daughters and stood to go join them.

Phelan's face lost its smile. "I was told that you are a friend of the coal miners," he said, standing up. "Don't you understand that coal mine communities are ripe for gangsters? Surely you know these vices are harmful to miners and their families?"

"You teach a miner to sound his top," Harley said. "You teach a man to hold his liquor. My wife is Italian. She was drinking wine before she lost all her baby teeth, and she's never had a drinking problem."

"Do you not support the cause of law and order?" Phelan asked.

"I support law and order for all Americans," Harley said as he dropped his half-smoked cigar and ground it into the grass, "regardless of their religion or skin color. That mess you were in down in Herrin hurt the reputation of coal miners all across America. It gave unionism a bad name, and it's going to take a long time for the United Mine Workers to come back from that tragedy. As far as I'm concerned, Klan is just another name for gangster." Harley left the little man and walked toward Mary Kate and the girls.

Felina hurried away from the picnic area and went to her husband's side. "Well, what did he say?" she asked. "Is he going to give us the money?"

Phelan shook his head. "He is a very stupid man. When the time comes, I will remember Mister Harley Eng."

<><><><><><>

While Sam always had a powerful appetite, Vinnie was worried when he saw her finish off her third piece of fried chicken and fourth dill pickle. Everyone else at the picnic was chatting happily. It was not unusual for Sam to be quiet. He liked that about her, but it worried him that she refused to talk about her getting sick the last several mornings.

Vinnie had lost two brothers. He didn't know what he'd do without Sam. He couldn't explain it, but he didn't feel she was as much his wife as his best friend. Even though Vinnie looked forward every day to coming home to Sam from work, their relationship wasn't at all like Bullo and Mary Kate's or his parents'. Sometimes the couple talked; more often they just enjoyed the peace and quiet of their home. Sam had built and hung several birdhouses from the oak trees in their yard, and even put up some big boxes for the squirrels. The chirping of the birds woke them at every sunrise and the squirrels provided entertainment on evenings when they sat on the porch.

Life was good. Although Vinnie and Sam took advantage of marital enjoyments on a regular basis, it was just as much the other things that made Vinnie feel he would be awfully lonely without his best friend at his side.

When he saw his mother get up from the picnic table for more lemonade, Vinnie followed her to the big ceramic container.

"Mama," he whispered, "would you talk to Sam? I don't think she's been feeling so good."

His mother surprised him with her knowing smile. Vinnie couldn't imagine what his mother knew that he did not. She reached up with both her hands and cupped his cheeks. "You are going to make such a good papa, my son."

<><><><><><>

Sam had been shot at in the Matewan gunfight and had squeezed thirty feet through a small hole in near total darkness to save her man, but when her mother-in-law and Mary Kate pulled her aside before the fireworks started and told her she was with child, she nearly fainted with fear. She slumped right down in the grass where she was and sat Indian style.

"Didn't anyone ever talk to you about where babies came from?" Mary Kate asked.

"No." Sam shook her head slowly. She felt so stupid, she didn't blame people for calling her a hillbilly. "I guess nobody back in the hills ever thought I'd need to know such things."

Mary Kate sat down on the lawn beside her and took her hand. "Sam, do you want me to leave while Mama talks to you about this?"

"Ah, heck no, Mary Kate," Sam said. "I reckon I'm so ignorant it may take both of you all night t' educate me."

"Do you have any questions?" Angeline asked as she joined her daughters-in-law on the grass.

"I suppose I have one question." Sam put both hands on her enlarged breasts. "Do I get to keep these after the baby's birthed?"

30.

Keiran Phelan's wife had expensive tastes. For a while, the Ku Klux Klan was his ticket to easy money. The Klan ran vigilante raids on the Bootleg joints, arresting the owners as well as the patrons. Phelan and other raiders pocketed much of the confiscated loot. Phelan's only problem was, Felina loved her cocktails and the very life her husband was condemning. She thrived on smoke-filled rooms with dancing, gambling and drinking. On nights when he was not raiding these types of establishments, he was driving Felina fifty miles away to frequent bars just like them.

Everything changed on the night of February 8. Phelan was patrolling the streets of Herrin with two other men when they received word that the bootleggers had shot a Klansman. Hundreds of armed men rushed through the streets toward Herrin Hospital. Upon arrival, Phelan saw Glenn Young, the Klan leader, standing on the running board of an automobile shouting for quiet. Young was a short, stout man in his mid-thirties. He had a reputation for ruthlessness and purportedly killed as many as twenty men during his time as an agent for the U.S. Treasury Department's Prohibition Unit.

"Caesar Cagle is dead!" Young shouted. "His killers are in the hospital right now, but they say we can't come in and get 'em!"

Instigation was Kieran Phelan's gift. *"Shoot 'em out!"* he screamed, waving his arms for the crowd of Klansmen to join him. The armed men poured bullets into the glass doors and windows of the hospital. After the first round of shooting, there was a brief moment of silence before a few gunshots were returned from inside the building. After that, a steady stream of gunfire began that lasted until daybreak.

Phelan was the first to leave the scene when the National Guard trucks pulled up that morning and began dispersing the Klan. Felina was waiting for him near the European Hotel and rushed out to meet him when he rounded the corner onto Monroe Street.

"Did you kill anybody?" she asked.

"Ah, those dirty cowards wouldn't show themselves."

Felina pulled him toward the hotel entrance. Phelan saw a man with a shock of coal-black hair combed back across his head standing in the entrance smoking a cigarette.

"I have an answer to all our problems." Felina held her hand out as if making a formal introduction at a dinner party. "Keiran Phelan, meet Bernie Shelton."

<><><><><><>

"The coal mine communities are perfect for our organization," Bernie told Phelan when they were comfortable in the chairs of his big hotel room. "The miners supplement their incomes by selling bootleg liquor to my brothers and me. We sell it to the tavern owners and help them set up slot machines, dice games, whatever. The coal miners get their booze and entertainment, and we charge the tavern owners for protection so nobody gets bothered. Then we slip a few bucks to the local cops and everybody is happy."

"Tell him how big your operation is, Bernie." Felina poured them each another whiskey.

"We plan on running everything from Peoria to Cairo," Bernie said. He threw the drink down his throat like it was water.

Phelan knew he was about to lose control. In the Klan, he was a big shot who could manipulate his comrades into doing whatever he wanted. The Sheltons were gangsters, and tough ones at that. Bernie had a reputation as a hot head not hesitant to kill. If Phelan switched sides, the Sheltons would probably never fully trust him. But if he did join the gangsters, he would have greater opportunities for financial gain and could openly live the lifestyle that he and Felina had to hide from the Klan.

He watched Felina cooing over the thug like the man was Rudolph Valentino. She had no idea the dangerous situation she had placed him in. He was certain that she was sleeping with Shelton, he could smell it on them both. If he turned the man's offer down, Phelan knew he might as well leave the state. Otherwise, he would most likely be found in a ditch with his body full of bullet holes.

"What happened to Caesar Cagle tonight?" Phelan asked, though he was afraid of the answer.

"Funny you should ask that," Bernie said. "My brothers Carl and Earl walked up to him and told him to get his hands up. Cagle must have been scared 'cause he didn't move so fast. Carl put his gun to his head and said, 'Too slow,' and he blew his brains out." The gangster roared with laughter. "Ain't that a riot? 'Too slow.' Carl always was the funny one in the family."

"What would you have me do if I join up?" Phelan asked, trying to not show how much the piercing laugh of Shelton scared him.

"Well, your wife says she has family up in Christian County," Bernie said, lighting a cigar. "You work down here awhile with us 'til you get acquainted with the business, then we set you up with an operation up there."

Phelan perked up a little at the idea of being the boss of his own business.

"When do I start?" Phelan said.

Bernie reached out to shake on it. When Phelan touched the gangster's hand, it felt cold and sweaty.

"First, we want you to help us take care of that bastard with the hood, Glenn Young," Bernie said, holding his glass out for Felina to refill. "Then we'll talk shop."

Sixteen Tons

<><><><><><>

Later that spring, Glenn Young stood on the running board of the Lincoln sedan that the grateful townsfolk had given him. He gallantly waved his hat at the small group of applauding Klansmen gathered on the Herrin town square to see him off. "I'm off to clean up East Saint Louis like I cleaned up Williamson County!" Young's pretty wife Grace waited patiently in the car seat. When her husband finally got in beside her and headed the car out of town, no one noticed the four men who jumped into a Dodge touring car and followed.

Kieran Phelan and the three Shelton brothers arrived in town at the right moment to hear Young's boastful remark. They also had a small arsenal in their car. Phelan drove the Dodge along the Atlantic-Pacific, Highway keeping a safe distance behind Young's Lincoln.

"Don't get close to him 'til we hit the Okaw bottoms," Carl Shelton told Phelan from the backseat.

Bernie Shelton sat in the front passenger seat and checked his pistols. In the back, Carl and his other brother Earl raised the curtain they had placed over the vehicle's rear windows. Carl rested the muzzle of a sawed-off shotgun on the window just below the curtain. Earl leaned over him and did the same with a carbine.

It was a pretty day in late May. Phelan wished that Felina could be with them. She was always so amorous after a killing. Unfortunately, her excitement sometimes caused indiscretions, such as the time he found her in Bernie's bed the night they cut the two dago's throats. When Phelan walked into the bedroom, they ignored him and continued their pleasure. Then Felina motioned for him to join them. Bernie was so drunk, Phelan knew he wouldn't remember any of it the next day. He was right.

As Phelan drove the ambush car, the Kaskaskia River Valley

was coming up fast and he had to concentrate. He gunned the engine, closing the gap with the Lincoln. Even if Glenn Young saw them through the thick cloud of dust his own car was making, he would never be able to outrun them. Phelan downshifted just as he came alongside the car. He wanted to turn his head and watch, but had to keep the vehicle on the road and be ready in case Young swerved into him.

The shotgun blast came first, with the rifle and pistol firing immediately after. As Phelan had feared, the Lincoln swerved and rammed the Dodge. The squeal of metal against metal was like fingernails on a chalkboard. Phelan braked hard and felt his front bumper catch on the rear bumper of the Lincoln. Young was trying to accelerate away from the gunmen's car but couldn't. Phelan tried to accelerate and break away from the other car. When his second attempt worked, Young's car ran off into a small embankment.

Phelan braked hard. With his flivver sliding sideways, he finally stopped in the middle of the road. The Sheltons opened their car doors and used them as shields as well as mounts for their weapons. Young limped out of his car and dove beneath it. For thirty hot seconds, he exchanged gunfire with the brothers.

"We'll never get the dirty coward like this!" Carl yelled to Bernie and Earl. They got back into the Dodge and Phelan sped it away.

They found out later that Glenn Young had been hit with a forty-five-caliber bullet below his knee. His wife had taken a face full of buckshot. She would be blind for the rest of her life. Phelan regretted his role in the affair. He knew he would have had a lot more fun if Bernie would have been driving so he could have done some shooting.

<>

August 30 was a great day for Carl and Earl Shelton. After charges were dropped for the murder of Caesar Cagle, their friends Sheriff Galligan and Deputy Allison escorted the brothers from the courthouse. Even Cagle's own father had said he didn't think the brothers had shot his son. They could thank Kieran Phelan for that bit of persuasion.

The dozens of Klansmen gathered outside the building to await the verdict were hot and angry. They were a tough lot when they were in a group, but few were as hardcore as the Sheltons. The brothers had brought in gangsters from East St. Louis who had plenty of experience with weaponry. It was even rumored that Carl was having an armored truck built with mounted machine guns.

As they walked through the angry crowd, Bernie Shelton, Keiran Phelan and fellow gangster Ora Thomas joined them. Each man touted no fewer than two pistols beneath their suit jackets, while Bernie carried his brother Carl's favorite sawed-off shotgun.

"We might as well go get the Dodge, since we won't need it anymore for evidence," Sheriff Galligan said in a mocking voice intended to incite the men gathered outside the courthouse. He led his group toward the garage as the Klansmen dispersed. No match for real gunfighters, the Klan was made up mostly of businessmen, farmers and even clergymen. Their faces were full of anger and hatred as they watched the brothers walk away from what should have been the worst day of their lives.

Bernie Shelton was particularly cocky about his siblings getting away with the murder. The youngest brother strutted along beside the sheriff. When they entered the garage to claim the car, he waved his shotgun at the six Klansmen hanging out there.

"We came to get the Dodge," Bernie said.

The men in the garage hadn't heard the result of the trial and were shocked to see the accused Sheltons walk so boldly into their shop. Bernie didn't wait for the sheriff to explain the situation. He slammed the butt of the shotgun into the stomach of one of the men. Both sides broke into a brawl. Not liking a fair fight, Phelan watched as the Sheltons pummeled the six men.

Footsteps ran toward the garage. Before Phelan could turn, the three brothers had their guns out and were blasting away at anything that moved. Phelan dove behind a flivver and pulled his gun from his jacket. He was shaking so badly he couldn't rise up to see what was happening.

"Get in the car!" Carl yelled.

Phelan scrambled to his feet and jumped into the middle of the backseat. Bernie and Earl continued shooting as the sheriff drove the flivver out of the garage, down the street and out of town. Four men, including Deputy Allison, lay dead in the garage. Two innocent pedestrians on the street were also killed as the Shelton Gang made their getaway.

"We're going to need to get out of the county for awhile," Carl said from the front seat as the car sped toward their heavily fortified farmhouse. He looked at Phelan. "You said something about a bank in Christian County that would be easy."

Phelan struggled to look as calm as the others. "The coal company payrolls come in at the end of every month," he said in a shaky voice. "There are several small town banks that'd be easy pickins. Those hicks would shit their pants if the Shelton Gang rode into town."

<><><><><><>

"Are you sure you know how to drive this contraption?" Sam Vacca asked. She sat in the passenger seat of the Ford Fordor Sedan waiting for her sister-in-law to get the vehicle moving.

"Oh, sure," Mary Kate said. "All you got to do is aim it in the right direction and push up and down on these foot thingies."

The automobile leapt forward so fast Sam lost her death grip on the door handle. Though they seemed to have nothing more in common than being married to the Vacca brothers, Mary Kate had come to think of Sam as a sister. She loved the sweet innocence of the mountain girl. When Sam's little boy Sid arrived on Christmas day, she had barely whimpered during the seven hours of labor. Their mother-in-law kept telling her that it was okay to scream if she needed to, but the laboring mother just kept looking at a point on the ceiling and breathing heavy. Now Sam was taking similar breaths as Mary Kate guided the car along and sometimes off the dirt road. This was the girls' first outing alone together in the new family car and Mary Kate wanted to make it special.

"There's a big, new store in Kincaid that has everything," Mary Kate said merrily as she swerved into a grassy field to avoid a pile of horse droppings. "I'm so glad you're getting used to wearing dresses," said Mary Kate, turning the wheel hard and skidding back on the road. "You look so nice in that blue one."

"I took a bath this morning, too," Sam said, putting both hands on the dashboard, "but that don't mean I'm ready for buryin'."

Once they were on the main road, it was a straight shot, making it easier for Mary Kate to aim her vehicle. It was also one of the county's hard roads, so there was less dust. Sam gradually relaxed and began to enjoy the ride.

"They are thinking of changing the name of Kincaid to Electric City because the coal in this area generates so much electricity," Mary Kate said as they drove into the little village of fifteen hundred. "I wouldn't be surprised if this town becomes a big city someday."

Sam looked at the faces of the people milling around the stores. "I reckon there's already enough big cities. I kinda like this one small."

Mary Kate stopped the car by turning it off before it was stopped and letting it roll into a hitching post. She ignored the shaking heads of two old men who jumped off the sidewalk bench at the sound of the collision. The girls got out as if nothing had happened and walked along the sidewalk. Mary

Kate sported a flat, broad brimmed hat. Her sister-in-law preferred to be bare headed. Sam only wore hats to hold her lures when she fished. The businesses were just beginning to open on a lazy, Saturday morning.

"Good morning, Mister Aull," Mary Kate said to a man who tipped his hat to the ladies. "That was the cashier at the bank," she told Sam as they entered the store.

The girls spent a few minutes looking at children's clothes and toys. When Mary Kate moved on to the dresses and hats, Sam wandered over to the gun display. She lifted a .45 caliber pistol and checked it for balance.

"You thinking of buying a gun for your husband, missy?" the store clerk asked.

"Nah," Sam said, "but I do like the longer grip on this nineteen-eleven. Prevents hammer bite, don't ya think?"

Mary Kate smiled when she saw the expression on the salesman's face. Just then she heard a quick series of loud pops followed by the even louder ringing of an alarm.

"That's the bank alarm!" the storekeep shouted.

They looked out the big store window and saw three men wearing suits and ties emerge from the bank and spray the surrounding buildings with bullets from their handguns. One was carrying a sack and the other two were dragging a frightened Mr. Aull toward a green Cadillac as they fired.

A bullet shattered the window to the store, sending the storekeep to the floor, covering his head. Mary Kate felt her sister-in-law grab her and throw her to the floor beside the man. More shots came from the street as the engine from the Cadillac roared. Sam was suddenly shoving a magazine in the handle of the pistol she had been looking at.

"Sam, what are you doing?" Mary Kate yelled, then watched as Vinnie Vacca's wife ran out the door holding the pistol at arm's length, her gun blazing.

<><><><><><>

"Earl got shot by a broad!" Bernie Shelton gleefully told Kieran Phelan when they picked him up on a side-road south of Kincaid.

"No, I didn't," Earl hissed. He was holding a handkerchief on a wound just below his knee. "That fella that came out of the grocery store shot me and he shot Carl in the hand too. Ain't that right, Carl?"

"Where's my shotgun, Bill?" Carl asked the man in the front seat.

"I dropped it when that gal started shootin' at me," the gangster called Bill said.

"That's just *fine!*" Carl slammed his fist into the back of the seat. "You drop my favorite sawed-off shotgun and Earl gets shot and drops the loot. Fine bunch of gangsters you guys are." He glared at Phelan, who sat between him and the door. "You said this was a hick town and an easy take!" Carl pistol-whipped the dark-skinned little man in the head.

The Cadillac never slowed down when they opened the car door and rolled an unconscious Kieran Phelan into a shallow creek bed.

31.

"Ladies and gentlemen, please welcome one of the great humanitarians of our time. A miner's angel who has come to be known throughout the world simply as Mother Jones."

The applause and catcalls could be heard for miles. Harley and Lena Eng had heard of Mary Harris Jones, but were not prepared for the tiny, gray-haired woman who walked to the front of the stage. The crowd didn't stop cheering, even when the great lady, who always wore a black dress and black leather boots, raised a hand for them to stop. Then a group in the front of the crowd began singing:

She'll be coming 'round the mountain when she comes,
when she comes.
She'll be coming 'round the mountain when she comes,
when she comes.
She'll be coming 'round the mountain, she'll be coming
'round the mountain,
She'll be coming 'round the mountain when she comes,
when she comes.

"They wrote that song about Mother Jones coming to help the miners in the mountains of West Virginia!" Lena shouted to her husband, then joined in the song.

Harley glanced at his wife. He had never seen her so enthusiastic about anything.

She'll be wearing red pajamas when she comes, when she comes

Sixteen Tons

We will kill the old red rooster when she comes, when she comes

Amazed, Harley studied the crowd in the assembly hall. Though mostly men, their devotion to this lady, who her opponents called the most dangerous woman in America, reminded him of the enthusiasm he had seen at a tent revival when he was a boy.

We'll be havin' chicken and dumplings when she comes, when she comes
She will have to sleep with Grandma when she comes, when she comes

Tears formed in Lena's eyes. Like many in the crowd, she began throwing her right fist up in the air each time she shouted, "When she comes!"

The song ended with another long ovation. When Mother Jones again lifted a hand, this time the crowd became quiet but for the usual chorus of miner's cough. She smiled. It was as if her piercing blue eyes were making some sort of connection with each one of the thousands of people in attendance. She looked so small and frail, Harley figured he wouldn't be able to hear her. She paused even after everyone was still, creating an intensity he'd never before felt. Then she spoke in a clear, powerful voice that he couldn't believe came from such a petite lady.

"Get it right. I'm not a humanitarian, I'm a *hell-raiser*."

The audience broke into still another and even louder ovation. Grown men stood with tears running down their faces, clapping their hands together as hard as they could. When the room became quiet again, thousands of ears waited for the next words from the famous woman's mouth. She began in a low tone that filled the room.

"I was born in the city of Cork, Ireland, in eighteen-thirty.

My people were poor. For generations they had fought for Ireland's freedom. Many of my folks have died in that struggle. My father, Richard Harris, came to America five years later, and as soon as he had become an American citizen, he sent for his family. Here I was brought up, but always as the child of an American citizen. Of that citizenship I have ever been proud.

"I was married in Memphis, Tennessee, in sixty-one. My husband was an iron molder and a member of the Iron Molders' Union. Six years later, a fever epidemic swept Memphis. Its victims were mainly among the poor and the workers. The rich and the well-to-do fled the city. Schools and churches were closed. People were not permitted to enter the house of a yellow fever victim without permits. The poor could not afford nurses. Across the street from me, ten persons lay dead from the plague. The dead surrounded us. They were buried at night quickly and without ceremony.

"All about my house I could hear weeping and the cries of delirium. One by one, my own four little children sickened and died. I washed their little bodies and got them ready for burial. Then my husband caught the fever and died. I sat alone through nights of grief. No one came to me. No one could. Other homes were as stricken as mine. All day long, all night long, I heard the grating of the wheels of the death cart.

"After the plague, now alone, I moved to Chicago and went again into the dressmaking business with a partner. In October of seventy-one, the great Chicago fire burned up our establishment and everything that we had. The fire made thousands homeless. We stayed all night and the next day without food on the lakefront. Old St. Mary's Church at Wabash Avenue and Peck Court was thrown open to refugees, and there I camped until I could find a place to go.

"Nearby, in an old, tumbled down, fire-scorched building, the Knights of Labor held meetings. The Knights of Labor was the labor organization of those days. I used to spend my evenings at their meetings, listening to splendid speakers.

Sundays we went out into the woods and held meetings.

"Those were the days of sacrifice for the cause of labor. Those were the days when we had no halls, when there were no high salaried officers, no feasting with the enemies of labor. Those were the days of the martyrs and the saints. I became acquainted with the labor movement."

Mother Jone's voice grew in intensity.

"Since that day, my address is like my shoes. It travels with me. I abide where there is a fight against wrong."

The crowd cheered again and again, each acknowledgement growing louder and more intense.

"I learned in the early part of my career that labor must bear the cross for others' sins, must be the vicarious sufferer for the wrongs that others do."

"*Hurrah!*" the crowd cheered.

"I am not afraid of the pen, or the scaffold, or the sword. I will tell the truth wherever I please."

"*HURRAH!*"

"If they want to hang me, let them. And on the scaffold I will shout, 'Freedom for the working class!' Injustice boils in men's hearts as does steel in its cauldron, ready to pour forth, white hot, in the fullness of time."

Her voice changed to somber, as did the crowd.

"The only time you miners have ever lost was because you only had the United States Constitution on your side. The other side had bayonets. Bayonets always win."

Whether those in the audience hung their heads or stared at Mother Jones, their eyes were full of angry tears.

"So I want you men to remember this. When injustices are done by your mine companies, I want you to rise up and *strike.* Strike until the last one of you drop into your graves. We are going to stand together and never surrender. Boys, always remember you ain't got a damn thing if you ain't got a union!"

The cheering and applause erupted and continued for Mother Jones as she was gently and lovingly escorted off the stage and through the audience. While the band played "She'll Be Coming Around the Mountain," she moved slowly, shaking hands, hugging and kissing her boys.

Perhaps because Lena was one of the few women in the crowd, Mother Jones came toward her and took both her hands in her own. "Where are you from, child?"

"From the coal fields of central Illinois!" Lena said, shouting above the still cheering crowd.

Harley was happy with his wife's answer. He was embarrassed to be a millionaire, and even more embarrassed to be wearing a fine gabardine suit with a bright red bowtie.

"Oh, my, that reminds me," Mother Jones said, still clutching Lena's hands. "I must write the miners in Illinois. I want to be buried next to my boys who were killed in the Virden Massacre of 1898. Thank you, dear. You are a beautiful lady, but remember, whatever your fight, don't be ladylike."

"I will pray for you," Lena said as the little woman moved away.

"Don't pray for me yet, dear," Mother Jones said over her shoulder as she moved away from her through the crowd. "Pray for the dead, and fight like hell for the living."

<><><><><><>

That night, Mary Jones took off her trademark steel-toed, black leather boots, giving each foot a good long massage as she did so. The mining couple she was staying with had not come home yet. She had the place to herself. She liked that. So often, she had people wanting her attention. She was eighty-eight years old, though she liked to tell people she was ninety-five, and she knew that her time on Earth was coming to an end. She sat back on the bed, put her feet up, and rested her weary back against the pillows. It was nice to have a moment just for herself.

It seemed she had only closed her eyes for a moment when

she heard a knock at the front door. With a quiet sigh she got out of bed, pulled her shoes back on and walked into the front room.

"Who is it?" she asked, placing a hand on the doorknob.

"Jack Felton, ma'am," a voice said. "I'm a neighbor down the street. Someone had an accident out here. Do you have anything we can clean a cut with?"

Mary turned the lock. The door flew open, hitting her shoulder and knocking her to the ground. Two men rushed up, lifted her off the ground by her arms and legs and carried her into the bedroom. They dropped her in front of the bed.

"We have a present for you from a friend of yours," the man said. He bent down to pick her up again.

Mary's hands reached under the bed for something to brace against. She felt something hard in the corner where she kept her little duffle bag full of mementos from past labor strikes. She grabbed onto the first large object she could find. It was a heavy shoe, the one that spunky gal from Matewan had given her. When the man brought her to her feet, she let fly with the flat of the leather sole as hard as she could to the man's nose. Blood didn't bother Mary Thomas. She had worked in sweatshops where she'd seen ten-year old children get arms and legs torn off by machines. The blood that gushed from the man's face did, however, unnerve his accomplice. That thug ran out of the building as his partner with the broken nose dropped to the floor.

Steel-toed boots had protected Mary's feet many times when she visited her boys in the coal mines. She had never imagined she would ever use them as a weapon, but use them she did as she kicked the man over and over in the face and throat. The thug who thought he would have no problem taking care of a little old lady died the next day.

32

"'Member me? I'm the one told you to shoot the grasshopper," Art Cabassi said.

Though he had known him his entire life, Joe Harrison looked at the old tavern owner as if seeing him for the first time. The man had been his father's mine partner at one time.

"I forgot you were on that ridge," Joe said. This was not a conversation he had wanted to have when he stopped at the Villa for a sip of the homebrew that Art kept hidden behind the milk cans.

"I know what you mean," Cabassi said. "I try to not think about it either. A lot of the men moved away after it happened. A lot a' others have died off. I reckon I'm 'bout the oldest one left now. I was near fifty when it happened."

Joe looked at the wrinkles on Art's face. He figured there must be at least one for every year the man had lived on Earth.

"Why did you do it?" Joe asked.

Cabassi shook his head. "I was just following everyone else, I guess."

"Did you know that Staples was going to . . . ?" Joe stopped, remembering the bullet moving like an arrow toward the black man's face.

Cabassi shook his head again. "I s'pect most of us knew what we was doing."

"Then . . ." Joe hesitated again. He took another shot from his glass.

"Why'd we do it?" Cabassi filled the younger man's glass again. "We did it 'cause we felt we were fighting for our family's survival. Joe, you was just a boy at the time. You never stayed

265

awake nights wondering if you could put food on your baby's plate."

"I have a child now."

"Yes, and now you're a company man." Cabassi looked down at his own big hands that were clasped in front of him on the bar.

"Does being a mine boss make me any less eager to feed my child?" Joe felt his face getting hot.

"No, just a lot easier."

It was the truth. He made good money now, nearly eight dollars a day, and he was able to work six days a week instead of just five. Behind his back, miners said the only reason he'd gotten promoted was because he was a Johnny Bull, but he knew plenty of workers from the British Isles who never got promoted. Joe knew that much of his success was that a long time ago he had followed Cabassi's advice and shot a grasshopper.

"I can't help it that I can speak English better than you wop dagos," Joe said. Somehow hurdling the insult made him feel better. He laughed, and so did Cabassi.

"You and I are family, Joe," Cabassi told him. "We're not related by the blood in our body but by the blood we have spilled for working men everywhere."

"Why tell me this now?" Joe asked.

"'Cause I need you by my side one more time." The old man looked Joe in the eyes. "I want you to help me kill a man."

<><><><><><>

Joe lay awake all that night staring up at the ceiling. Since Myrna had revealed that he slept with his eyes open, he didn't even try to shut them when she got up in the middle of the night to go to the outhouse. He was afraid that if he did close his eyes, he would see grasshoppers.

He rose before dawn the next morning and drove his car to

Mine Number Seven in Langley, then walked the last mile to the Villa Tavern. The sun was just beginning to pop up when he slipped in the back door.

Art Cabassi crouched between the bar and the window. Two shotguns and a pistol lay on the floor beside him.

"He said he'd be here at sunrise," Cabassi told Joe without taking his eyes off the wooded area next to the road. "I figure he'll park at the lake and walk here through those woods."

"You sure he'll be alone?" Joe asked.

"No, that's why you're here. Take that gun and get behind the bar. It's solid oak and should stop a cannonball."

"Art, I never—" Joe caught himself before he said he'd never fired a gun. He hoped Cabassi wouldn't tell him again to just shoot the grasshopper.

"You'll know what to do when the time comes," Cabassi told him. He jerked his head at a sound outside. "Looks like the time has come."

Joe quietly pulled one of the shotguns off the floor and assumed his position behind the bar. He kept his head down, listening to footsteps on the leaves outside. When he had walked toward the house, leaves had been scattered all across the wooded area and in the yard around the house. Cabassi must have raked the leaves there to provide a kind of alarm system.

The sound of footsteps moved slowly toward the front door, where they stopped. Then came three quiet knocks. Cabassi turned and motioned for Joe to stay put. He put one hand to an ear, then pointed at the back door. The old tavern owner stood, took the pistol in his right hand, and with his left opened the door.

"Good morning," said a man on the porch. "Glad to see you're up. Got the money?"

"Yes," Cabassi said. He kept his right hand with the pistol above his shoulder and hidden behind the door. "You say you'll come by once a month at the same time?"

"That's right," the man said as if he were a newspaper boy making a monthly collection. "As long as you pay you'll have protection and you can keep selling that homebrew you keep behind those milk cans. We'll make sure the cops and the feds leave you alone."

"And if I decide not to pay?" Cabassi said.

Joe heard the man on the porch make a sudden movement, followed by two loud gunshots. After the body fell there was a long moment of silence, then the sound of heavy steps running through the leaves toward the back door. Joe rose and aimed the shotgun at the entrance. When it burst open, he didn't hesitate. This time he had braced the gun firmly against his shoulder, but the explosion as he pulled the trigger echoed throughout the room. For a second time in his life, his ears rang from a gunshot.

The man who had come through the door was blasted all the way back into the grass.

"Good," Cabassi said as he took the shotgun out of Joe's hands and put it back on a set of hooks under the bar. "No blood inside to clean up."

For the next several seconds Cabassi ran around the inside of the tavern putting away the other guns. "I'll clean them when we get back," he said as he passed Joe and went outside.

Joe followed the tavern owner out the front door and with shaking hands struggled to light a cigarette.

Cabassi pushed a wheelbarrow toward the man lying on the ground. "Help me get him up."

Joe reluctantly took one arm and a leg and helped lift the body. When they had him lying on his back with his limp legs hanging over the front, Cabassi took the handles of the wheelbarrow and pushed it to the other side of the building.

The man Joe had killed lay on his back with his eyes wide open, his arms and legs flailed out to his side. It was eerily like a scene from twenty-nine years before. In fact, he realized it was twenty-nine years almost to the day. *I've only pulled a trigger twice in my whole life and two men are dead.*

They lifted this corpse in the same manner, flipping him over onto his stomach so they wouldn't have to look at his blood-soaked chest. Handing Joe two shovels, Cabassi wheeled the two bodies toward the woods and along a narrow path. Joe followed behind until the old man stopped to take a breather. Without a word, he took over the wooden posts of the wheelbarrow and followed behind Cabassi deeper into the woods. At last they came to a little clearing. The pile of dirt made Joe think of a similar scene on a ridge long ago.

"You've already dug their grave?"

"No, a well." Cabassi put his hands on his knees to catch his breath. "I had planned to build a cabin back here and dug the well first."

Joe looked down into the dark hole. Not seeing the bottom, he picked up a thick stick and dropped it in. After what seemed a long couple of seconds, he heard a splash. When Cabassi recovered, the old man went through the pockets of the two dead men and pulled out their wallets, two long pocket knives the likes of which Joe had never seen, a few papers, and another small gun. Joe then wheeled the barrow over to the edge of the hole, raised the handled end and dumped the two bodies down the well. The bodies made a much loader splash than the stick. Then they began filling the hole. It was close to noon by the time the work was done. Cabassi transplanted a little silver maple tree to mark the spot.

"Maybe when you're as old as me," Cabassi said, "you may take a notion to come sit under this tree and remember our adventures together."

Joe stared at Cabassi for a long time. Finally, he mumbled, "Not likely," and walked away.

<><><><><><>

Two months later, Art Cabassi died quietly in his sleep.

Everyone in the community wondered why he left instructions to be buried up on Williamsburg Hill way over in Shelby County. Few of the mourners at the church services were able to make the twenty-five mile trip to see the old man interned in the grave. Antonio, Angeline and Bullo rode in Joe's car with him. Myrna stayed home with one of her headaches.

The funeral procession followed the hearse up the steep hill. Bad memories leapt at Joe at every turn. They stopped at the ridge between the two gravel pits. The landscape had changed little in twenty-eight years. As far as Joe could tell, Art Cabassi had picked himself a spot right over the area where the Negro strikebreakers were buried. He walked over to the hole where his friend would rest and looked down, half expecting to see bones lying at the bottom of it.

Two headstones rested nearby—two other men who had been there that terrible day in 1898.

After Art Cabassi was laid to rest, Joe asked Antonio to drive them back to Taylorville. Bullo sat in front with his father and chatted the entire way. Angeline allowed Joe his space, and when he fell asleep with his eyes open, she softly shut them. Joe slept better during that thirty-five minute ride home than he had in twenty-eight years.

33.

Phelan's first attempts at crime organization had been a disaster. The two thugs he sent to shake down the tavern owners in Christian County had disappeared from the face of the earth. He tried to ally himself with his former partner's primary competition, Charlie Birger. The Shelton and Birger gangs were fighting a war throughout downstate Illinois that was as violent as anything in Chicago between Al Capone and Bugs Moran. Both sides used homemade armored cars to protect their rural home bases. After Shelton gang member Ora Thomas walked into a cigar store and shot it out with Glenn Young, leaving both men dead, the Ku Klux Klan virtually disappeared as an enemy of organized crime.

Birger helped Phelan get his small-time syndicate started, promising to set up shipments of bootleg liquor from Canada. But that association came to an abrupt ending when Birger was hung for one of the many murders he'd committed.

"Charlie was a joker all the way to the gallows," Phelan told Felina when he returned from the hanging in Benton, Illinois. "He said he wanted to be buried in a Catholic cemetery 'cause that's the last place the devil would look for a Jew."

"Well, what the hell are you going to do now?" Felina asked, not amused. She didn't even move from the chaise lounge to welcome her husband home. "I'm tired of driving that rusty old flivver, and I'm tired of living in this dump. Hell, you might as well be a coal miner for what little we have."

"*Coal miner?*" Phelan laughed. "I'll not be goin' in that hell hole again. The company is hiring men to protect the yards. That'll be the job for me until I get my own business going again. You'll have your fine home soon enough."

<><><><><><>

"All job sharing means is we'll all starve together," Joe told Antonio and Harley one evening as they lounged in the Vacca back yard. The argument had been ongoing for years. The Socialist Party, especially popular in the southern counties of Illinois, had been advocating redistribution of wealth.

"Not if the company pays workers what they're worth," Harley said. "They are making millions off your blood and sweat, and they've never worked a day in their lives."

"I guess you'd know about not working," Joe said. "Next thing we know you'll be wearing a red scarf around your neck like Sam used to."

Harley stood, his cheeks turning bright pink. He wanted to grab Joe by the shirt front and make the man see how much he'd done for the miners, but knew Joe would never accept it.

"I'm going to get some more sassafras tea," he said. "Anyone want anything?"

Joe looked away, but Antonio smiled and shook his head as Harley rose and went inside.

"That wasn't right, Joe," Antonio said when their friend was gone. "Harley has done more to help the miners than anyone."

"What's a man with his money care what happens to us?" Joe asked. "Why doesn't he just go to Cape Cod and vacation with his millionaire friends?"

"I don't think that he or Lena are comfortable around the wealthy," Antonio said. "He's a working man at heart."

"Well," Joe said, "I don't need him telling me what the working man needs."

"They'll be laying another hundred hand-loaders off next month," Antonio said. He coughed hard into a small, white towel.

Joe noticed the black stains on the cloth. He wished his

friend would take the job he offered him above ground as rock picking boss. At least that would get him away from the dust.

"Half the coal is being mined by cutting and loading machines," Joe said. "If you want to keep working in the mines, you'd better learn how to run a machine."

Antonio leaned back in his wicker chair and looked up. The big oak trees provided a beautiful green ceiling to the yard. Joe was right. He and Vinnie could no longer compete with Bullo and his machines. He raised his glass and took a long sip of homemade wine.

"Joe," Antonio said slowly, "look how many man have been injured from the machines. The company doesn't care about you if you get hurt. They give you a small compensation and a pat on the back as they send you out the door."

Joe couldn't argue with that. When the cutting machine ripped through Bullo's boot and took the toenail off his big toe and the boy missed work for almost a week, all the machine boss told him was that if it happened again he'd be fired.

"Even John L. Lewis said you can't stop progress," Joe said. "He knows that if the United Mine Workers are going to survive, they have to adapt. Unemployment is up and wages are down."

"Everything's getting so specialized," Antonio said, his eyes distant. "I used to be responsible for my own safety. Now I have to rely on timber men, shot firers, and trackmen. If they don't do their job right, I'm the one gets killed."

"Augustus Ware put Poison Corso in charge of the timbering at the Langley mine," Joe said to change the subject. His right eyebrow arched. "It seems Ware and Ada Corso have become good friends."

"Is that why Poison always get overtime on the dirt gang?" Antonio asked. Clearing tracks of coal that had fallen out of bouncing boxcars was extra money on idle days.

"They say when Poison gets the shaft," Joe said, a wry smile on his face, "it means Ware is in the hole."

Antonio milled that around in his head for a few seconds.

Then he almost fell out of his chair laughing.

<><><><><><>

Later that afternoon, the men went into town. Angie Eng spent her sixteenth birthday in the Vacca's shady backyard visiting with Mary Kate and Sam. While she thought of Angeline as her aunt, these two were her surrogate cousins. The three girls lounged in a couple's swing that had two double seats facing one another.

Nearby, little Sid sat in a sandbox playing with his wooden soldiers as he sang his favorite song. "See my pony, jet black pony, I ride him each day." He only stopped singing when his cousin Willie shouted at him to start counting.

"One, two, three..." shouted little Sid in a slow cadence.

On the other side of the yard, Tony heeled their black Shetland pony named Coal to a full gallop toward his older brother, who stood crouching like a lion on the ground. As Tony circled Coal in a short turn, Willie grabbed the back of the saddle and swung on behind his brother. The boys rode double at full gallop back to the starting point.

"Eleven, twelve seconds!" Sid shouted as he jumped up and clapped his little hands as loud as he could. Dropping back onto his sandy bottom he resumed singing and playing.

Willie slid off the rump of the pony before Tony reined it to a full stop.

"You gotta turn him closer to me!" Willie yelled at his brother.

"He's shyin' away from ya cause you look like a mountain lion all scrunched up like that!" Tony shouted back.

"*Boys!*" Mary Kate warned from her seat in the swing.

Giving his brother an angry glare, Willie jogged back to his pick up point to try the pick-up race again.

"Sam," Angie said as they resumed their conversation, "how did you know that Vinnie was the one you wanted to marry?"

"Ah, heck," Sam said in her hill folk slang that Angie adored, "I reckon I was pretty ignorant of boys when I met Vinnie. We were just pards for 'bout a year before I saw that he looked better'n most men. I remember the first time I took notice was one day when we was fishing and he caught a pike. Now a pike's a junk fish, you know, and most men would have just cut its head off and thrown it away, but Vinnie released it back into the water as gentle as he would an undersized catch. I asked him why he didn't just kill it and he told me he figured everything's got a right to live. Right after that I started feeling real funny whenever he'd brush up against me."

When Sam looked away into the canopy provided by the green oak trees, Angie and Mary Kate glanced at one another and smiled. The mountain gal had taught them both to enjoy fishing and wading out into the pond to skip stones on the water. Angie's mother told her that Sam's influence on her mother-in-law was nothing short of remarkable. Everyone in the Vacca family, including Angeline, always tried everything that Sam proposed, from eating frog legs to cooking with possum fat. If anyone had any reservations about these hillbilly dishes, they didn't express them. Sam was the quietest of the Vacca women and only spoke when spoken to, accepting hugs graciously, but like Vinnie never venturing to offer one.

"Sam," Angie said, "did you really shoot one of the Shelton gangsters when they tried to rob the Kincaid Bank?"

"Nah," Sam chuckled, "not unless I got him with a ricochet. He was on the other side of the automobile. I'd s'pect the grocer shot him. There were a lot of us firin' at 'em that day. I guess those hoodlums learned not to mess with Christian County. It's too bad the court let 'em go."

Sam looked away again and Angie could tell she wanted to change the subject.

"I'll bet Bullo was as suave as Rudolph Valentino when he started courting you," Angie said.

"Oh, no," Mary Kate said, "Bullo was the clumsiest boy I

ever saw. He nearly knocked me down twice the day we met."

"Then why did you start seeing him?" Angie asked.

"Because he didn't try to be something he wasn't," Mary Kate said. "Antonio Vacca taught his sons to work, and Angeline Vacca taught them the importance of family."

"I remember Filberto and Libero," Angie said. "They used to protect me from Felina."

"I didn't get to know them very well before they died," Mary Kate said, "but I remember how lost Filberto was when Libero passed. I like to think they're together right now playing kick-the-can."

<><><><><><>

While the girls celebrated Angie's birthday, Bullo and Vinnie snuck out to the picture show. Their wives had been begging them to take them to see *The Jazz Singer*, the first picture with synchronized talking, but the brothers wanted to watch it together as a private tribute to Filberto and Libero.

"Filberto had it right, didn't he?" Vinnie said when they took their seats in the little schoolhouse where the film would be projected onto a white sheet nailed to the wall. "I remember I made fun of him for saying there would someday be talking pictures."

"I'll bet he would have been another Thomas Edison," Bullo said, glad that the room was dark enough to hide his tears. "Of course, he would have made Libero his assistant."

The movie began like most silent films, with captions for dialogue. Mrs. Foster, the school marm, played background music on an organ as she followed the action on the screen. Old Mrs. Foster was the most popular movie accompanist in Christian county. She not only played the music provided by the movie studio, she also improvised her own sound effects with drums, cymbals and a variety of other percussion instruments. Her flourishes heightened the drama, comedy and romance on the movie screen. She was most famous for her ability to almost perfectly create the sound of galloping horses using nothing more than two-by-four pieces of lumber.

The famous, black-faced singer, Al Jolson, played the jazz singer, a young man who defies his Jewish father and goes out into the world to become a cabaret singer. Fifteen minutes into the film, Mrs. Foster moved away from her organ and became a spectator as the first sound came to the screen. Jolson stood in front of a cabaret crowd and sang, "Dirty Hands, Dirty Face." Immediately following this song were the first words ever heard spoken in a film.

Jolson looked straight into the camera and said, "Wait a minute, wait a minute, you ain't heard nothin' yet. Wait a minute, I tell ya, you ain't heard nothin'. You wanna hear Toot, Toot, Tootsie? All right. Hold on. Hold on. Lou, listen. Play Toot, Toot, Tootsie—three choruses, you understand? In the third chorus, I whistle. Now give it to 'em hard and heavy. Go right ahead."

The music from the next song was completely drowned out as many of the men and women attending the Taylorville film jumped out of their seats and began cheering and hugging. Bullo and Vinnie rose with the others, but instead of shouting they just looked at one another and laughed until tears came to their eyes. This moment was for Filberto and Libero.

34

Lena Eng thought of the 1920s as the crazy years. By the end of October, 1929, as the decade came to a close, she hoped for the "return to normalcy" that the late President Harding had promised. The world was changing so fast she was beginning to feel she couldn't keep up. Automobiles, pictures with sound, and now radio seemed to dominate every minute of her life. Kids were acting crazier than ever with their music and dance, while many Bible thumpers were saying the decadence meant the end of the world was near.

The only piece of technology that Lena truly liked was her telephone. She and Angeline had developed a morning and afternoon ritual of calling each other to chat for as long as those on their party line would allow before rudely telling them to get off the phone and give other people a chance.

These calls were mostly carried on in Italian so the eavesdroppers wouldn't understand. The ability to communicate easily by telephone made the two women closer than ever, despite their differences in social standing.

That social standing became even less prevalent on October 29, 1929. Lena would tell Angeline later that she knew her husband was in trouble, because he had held her close to him that entire night. At four o'clock Wednesday morning, after leaving her side, Harley Eng snuck quietly out of the bedroom, dressed in the kitchen, packed a dinner bucket and drove his Chevy the three miles to Number Nine Mine in Langley.

When the mine boss, George Howsham, saw Harley standing at his office door wearing bib overalls, he knew immediately what he was up to.

"Well, well, I told people I didn't figure you for a suicide like all those other millionaires," Howsham said matter-of-factly. "How much'd you lose?"

"All of it, I guess," Harley said. "But I got a strong back, if not a weak mind. Think you could use a rock picker?"

"Planning on startin' at the top, are ya?"

"I'll start wherever you tell me to," Harley said. "I got a family to support."

"So does everyone else in this town," Howsham said flatly. He didn't appreciate Harley Eng taking the loss of his entire fortune so lightly. When Howsham lost all of his savings in that week's stock market crashes, he considered leaving his nagging wife and spoiled kids and hitting the tracks for Chicago. Now, the wealthiest man in the county walked into his office and offered to sit at a table with children and pick rock out of the coal for less than three dollars a day. Howsham was ready to throw the man out of his office.

"George," Harley said, looking in Howsham's eyes. "I'll do what I have to do to take care of my family."

Howsham had seen that look in the eyes of many men who asked him for a job. They were his biggest weakness and he hated himself for it. Now this man, who had been a millionaire just a few days before, was looking at him with the same hungry, sincere eyes that had been haunting his dreams since he'd become a mine boss.

"We're looking for mine safety inspectors," Howsham said. "You've got some knowledge in that area, but you'll need some basic experience as a miner before you take classes. I'll start you out as a trip rider assistant. You look quick enough, but I'm going to make you sign a paper that you don't get compensated if you lose a finger or hand."

"I've already got a Chevy," Harley said, smiling. The miner's expression, "Lose a finger and buy a Chevy with the compensation," was small recompense if you were also fired.

<><><><><><>

He worked that day with an Italian trip rider named Emilio Macchiarolo, nicknamed "Top Hat." Everyone in the mines had a handle, and Top Hat quickly christened Harley with the unflattering nickname "Drugstore." Drugstore Cowboys were what miners called Americans who thought they were better than foreigners. Hoping the nickname didn't stick, Harley kept his mouth shut and tried to concentrate on the tricky business at hand.

He tried to disguise his inexperience from the rest of the men, but Top Hat wouldn't hear of it. The two followed fourteen others onto the cage for the ride down into the mine. There were two bars; each man put one hand on the bar while holding his dinner bucket in the other. He thought of the seventh cage he had missed at Cherry back in '09. His moment had finally arrived.

"We've got a new man going down!" Top Hat shouted to the engineer running the cage. "Cut the rope!"

As the elevator floor seemingly dropped out from under him, Harley dropped his dinner bucket and grabbed the bar with both hands. For several terrifying moments they were plunged into total darkness as the cage went down deeper and deeper into the ground. Harley knew that a solid wall of rock was passing swiftly just inches from his shoulder. If he moved he might brush up against it and scrape away the flesh right to the bone.

Finally, the cage began to slow its descent, and just as quickly as they had started, it stopped. They were on the bottom. At first Harley could only see a few flickers of electric lights and shadows moving about. Then the men who arrived with him began lighting carbide lamps and putting them on their canvas caps. He had trouble lighting his own, and after several clumsy attempts, Top Hat helped him.

When his eyes finally grew accustomed to the dim light, he

picked up his dinner bucket. The shaking of the cage during the descent had bounced the bucket against the rock wall, causing the clasp to break. The lid had popped open and the two sandwiches he had wrapped in paper had fallen out, to be trampled on by the exiting miners. He picked up a bruised apple and his jar of water, and put them back in the bucket.

"It'll be a long time till supper," Top Hat said with a chuckle.

While Top Hat loved to boss and criticize, he was also a good teacher. By midday, Harley was able to ride between two coal cars weighing three tons apiece, jump off while they were still moving, slip a coupling pin in the link, and get his hands out before the two heavy cars smashed into each other.

"Don't be too proud of yourself just yet," Top Hat told Harley while the newcomer was devouring his apple at lunchtime. "Beginners rarely get squeezed. It's usually when you get more experienced and become careless that you get a collarbone broke or lose a finger. I got squeezed one time and it made a believer out of me. My boss said, 'I told you about coupling on the inside of a turn.' By golly, he kicked me in the butt while I was still caught between those cars. I missed work for a week, but I sure did learn from that experience and coupled a lot faster from then on."

<><><><><><>

When Harley got home that night, his clothes were covered with coal dust, having forgotten to take something to change into after work. The job had taken every bit of concentration he had just so he could finish the day without an injury. This was complicated by the resentment from timber men and tracklayers who had been waiting for months and sometimes years for a job as a higher paying trip rider.

Though he had cleaned up at the washhouse when he came out of the shaft, Harley drew himself a bath and sank slowly up to his ears in the hot water. He was lying that way, feeling the soreness throughout his body, thinking that he had to go back down in that damned hell-hole again in just a few hours. He was just about ready to cry when he felt his wife's hands reach into the water and start massaging his legs.

"Angeline says she does this for Antonio when he has a bad day," Lena said.

"I don't know how that man ever had strength enough to sire four sons," Harley said. With her one touch he immediately felt his responsibilities overriding his self-pity.

Lena ran her hands up her man's body to his upper torso. She let her fingers knead his flesh in the same motion as she did her bread dough: deep into the skin of his chest and shoulders.

Harley loved his wife more deeply at that moment than ever before. He had to take care of her and the children. She deserved to have happiness and security. Before going to bed the night before, he had placed his life insurance policy in a dresser drawer where she would find it if something happened to him. On his way to the mine that morning, he had pushed his car to the max on Langley Road, trying to get the courage to ram it into a tree. The courage never came, and he found himself standing in George Howsham's office, begging to work alongside sixteen-year old boys picking rock.

Lena bent forward across the tub and kissed him on the wounds he had suffered that day in the mine. She lifted his left hand gently to her mouth and kissed each blister with an open mouth. Then she kissed his wedding ring and let a tear fall onto it.

"I want a new house," Lena said, her mouth still on his hand.

"*What?*" Harley thought he must not have heard her correctly.

"I want what Angeline has." Lena looked in his eyes. "I want a little home where you can't get away from me. I want a home where I can see you from every room. I want a home where we have to make love quietly on the floor because the children are in the next room. Oh, darling, I don't want other women cleaning my house and telling everyone in town all my secrets. I just want it to be you and me for the rest of our days, happy and together until the end. Please, please, for once give me what I want and not what you want me to have."

Harley sat with his teeth clenched. Finally he said. "Lena, this house is paid for and we would never get what its worth, not after the runs on the banks this week."

"Augustus Ware wants to buy it. I talked to his wife today." Lena brushed his hair with her hand. "He won't give us much, but it will be enough that you won't have to work in the coal mine."

"*No!*" Harley shouted and set up so suddenly Lena jumped back. "I want to work in the mine!"

His words surprised himself as much as they did his wife, but despite his thoughts of a few moments before, he was certain that he meant it.

"I need to work in the mine," he said more quietly, reaching out a hand to her. "That is what I need for me. I can't explain it, but now that I can work because I want to and not because I have to, it feels good. For once in my life to go to bed exhausted knowing that I did an honest day's work. . ." He hesitated. "That feels so good, Lena." He pulled his wife close and stroked her hair. "Do you understand? Maybe I'm going nuts, but it feels good to be like everyone else."

"No darling, I do understand." Lena hugged her husband's head. "That is how I feel about our little house."

A week later the Eng's moved out of their six bedroom, two and a half bath mansion and into a two bedroom home with a pump well outside. The only improvement they made to the estate was to build a two-seater outhouse. That way there could be no room where Harley could get away from Lena.

35

For over a year, the Eng family struggled to make ends meet as the recession turned into a depression that devastated the United States, as well as much of the world. Families and friends banded together to survive the terrible days that seemed to get worse almost every day. Out-of-work men traveled the country in search of jobs so they could send money home to their families.

December of 1930 found Angeline and Lena standing in the cold winter air at the Union Miner's Cemetery in Mt. Olive, Illinois, their husbands' arms wrapped around them. Automobiles lined every country road for miles. Somewhere in the audience of fifteen thousand were Bullo, Mary Kate, Vinnie and Sam. Rather than risk losing them in the crowd, the children had been left at home with Angie. People came from all over the country to see the great woman who was now being buried alongside the four miners who had died years ago at the Virden Massacre of 1898.

Rev. John Maguire's voice was carried by loudspeakers to the thousands of mourners: "Wealthy coal operators and capitalists throughout the United States are breathing sighs of relief while toil-worn men and women are weeping tears of bitter grief. The reason for this contrast of relief and sorrow is apparent. Mother Jones is dead."

"She had a small, frail body," Rev. Maguire continued, "but she had a great and indomitable spirit. She was relatively uneducated, but she had a flaming tongue. She was poor, but she had a great blazing love for the poor, the downtrodden and the oppressed. She was without influence but she had a mother's heart great enough to embrace the weak and defenseless babes of the world."

After the service, the two couples waited in line for two hours to get a chance to say goodbye to the Miner's Angel.

"I don't know if the United Mine Workers will survive without her," a miner from West Virginia told Antonio and Harley as they shivered in the cold. "A lot of miners are starting to show support for the company. It kinda makes sense. At least it gives us some security."

"Isn't that like living at home with your parents?" Lena said.

"What?" The miner looked at Lena as if he had just seen her.

"I mean, if you don't feel you are grown up enough to make decisions for yourself," Lena said. "I guess if you live at home with your parents and have them think for you when you're grown, you'd have a pretty easy life. You wouldn't have to think at all, would you?"

"Where I come from," the miner said, his face turning red, "women know how to hold their tongue."

"Sir, I meant no offense," Lena said quietly. "I was just quoting the woman whose life you have been standing here waiting to celebrate."

The miner studied Lena's face. Several minutes passed in silence. Finally, he extended his hand to her. "I met Mother Jones twenty years ago at the Westmoreland Strike. She gave me a good talking to, much as you just did. If we men are going to win this thing, I figure we're gonna need women like you backing us up."

"How about instead of backing you up," Lena said as she accepted his hand, "we fight alongside you?"

<><><><><><>

The spring of 1931 brought forth another opportunity for the United Mine Workers to remedy one more injustice.

"I'm not buying that damned health insurance!" Antonio's hands moved in perfect synchronization with his mouth.

"You have to buy it," Joe argued. He had never seen his friend so angry. "You need to accept the fact that Peabody Coal Company wants miners to be protected. Get it through that thick dago skull of yours. The company is not the enemy."

"I have protection!" Antonio shouted. "If I get hurt working, the mine company has to pay my expenses. It's the law."

"But you're not always *in* the mine!" Joe shouted back in a manner that only a close friend can get away with. "What if you fall and break your leg while walking down the street, or what if that cough of yours gets worse?"

"I'm only forty-eight years old," Antonio said. "I don't get sick. And besides, all miner's cough. It goes with the territory."

Joe threw up his hands. He had expected problems like this when he became the mine boss, but not from his best friend. Since Mother Jones died, the union members, especially Antonio, had been looking for a way to test their strength.

"If the company wants to do me a favor," Antonio said, "they can insure our wives and children. Then maybe I'll consider their insurance."

<><><><><><>

Antonio waited until the last men had descended the cage for the day. He walked to the center of the entry room with his dinner bucket and raised it above his head. Slowly, every eye in the dark room turned toward him. The face boss, knowing immediately what the Italian was up to, stepped back onto the cage with a frown. Antonio very slowly turned his dinner bucket over.

"What's he doing?" a young miner asked.

"If the water stays in the air," the boy's father told him, "we go to work."

Water trickled from the container and fell, as water will,

splattering onto the ground.

"Throw out the water, boys," Antonio said, "we're going home."

The men in the mine didn't even ask why. When Antonio Vacca said they were going home, they knew there had to be a good reason. The company had been pushing the miners hard for a long while. Dropping their picks and shovels where they stood, they picked up their dinner buckets and began loading back onto the cage alongside the disgusted face boss.

When the first load of men filed out of the elevator at the surface, they walked straight up to Joe Harrison, who stood with a pit committeeman studying a worksheet. One at a time the miners opened their dinner buckets and dumped their drinking water on the ground at his feet.

Antonio was the last to walk past Joe.

"Damn wop," Joe quietly said to his friend, "you've done it now."

<><><><><><>

That afternoon, Antonio drove to Tovey. He wanted to catch the miners as they came off work. If he could convince them to go along with the wildcat strike, he thought the other Peabody mines in Tovey and Langley would follow suit.

The mine yard stood on a small hill just beyond a street with long rows of company owned houses. As Antonio drove between the houses, he was thankful that the mine in Hewittville did not have company houses. Every one of them was exactly the same. Small, white, two bedroom homes with no porch to sit on, no shade trees, and barely enough room in the yard for the children to play, much less plant a garden. And the miners were paying far too much to live there. They would never be able to save enough money to purchase their own place because the company kept them in debt, not only with the houses, but by requiring them to buy goods from the high-priced company store. Now Peabody was adding to all this by forcing them to purchase health insurance they didn't want or need.

By the time he entered the mine yard, his blood was boiling. The first person he saw as Jerry Milner, the mine boss, standing on the steps to the main office smoking a pipe. When Milner spied Antonio, he opened the office door and said something to those inside. Four security men walked quickly out and stepped in front of the Italian.

"Ware wants to see you," the largest of the four men said.

"I figured he might," Antonio said and followed the big man. The other three walked behind, shutting the door when they were in the building.

Augustus Ware sat behind his desk, sorting through a stack of papers. The men escorted Antonio to a row of four wooden chairs, then took two steps backwards, blocking the door. After several silent moments, Ware signed his name at the bottom of a paper, stuck it in a file folder and looked up. There was little expression on his rotund face.

"I can't tell you what to do," Ware said, "but I strongly advise you to buy the health insurance that we are offering."

Antonio knew better than to say anything. He knew the thugs were for intimidation. Several of the workers in the mine yard had seen him being escorted into the office. Still, he would need to tell Bullo and Vinnie to tread carefully until this was all over.

A knock sounded at the office door. The four thugs looked at their boss, who continued to lock eyes with Antonio. A second, much louder knock echoed through the room. The mine boss nodded at one of the men, who opened the door.

The men in the office looked out the door. Fifty union miners stood outside. The union men didn't need to say a word. Antonio turned and walked out of the office, passing the miners silently. Each man he passed took his lunch bucket and dumped the water on the ground.

Sixteen Tons

When he left the mine yard, Joe Harrison walked toward him. Joe motioned for him to follow and walked around to the east side of the mine. A long, dirt area lay between the mine and the nearest houses. The two moved slowly as they talked.

"This ain't your mine." Antonio said quietly."

"I drove over here to try and talk some sense to you," Joe said. "Tell me what it is you're tryin' to accomplish."

Antonio picked up a long strand of grass and put it between his teeth. "Remember when the old miners used to call us sounders, Joe? We understood we were responsible for our own safety in the mines. Well, we still are. Now they are bringing in these machines, and I've heard talk they want to replace even more workers.

Joe listened, saying nothing.

"In the old days, we used to let the dust settle by blasting before we went home. Now the dust is worse than ever with all these infernal contraptions. Men don't have time to sound the tops 'cause they have to worry about losing fingers or even a hand in the machines. No, sir, give me back the days when I was teased for being a sounder. A wildcat strike wouldn't have gone this far if other miners and the UMW weren't behind me. We can't let the company take our money and give us nothing in return."

"What is it that you want?" Joe asked.

"If we have to pay for health insurance, then our wives and children should be included." Antonio drew a line in the dirt with his foot, then turned and walked back to be with the miners.

Joe shook his head. He looked at the line that Antonio had drawn, a sign as clear to him as a cross on a church. He turned away and went back to the company office.

<><><><><><>

The strike lasted almost a month and closed all four

Peabody-owned mines in the county. When workers at seven other Peabody mines in Illinois also threatened to strike, the company proposed a compromise.

A knock sounded at Antonio Vacca's door. When he opened the door, a small, bespectacled, middle-aged man wearing a brown suit and tie stood there. The man looked familiar.

"Do you remember me, Antonio? I'm RJ Hiler. I met you in Kentucky some fourteen years ago," the man said, extending his hand. "I'm sorry to disturb you so late. May I speak to you for a moment?"

Antonio took Hiler's hand and shook it warmly. "Of course I remember you. Rolfe. You saved my life. In fact, I wrote you after Ludlow. I remember you were headed that way and I wanted to see if you had come out of there all right. I guess you never got the letter. How's your wife? Carmela, wasn't it?"

Hiler turned his face toward the wall. "She died at Ludlow, Antonio."

"I'm so sorry." Antonio didn't know what to say. "I liked her."

"I understand that it's because of your efforts I am here," Hiler continued, "and I wanted yours to be the first hand I shake in this community. I have been hired as the new company doctor."

Antonio stared at the man. Representatives of the United Mine Workers had been meeting with the company that evening, but he hadn't expected this to be the result.

"Come in, Rolfe." Antonio offered his wife's rocking chair next to the fireplace. Angeline came in from the kitchen, her arms and apron speckled with flour.

"I go by RJ, now, Antonio." Dr. Hiler smiled warmly.

Hiler's mouth dropped open when he looked at Angeline. Antonio suddenly remembered how much Angeline looked like the doctor's late wife, Carmela.

"Mrs. Vacca," RJ said after an awkward pause. "I'd love for you to join us."

Angeline looked at her husband, and he nodded. She took

Antonio's rocking chair, leaving him to sit on the couch.

"Our friend Harley Eng speaks very highly of you," Angeline said. "Antonio and I didn't know that you were the Rolfe Hiler who saved his life in Kentucky."

"I can speak just as highly of Harley," RJ said. "He would've made a mighty fine doctor."

"He's training right now to become a mine safety inspector," Antonio said.

"Then I can guarantee," RJ said, "that he will find ways to make your mines less dangerous."

"Will you be tending to the miners, Doctor?" Angeline asked.

"That's what I wanted to discuss with you and Antonio. The reason the union decided to accept the health insurance is because the company went along with Joe Harrison's suggestion to have me also treat the wives and children of the miners."

Antonio and Angeline exchanged glances.

"That was originally your idea, I understand," Hiler said.

Antonio leaned forward. "How can one doctor take care of all the workers and their families in a community with four coal mines?"

"I can't," Hiler admitted, "but they gave me an automobile, and I plan on setting up a regular circuit with home visits to the really bad cases."

"Rolfe, I mean RJ, at least one miner gets hurt every day in one of our mines," Antonio said with a look of skepticism.

"That's why I wanted to meet your wife," Hiler said, looking at Angeline. "My dear, I am going to train wives to deal with as many medical problems as possible. Most of you already have midwife skills, but I want the ladies in your community to know how to treat other injuries. I have studied several mine disasters, and I have some ideas that I believe will help if there is, God forbid, an emergency."

"God forbid," Angeline said and crossed herself.

"I know it's a big task," RJ said, "and I don't expect to be able to solve all your problems, but there is one advantage to agreeing to this proposal."

Antonio and Angeline waited for the little man to finish.

"You'll have one more person on your side who is looking after your interests."

36

"Miners go on strike every summer," Myrna told her husband. "Is this a joke?"

Joe scarfed down his breakfast as quickly as he could. Hot oatmeal was the one food his wife hadn't found a way to ruin, and he wanted to eat it in peace. The coffee was weak but he refrained from comment.

"No, it's not a joke. Mines slowdown in the summer because coal isn't needed as much in the hot months. That's when the union negotiates their contracts. I tell you that every year."

"You should just hire strikebreakers and fire the ones who don't want to work," Myrna said. She put a bare foot across her knee and began picking at a toenail. "Well, what is it they want now?"

"Illinois miners make more than in other states," Joe said. "The coal companies want to lower wages across our state."

"I've told you for years that those miners get paid too much," Myrna said. "Why don't you just get more machines and get rid of the men?"

"We have already got rid of half the men," Joe said, "but someone still has to operate the machines."

"I wish you'd get a machine to operate the machines." Myrna put her foot down and raised the other one. "Do you think I like listening to you complain every spring?"

Joe took one last swallow of watery coffee and hurried out of the house.

<><><><><><>

As Bullo rolled on the ground from a punch to his jaw, it occurred to Vinnie that he had not had a fistfight with Bullo since they were kids. The older brother immediately rose to one knee and wiped his bleeding mouth.

"This is my house and you're not gonna stop me from leavin' it," Bullo said, breathing deeply. "Being able to knock me down doesn't make you right, Vinnie."

"I'd rather knock you down than disgrace our family!" Vinnie said, his fists clenched. "I'm not going to let you cross that picket line!"

"You and Papa are wrong," Bullo said, rising to his feet. "You can't stop the machines from taking over the mines."

"It's not just about the *machines*," Vinnie said, his voice growing louder. "The company don't have to lower our wages by over a dollar a day!"

"The country is in a depression!" Bullo shouted, waving his hands almost as much as his father. "Illinois miners get paid more than any miners in the nation. We have to take a cut so we can compete with other states that sell coal."

"How much of a cut in profits are the owners taking?" Vinnie yelled back. "Why do those of us who risk our lives have to be the only ones to take a loss?"

"The UMW is against you," Bullo said in a voice that was suddenly slow and deliberate. "John L. Lewis is against you. Hell, the whole town's against you, Vinnie. If you men try to organize a new union, there's going to be bloodshed."

"We're going to Springfield to give the UMW one more chance to hear us out," Vinnie replied in a strained attempt to be equally calm. "We will only accept a pay decrease if they also cut us to six hours a day and hire on a second shift of workers."

"They will never agree with your socialist ideas," Bullo said. "You're fighting a lost cause."

"Were the miners fighting a lost cause at Ludlow, Bullo? How about Matewan or Blair Mountain?"

"Those were different circumstances," Bullo said, then

changed tactics. "Both sides thought they were right in the American Civil War, too. It caused brother to fight against brother and father against son. Vinnie, this is our civil war. We each have to do what we think is right and respect each other's decisions even if we don't agree."

"If you strike break," Vinnie said slowly, "and take food off my family's plate, I will treat you like any other dirty scab. I'll shoot you myself if I have to."

For a long moment Bullo stared at his brother. Finally, he opened a drawer to the China cabinet, took out a pistol and thrust it under his belt. The screen door double slammed behind him as he left the house.

<><><><><><>

Joe Harrison looked down at the forty-five-caliber pistol in his hand and then at the strange scene before him. The hard road coming in from Springfield was lined with corn stalk torches that filled the night air with a yellowish smoke. Sheriff Watson and over two hundred well-armed deputies stood near three police cars, their lights shining in the distance. Behind that first blockade was a second row of vehicles, providing cover for over one thousand of the city defenders. Men with rifles lay sprawled across many of the cars, waiting.

The blood lust of the men surrounding Joe did not seem as great as it had been back in '98. This was not an ambush, these were merchants, clerks, bankers and lawyers. He doubted their resolve if trouble started. He also hoped the miners returning from their UMW meeting in Springfield would have second thoughts about shooting their friends and neighbors.

Though thousands of miners had shown their solidarity by gathering at the state arsenal in Springfield, the Illinois President of the United Mine Workers vetoed their request for support of their wildcat strike. The miners immediately declared they would quit the UMW and form a new union. The kingdom of the mine workers was now sharply divided. Those in favor of forming a new union agreed to meet in Taylorville for an organizational rally.

"They're comin'!" a young boy yelled from the top of a telephone pole.

Joe's stomach somersaulted. The boy reminded him too much of himself as a young man with his ear pressed against a railroad track.

Men who had been sitting stood as one. There was suddenly a great deal of talk as a caravan of car and truck lights could be seen snaking along the hard road toward Taylorville. Sheriff Watson jumped onto the back of a flatbed truck and shouted for the crowd to get quiet. In front of him, Kieran Phelan waved his rifle like a flag. A moment later, the only sound was the crickets and cicadas. Even the air was suddenly still, with the smoke from the lighted corn stalk shucks hovering above heads like a low cloud.

"No one is to talk except me!" Watson shouted. "Anyone who interferes or fires a shot will be arrested. Just to prevent an accident, no one is to cock a gun or even place a finger on a trigger. *Ya' all understand that?*"

Heads nodded, and many of those around Joe took a collective swallow. Others spat tobacco juice and wiped their mouths with shirtsleeves.

The lead car in the caravan pulled up and stopped fifty yards from the first barricade. For a moment, there was only the sound of brakes squealing, followed by car doors slamming. It took ten minutes for the last of the miners to leave their vehicles and join the formation that extended far out into bean fields on either side of the road. While the group easily numbered over fifteen hundred, few of the men carried firearms.

"Evenin', Antonio," Sheriff Watson said with a smile.

"What's goin' on here, Howard?" Antonio Vacca asked, not returning the smile.

"We're told you men plan to hold a conference here to

organize a strike against your union's advice," Watson said. "We want you to know that we support the United Mine Workers in Christian County."

An angry murmuring arose from the miners.

"John L. Lewis sold us out, Howard!" Antonio said in a loud but calm voice. The miners behind him grew quiet again. "We voted down the wage reduction proposal, but the union and the company banded together and stole the ballots. Now Lewis declares a state of emergency and we have no one to represent us. We aim to be heard."

The miners gave a loud shout of approval.

Phelan raised his rifle to his waist. Hundreds of men facing the unarmed miners did the same.

"Steady, men!" Joe Harrison told those nearest him. "Remember what the sheriff said. Don't touch those triggers."

Seeing Phelan's weapon was in direct line with Antonio's chest, Joe began moving slowly through the crowd toward his son-in-law.

"We don't want any trouble here," Sheriff Watson said. "Maybe it would be a good idea for you to just move your meeting elsewhere."

Antonio turned his back to the sheriff and spoke in a low voice to his fellow officers.

Phelan also whispered to a few of his men. One of them turned and nodded toward a car. The man in the backseat raised a wide-barreled gun. It was a weapon that shot tear gas bombs.

As Antonio turned back toward the sheriff after his conference, Phelan again casually pointed his rifle barrel toward the Italian.

"I'm right behind you," Joe whispered in his son-in-law's ear. "If any shots are fired, so help me, I'll blow your damned brains out."

Phelan lowered his gun.

"We'll set up our meeting on some land that old man Reese

is letting us use," Antonio told the sheriff. "There would be nothing illegal about that. It's just outside the city limits."

Watson took a deep breath, as did several other Taylorville defenders. The sheriff looked at Antonio and nodded. He motioned for his men to go home. The confrontation was over as quickly as it had begun.

The miners walked back to their vehicles, got in and began jerking them forward and backwards to turn them around on the narrow hard road. As Joe watched the lights from the miners' cars veer off the paved road and onto the various dirt roads around the town to the east, he felt his son-in-law's presence near him.

"You're a traitor to the company," Phelan hissed.

"And you're nothing but a cold-blooded killer," Joe said. "I'd better never catch you trying to instigate an ambush like that again."

"Oh, yeah?" Phelan said with a sneer. "I've heard that you've got some pretty good experience at ambushing. Or are you only a brave man when confronting unarmed niggers?"

Joe was so startled he felt as if his knees were about to buckle out from under him. No one except Art Cabassi had ever mentioned that bloody day. Even the men who had helped him develop his mining craft during his youth had remained silent on the episode, though many of them had been on Williamsburg Hill in '98.

"You'd better decide which side you're on, fella," Phelan said. "I'm bringing in boys from down south and some even tougher ones from Chicago."

"Thugs like you?" Joe kept his eyes locked on Phelan's.

"The war is about to begin, buddy boy." Phelan laughed. "You'd better stay out of the way."

<><><><><><>

"Just because those company thugs stole the ballots doesn't

mean you can't be heard," Lena Eng shouted to the men and women gathered in the open field. "Remember what Mother Jones said. You don't need a vote to raise hell. All you need are convictions and a voice."

"Well, Mother Jones ain't here!" an old miner from Gillespie named Homer Keel yelled, "and we don't need no dames telling us what to do, neither."

A roar erupted from the crowd with a thousand men shouting either in favor or against the old man's comment. Antonio Vacca climbed on top of a big tree stump and raised his hands for quiet. Several men carrying torches came and stood around him so everyone's attention would be focused on the Italian. Still, it took five minutes for the crowd to quiet.

"Homer," Antonio said in a voice he hoped sounded calm but loud enough to carry across the field, "I have to disagree with you on that point. I believe Mother Jones *is* here. Most everyone gathered in this field was at her funeral, and I sense that we all carried a part of her spirit away with us that day."

Many men removed their hats and nodded in agreement.

"Now we're going to need to keep that great lady close to our hearts in the difficult days ahead," Antonio said, remembering the lesson he had learned from Rolfe Hiler during his brief time as a union spokesman. "The first thing we implore all of you to do is be patient while we organize. If you all would oblige me, I'd ask that the union leaders from each mine gather down here by the creek. While we are meeting to make plans, we will allow one man or woman to stand on this stump and speak for no more than five minutes at a time. Homer Keel, I'd like you to go first."

The men with the torches stuck them in the ground to form a circle around the stump. As old Homer was helped up on the platform, Antonio and a group of men retreated to the creek bottom where, sitting on fallen logs, they began plans to shut down Illinois coal mines without the help or authorization of the United Mine Workers.

Sixteen Tons

<><><><><><>

The next day, the Eng and Vacca women worked alongside hundreds of others to provide food for five thousand strikers. Men had come to Christian County from all over the state to help shut down the mines. Since the weather was good, the miners slept on the ground at Reese's Woods or alongside the roads that went into the mines. Since they hadn't sanctioned the strike, the United Mine Workers refused to provide tents and other equipment.

Though Angeline's ten-acre garden was in full production with sweet corn, tomatoes, peas, green beans, spinach and many other vegetables, everything that was ripe was picked by the end of the day. Sam Vacca showed she had experience feeding multitudes of men, hanging a dozen big cauldrons from tripods over open fires. The West Virginia mountain girl showed the other women how to make a variety of stews seasoned with fatback, as well as one that she called a "this and that soup."

"We got to keep the men fed and happy and away from the hooch," Sam told the other women as they added as many meats and vegetables as they could find to the soup.

"Sing to 'em, gals," Mrs. Borgononi said in a weak, crackly voice. Sitting in the wicker chair that Mary Kate provided her, the one-hundred-year-old lady broke green beans into a bowl resting on her lap. "That's what Mother Jones always had us do. Men like singing and good food almost as much as they like—"

"*Dancing*," Mary Kate said quickly. "Men like dancing, and our Sam can dance as good a jig as anyone."

"Well," Mrs. Borgononi said, shaking her head, "that isn't what I was going to say, but I think you're right. Young Sam does wiggle kinda cute when she cuts loose."

<><><><><><>

Angeline was worried about keeping her friends and family together. Lena was mad at Antonio for letting Homer Keel be the first to speak at the rally after the old man had criticized her. Bullo and Vinnie were not talking, and she was pretty sure blows had been exchanged at least once. Antonio was so involved in organizing the strikers' camp, many nights he didn't even come home until almost dawn. Now, from their house next door, she could hear Bullo yelling at Mary Kate for helping to feed the strikers.

"I'm risking my life by crossing the picket line so I can feed my family, and you are helping the very men who want to kill me!" he shouted.

"They are your family too, Bullo!" Mary Kate yelled back. If the argument were not so tragic, she would have smiled at her daughter-in-law's Irish grit.

"I forbid you to help them!" Bullo said.

"*You? Forbid* me?" Mary Kate said, her dander clearly up. "No one is going to forbid Mary Kate Vacca from helping her family!"

"They are not our family anymore!" Bullo yelled. "You and I and our boys are our only family from now on!"

"*No!* Out of respect to my husband, I will no longer help the striking miners, but you will *never* forbid me or our sons from being part of the Vacca family."

Angeline heard a loud slam and knew the conversation was ended. There would be no kicking doors down in a Vacca home. Her son would give his woman the space she needed and he would sleep on the porch hammock. The little Italian mother could not control the rest of the world, but on this matter she was positive. She had taught her boys to respect their women.

37

The next day five thousand miners surrounded Mine Number 58 in Hewittville. Even as he walked toward the picket line with two hundred loyal United Mine Workers, Bullo knew this time his crew would not get through. The strikers were armed with baseball bats and axe handles, which they thumped menacingly against the palms of their hands.

In the middle of the road that ran into the mine yard, his father and brother stood in the front of the angry crowd. With his eyes narrow and lips pressed tightly together, his brother looked like the Vinnie of their youth: angry and ready to take on the world. He appeared especially menacing, wearing a sleeveless, skin-tight tee shirt and the head of a heavy, ball-peen hammer sticking out of his trouser belt.

"You boys can just stop right there," Antonio said, holding up a hand.

The workers stopped walking. Some of them reached slowly inside the jackets they wore despite the warm, summer day. Bullo had his own pistol tucked beneath the belt under his shirt. But with his father and brother standing so close, he could not imagine using it, even though Vinnie looked like he would not hesitate to split his brother's skull with the hammer if a battle began.

The sudden blare of the emergency siren in the mine yard startled everyone. A ruckus sounded behind the picketers. A moment later, Joe Harrison, Keiran Phelan and several dozen men armed with Thompson submachine guns cleared a wide path between the workers and the mine gate. Most of the men wore well-tailored suits and fedora hats.

Shouts of outrage erupted from the strikers, who quickly came around behind the workers, effectively surrounding them. Among those who didn't retreat from the armed thugs were Bullo's father, brother and Harley Eng.

"Joe, Keiran." Harley nodded as calmly as if they had just met in the church parking lot. "What's with the tommy guns? It's not Valentine's Day."

"*Tommy guns? Valentine's Day?*" Phelan shouted, his eyes showing white all around the pupils. He raised the weapon to Harley's face. "You're funny, big man. Me and Al call 'em Chicago typewriters."

"Capone's in prison," Harley said, the muzzle of the gun not inches from his nose.

"Not for long," Phelan sneered.

"Lower that gun, Keiran," Joe said quietly to his son-in-law.

Phelan smiled as he brought the gun part way down but still aimed in Harley's direction. He was the only one smiling. Everyone else seemed to understand the tension and danger of the moment. Even the company thugs recruited from Chicago and the Shelton and Birger gangs of southern Illinois watched the strikers with concerned eyes. Hundreds of pistols slowly emerged from within the ranks of the strikers.

Only Kieran Phelan seemed crazed with blood lust. While everyone else stood almost perfectly silent and still, Phelan was in constant motion. His eyes darted from one striker to another as if he were trying to determine whom he would kill first.

"What's wrong with that fellow?" Bullo heard one miner whisper. "He's actin' like a cat in a room full a' rockin' chairs."

Joe Harrison was also concerned. Moving close to him, he whispered a few words. Phelan immediately quit fidgeting, though his eyes continued to twitch. He slowly lowered his gun barrel the rest of the way down.

"These men are coming in to work!" Joe said loudly to no one in particular.

"Not without bloodshed, Joe," Antonio said before the

strikers could shout a response.

Bullo sensed that even a cough or sneeze would set off a battle. He couldn't believe this many men could be so quiet. The clucking of chickens could be heard from a nearby home. As his father took a few steps toward Joe Harrison, Bullo thought about what close friends the two men had been for over thirty years.

"Do you think this is what it was like at Virden in '98?" his father asked the mine boss in almost a whisper.

A glazed look appeared in Joe's eyes. The words had meant something profound to his father's former partner. Joe looked around at the workers, strikers and company thugs as if seeing them for the first time. Pointing at the mine, he ordered the men back inside the yard.

All of the company thugs except for Phelan turned and moved toward the gate. When they were out of sight Joe turned toward Bullo and the strikebreakers. "You all go on home for now. We'll contact you when we want you to return to work."

The rousing shout of victory from the strikers could be heard three miles away in Langleyville.

<><><><><><>

"Why did you do that?" Phelan screamed when he and Joe were back in the mine office. "We had 'em dead to rights."

"If I hadn't done that we'd have a hundred dead bodies lying out there right now!" Joe yelled back, "and you would have been the first one shot, wavin' that damned gun all around and grinnin' like a possum eatin' shit."

"You can't talk to me like that!"

"The hell I *can't*," Joe replied firmly. "Right now the people of this county and the newspaper are on our side. If we want to win this thing, we're going to have to keep the public's support, and we won't do it by startin' a mine war."

"If you won't let my men do it then you're going to need the

National Guard to get those workers past that many pickets."

"They're not going to send the Guard as long as the strike is peaceful," Joe said, "and I don't see Antonio Vacca doing anything unless he's provoked."

"The *Taylorville Breeze* is on our side," Phelan said. "Maybe they could get things stirred up."

"The newspaper is just barely on our side," Joe corrected. Besides, you'd have to put a bomb under Governor Horner's desk to make him move on anything."

Phelan looked out the window at the dynamite shed and smiled.

<><><><><><>

The next morning, strikers blocked all the roads going into the mines, successfully shutting down Peabody at all four locations in Christian County. Workers didn't even try to cross the picket lines. For the next few weeks, picketers slept on the ground around fires that housed a hot pot of coffee twenty-four hours a day. Mines across the state followed suit, and by the middle of August, all but a few in southern Illinois were shut down.

Lena and Angeline helped organize a Women's Auxiliary similar to the one they had helped with during the war. They set up a soup kitchen in Kincaid, and Sam, Angie and Margaret kept busy driving the food to the hungry picketers.

"We have to shut down the mines in the southern counties," Antonio said one evening to the seven men who had gathered in his back yard for an officers meeting. Lena and Angeline were walking around the picnic table pouring coffee. "How are we going to do that and have the manpower to keep the mines up here shut down?"

"Ahem." Lena cleared her throat, drawing the eyes of the men. "Angeline, I thought you had done a better job training your man."

"I thought I had." Angeline shook her head sadly. "Clearly, I was wrong."

"What are you talking about, Lena?" Harley said, ready to come to Antonio's defense.

"I mean," Lena said, "why don't you let the women walk the picket line? Mother Jones did."

The men looked at her as she and Angeline linked arms.

Antonio shook his head. "I don't know that this is the same type of situation. You know what happened at Ludlow, Angeline. Do you want to be the one responsible for that happening here?"

"I won't let that happen," Angeline said. "We will keep the children away from the mines."

The men looked down at their coffee cups. Antonio ran his hands across his forehead and through his hair. Lena sat down on the bench between her husband and Antonio, her back to the table.

"You men risk your lives in the mine every day," Lena said to no one in particular. "Nothing has ever been gained for you miners or us wives or our children without risking blood and death. We don't want that to happen," her voice became stronger and hard, "but, by God, these thugs are not going to bully us into living like medieval peasants."

<>< ><>< ><>< >

On August 24, a caravan of cars stretching for several miles left Christian County and drove south on Highway 51. Vinnie sat between his father, who was driving, and Harley Eng. The backseat was filled with food, blankets and other provisions necessary for a long siege of the mines. The other vehicles were likewise filled to capacity with burly miners, many of them proudly sporting American flags. The procession moved slowly, especially in small towns where people came running out of their homes to watch the impromptu parade. At first, most people cheered them, but when they moved into the more southern counties, men stood behind buildings and threw rocks at the cars.

"Why are the people down this way so against the union?" Vinnie asked.

"This is mostly an agricultural area," Harley said. "They don't have as much industry, so they don't understand the importance of unions."

"Plus," Antonio said as he drove, "after the war, there was a lot of anger toward Russia for becoming communist. There was a pretty big movement toward communism in these counties and a lot of division is still there. You are too young to remember, but there was a red scare in America. Newly arrived immigrants were harassed and sometimes run out of the country."

"I remember," Vinnie said. After a long pause, he asked, "Papa, you know that Sam is a socialist, don't you?"

"I figured so," Antonio smiled. "I don't think she'll ever have any trouble, though. America is a fine country and we learn from our mistakes. People are allowed the rights of speech and expression. I don't suspect we'll see any more such nonsense again in this land of freedom."

<><><><><><>

"Move your ass, little girlie-boy," Keiran Phelan said to Sam Vacca, who was dressed in overalls and standing like a rock in front of two hundred strikebreakers. Each one carried a pickaxe over his shoulder. Half weren't dressed for mining, but instead wore clean, well-pressed suits along with the fedora hats favored by the Chicago gangsters. Their bulging jackets did little to hide the artillery strapped to their chests.

"You one of them rednecks now, Sam?" Phelan continued. "Is that why you wear a red bandanna 'round your neck?"

Sam Vacca had walked alongside her mother-in-law and Lena Eng to meet the men. Several hundred members of the

Women's Auxiliary stood behind them near the mine gate. The ladies bore no weapons other than their sharp tongues and formidable cat-like claws. Though Sam had never had a conversation with Phelan, she thought that with their mutual friends and family, he would be civil to her. Instead, the dark little man seemed to relish being in the limelight of the situation.

Laughter came from the suits around Phelan, but the men who were dressed for mining looked scared and serious.

"You ain't comin' through," Sam said to Phelan, her feet planted firmly on the ground.

Phelan laughed again, as did the small army behind him. Then he walked a step closer to her and said in a voice low enough the women behind her couldn't hear. "When this is over I'm going to rip those stupid britches off you and—"

Sam stepped forward and kicked. Phelan caught her foot like a baseball player fielding a ground ball and flipped her hard onto her back.

"Not this time girlie-boy!" Phelan shouted. "I heard all about your little tricks when I was in West Virginia."

Sam knew instantly that her right shoulder had dislocated. She heard the screams of outrage from the women behind her and the laughter from the strikebreakers and thugs. When some of the women started to charge forward, Angeline spun around and threw up her right hand. The women stopped in their tracks.

Angeline looked back toward the strikebreakers, who immediately quit laughing. Phelan had been smiling over his shoulder at his men, and when their eyes suddenly showed bright white around their pupils, he jerked his head back around just in time to meet the full impact of Angeline Vacca's fist directly on the bridge of his nose. Phelan's head snapped back even as the weight of his body collapsed forward, driving his knees hard into the ground. The only noise was the clicking of the cicadas as the top half of Phelan's body continued its slow deflation into unconsciousness. When the final fall forward came, none of his men moved to stop his face from its heavy bounce against the surface of the hard road. With disgusted shaking of their heads, the strikebreakers turned and walked toward home, leaving their humiliated leader to lie in the street.

Angeline bent down, grabbed a handful of Phelan's hair and turned it so he could breathe. "I told you not to insult my Sam," she said quietly, then added, "I expect a kick in the groin would have hurt less."

<><><><><><>

By the time the caravan of striking miners reached the southern counties, it had been joined by so many vehicles that it snaked along the narrow highways for over twenty miles. Franklin County was heavily forested with oak, maple and hickory trees, creating an arching canopy of leaves above the road.

Antonio's car had dropped back a half mile to allow additional strikers to join the procession. He planned on taking the lead again when they reached the next village called Mulkeytown.

"I don't like that lowland area up ahead," Vinnie said as they began descending a high hill into a river valley. He was reminded of the valley in West Virginia where he and Sam had helped ambush the state police.

"I'm not sure what we can do about it from way back here," Harley Eng said, "although we're going slow enough I could just about run up ahead and warn them."

"And what good would that do?" Antonio said. "We are weaponless—unless some of the men broke orders and snuck guns in with their blankets."

Vinnie squirmed and rubbed one foot against the other. He moved forward in his seat a little so he could see more clearly through the windshield. Their own car was now passing over a rickety bridge, and the loud creaking sound of the boards beneath the tires echoed like gunshots through the valley. They were only a hundred yards past the bridge when Vinnie noticed a flock of pheasants running out of the woods toward the cars in front.

"Stop, Papa!" he shouted.

The brakes squealed as Antonio brought the vehicle to a rapid stop. The cars and trucks behind them also came to a sudden halt and many began sounding their horns. Vinnie reached across Harley's body, pushed the door open and rolled across him and out of the automobile. He paused only a second to pull a forty-five caliber pistol from the right boot beneath his trousers. The next moment, he sprinted toward the vehicles that had continued to move forward through the river valley. Running alongside a narrow ditch, he fired a warning shot in the air. As if it were a signal, it was answered by the thunder of hundreds of gunshots from behind trees and bushes. Cars careened sideways as they simultaneously braked hard. The screeching sound of metal against metal made Vinnie clench his teeth as a few cars crashed into the vehicles in front of them. He opened his mouth and screamed the Rebel yell he had learned in West Virginia, "Woh-who-ey! who-ey! who-ey! Woh-who-ey! who-ey!"

He was still an eighth of a mile away as he watched hundreds of men run out of the wooded area swinging axe handles and rifle butts at the strikers, who fumbled to get out of their vehicles. With a dozen men helping, the ambushers quickly turned several cars over with the shouting occupants still inside. One old truck went up in a loud explosion as a bullet ricochet off a car door and sent sparks into gas that had spilled onto the ground.

When he got close enough, Vinnie emptied his gun into a crowd of men trying to overturn a flatbed truck. The men scattered, but not before Vinnie smashed his fist into the face of the slowest of the bunch.

From behind him, two men grabbed his arms and another punched him in the stomach and then twice in the face. Vinnie leaned back into the men holding him and kicked up into the assailant's jaw. The man's false teeth shot out of his mouth as he fell back into the ditch.

Vinnie felt his left arm pull free.

Harley Eng had ran up and struck one of the thugs in the head with a tire iron.

Vinnie dropped to the ground as the man holding his right arm tried to hit him with a metal pipe. He swung his feet in a hard loop and kicked the man's legs out from under him.

Another barrage of gunshots began. One of the men from the caravan spun to the ground with a red hole in his jaw.

A moment later, hundreds of strikers ran past him while the ambushers fled back into the forest. After another smattering of gunshots, the assault ended as quickly as it had begun.

Vinnie felt Harley Eng ease him down onto the ground.

"You're bleeding pretty bad from the stomach," Harley said above the shouts from men who were running around the devastation trying to help other wounded.

"Did we lose anyone?" Vinnie asked.

Harley tore Vinnie's shirt open and examined the wound. "I don't know." He took the torn shirt and held it against the bleeding. "Looks like that fella that hit you in the stomach was wearing something sharp on his fist."

"Brass knuckles," Antonio said breathlessly as he suddenly appeared next to his son. He held out a piece of metal that looked like four finger rings welded together. "There must have been a spike in the middle one, but it looks like it got knocked off."

Vinnie winced as Harley pulled something out of his wound and held it up. It was a small, sharp, medal thorn shaped like a cat claw.

"Good thing it broke off in your stomach and not your eye,"

Harley said.

Nearly a thousand miners had now made it to the scene. They worked to upright overturned vehicles and place the most seriously wounded in cars that could make straight for the closest hospital in Du Quoin. After meeting for a few moments with the other strike leaders, Antonio returned to his son.

"Vinnie, we are going to rendezvous back in Benld to hold a meeting. I'm going to have Harley take you to Du Quoin and get that wound treated."

"What do you think you'll do?" Vinnie asked.

"We believe we were ambushed by the Franklin County Sheriff with the help of Peabody Coal Company and the United Mine Workers," Antonio said. "It looks like its time to form a new union."

38

"They call themselves the Progressive Mine Workers of America," Augustus Ware told the committee of men sitting around the conference table in the UMW office. "The PMW of A."

Keiran Phelan considered making a clever comment about the initials but kept it to himself. Since Angeline Vacca had humiliated him in front of the men, he had been taking more ribbing than he could handle. His confidence was down and his blood rage up, especially for the Vacca bitch.

Augustus Ware was now the Divisional Superintendent of Mines for Peabody Coal Company. Phelan hated the fat, arrogant man's condescending way of talking to him and his downstate friends. Ware and the gangsters from Chicago were always acting as though they were sharing a laugh at the rural thug's expense.

"These Progressives have the mines bottled up," Ware told the men. "Public sympathy is on their side right now because of that fiasco down in Franklin County. The governor refuses to send in the National Guard to break the strike as long as this new union remains law abiding. Knowing their leaders as I do, they aren't going to do anything stupid."

Phelan took offense to Ware's words. It made the Progressives sound like they were smarter than he was. He was determined to do something extraordinary.

"Archie," Ware addressed a short man with enormous jowls, "you boys ever do much with dynamite?"

"Not as long as our choppers work," Archie Norton said, caressing his Thompson machine gun. "A few of the boys use powder to blow a safe, though."

"I've used both black powder and dynamite," Phelan said.

Ware and Norton exchange smirky grins.

"What'll ya wanna blow up?" Phelan asked, ignoring the quiet snickers.

Ware walked around his desk and looked down at Phelan. "I want to blow up this office."

Phelan smiled. He had been formulating a similar plan for weeks. Now was the time to regain the confidence of his peers.

"How about bombing the Taylorville Daily Breeze?" Phelan said.

"What's wrong with you?" Norton said. "The newspaper's on our side."

The men in the room shared a laugh on Phelan, but he had expected it. "Yes, they're on our side," Phelan said sarcastically, "and that makes them the perfect target, now doesn't it?"

The man with the jowls shook his head, creating ripples of movement. "You mean—"

"Yes. Frame those bastards."

The men grew quiet as Phelan told them the rest of his plan. "We miners know how to fire a shot so all the damage is done to just one area. So if I blow the wall to the front room of the office facing the street, the printing machines in the backroom will be ready before morning to run an edition blaming the PM of A."

"What if the explosion kills the typesetters?" Norton said, looking miffed.

"That's why," Phelan said, his head tilted back so the crooked nose Angeline Vacca had given him was less prominent, "we do it early Sunday morning when no one's around."

<><><><><><>

When Joe Harrison heard the explosion the following Sunday morning, he jumped out of bed, threw on his clothes and raced out of the house. Her white face mask over her eyes, Myrna simply rolled over onto her stomach, placed a pillow over her head and went back to sleep.

The second explosion came as Joe was getting in his car. It was so loud he was tempted to simply run toward the town square where white smoke was rising above the trees and buildings into a moon bright sky. Men began running out of houses. Many piled into cars and the backs of pickup trucks as they hurried to find out what had happened.

Joe's mind came fully awake with an unsettling premonition. He did a u-turn in the road and went in the opposite direction of everyone else.

A few minutes later he pulled up beside his daughter and son-in-law's house. Joe got out and hurried to the Phelan Chevy, which was in its usual spot in front of the carriage house. He placed his hand on the hood, raised it and looked at the engine. Slamming it shut with a loud bang, he went to the front entrance and knocked hard. He thought it took much too long for Phelan to finally open the door. His son-in-law's nightshirt hung down to his boney, bare knees, and his expression of shock at seeing his father-in-law at his doorstep at three in the morning seemed to be forced.

"*What did you do?*" Joe said, resisting the urge to choke the man.

"What are you talking about?" Phelan asked. "Felina and I have been asleep all night."

"Your car engine is hot and still dripping oil." Joe pushed Phelan inside and shut the door. "You set off that bomb, didn't you?"

"What bomb, Daddy?" Felina said from the doorway to the bedroom. She wore a thick, black robe. "Why are you here?"

"Because this imbecile husband of yours might have just killed innocent people!" Joe shouted.

"There's no one on the town square at this time of night!" Felina said. Her husband gave her a "shut-up" look.

Sixteen Tons

"How did you know it was on the town square?" Joe said, not surprised that his daughter was in on it.

"Get the hell out of our house." Phelan grabbed his father-in-law's arm and pushed.

Years of hard labor in the mines had not deserted the older man. Joe spun and punched Phelan in the nose, sending him onto the wooden coffee table and shattering it.

When he returned to his own home, so many vehicles blocked the roads to the downtown, Joe decided to park and walk. The sirens from ambulances, fire trucks and police cars filled the air. There were small fires on both the east and west sides of the square, while the familiar smell of nitroglycerine fumes lingered in the still, morning air.

Five minutes later, Joe was close enough to recognize that the crowds around the courthouse were quickly dividing into rival factions. The newly formed Progressive Mine Workers massed around the east side near a smoking *Taylorville Daily Breeze* building. Angry and shouting supporters of The United Mine Workers and Peabody Coal gathered on the west side near their bombed out headquarters.

The UMW office was a near total loss. The newspaper building seemed to have less damage, although the debris in the street was extensive. The owners of the *Breeze* were already sifting through the rubble. Several employees were cleaning up the printing press room.

"Joe!" someone yelled.

He turned and saw Bullo Vacca making his way through the mob of UMW supporters. When they met, the young miner took Joe's arm and guided him to the less crowded north side of the courthouse. "Joe, you've got to keep our men under control until the National Guard arrives."

Joe shook his head and looked back at the two mobs of angry men. They were facing one another, shouting accusations and insults. Events were once again escalating out of control. Joe wished he could just go back home and climb under the

320

blankets of his bed.

Bullo grabbed his arm. "Joe, what are we going to do?"

A farm truck pushed its way slowly between the two sides. Antonio stood on the back, waving his arms at the Progressives. The hired company men from Chicago tried to board the vehicle from their side, but Vinnie Vacca jumped into the truck bed and laid the lead thug out with a metal pipe. The others fell back.

A dozen strikers surrounded the truck. Someone handed Antonio a bullhorn. He began shouting into it. The Progressive side grew quiet and listened.

"Meeting in Manner's Park!" Antonio shouted. "All Progressive Mine Workers are to report to Manner's Park immediately for an important meeting!"

Many faces on both sides looked relieved as the strikers turned and walked south toward the park. Some of the company men began throwing rocks as the group retreated. Vinnie caught a rock that was headed toward his father's head and hurled it back toward the crowd.

Joe turned to say something to Bullo, but the oldest Vacca brother ran with clenched fists in the direction of the man who had thrown the stone at his father.

The sun was beginning to come up as the rest of the crowd dispersed. Joe took the side streets home. He didn't want to talk to anyone. Each time he heard a gunshot or a scream, he had to help his mind distinguish whether it was real or just a terrible memory.

"Just shoot the grasshopper, son," the shadow of Art Cabassi whispered in his ear. "Both barrels."

As he walked faster toward home, Joe bit down on his lip until it bled. Why had he not told Antonio that it was Phelan and the company who had done the bombing that night? His mind raced between loyalty for the man who had saved his life and his dislikable son-in-law. Antonio was his best friend, but Phelan was his family—and the mine company paid his wages.

"You and I are not related by the blood in our bodies but by the blood we sacrificed for working men everywhere," Cabassi's haunting voice continued. "I want you to help me kill a man, Joe."

Joe began to run. By the time he got to his house, he didn't want to be there, either. As another explosion erupted somewhere in the town, Joe's head pounded. Myrna would never give him any peace with her endless stupid questions, so he turned toward the smokehouse. Flipping open the side door, he went inside and blocked the entrance behind him with a rake. The room was dark and smelled of old, musty wooden tools.

He looked at the big bathtub with its lion claw legs. He and Myrna would drag the tub out into the yard on hot summer days and fill it with buckets of water from the pump. He remembered the feel of the sun-warmed water on his body. Now it was stuffed with old towels and burlap potato sacks that looked strangely inviting. Joe walked over the dirt floor, climbed into the tub and lay down. He pillowed his head with some of the towels and pulled burlap sacks over his body. Within moments, the worries of the day began to fade. He thought of what it would be like to lie in that bathtub forever. It seemed such a comfortable place to spend eternity—much better than a common grave or the bottom of a well.

<><><><><><>

Before the sun was fully up that morning, an extra edition of *The Taylorville Breeze* hit the street. No one could remember when the newspaper had last put out a Sunday paper. Word quickly spread that the publishers had left the lead melting pots on the night before. The headline article condemning the Progressives for the bombings seemed extremely well-edited, considering it had taken less than one hour to write.

"We've been set up!" Antonio told the miners. Standing in

front of the podium on the Chautauqua stage where John L. Lewis had once spoken, he held at arm's length the newspaper that had just been handed him. The thundering of boos and jeers shook the rafters of the open building.

When the bellows finally subsided, old Homer Keel stood in the front row and shouted, "Why're they blamin' us for that bombin'? We didn't do it!" Homer looked at Antonio and hesitated before asking. "Did we?"

"No, we didn't, Homer!" Antonio said. "But we can't prove it, so we can expect the National Guard here in the next day or two."

"We'll just send those boys a packin', I'll tell ya!" shouted a miner.

The men in the building roared their approval. Tempers were high and it took several moments before Antonio's shouting and hand waving brought the crowd back under control.

"We will not let this become another mine war!" Antonio hollered above the din. The men who still had their senses urged their angrier colleagues to calm down and listen. "The Guard will have machine guns, tear gas, and armored cars," Antonio said. "Do you really think we can fight them with squirrel guns and shotguns? We have *got* to remain within the boundaries of the law if we are to win this. We need to get the public back on our side."

"How do we do that when even the newspaper is against us?" someone shouted.

Before pandemonium could return, Antonio said, "Our Women's Auxiliary is at this moment telephoning newspapers from around the country to tell them what is happening here in Christian County. If we conduct ourselves as peaceful protesters who are being bullied by the National Guard and Peabody's goon squads, we will get public sympathy. *The Taylorville Breeze* will side with the majority of the people so they can sell newspapers. We can win them over if we show the public that we are in the right and that we are the victims."

<><><><><><>

By seven o'clock that morning, every mine in Christian County had at least a thousand strikers blocking the main gates. The National Guard didn't show, but word got around that they would be there the next day. By the time military trucks began arriving on Tuesday morning, over ten thousand miners had appeared from around the state to man the picket lines.

That afternoon, Vinnie took Sam on a casual walk around the town square, making mental notes of what they saw. He estimated the State Militia had over one hundred uniformed men walking the streets of Taylorville to maintain order. There were at least twice that many thugs from Chicago, as well as recruits from the Southern Illinois Birger and Sheldon gangs. Most of the latter seemed to be under the direction of Kieran Phelan, who peacocked through the streets shouting orders to the goons as well as the guardsmen.

The militia was being housed in the big, three-story county courthouse in the middle of the square. Two guards dressed in trench coats and doughboy helmets were positioned at the entrances on all four sides of the building. Each Guardsman's left hand was behind his back. The other hand held his rifle by the top of the barrel at arm's length while the butt remained on the ground by his right foot.

"Someone sure wanted those poor soldier boys to look intimidating," Vinnie told his father that evening as they sat in front of a picket fire sipping coffee. "They even placed machine guns on top of the buildings around the square."

Antonio nodded. "We caught a company man trying to sneak a machine gun into the mine in Tovey."

"What did you do?" Vinnie asked.

"They rolled his car off into the ditch . . . with him in it."

"Not the big ditch that drops down into the South Fork?" Vinnie said, trying to remember if there were any trees that would have prevented the vehicle from rolling into the river.

"That's the one," Antonio said. "Some of Phelan's goons pulled him out before he drowned. His ribs were busted, but he'll live."

"What did they do with the machine gun?" Vinnie said.

"It's in a safe place in case we need it later."

Vinnie recognized that his father didn't look very enthused about the prospect of using the weapon.

"Vinnie, I know you're itchin' for a fight, but I have a more important job for you and Sam. Your Uncle Vincent said the two of you brought in more game than any of the other hunters during the West Virginia strike. I want you to teach the young people everything you know. We'll provide trucks for you to go down into southern Illinois and Missouri when the game gets scarce here."

Vinnie sat for a long time with his head down. "This is Mama's idea, isn't it? She wants to get me and Sam away from the fight."

"No," his father said, though he averted his eyes. "It's a simple matter of survival. We have thousands of men to feed. The fields are just about done, and the government surplus the Women's Auxiliary brought us was no good. That pork had so much salt in it you could boil it for a week and still not be able to eat it. We are starting to get money in from miners who joined the Progressives in other parts of the country, but it won't be enough to get us through the winter. We need to do everything we can to feed our men."

Vinnie took a sip of coffee and spat a thin stream between his teeth onto the fire, weighing his father's words.

"Sam will like the hills of Missouri," he said. "We'll leave in the morning."

39

For the next several weeks, Antonio worked with the Progressive leaders to keep the strike going. Angeline and Lena marched with the local Woman's Auxiliary leader, Agnes Wieck, and hundreds of other women through the Springfield streets to gain assistance from the Red Cross and Salvation Army. Opposition from hundreds of supporters of the United Mine Workers turned them back in what almost became a bloody riot.

As the weather became colder, the Progressives began clearing fields for farmers in exchange for firewood to take home. Young boys walked the railroad tracks picking up coal that had fallen off the train cars.

Vinnie and Sam traveled far and wide to hunt game and fish. They showed young boys how to set a drop line and a trotline. Older, braver boys tried noodling by sticking their hands in a catfish hole. When the catfish bit their hand they would pull it out of the hole. Sam was careful to warn the boys that they should never do this alone, as a big catfish could pull them under water and drown them.

Meanwhile, many of the National Guardsmen tried to provoke the strikers into fighting. They poked loiterers with their bayonets, and even used gas bombs if they saw a large group of men standing in the streets talking.

Even students going to and from school weren't safe. Margaret Eng and Doris Dalton, freshmen in high school, twice had rocks thrown at them from someone hiding behind the mine yard fence. When they began taking a different route a block away, a gunshot came from the mine tipple and a bullet ricocheted off the road and into a building next to them. After that, their mothers insisted on driving them to school.

"Did you know that the school is being heated with Peabody Coal?" Doris told Margaret one day after they were dropped off at the school. Doris had curly red locks and a poor posture that caused boys to call her "Hunchback." "I have half a mind to burn this place to the ground."

"You do that and you'll prove you do have half a mind," Margaret said. Taller than the boys her age, she had her mother's blond hair as well as her grit.

"Well, what do you think we should do about it?" Doris asked.

"Our parents are picketing," Margaret said. "Why shouldn't we?"

The vast majority of students at Memorial High School were the children of Progressive Mine Workers. On a warm day in early October when the bell rang at the end of the lunch period, two hundred students failed to report to classes.

The students fondly called their principal Peg Leg Kroll. He was popular because at the end of each year he picked one high school graduate who had displayed especially good behavior throughout the school year to throw a dart at his wooden leg. So far, his oak leg had sixteen tiny holes, one for each year he had been principal.

"The doc tried to give me a new wooden leg a few years ago," Peg Leg Kroll told his students each May as he rolled up his pant leg for the ceremonial dart throw, "but I told him he'd have to wait 'til I retire. I'm mighty proud of these punctures." He always pointed at one hole where the dartster had nearly missed. It was near his knee where the stump of his real leg began. "Joe Norris gave me that one seven years ago, and he was a baseball pitcher, for gosh sakes."

The student walkout worked well, even among the seniors. Some of the boys walked because they couldn't say no to the pretty Margaret Eng.

"What's going on out here?" Mr. Kroll said when he came outside to confront the picketers. "You seniors are going to lose your shot at my leg if you don't get to class."

Two senior boys ran into the building. A moment later, three more followed. Margaret figured she'd better talk fast or she'd lose the entire senior class. "We want you to quit using Peabody Coal in your furnace!" she said in a voice more shrill than she had intended.

"Why, Marge, we don't even have the furnace burning," Mr. Kroll said. "It's a nice, Indian summer day, don't you think?"

Margaret hadn't thought of that. "Well, then we'll just stand out here 'til the weather turns."

"All right," Mr. Kroll said with a smile. "I'll bring the classes out here then."

Five minutes later, the schoolyard was divided into a dozen classes, with students sitting in front of their teachers on the ground. Margaret looked at Doris and shrugged. When it began raining the next day and kept up a steady drizzle the entire week, the students postponed the strike. Mr. Krohl didn't turn the furnaces on until it got so cold the students started wearing coats in their classes. Eventually they were begging the wily principal to burn the scab coal.

<><><><><><>

Angie Eng wasn't as pretty as her little sister, but she was smarter. She was in her third year at Illinois State University in Normal when the Progressive Union was formed. She already had a two-year degree in education, so when she heard that after forty years, Mrs. Foster had given up her job as schoolmarm and moved to Indiana to live with her mother, Angie dropped out of school and took the next train home.

She couldn't believe that old Mrs. Foster could have a mother that was still alive, but she was grateful the old teacher was finally calling it quits. Mrs. Foster had lived in a little house next to Jack Stanley, who was the president of the local Progressives. Rumor was that she got tired of being awakened at night by gunshots, and when a small bomb went off as she was sitting in her outhouse, she packed her trunks and skedaddled for Indiana.

The moment Angie stepped out of the passenger compartment at the Taylorville train station, she heard the rat-a-tat-tat of machine gun fire. Everyone around her ran for cover.

"Get down, girl!" yelled a man in a military uniform.

When a bullet buzzed over her head and struck the building behind her, Angie's mind froze. Unable to get her body to move, she saw a strange, yellow smoke rising behind the trees to the south. Suddenly she felt a powerful arm around her waist, and the next moment she lay spread-eagle on her back next to the train track. The uniformed man was on top of her. She felt the burly stubble of his unshaven face against her cheeks.

"Ouch!" Angie squealed. "Don't you ever shave?"

"Shut up and hold still 'til the shootin' stops!" the man said. "Those machine gun bullets can go right through a wall from half a mile away."

Angie heard a loud pop and a dull explosion.

"They're using tear gas!" The man held up a big gas mask. "If it drifts this way, I'll put this over your face."

"You most certainly will not!" Angie shouted. "No gas can be worse than that toilet water you're wearing."

"Shut your eyes and that big mouth of yours!" the man yelled.

Angie felt a powdery mist come down on her face. When she took a breath through her nose, her nostrils burned like she had just inhaled fire from a candle. The Guardsman pulled the gas mask over her head. Keeping her eyes shut, she wondered if he had a mask for himself. She heard more gunshots, shouts from men, two more explosions, and the strange pop of more tear gas canisters being fired.

After an eternity of waiting, the battle abruptly ended. The man kept his face buried against hers for several minutes after the last shots were fired. She heard people moving around them and opened her eyes. The Guardsman's body was still pressed heavily on top of her.

"Get off me, you big oaf!" she yelled in his ear.

The man rolled off her and onto his side. She tore the mask off her own head and looked for the first time at his face. All she saw were swollen, red-blotched eyes with lids twice the normal size. His breathing was swallow. He went into convulsions.

Angie screamed for help.

<><><><><><>

When Angeline Vacca opened the door to her house, the last thing she expected to see was an extremely tall National Guardsman being held up by little Angie Eng.

"He risked his life to save me, and he's been gassed something awful!" Angie said. "Your house was the closest place for me to take him. His guardsman friend says he'll be in terrible trouble for letting me wear his gas mask."

Angeline helped get the big man into the boy's old room and dropped him somewhat roughly onto a bottom bunk.

"Get me some baking soda and warm water," Angeline said as she undid the top buttons on his jacket. She had learned several medical techniques from Dr. Hiler, but preferred to try good, old-fashioned home remedies first.

"Thank you, ma'am," the Guardsman said weakly. "My name—"

"No need for names, young man," Angeline interrupted him. "You may wind up shooting one of my men. The less we know about each other, the better."

When Angie brought in a bowl and a dishrag and began treating the soldier's eyes with extreme tenderness, Angeline bolted from the room. "I'll call your Mama and tell her you're

331

here," she said over her shoulder.

"I can't believe you're not screaming in pain," Angie said to the Guardsman.

"I didn't want to embarrass myself in front of you. I take it your friend is one of the militants."

"If that's what you call a Progressive, then yes, she is, and so am I. She's my godmother, and I'm named after her."

"I'm sorry if I insulted you. I'm from a neighborhood in Chicago called Canaryville, and I don't even know what all this is really about. I'm just following orders."

"Is that the excuse you guardsmen give when you shoot or gas your fellow Americans?"

"I've never shot or gassed anyone," he said and flinched when she touched an area that was beginning to bleed.

"Can you see?" she asked.

"No. From what I've been told, I probably won't for several hours." He tried to sit up. "If you'll let me call my commander, I'll get out of your way."

Angie pushed him back down on the bed. "Just like a man to pretend to be noble. You just lie there and I'll send you home when this swelling goes down and you can see again."

"Not before I see if you're as pretty as you sound."

"I'm not. So you might as well go home before you're disappointed."

<><><><><><>

By the time Antonio arrived home that night, there was no place to sit. Harley and Lena were in the living room with Angeline, along with Vinnie and Sam. Margaret Eng sat at the kitchen table with Doris Dalton and Little Sid. They were taking turns turning the ice cream maker. Sid waved at his grandpa, then stuck his finger into a hole in the wooden barrel and licked the salt off it.

"What's going on here?" Antonio asked.

"First, tell us what happened at the mine," Harley said.

"We lost Hewittville." Antonio took his boots off and set them by the door. "We put up a battle but they gassed us."

"Anyone hurt?" Lena asked, her hand over her mouth.

"Plenty." Antonio pulled up a footstool and sat on it. "Doc Hiler doesn't think anyone will die, though."

"So now they've got Hewittville and Langleyville." Harley shook his head. "Any chance of getting them back?"

Antonio shook his head. "Most of the scabs will likely be sleeping in the mine yard. They'll probably send a third of 'em out at a time. So what's going on here?"

"Angie's home," Lena said, "and she dragged in a stray."

<><><><><><>

Private First Class Michael O'Sullivan didn't want to leave until he got a better look at Angie Eng. So far things were mostly a blur, but still he liked what he saw. Though she had been right and was no beauty, she had a strong, motherly appearance that he liked. He wanted to get to know her better, but the stout little lady with the thick Italian accent came into the room.

"My husband will take you to your quarters in our courthouse," Angeline said, then turned and walked out.

"Whew, that lady does not like me," O'Sullivan said as he sat up in the bunk.

"She doesn't like your *uniform*," Angie corrected.

"If I came to visit you without the uniform when this is over, do you think she'd give me a break?" he said, wishing they had met under different circumstances.

He let the girl take his arm as he rose to his feet. He was six-foot, five inches in his stocking feet. Angie was barely five feet, if that.

"I think it depends on how things go," Angie said.

When they entered the living room, he felt that he was facing a gauntlet. Three men and three women stood between him and the door.

"Are you a giant?" a little boy asked him from the kitchen.

Turning, O'Sullivan saw with blurry eyes the boy and what looked like two young girls sitting in front of an ice cream maker on the table. "Better keep that churn goin' or that ice cream won't get hard," he said.

One of the girls grabbed the handle and started turning it.

"I'm sorry to have inconvenienced you folks," O'Sullivan said to no one in particular as he turned back toward the door. "I swear to you all that I don't want to cause any of you any trouble. I didn't sign up with the guard to harass American citizens." O'Sullivan felt something pulling his trouser leg. He looked down to see the little boy standing at his feet.

The little boy said, "You sound like Grandmamma when she tells the story of the giant. He says fee, fi, fo, fum."

Hard as they tried not to, the adults in the room couldn't hide their smiles.

O'Sullivan saw the youngest of the men in the room step toward him and pick up the little boy. "He's my son," the man said, "and he's too young to understand what's happening."

"Well, I'm old enough, but I don't understand," O'Sullivan said. "I just don't know what to do when I'm ordered to do something I know is wrong. You can't imagine what it's like."

The man holding the little boy looked at him. "I do understand," the man said. "I was in that situation once when I was in West Virginia. I was told to fire on a group of men that I had no quarrel with."

"What did you do?" O'Sullivan asked.

"They told me to shoot," the man said, "but they didn't say I had to hit anything."

That night Michael O'Sullivan had a long talk with his fellow National Guardsmen from Chicago. The next day, they began an organized defiance of the authority of Kieran Phelan and his hired thugs. A week later, his entire regiment was sent back to Springfield and replaced with fresh troops.

40

On October 12, the same day that Michael O'Sullivan and his Chicago Guard were relieved, the Progressives held a rally in Taylorville in commemoration of the 1898 Virden Massacre. Lena Eng was one of the women asked to speak in Manner's Park. Vinnie and Sam were in charge of setting up food while she spoke from the Chautauqua stage.

Lena shouted into the microphone that squealed with feedback every thirty seconds, "Mother Jones told us when injustices are done by your mine companies, we have to rise up and strike! Strike until the last one of us drop into our graves. We are going to stand together and never surrender. Boys, always remember you ain't got a damn thing if you ain't got a union! Union forever, boys!"

Two thousand men who heard her words over the speakers roared their approval, while another thousand too far away to hear followed suit anyway. The park was abuzz with energy.

"You men work hard to feed your families," Lena continued. "You don't want handouts, but you deserve fair pay for the dangers you face each—."

"The Guard's coming!" a voice cried out. The audience rose from their seats and craned their necks in the direction of the nearest park entrance.

Vinnie jumped on top of the picnic table. Two lines of guardsmen, bayonets extended, spreading out near the west entrance of the park. A gunshot sounded from the north. Vinnie turned. A similar formation of guardsmen formed at that entrance. He looked to the only remaining gate to the west that went out toward the cemetery. Miners were quickly moving women and children in that direction to get them away from danger.

"Take Sid and get out the east gate!" he yelled to his wife. Sam threw down the bushel basket of tomatoes she was carrying, grabbed her son and shouted above the chaos for the women to follow her.

The Progressive leaders had been adamant that miners not bring guns to the rally. Vinnie grabbed up the only weapon he could find, the basket of tomatoes. Throwing it on his shoulder, he pushed his way through the crowd to the front of the defensive line that was slowly retreating from the sharp bayonets. Most of those bold enough to hold their ground were stout young men with more attitude than wisdom.

"You boys with strong, chuckin' arms," Vinnie yelled at his comrades, "grab a handful of these here love apples and fire on my command!"

Besides cache-cheeked squirrels, the trees on the grounds to the south were populated with young boys and newspapermen. Many of the latter were attempting to aim big, clumsy cameras while hanging precariously from tree limbs. Knowing his father wanted the militia to appear to be the ones who were bullies, Vinnie figured a little instigation might be appropriate. It was apparent by their stoic expressions that most of the guardsmen didn't like their jobs. Vinnie did see a few, however, with wild eyes like they couldn't wait to stick someone with their bayonet. He decided to target them first.

"Let 'em have it, boys!" Vinnie yelled as he hurled a strike into the sour face of a uniformed man. He saw one soldier go down and several turned and ran as the blood-red tomatoes spattered like angry wounds off the heads of the retreating Illinois National Guard. Dressed mostly in overalls and short-brimmed caps, hundreds of the Progressive hotheads attacked the guardsmen and began pummeling them with angry fists and kicks. The victory was short lived when a series of tear gas bombs bounced like baseballs between the legs of the protestors.

Vinnie was suddenly knocked to the ground by a fleeing protestor. When he brought his head up he saw a gas-masked Guardsmen swinging the butt of his rifle toward him. Then a bright light exploded inside his head and the sound of screams and gunshots went silent.

<><><><><><>

When Vinnie regained consciousness, the excited voices of the men around him seemed muffled and far away. It took a long time before any of the words made sense, and when he was finally able to decipher them, he realized he was lying on the cold, tile floor of the Christian County Courthouse.

"They arrested so many strikers they're using the courthouse as a jailhouse," Dr. Hiler told Vinnie when he was well enough to sit up. "Your head took about twenty stitches."

"How . . . long?" Vinnie asked.

"About twenty-four hours. It's noon, Thursday."

"What is keeping us in here?" Vinnie asked. Though his brain was fuzzy, he couldn't imagine why so many men didn't just knock the doors down and leave.

"About every hour the militia fires off a few rounds from their machine guns on the rooftops," Hiler said as he changed the bandage wrapped around Vinnie's head.

"They're bluffin'," Vinnie said with a painful wince as the doctor patted at his wound with a wet cloth. "That tall guardsman Angie Eng brought home was scared to death that he'd have to shoot someone."

"I guess no one wants to call their bluff," Dr. Hiler said. "The fellow that brained you didn't hold back any, I can tell you that."

"Why'd the company let you come in here and help us?" Vinnie asked.

"They didn't." Hiler smiled. "I'm a double agent."

By evening, Vinnie was up and walking, though he had

occasional dizzy spells. The prisoners seemed to have free rein to walk about the building, though they were not allowed to travel in groups through the wide hallways, which were patrolled by armed guardsmen. Vinnie saw that his fellow inmates had done considerable damage to a few of the rooms they were confined to.

The highest-ranking member of the Progressives who was being held prisoner was a man named Ray Tombazzi. As Antonio Vacca's son, Vinnie was quickly recruited to be one of Tombazzi's advisors.

"How many strikers are in here?" Tombazzi asked the men gathered in the courtroom.

"'Round a thousand I'd s'pect," one of the men said, a count that Vinnie thought high.

"Spread the word throughout the courthouse," Tombazzi told the men, "that when the church bells begin playing at eight o'clock, we cause such a ruckus the Guard will think the building is coming down. Then, when the bells stop, everyone is to run to the first floor, jump out the windows and hightail it for home."

Vinnie thought this a splendid plan. His only worry was whether or not he was well enough to make a run for it when the time came.

<><><><><><>

Kieran Phelan strutted the town square with Felina at his side. He not only wanted to show her what a big man he was, he also wanted the Guardsman and the boys from Chicago to get a load of his trophy wife. By the envious stares from the men in the fedora hats and the eye movement of the militiamen, he was successful on at least the second objective.

"This is our town, baby," Phelan said as they walked arm-in-arm along the sidewalk. "Anything you want, I'll get it for you, doll."

"Well, why don't you do something about those disgusting Vaccas?" Felina said. "I hate those people. Why couldn't the rest of them have died of the Spanish Flu like Filberto and Libero?"

Kieran lost some of the starch in his walk. He had been sure that his recent successes would allow him to regain the pleasures that Felina had been denying him since the humiliation of the Angeline Vacca incident.

"Why can't you be as gallant as Charlie Birger?" Felina said.

"Charlie got hung, Felina." Phelan said.

"Yeah, but he did it in style." Felina turned when she heard the church bells begin their musical salute to the evening. "And why can't you get rid of that stupid ringing?"

Every window in the courthouse suddenly exploded with glass and debris at the same time. The roar of the men inside the building made Phelan trip over Felina's long skirt and fall on his back. Before he could get to his feet, hundreds of men came out the windows like bees from a beehive. They raced past and over him. Some stepped on his back as they fled. When he was finally able to roll on one side, he saw a young coal miner grab Felina and kiss her. It was not just a quick peck on the mouth, either, but rather a long and extremely wet, open-mouthed kiss. To make it worse, instead of pushing the boy away from her, Felina embraced him, even wrapping a leg around his thigh.

Just as Phelan regained his feet and was ready to pounce on the young ruffian taking advantage of his wife, a man with a bandaged head moved toward him. Phelan tried to yell to a nearby guardsman to shoot him, but before he could get the words out, the wounded man swung a powerful fist into his nose. When he was finally able to get to his feet again, the entire courthouse was empty, except for a few guardsmen who, when they saw Phelan looking at them, snapped back into parade-rest position.

Felina stood in the middle of the yard with a faraway look in her eyes; a look he had seen only one other time. It was the same satisfied expression she showed the day he slashed the scabs throats in Herrin.

<><><><><><>

There were two casualties for the Progressives during the month of October. A young boy named Andrew Gyenes was shot and killed by a National Guardsman and a mail carrier in Langley caught a stray bullet and died.

Since young Gyenes was a Progressive, there were thousands of mourners at his funeral. The newspapers came from far and wide, speeches were given, and the Progressives seemed to finally gain a little nationwide sympathy from the public. The mine war, though, was just beginning.

41

On Christmas Eve morning, Harley and Lena drove twenty miles to a tree farm near a little community called Moweaqua. The proprietor of the farm was a coal miner, Thomas Jackson, who had been mining for forty years and was proud of the fact that he had never had an accident.

The Engs drove across a quaint covered bridge and onto a hilly lane surrounded on both sides by blue spruce, Scots pine, and Douglas and Balsam firs. Thomas' wife Frances was standing in front of a little log cabin her husband had built to help Christmas tree shoppers get into the mood of the season.

The inside of the cabin would be decorated with Frances' homemade crafts, the fireplace would be ablaze, and there would be hot chocolate warming in a pan.

When Harley parked his car and got out, two little boys wearing matching plaid jackets and hand-woven gloves helped their parents load a tree in the back of a Ford pickup.

The wreath-covered door to the cabin opened and Francis greeted them with a joyful, "Merry Christmas."

Lena returned the greeting and handed her friend a colorfully wrapped fruitcake.

"Where's Thomas?" Harley asked after giving Frances an affectionate hug.

"Where else?" Francis said. "He wanted to get in a few hours work at the mine. I think he's so excited about playing Santa Claus tonight at the Moweaqua Christmas Party, he just couldn't sit still."

"That's our Thomas," Harley said. The Jacksons had been unable to have any children of their own, so handing out the candy canes at the community party was quite a treat for him.

Having secured their tree on the truck, the two little boys ran back into the cabin, followed by their father.

"Why don't you two go pick yourself out a nice tree while I take care of these people?" Frances asked, handing Harley a long, razor tooth saw.

Harley and Lena spent a blissful half hour walking through the tree farm and arguing amiably about the perfect tree.

"I like this one," Harley said.

"Oh, no, that's way too big." Lena pointed at a much smaller blue spruce nearby. "Now that one would look good in our living room."

Since it was beginning to drizzle, Harley bowed to his wife's discretion and cut the smaller tree. He tied some twine around it and hefted it to his shoulder.

"See," Lena said, "you couldn't have done that with that big old tree you wanted."

When they came up over a hill to the cabin, a car skidded down the dirt road and bounced across the covered bridge.

"I'd say that fella's in a hurry to get a tree," Harley said.

As he and Lena came across the field, a man jumped out of the vehicle and ran inside the cabin. By the time they reached the porch, the man and a frightened Frances were running out.

"There's been an accident at the Moweaqua mine!" the man said, his eyes wide. "They said it sounded like a methane explosion. There's a fall barricading the tunnel mouth about a mile in." The man turned and whispered to Harley so the women couldn't hear, "The overcast was destroyed by the blast."

Harley immediately recognized the danger. Without the overcast that blew fresh air into the tunnel, the men would be at the mercy of the black damp.

<><><><><><>

Antonio was helping Angeline in the kitchen when Bullo

burst into the house. "There's been a mine explosion at Moweaqua," their son said more calmly than he looked.

Even as Antonio heard the shocking information, his mind went into disaster drill mode. Ignoring the animosity that had existed between him and his eldest son for the past six months, he began reciting orders.

"Make sure the mine safety inspectors are notified," Antonio told Bullo, who raced back out of the house. He turned toward his wife. "Angeline, start the Women's Auxiliary calling tree and tell them to spread the word they are to meet at the high school in one hour with the emergency packets RJ gave them."

"Where will you be?" Angeline asked.

"The disaster plan is for the Progressive leadership to meet at the Scout Cabin at Manner's Park," Antonio said. "We will use that as a headquarters. Call me there when you get to the high school, and I'll talk to you before you start your meeting. If this is a disaster, it is important the PMW respond quickly and efficiently."

Angeline nodded and went straight to the telephone where, standing on tiptoes, she put the receiver to her ear and shouted into the mouthpiece. "Thelma, this is Angeline! Clear the line, Thelma, we have an emergency!"

<><><><><><>

With the entire community out in front of the mine gate, Harley had to park a half-mile away. He headed for the mine office while Lena and Francis worked their way through the crowd toward the mine tipple.

"I'm a mine safety inspector," Harley told guards standing in front of the office. They ushered him inside.

Fifteen minutes later, he was dressed in an orange safety inspector jumpsuit and following a group of other inspectors into the mine. A cold drizzle of icy rain made the many concerned spectators shiver and huddle together. Crying women held scarves tight against their heads and water dripped off men's white hats onto Sunday best clothes they had donned for the day's celebration. Someone handed Harley a battery-powered flashlight, and the lead man, named John Millhouse, motioned for the men to follow him down the sloped shaft entrance.

A quarter of a mile in, the inspectors saw signs of the explosion. The rescue crew had already replaced a long section of broken and damaged props. They came upon those men after another short walk. The rescue crew was working carefully but frantically to clear an immense rock fall. They not only had to remove debris of shale and rock, but also replace damaged timber with new. Several weak places in the top had required an extensive amount of propping.

"We've been sounding," a black-faced man shouted through his gas mask. Sweat poured off his body and he looked ready to collapse. "We haven't heard any response."

"We have another crew coming in to relieve you men in about an hour," Millhouse told the weary men.

"We can make it," a brawny miner said as he swung a pickaxe. "Those are our mates down there. We'll get 'em out."

One of the other men dropped to his knees and started crying. Every man working the entryway understood the odds were against any of their friends being found alive. The only good thing was that since it was Christmas Eve, there would be far fewer causalities than if it had happened even a day earlier.

"There is only one thing I can think to do," Millhouse told the other five inspectors when they huddled away from the workers. "Until we get an opening through this corridor, I would like to get back behind this fall by traveling up the back entry. Maybe we can work our way back from the 15th South and open up the Main West entry."

Even in the darkness, Harley could see the looks of concern.

"You all know the risks," Millhouse continued. "The air may be foul in the back entry. The rescue crew is using all of our gas masks. Other than our own senses and this safety lamp, we don't have any instruments to test the air."

"You could have three men spread out in back of us about fifty feet," Harley suggested, "then if you and I get in trouble, they should be able to get us out."

"That sound okay to you fellas?" Millhouse asked. When they all nodded, he patted them each on the shoulder. "You three are our caboose. If Eng or I go down, you come running. But if you find you can't get us out, you leave us. Understand?"

The men all nodded again. Though he didn't know the men personally, Harley was certain they would each rather bust a lung than leave a fellow miner to be gassed to death.

When they arrived at 15th South, Millhouse raised the closed flame safety lamp to the return airway. The flame inside the wired enclosure remained constant.

"No firedamp anyway," Millhouse said, his voice quivering.

"I don't smell anything unusual," Harley said, though he knew the most dangerous gas, carbon monoxide, was odorless.

"I believe the good Lord is with us," Millhouse said, "but let's travel carefully anyway."

The two men moved slowly through the dark corridor. Occasionally Harley looked back at the three faint lights following them at a safe distance. The second and third men were spread out about fifty and one hundred feet behind the one in front. He began to doubt that he and Millhouse would be saved if gases overcame them. A sudden sensation of claustrophobia came over him. The dark walls in front seemed to be narrowing, though he knew that was impossible. He struggled to push the specter of dead bodies out of his mind.

"I wish I'd brought a canary," Millhouse said in a whisper. "Remind me tomorrow to bring one along, would you?"

"One canary," Harley said. "Check."

"Oh, my God, no!" Millhouse said suddenly.

Harley recognized they were at the Main West Entry, and there was a fall that looked worse than the one at the other end. Now he understood why the walls seemed to have been narrowing. He looked at Millhouse. The man's head seemed to sway. "Are you—?"

The supervisor raised a hand.

Not daring to take a breath, both men turned and stumbled toward the distant lights of their fellow miners. Harley tripped over a rock, but Millhouse lifted him with one hand and the two staggered forward as fast as they dared. Harley's lungs burned from holding his breath, but he knew that to inhale would mean certain death. They had both recognized the symptoms associated with the poisonous carbon monoxide that formed after a coal dust explosion.

<><><><><><>

Angeline was just about to leave for the high school when Sam stumbled into the house. A very weak Vinnie leaned against her shoulder.

"What happened?" Angeline took her son's free arm and led him into the room of his childhood. He fell unconscious onto the bed.

"Squirrel fever." Sam's face was strained and tired. "Call Doc Hiler."

Angeline stood frozen in place. "All the doctors are in Moweaqua. There's been a mine explosion."

Sam wiped Vinnie's feverish head with a wet cloth. Tears rolled down her cheeks. Angeline had never seen her daughter-in-law cry.

"Mama," Sam said without taking her eyes off her husband, "My Vinnie is dying."

<><><><><><>

Antonio paced. The fledgling union was in trouble. They had not been as prepared for this disaster as the United Mine

Workers were. He had already received word that the UMW had set up a railroad car to cook meals for the workers and were sending in money and equipment to help with the rescue attempts.

The Progressives were hampered by inadequate communication. The telephone lines were so jammed he couldn't get through to anyone, including Angeline and the Women's Auxiliary. Frustrated, many of his fellow union officers had given up and decided to drive on down to Moweaqua. Without an organized plan, they would simply join the thousands of other spectators standing outside the mine yard in the rain and getting in the way of the rescuers.

Still, he was about ready to give up and join them when Mary Kate rushed into the headquarters with the news about Vinnie. Antonio didn't hesitate; he rushed to his son's bedside.

<><><><><><>

Lena wasn't dressed for standing in the cold and rain, but neither were any of the other men, women and children who continued the silent vigil outside the mine gates. Frances Jackson had gone to join the wives and children of the other miners still trapped in the mine along with her husband. Lena had heard that as many as sixty were still down there.

It was well past noon when she heard the first group of mine inspectors had been overcome by white damp. Thus far only one had made it back to the surface. An hour later they posted the names of the inspectors who were still in the mine. Waiting for five long minutes in the line to see the names, Lena nearly collapsed when she saw Harley Eng written on it.

"That's my husband's name!" she shouted to no one in particular.

A miner took her arm. "Come with me, ma'am. I'll get you to the tipple."

"This woman's husband is in the mine!" the man shouted.

"Let me through!"

The crowd parted as the man continued to shout. Several people put their hands on her and shouted condolences as she passed them.

"We'll pray for you and your husband, dear."

"God bless you and your husband."

When she arrived at the tipple, a woman carrying an open umbrella hurried up and put an arm around her. "I'm Mrs. Millhouse, dear," the woman said. "My husband is down there, too."

Lena was too shocked to speak. Instead, she stood close against the woman so the umbrella protected them both. From their vantage point on higher ground she watched as a railroad passenger car was slowly backed through the parting crowd toward the mine gate.

"Thank God for the United Mine Workers," Mrs. Millhouse said.

Lena remained silent. Throughout the morning the miners had been asking where help from their Progressive union was.

"As soon as our men come up, why don't you and I go lend a hand with the cooking?" Mrs. Millhouse said with a reassuring confidence that their husbands would survive. "The United Mine Workers are going to be serving soup and coffee in a little bit."

"My husband is a Progressive," Lena said.

"I don't think that matters in a situation like this," Mrs. Millhouse said kindly. "Do you?"

"No, of course not." Lena felt immediate affection for the older woman.

It seemed an eternity before any activity appeared from the mineshaft entrance. Finally, a group of black-faced men came out in single file carrying men on stretchers. Mrs. Millhouse handed Lena the umbrella and ran toward one of the men who walked alongside a stretcher.

"John!" Mrs. Millhouse shouted, jumping into her husband's

arms.

"It's all right, Mrs. Millhouse," her husband said as he returned her embrace. "Thanks to Harley Eng here, I made it out safely."

It wasn't until Lena heard his name that she realized it was her own husband lying on the first stretcher. He held a gas mask over his face but threw it aside when he saw her.

"Get me up," he said, then went into a coughing fit.

R.J. Hiler put the mask back over his face. "You leave that on until I get you into the office or you won't be getting up ever again."

Lena took her husband's hand and walked alongside the stretcher as they carried him toward the mine office.

"We'll try again in a few hours," Mr. Millhouse told Harley. "Get some sleep."

<>< ><>< ><>< >

Even a soul with the strength of Angeline Vacca was weakened by the threatened loss of her third son. First it had been Libero, then Filberto, and now there was little doubt the angels would come and claim Vinnie as their own. God seemed to be reclaiming her boys in reverse of their birth order. The first two lay side by side at Oak Hill Cemetery. With her second son's passing, Angeline had insisted that Antonio purchase enough plots to accommodate their family for generations to come. If she couldn't keep her family together in life, she would do it in the hereafter.

While the two women sat by his bedside, Sam told stories of her friendship with Vinnie before they fell in love. "Vinnie and I was trackin' a wild boar one time up around Blair Mountain way," she said as they took turns patting a wet towel on his forehead. "She was about eight hundred pounds of the meanest critter that I ever saw. We'd seen her attack and take down a young fawn, but she ran away when we got close enough to fire a shot. We finally spotted her rootin' around a holler one day, so we got down wind and started sneakin' up on her real patient-like. Vinnie had been practicin' his marksmanship and he was gettin' pretty good, and not just a little cocky about it."

"That's my Vinnie," Angeline said, wiping her eyes with the end of her blue apron.

"Well, this was a day when he thought the sun came up just to hear him crow, so he done says to me, 'Sam, I'll bet you a nickel I can shoot a tit off that mean old sow'. Now mind you, I knowed my Vinnie didn't got no nickel to his name, and neither did I, but I took his ol' bet anyway. So that Vinnie of ours licked his sight and done took careful aim. He was holding that ol' Enfield as steady as a hitchin' post in a snowstorm and damn if he didn't shoot the front nipple off that mean ol' sow from a good seventy yards away."

Angeline couldn't help but smile at the way Sam told the story. "What happened next?" she asked.

"Well, you wouldn't *believe* it, Mama." Sam slapped her thigh. "That dang ol' boar turned her head and looked right at me and Vinnie. She was as mad as a mule chewin' on bumblebees, and she charged us faster than green grass through a goose. We done run a good two miles before we slowed down to squat us a rest."

Angeline laughed and cried and struggled to breathe. She wrapped pudgy forearms around Sam. "You won't go back to the hills, will you?" Happy tears mixed with sad ones rolled onto the young woman's shoulder. "I don't know what I'd do without you to help me get through this."

"Well, I reckon I'm a Vacca long as you let me keep the name."

Angeline held on to her Sam and sobbed harder.

That evening, Sam set on the edge of the bed holding Vinnie's hand. His face and eyes were reddened. He had lesions on his chest, and the lymph nodes under his neck and chin were swollen. His breathing was shallow and he hadn't regained consciousness since they'd lain him on the bed. Antonio and Angeline took turns sitting with him, while Sam never left his side. Not even to eat.

Mary Kate had gone to Moweaqua to find Bullo but hadn't made it back yet.

An hour after sunset, Vinnie moaned and opened his eyes. He looked at Sam and raised his swollen cheeks into half a smile.

"Don't try to talk," Sam said. She sensed his parents were standing behind her and saw him look up and acknowledge them with his eyes. "You know something, Vinnie," Sam said in a slightly breaking voice, "you and me just understand each other." She laughed, tears rolling off her face and landing on her husband's cheek. "We never had to act all lovey-dovey like some folks do. We're just best friends." Her in-law's hands rested on her shoulders. "Best friends who fell in love."

The sick young man's eyes watered. A tear rolled down to join those of his wife's. His face suddenly went lax.

Sam gave a forlorn gasp. As she released his hand, he made a long rattling sound, then took a deep breath. A moment later Vinnie Vacca opened his mouth and whispered, "You never did pay me that nickel for shootin' the tit off that old sow."

42

Antonio paced. No one respected his right to stay and take care of his still very sick son. The Progressive leadership gave him only two days before they began hounding him that they needed his help with the strike. While Harley Eng was sympathetic, he was also busy investigating the cause of the Moweaqua disaster which had killed fifty-four men. Joe had made a showing at the house with some soup, but other than a warm handshake, he said little else to his former partner. Even Angeline seemed to put on a show of strength and courage in his presence while seeking comfort from her daughters-in-law and Lena Eng instead of him. The only person Antonio had to talk to was Bullo, who had, since Vinnie's illness, come around every morning and had coffee with him before getting on the heavily armed strikebreaker's truck to go to work. Doctor Hiler had been to the house twice a day and was cautiously optimistic that Vinnie would completely recover, though he said it could take several weeks.

As the year 1933 came in, Antonio became increasingly disgusted with the situation in the mines. The Progressives were also becoming frustrated. They had failed to adequately respond to the Moweaqua mine disaster and the UMW had looked like guardian angels by providing for the injured as well as the families.

Day after day tempers flared and fights broke out throughout all the mining communities. The militia had been withdrawn, but the pickets were still not strong enough to stop the heavily armored trucks from getting workers in and out of the mine yards. Keiran Phelan was again in control of the company thugs, and even the Chicago gangsters answered to him like he was a little Al Capone.

Finally, on the night of January 3, tensions rose to a peak. A lynch mob mentality broke out in the PMA headquarters. Over one-hundred fifty men decided they'd had enough. That evening they met at the patch community of Tovey, armed to the teeth. A gloomy and frustrated Antonio Vacca joined them.

<><><><><><>

"Tear up some white cloth into strips," Phelan screamed at the men in the Tovey mine yard. "Have everyone tie a piece around each arm. When the bastards come in the mine gate, shoot anyone who isn't wearing an armband. By the time they figure out what's going on, it'll be too late."

The men understood the plan. While most nodded they liked it, Joe Harrison didn't. But he knew better than to say so. It was going to be a massacre. Every man in the mine yard had been issued either a bolt-action carbine rifle or a .44 caliber revolver. A few had shotguns, which would be just as deadly at close range. Joe had to believe that most of the men didn't really think there would be anyone killed—that cooler heads would prevail when the Progressives saw how well-armed the company men were.

"We'll just give 'em a good scare and they'll go home," one miner said.

"Sure," the man's friend said, "just fire over their heads and they'll high tail it for home."

Joe couldn't help but feel he had lived through this moment too many times before. Looking across the mine yard at where men were taking cover, he realized that if they shot over the heads of the Progressives, the company houses would be in direct line of the fire. There were women and children in those homes.

"Keiran!" Joe shouted at his son-in-law and pointed. "The

company houses!"

"Let them worry about their own!" Phelan yelled back as men scampered to get in position. "In fact, a few well-placed shots into the houses might be a good idea. You hear that, Howsham?"

"Got it, chief," Howsham said. "You two men come with me."

Joe watched as the mine boss and two men with carbines climbed to the top of the tipple. His first impulse was to run across the yard screaming at the men, pleading with them to give up this insanity. His heart raced as it had never done before. He was more nervous, than back in '98; even more than that day at the Villa with Art Cabassi. He felt like he was the only person who knew what could happen; what *would* happen.

First, he had to get control of himself. There was no way he could stop the fanatical frenzy of the men on the company side of the stockade. That left him with no choice. He had to get word to the Progressives; had to get them to go home and fight another day, without guns. But how? And who would believe him? They would think he was a company man, and was trying to trick them.

Antonio? Antonio hated him. But of all the Progressives, Joe believed his old pard was the one person who might listen to him. How could he find him? There were hundreds of men on the other side of that wall.

<><><><><><>

When Harley Eng pulled into the Vacca driveway to pick up his wife, she ran out with a frantic Angeline beside her. The women jumped into the car.

"Get us to Tovey, fast!" Lena shouted.

"What?" Harley backed the car onto the road before getting an explanation. He had just returned from a long meeting on the Moweaqua mine disaster and was looking forward to a warm bed.

"Antonio and a group of men are trying to shut down the mine," Lena said. "They are heavily armed."

"Have they lost their minds?" Harley asked.

"Yes," Angeline said quietly, "they've lost their minds."

Harley stepped on the accelerator.

Ten minutes later, he parked at the first of the two entrances to the small community. A line of cars prevented them from getting closer. They got out and ran between the cars toward the mine, Harley in the lead. When they came to the last company house before the gate, a group of miners' wives stood on the porch. Harley stopped running and grabbed his wife and Angeline by the arms to stop them.

"What's going on?" Harley asked the women on the porch.

"There's a group of our Progressive men trying to close the mine exits," one of the women answered. "I wouldn't go no nearer 'cause they'll shoot anyone they don't know. We're fixin' to take cover inside. Those company hoodlums have a machine gun up on the tipple."

Harley looked at his wife. "Take Angeline and stay inside with these women. I'll get Antonio and bring him back here."

Angeline touched his arm. "You won't let me lose anyone else, will you, Harley?"

"Not a chance," Harley said, hoping beyond hope he told the truth. He ran toward the mine yard.

<><><><><><>

Joe Harrison and Antonio Vacca had stood outside the east wall together one other time, when they argued about health insurance. They had been on different sides then, too. Remembering this, Joe ran toward that same east wall. There were few company men on that side because of the wide open area. Everyone knew that the Progressives would not try to cross such a large killing field without cover.

"Phelan changed his mind!" Joe shouted. "He wants you men on the west wall!"

The men left immediately, leaving Joe alone. There likely would be a few Progressives behind the buildings across the field under orders to fire a few shots, if nothing else, to draw company men away from the main conflict. He needed to get Antonio to come to that side so he could talk to him. Lighting a kerosene lantern, he held it in front of his face.

Voices traveled from across the field. So that they would know he was unarmed, he took off his coat, held up his hands and turned all the way around. He then dropped to the other side of the wooden stockade.

"Tell Antonio Vacca that Joe Harrison wants to talk to him," he said in a voice loud enough to be heard by the Progressives.

Their high voices gave away that they were but boys. One of them ran like a deer behind the buildings and out of sight. Endless minutes passed. Joe feared the battle would begin before he had a chance to talk to his friend. Finally, he heard footsteps running down the alley toward him.

"What do you want, Harrison?" Antonio's out of breath voice startled Joe and he almost dropped his lantern.

"I'm gonna turn this lantern off and come over to talk to you."

"You do and I'll shoot you where you stand," Antonio said, followed by the cocking of a carbine.

Joe turned the lantern off and began walking across the field. He knew Antonio wouldn't shoot him, though he wasn't sure about the boys.

"Tell the boys not to shoot," he said quietly.

"I sent them home to their mothers." Antonio's voice was full of spite that Joe knew wasn't for the boys.

"That's far enough," the Italian said, stepping out from behind a woodpile. Joe hadn't seen him for several weeks. He noted that Antonio had lost weight.

"The company men are wrapping their arms with white

cloth strips," Joe told him. "Your men won't know who to shoot at but the company men will."

"Why are you telling me this?"

"Because it will be a massacre, Antonio." Joe's voice was pleading. "I don't want your side to win, but those Progressives used to be my friends. I know their wives and children. This thing isn't worth dying for."

Antonio remained quiet.

Joe took another step forward and lowered his voice. "Antonio, I was at the massacre of the colored scabs in ninety-eight and I helped Cabassi kill those thugs in twenty-five."

"I thought both those killings were just wild talk," Antonio said quietly. He seemed skeptical.

"I can tell you where they're buried. If I'm lying about the white arm bands, you can have me charged with murder."

Again, Antonio said nothing.

"The coloreds," Joe said loudly, "are buried on—"

"Shut up," Antonio hissed. He turned and yelled at someone behind a tree. "Go tell the boys to put white armbands on."

A man ran toward the front of the mine.

Antonio suddenly raised his carbine and pointed it at Joe. "Let's go!"

"I'm not going with you," Joe said. "I may not like what Phelan was going to do, but I'm a company man, Antonio." He headed back toward the mine but turned back when he heard Antonio moving toward him. He felt the crash of a powerful fist against his jaw. Then there was nothing but darkness.

<><><><><><>

Keiran Phelan had a new toy. It was a brand new Mosin-Nagant M1891 sniper rifle with a telescopic sight. He had been practicing for weeks and could consistently hit a human-sized object at two hundred yards. When Phelan took his position near the top of the tipple he did a quick scan of the community with the scope. He saw several men running between buildings carrying guns, but when he saw both his in-laws with Angeline Vacca in tow, he almost took a shot at the fat little dago bitch right then. He refrained himself and watched as the two women followed several others into the house.

He then concentrated on following Eng as he ran through the community talking to men. Sometimes Eng would throw his hands in the air when the Progressives pointed their guns at him. Phelan said, "shit" each time they lowered their weapons and let him move away. Finally, Phelan aimed his scope back at the door to the house, deciding he would rather kill the Vacca woman more than anyone else. She had embarrassed him in front of his men, and she was the reason Felina had made him sleep on the couch for the past several months. He released the safety on the long rifle and waited.

<><><><><><>

Joe awoke to find he was being carried across a broad shoulder. When Antonio threw him on the ground, he grabbed at the Italian's foot and flipped him onto his back.

"Antonio!" Joe shouted, still on both knees. "I have to get back in there to stop them from—"

Another fist landed on his face, but this time Joe saw it coming and deflected it off his cheek.

A volley of gunshots erupted. Antonio bounded to his feet and ran.

"The houses, Antonio!" Joe screamed as he also jumped up and sprinted after his friend. "They're firing on the houses! That's why I needed to get back inside."

Antonio stopped and looked toward the company houses.

"*Angeline!*" he shouted, running toward the house.

<><><><><><>

"Antonio!" Angeline screamed when she heard the first shots fired. She ran out onto the porch.

"Angeline, no!" Lena followed behind her. A sound like the buzz of an angry bee followed by a thump replaced the quiet. A bullet went through Angeline's chest and out the back. She froze, then looked down when the spent bullet bounced off the wall of the house, clattered onto the wooden porch and rolled to a stop next to the back of her foot.

Angeline remained standing for several seconds before her knees buckled. Lena caught her around the waist and lowered her gently onto her back on the floor of the porch. Suddenly, as the sound of gunshots rattled as fast as machine gun fire, Dr. Hiler came running up to the two women.

"I knew something like this would happen," RJ said as he tore open Angeline's dress and put a cloth over the wound to control the bleeding.

Just as suddenly, Antonio dropped onto his knees next to his wife. RJ looked at him and answered his unspoken questions with his silence. The miner cradled his wife's head in his big hands and looked into her dying eyes.

"My Antonio," Angeline whispered.

"Don't leave me," he begged.

"You sit on your porch and drink wine." Angeline put her hand on his cheek. "I will watch over our sons for you."

With those words, Angeline Vacca died.

43

Rooms
Life begins in some
Others are where final breaths are taken
Some are where many souls come
And some are God-forsaken.
Some rooms have walls and others have none
But rooms with stories and secrets are the ones that will most
awaken

RJ lowered the little journal that was filled with his beloved
wife's beautiful, old-style penmanship. He spent every Sunday
evening reading Carmela's journal entries and poems. He was
always amazed by how often they gave him understanding.
Lately, he had been thinking about those remarkable chambers
of coal that lie far beneath the spot on the earth where he now
sat so comfortably, just rocking and reading and remembering.

Yes, Carmela had been right. Even those God-forsaken
rooms had their share of untold stories and secrets. Rooms
that had felt the presence of so few human souls—where
men sought to return the remains of prehistoric plants back
to the air and sunshine that had created them. He thought of
the stories that his friends Antonio and Joe had told him, his
favorite being the explosion that almost killed them back at the
turn of the century. In fact, "Are the mules okay?" had become
a standard line at the Christian County mines for any and all
accidents that were not serious or life threatening.

RJ wished his Carmela could have met spunky Angeline and
energetic Lena Eng. What a trio the three women would have

been. Watching Angeline Vacca die had been like watching Carmela's death all over at Ludlow. While over a dozen were wounded that bloody night, only Angeline and one Progressive named Vincent Rodems were killed. The state's attorney's office, which was a close ally of Peabody Coal Company, claimed both deaths were the result of the victims being in the wrong place at the wrong time. While no company men were even investigated for the deaths, over thirty of the Progressives were arrested and later released. Investigators determined the reason more men weren't killed at the gun battle in Tovey was because both sides were wearing white armbands. Neither side knew whom to shoot.

The next morning, RJ stood beside Harley and Joe at the entrance to the Tovey mine and watched the National Guard trucks return to Christian County. The Guard immediately declared martial law and, fearing a riot, announced that only family members would be allowed to attend the lying to rest of Angeline Vacca. To ensure this happened, they blocked the main streets and roads going into Oak Hill cemetery.

Regardless, the Women's Auxiliary that Angeline had helped form would not be denied. Hundreds of vehicles wound their way through cow pastures and along muddy, country roads to get to the funeral. The resting place of the little lady was next to that of Libero and Filberto. Newspaper reporters came from across the country, forcing the militia to finally step aside rather than appear the villain. In the end, over ten thousand people attended her funeral. Still, the peacefulness of the cemetery and the comforting words of the priest were constantly interrupted by U.S. bomber planes that flew menacingly low throughout the proceedings.

"Angeline told me to sit on the porch and drink wine," Antonio told RJ, Harley and Joe as they stood around Angeline's casket, surrounded by the Vacca family, and watched the planes buzz the cemetery. "I intend to fulfill her last wish. I'm done with the mine."

Still weak from the fever, Vinnie was supported on either side by Sam and Bullo. Off to the side, well-mannered little Sid silently stood between his cousins Willie and Tony. The three boys twitched and scratched at their suits and ties now and then but kept respectfully quiet. Angie and Margaret Eng hovered over the boys like doting aunts and gave occasional pats on the boy's shoulders.

"How would you like to open that restaurant she always wanted?" Joe asked. "I think it's about time Mary Kate and Sam share that tortellini recipe that Angeline taught them. RJ, Harley and me would like to go in on it with you, if you'd let us."

"We'll talk about it," Antonio said with his first smile in three days. After a long pause he added. "Vacca's Restaurant. That does have a nice ring to it."

Mary Kate stepped forward, put her arm around her father-in-law's waist, and rested her head on his broad shoulder. "Angeline's Place sounds much better," she said.

<><><><><><>

The next day, Joe Harrison cleared out the desk in his office, walked away from the coal mine and never looked back. At first Myrna was outraged, but when she saw that her husband had a knack for business, she helped him open a general store in the little town of Herrick just south of Williamsburg Hill, the site of Art Cabassi's grave. While Joe did better than ever financially, he became increasingly recluseive, spending many evenings walking the hill near the peculiar burial place.

In the meantime, the Christian County coal mine war was in full gear. Bombings and shootings became the order of the day as dozens of people on both sides died. Men like Kieran Phelan recruited miners from southern Illinois to strike break.

"Tell those swampies they'd be better off living someplace else besides Taylorville," Antonio told Bullo one day in 1936. Vinnie gave him a thumb's up. The brothers had been enjoying early morning coffee with their father ever since their mother's death. Angeline's Place in Hewittville made a fine rendezvous place for the Vacca men before the rush of customers began. Bullo always made it a point to leave for work before the mostly Progressive crowd arrived to sit with his father and Vinnie. Mary Kate and Angie were in the kitchen chatting up a storm as they prepared food, while Sam rushed about setting tables.

"I wish people would quit calling the miners swampies," Bullo said. He and his father had learned to speak their minds on the mine war without taking offense. Vinnie had learned to stay clear of the discussion. There had been two explosions that night, although no one had died. "You know they can't live anywhere else. The Progressives in the towns around here would make mincemeat of them."

"Have you heard how Harley is doing with his patents?" Antonio asked.

"It looks like there's a pretty good chance he'll make back his fortune on his safety equipment ideas," Bullo said. "He's a lot smarter than I was. At least he kept his ideas a secret from the company until he had his patents filed."

"If it makes you feel any better," Antonio said, "he told me he wouldn't have known better if he hadn't seen the company steal your ideas and patent them for themselves."

"Ever wonder what inventions Filberto would have come up with?" Vinnie asked.

"Every day," Antonio said with a smile then quickly changed the subject. "Lena plans to go up to Chicago to help organize meatpacking women."

"I heard she's finished raising money for the Mother Jones monument in Mt. Olive," Vinnie said. "The dedication ceremony is going to be in October. You gonna go?"

Placing a large hand around his coffee cup, Antonio said, "I wouldn't miss it for anything."

<><><><><><>

The twenty-two foot high headstone was built out of several tons of pink Minnesota granite and placed at the grave of Mother Jones in Mt. Olive. On October 11, Harley and Lena Eng, Antonio, Vinnie and Sam Vacca and Joe and Myrna Harrison gathered at the cemetery along with over fifty thousand people for the dedication ceremony. Five special trains and twenty-five Greyhound buses brought people to Mt. Olive. Others came by car and some even hitchhiked.

Many politicians took advantage of the crowds to share their thoughts and memories of Mother Jones, but it was the final speaker, Lillie May Burgess, who Lena Eng thought was most in tune with the hearts of working men and women. It was her home in which the great little lady had lived during her last years. Burgess told the crowd that Mother Jones had wanted to live another one hundred years to "fight to the end" so "there would be no more machine guns and no more sobbing of little children."

Following the speeches and the unveiling, a song was played over the loudspeakers as the crowd waited to get a closer look at the statue. Gene Autry, a young cowboy who was just beginning to make his mark on radio and in motion pictures, sang "The Death of Mother Jones."

The world today is mourning the death of Mother Jones
Grief and sorrow hover around the miners' homes
That grand old champion of labor has gone to a better land
But the hard-working miners miss her guiding hand

Lena took Antonio Vacca's hand as the song ended. Sam stepped forward and surprised everyone by giving her father-in-law a kiss on the cheek. Myrna Harrison turned toward her own husband, who stared wide-eyed at the ground. She muttered to him in a low voice, "They spent all that money on a silly headstone. Do they think anyone will ever come out here after today?"

"They will," Joe said without looking at her. "Sometimes the dead have more effect on us than the living. People will most definitely come."

44

On Christmas Eve, 1939, RJ Hiler sat in front of the warm pot-bellied stove in his office reading the annual letter from his friend Mary Thomas for the third time.

> My dearest Rolfe,
>
> The years have been good to me and I remain in good health. My store in Hollywood is doing well, but I do miss the days when I could sing in our dance hall with my loving husband Don by my side. He has been such a comfort to me despite his nagging at me to audition for a role in a musical picture show. He hasn't been as bad though these past few years now that I'm pushing fifty.

RJ heard Giovanna enter the room and begin tidying the bookshelf behind him. She was a competent nurse, though sometimes her tendency to linger was a nuisance. He tried to overlook this annoyance. She had been living alone since her husband died in the Moweaqua mine disaster in '32, and he suspected she didn't like going home to an empty home. Still, he lived in an empty house himself and he didn't hover over anyone when they were reading a private letter from an old friend. He quickly lowered the papers and turned to her.

"Didn't you just do that?" he asked with a little more irritation in his voice than he intended.

"I'm sorry, Doctor," Giovanna said. "I just wanted to make

sure everything was in order for your Christmas."

RJ's face burned. Giovanna was a good woman. She was trying to give him the only Christmas present she could probably afford—her time and loyalty.

"I'm sorry, Giovanna," RJ said. "I just don't want you to put yourself out. Thank you, though."

He turned back to the letter and skipped to the last page.

> I can't tell you how much I look forward every season to the moment when I sit down at the table in my parlor and send my holiday greetings to the man whose wife saved my life— and my daughters' lives—and so many others. It is so comforting to know that you and I both have a place in our memories where our dear Carmella shall remain so long as our hearts beat.
>
> But I come to the point now that I have spent many months considering how to phrase it. Oh, my dear Rolfe, you have such a big and compassionate heart. Don't you think there is room in there for one more? If you would forgive me for trying to speak for Carmela, I know she would say that she doesn't want to selfishly possess a lonely heart. She knows that you will choose wisely and the love you find will be as much a comfort to her soul in heaven as it will be to yours here on Earth. Remember that God is gracious.
>
> Now there, I've said what I've needed to say and I pray that you will forgive me if I have overstepped. I would never be able to bear losing your friendship.
>
> Always yours,
> Mary O'Neal

"Goodnight, Doctor," Giovanna said from the doorway. "And Merry Christmas."

"Goodnight, Giovanna," RJ said. He looked at her standing with her hat and coat on, her eyes looking shyly toward the middle of his chest. "Giovanna. That is such a pretty name. What does it mean?"

"It means *God is gracious*, sir." Giovanna raised her eyes for a moment and looked into his.

RJ looked for a moment at the letter in his hand. "How old are you, Nurse Giovanna?" he asked.

"Why, Doctor, you should never ask a woman her age." Giovanna smiled a smile that was prettier than he had noticed in many years.

"Just you never mind that!" RJ said in mock anger. "How old are you, Nurse Giovanna?"

"Well, I guess I'll be forty-five this April twenty," she said, stepping forward out of the doorway. "Why do you want to know?"

"Why, because it wouldn't be proper for me to be seen in public with someone younger than forty, don't you think?" RJ set the letter down on his desk, rose quickly to his feet and took his coat and hat off the back of his chair. "Are you hungry? I happen to know a little restaurant in Hewittville that makes the best tortellinis between here and Italy."

RJ was a little worried when he saw the hesitancy in the nurse's face. Then her pretty smile returned. She slipped her hand snuggly beneath his offered arm. The two stepped through the threshold into the crisp winter evening.

45

One day in 1941, Joe Harrison decided he could sleep himself to death. Once, several years before, he had slept for three days without food or water, only occasionally turning on one side to relieve himself into a milk container. He felt that if he had been left alone for another few days he would have slipped right into death, but Myrna had spoiled it by sending for Antonio. The little Italian took Joe home with him and made him sleep in the boys' old room. Each morning he had coffee with him on the front porch, where they watched the miners walking to work. Eventually, Joe recovered.

This time, though, Joe drove over to Pana, the town where he had grown up, and paid a two-month advance for a cheap hotel room. He told the manager that he was writing a novel and was not to be disturbed. Thirty days later, the manager had so many complaints about the smell coming from the room, he used his own key to gain entry. Joe Harrison lay on his back on the bed, his eyes wide open.

Myrna wasn't surprised when she found out her husband was dead. She called Antonio and asked him to make the arrangements.

"Joe wanted to be buried on Williamsburg Hill alongside Art Cabassi. I told him that was fine, but I wasn't going to be buried in those weeds, so he'd just have to rest there all by himself. I guess that's okay. We never were together very much when he was alive, so we might as well not be together in the hereafter."

Antonio hired an old colored man to dig a grave next to where Art Cabassi was buried. Rochester Hemings, the only black person in Shelby County, had lived there almost his entire adult life. A quiet and humble man, he was well liked and trusted. He made a good enough living as a mailman that he was able to buy a tractor, enabling him to deliver the mail on the steep hills even in the worst snow. Rochester loved big machines, and the tractor was his pride and joy.

"I came from Birmingham with my auntie when I's a young man," Rochester told Antonio as he began digging in the designated spot. "That was 'bout nineteen-hundred. We was looking for my brother, Willie. Never did find that boy, but we stayed on, and auntie took a job taking care of old Mrs. Kennedy. I surely did love that woman. My auntie, I mean."

When Antonio saw a tear start down the old man's face, he patted him on the shoulder, slipped a ten-dollar bill into his calloused hands and went back to his car.

The next morning, Joe Harrison went one last time underground. As were many miners, he was buried with a pick and a number two banjo next to him.

46

October 12, 1948

Though it was well out of his way, Antonio drove to Herrick, Illinois, to pick up Myrna and take her to Mt. Olive for the commemoration of the fiftieth anniversary of the Virden Massacre. Vinnie, Sam and Sid had taken the train to West Virginia to visit one of her sisters, and Antonio didn't want to make the trip alone. Just the day before he had come up with the idea to call Myrna. He was surprised when she accepted the invitation, but not surprised by the reason she gave him.

"I need to pick up some supplies for the store!" she yelled into the telephone receiver. "You'll have to pick me up early enough so we can stop off in Litchfield on the way."

The drive downstate was uneventful. At first Antonio shared news of his family and the success that Mary Kate and Sam were having with the restaurant. Myrna seemed uninterested. When he finished, she talked nonstop about the local gossip. Antonio forgot most of what she'd said by the time they arrived in Mt. Olive.

The ceremony was a somber one compared to others he had attended. Antonio believed that the Progressive Union had been destroyed as much by the United Mine Workers collusion with the coal companies as by the state and federal government. Progressives were being branded communists. Despite Antonio's prediction that such labeling could not happen again in the United States, a second red scare was beginning to take place in the land of the free. Even President Truman was throwing around the term "un-American" as a political weapon.

Antonio and Myrna stood apart in the crowd of thousands attending the ceremony. Many of the miners he once worked with had retired or moved on to other careers, often in areas far from central Illinois. Others, like Bullo, who were still working in the mines, avoided any connection with what they considered the more radical labor groups. Antonio had to admit, Bullo had been right about one thing. The machines had been as inevitable as the greed of the mine companies. The new world of technology would be for those who made the effort to keep themselves educated as the world continued to change.

Many of those at the ceremony acknowledged Antonio but kept their distance. He suspected this was because he was with Myrna, who had never shown much respect for the miners. On their way home after the ceremonies, Antonio asked her if she would like to stop at Williamsburg Hill and visit Joe's grave.

"I suppose we may as well get it out of the way while we're out," Myrna said, then let her head nod forward to rest.

The sun was low in the sky when they began driving up the long, steep hill. It was a perfect fall day, with trees aglow with various reds, greens and gold. Antonio saw old Rochester Hemings' coming down the narrow road on his tractor. He pulled over and left Myrna sleeping with her head against the window while he got out of the car to talk to the man.

"I'm glad to see you, sir," the old gentlemen said as he climbed slowly from the tractor and shook hands. "There's something that's been botherin' me these past many years."

"What is it, Rochester?"

"Well, sir, you remember when I dug that grave for you? Well, sir, you paid me a heap of money for doing that, but I just got to give it back to you."

"Why do you think that, Rochester?"

"Well, sir." The old man hesitated before letting the words spill out of him. "It's 'cause your friend ain't alone in that there ground."

Antonio didn't know what he had expected, but it wasn't this.

"You see, sir," Rochester continued, "when I got that grave dug to about six feet it was getting on toward dark. I climbed out of that hole and looked back down so as to make sure it was dug even on both sides. I had to hold a lantern down in it so I could see, don't you understand? Then I saw somethin' terrible, Mr. Antonio."

"What was it, Rochester?"

"It was a skull."

Antonio looked back to the car, thankful that Myrna was still asleep.

"I wanted to tell you, Mr. Antonio, but I was tired and scared. That skull had the top of its head gone and one side of its jaw. I fell down on my knees right there, I tell you, and I prayed for that poor fellow. I mean, I prayed and prayed. Then I done something terrible. I threw a shovel of dirt over those staring eye sockets and went on like I never seen nothin'."

Antonio stared at the crying old man.

"I know you're angry at me, Mr. Antonio. I'll move your friend to another spot if you wants. You don't have to pay me nothin', and I'll give you back the ten dollars to boot."

"No, my friend," Antonio said, smiling at Rochester. "Let the dead sleep. I imagine Joe was grateful for the company. My guess is that he took that poor soul and taught him how to be a coal miner."

Antonio shook the old man's hand again, got back in the car and drove on up the hill. Waking Myrna, he led her up the path to the grave. His heart sank a little when he saw the condition of the place. It was covered over with so many weeds it took several moments to find Joe's headstone. Thousands of insects crawled and jumped out of their way as the two approached the resting place.

"Joe wouldn't have liked this," Myrna said as Antonio pulled weeds away from the marker.

"I'll pay old Rochester to keep this area mowed," Antonio

said. Finishing with the weeds, he gently brushed the stone with his hand. "I agree. Joe wouldn't like to be covered with all these weeds. He was vain about his appearances."

"Oh, I don't mean the weeds would bother him," Myrna said. "It's these damned bugs hopping all over him. They'd terrify him."

Antonio smiled. "I never knew Joe to be afraid of anything."

"That's 'cause you was always underground when you was with him," Myrna said. "I thought he was your best friend. You sure didn't know him very well, did you?"

Antonio didn't answer. She was obviously right.

"There was only one thing that Joe Harrison was afraid of."

"What's that?" Antonio asked.

"Grasshoppers." Myrna turned and walked back to the car.

END

Author's Note

With the closing of the Christian County Mines in the 1950s an era ended. As one by one the mines were stripped of all their valuable machinery and the mine shafts finally filled in, those miners who spent a major part of their lives in them must have felt as one does at a funeral when the casket is laid to rest. Voices in many languages must surely still echo through abandoned chambers where boys became men and sometimes lost their lives. If we listen we may still hear them singing:

> We will win the fight today, boys,
> We'll win the fight today,
> Shouting the battle cry of union;
> We will rally from the coal mines,
> We'll battle to the end,
> Shouting the battle cry of union.
>
> The union forever, hurrah, boys, hurrah!
> Down with the Baldwins, up with the law;
> For we're coming, Colorado, we're coming all the way,
> Shouting the battle cry of union.
>
> We're Coming Colorado

ABOUT THE AUTHOR

After retiring from a career as an educator, Kevin Corley turned to his love of writing as a way to retell the stories he had shared with history students in his classroom. He recognized that the coal mining communities of Illinois were center-stage in the development of unions in the first half of the 20th century. From the Virden and Pana massacres of 1898-99 to the migration of miners after the Cherry mine disaster of 1909, Christian County became the rallying place for unionization.

Teaching history to many of the descendants of the coal mine wars, Corley developed a bond with the working man, a bond that was strengthened in 1986 when he was selected to research, through oral history interviews, the men and women who had lived through these powerful and often terrifying events. His research was used by Carl Oblinger to write his book, Divided Kingdom, which was published in 1991.

In addition to recording a vast collection coal miner stories, Corley discovered a wealth of old coal mining photographs dating back to 1898 in the homes of the Frank, Fritz, Otto and Max Boch family. Many of these photos are on display at the Abraham Lincoln Presidential Library and Museum in Springfield, Illinois. Taking inspiration from the Boch brothers' story, Corley loosely pattern his fictional Vacca brothers after them in Sixteen Tons. It is the four Boch brothers who are pictured on the cover of this novel.

TITLES FROM HARD BALL PRESS

The Lenny Moss Mysteries, by Timothy Sheard

THIS WON'T HURT A BIT
SOME CUTS NEVER HEAL
A RACE AGAINST DEATH
SLIM TO NONE
NO PLACE TO BE SICK
A BITTER PILL

HARD BALL PRESS Standalone Books

LOVE DIES, A Thriller, by Timothy Sheard

MURDER OF A POST OFFICE MANAGER,
A Legal Thriller, by Paul Felton

SIXTEEN TONS,
An Historical Novel, by Kevin Corley

WHAT DID YOU LEARN AT WORK TODAY? THE FORBIDDEN LESSONS OF LABOR EDUCATION, nonfiction, by Helena Worthen

Made in the USA
San Bernardino, CA
15 October 2016